Once Upon a Tower

Center Point
Large Print

Also by Eloisa James and available from
Center Point Large Print:

The Duke Is Mine
The Ugly Duchess

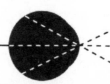

**This Large Print Book carries the
Seal of Approval of N.A.V.H.**

Once Upon a Tower

Eloisa James

CENTER POINT LARGE PRINT
THORNDIKE, MAINE

This Center Point Large Print edition
is published in the year 2013 by arrangement with
Avon Books, an imprint of HarperCollins Publishers.

The text of this Large Print edition is unabridged.
In other aspects, this book may vary
from the original edition.
Printed in the United States of America
on permanent paper.
Set in 16-point Times New Roman type.

ISBN: 978-1-61173-805-6

Library of Congress Cataloging-in-Publication Data

James, Eloisa.
Once upon a tower / Eloisa James. — Center Point Large Print edition.
pages cm
ISBN 978-1-61173-805-6 (Library binding : alk. paper)
1. Large type books. I. Title.
PS3560.A3796O53 2013
813'.54—dc23
                                          2013011754

This book is dedicated to a very special, eccentric, and hilarious group of women called the Duchesses. They have brightened my life with their laughter:
Thank you, Your Graces!

Acknowledgments

My books are like small children; they take a whole village to get them to a literate state. I want to offer my heartfelt thanks to my village: my editor, Carrie Feron; my agent, Kim Witherspoon; my writing partner, Linda Francis Lee; my Web site designers, Wax Creative; and my personal team: Kim Castillo, Franzeca Drouin, and Anne Connell. In addition, a kind fan, Ann M., gave me the idea of using a horsehair rope at a crucial moment in my "Rapunzel"-inspired plot. And a gifted and deeply knowledgeable cellist, Jeffrey Ericson Allen of the Chronotope Project, lent his expertise as regards the cello and the history of its use. When I wandered from the historical truth (as with the endpin), it was not without his advice.

One

Whenever possible, Gowan Stoughton of Craigievar, Duke of Kinross, Chief of Clan MacAulay, avoided rooms crowded with Englishmen. They were all babbling gossips with more earwax than brains, as his father was wont to say.

Though Shakespeare had got there first.

Yet here he was, nonetheless, entering a ballroom in the heart of London, rather than casting a line into a Highland stream, as he would have preferred. It was a disagreeable but inescapable fact of life—or of his life, at any rate—that fishing for a bride had taken precedence over fishing for salmon.

The moment he was announced, a flock of young women swiveled toward him, each face flaunting a gleaming array of teeth. To his mind they all looked constipated, though more likely the smiles were an automatic response to his title. He was, after all, an unmarried nobleman in possession of all his limbs. Hair, too; he had more hair than most Englishmen. Not to mention a castle.

His hosts, the Earl of Gilchrist and Lady Gilchrist, were waiting at the bottom of the steps, so the young ladies did not instantly pounce. Gowan liked Gilchrist—he was stern but fair, and had a brooding gaze that was almost Scottish. They were both interested in financial affairs, unlike most gentlemen, and the earl was a damned fine investor. Because Gowan was a governor of the Bank of Scotland and Gilchrist held a similar post at the Bank of England, they'd exchanged a good deal of correspondence over the last couple of years, though they'd rarely met.

"Your Grace, may I introduce my countess?" Gilchrist asked, drawing his lady forward. To Gowan's surprise, the countess was significantly younger than her husband, perhaps in her late twenties. What's more, she had sensual, full lips, and her lush breasts were framed by a bodice made of a twist of rosy silk. By all appearances, she was one of those aristocratic women who emulated the attire and manner of an opera dancer.

Gilchrist, on the other hand, bought to mind nothing so much as a stern churchwarden. It could not be a harmonious pairing. A man and wife ought to be complementary in age and interests.

The countess was telling him about her step-daughter, Edith, so Gowan bowed and expressed his ineffable pleasure at the idea of meeting the young lady.

Edith. What an awful name.

A long-tongued woman would have that name. A fusty nut, a flap-eared . . . *Englishwoman*.

Without warning, Lady Gilchrist slid her arm through his so he might accompany her to the adjacent reception chamber; he scarcely managed to suppress a flinch. In his youth, servants had always hovered around him, adjusting his clothing, touching his neck, wiping his mouth. But in the years since he turned fourteen, he had suffered no such familiarities unless absolutely required.

Because he had very little time alone, he preferred to maintain a barrier between himself and the world. He did not lament his lack of privacy; he felt it would be a waste of time to dress, for example, without simultaneously hearing his secretary's report. If there was anything that Gowan hated, it was wasting time.

Time wasted itself, in his opinion. All too soon, and out of the blue, you toppled over and died, and all your moments were gone.

It would be rank foolishness to pretend that those moments were infinite and endless, which—in his opinion—was precisely what people were doing when they dawdled in the bath or spent hours lazing about reading poetry. It was his inclination and his habit to do as many things at once as possible.

Indeed, this ball was a case in point: before he traveled to meet a group of bankers in Brighton on the morrow, he wanted to ask Gilchrist's opinion about a knotty point regarding issuance of the one-pound note. Gilchrist was giving a ball, which young ladies would attend. Gowan had an acute —not desperate, but acute—need for a spouse.

Ergo, two birds with one stone. He preferred three or four birds with a single stone, but sometimes one had to settle for less.

The only problem was that the room was filled with English ladies, and he had determined that it would be a bad idea to marry one of those. It was true that a Scottish nobleman always had good reason to tie himself to one of the great houses of England.

But it was also true that an English lass was, perforce, *English*.

Theirs was an indolent race, as everyone knew. Their gentlewomen sat about doing naught but quaffing endless cups of tea and reading novels, while their Scottish counterparts to the north thought nothing of running an estate with a thousand sheep while raising four children.

His own grandmother had worked from morn to dusk without complaint. If reading was to be done, she had always said it should be for improvement of the mind. The Bible and Shakespeare, with Montaigne's essays for light reading. His late fiancée was, by all accounts, cast in the same mold, which made sense given that his grandmother had arranged the marriage herself.

Miss Rosaline Partridge had died from a fever she caught while paying visits to the poor . . . virtue, in her case, proving less than rewarding.

Gowan rather thought diligence was his primary requirement in a bride (other than the obvious— that she be beautiful, maidenly, and well-bred). The future Duchess of Kinross could not be a time waster.

Lady Gilchrist had towed him through the ballroom, and they now entered a smaller chamber. A quick reconnaissance of the room told him that in matters of wealth or title, no unmarried man present matched him. In any case, there were likely only three contenders in all London.

So, strictly speaking, he needn't waste time courting a wife once he'd chosen her. Marriage was a market like any other; when he found the right lady, he would simply outbid his rivals.

The countess drew him to one side of the chamber and stopped before a young woman, whom she introduced as her stepdaughter.

It was the sort of moment that cleaves past from present, and changes the future forever.

Lady Edith did not belong in an overheated English ballroom. There was something other-worldly about her, as if she were dreaming of her home under a fairy hill. Her eyes were green pools, as deep and dark as a loch on a stormy day.

She was delightfully curved, and had hair that gleamed like the golden apples of the sun. It was pulled up in ringlets and curls, and all he wanted was to unwind it and make love to her on a bed of heather.

But it was her eyes that truly beguiled him: they met his with courteous disinterest, a dreamy peacefulness that showed none of the feverish enthusiasm with which unmarried young ladies generally regarded him.

Gowan did not consider himself a man given to carnality. A duke, to his mind, had no right to succumb to lust.

He had watched with bemusement as men of his acquaintance fell at the feet of women with saucy smiles and round bottoms. He had felt pity, as he did now for the earl with his lush wife.

But in the moment, looking down at Lady Edith, love and its attendant poetry made sense. A line came to him as if it had been written for that moment: *I never saw true beauty till this night . . .*

Perhaps Shakespeare was useful for something after all.

Lady Edith's rosy mouth curved into a smile. She dropped into a deep curtsy, inclining her head. "Your Grace, it is a pleasure to meet you."

To Gowan, it was as if the countess had ceased to exist; indeed, a roomful of people faded into the wallpaper. "The pleasure is entirely mine," he said, meaning every word. "May I have the honor of your hand for this dance?" He extended his hand.

His gesture was met not by rippling eagerness, but by a composure that drew him as surely as eagerness would have repelled him. He wanted nothing more than to make those serene eyes light for *him,* to see admiration, even adoration, in her gaze.

She inclined her head again, and took his hand. Her touch burned through their gloves, as if it warmed some part of him that had been cold until this moment. Rather than flinch, he had the impulse to pull her closer.

Once in the ballroom and in his arms, Edith danced as gracefully as the wave of the sea. And she was quiet.

The dance kept separating them and bringing them back together; they had progressed to the far end of the set before it dawned on Gowan that they had yet to exchange a word. He couldn't remember the last person who'd been so silent in his presence, yet she seemed to feel no need—nor inclination—to speak to him. Still, it was the most comfortable silence of his life.

He was aware of a feeling of profound surprise.

They turned and began to proceed up the room again. He tried to think of something to say, but nothing came to mind. He had mastered the art of polite conversation; a whole drawing room full of people unsettled by his ducal presence could be put at ease with a few well-chosen words.

But in his experience, young ladies did not need

prompting. Generally, they smiled feverishly, their eyes sending sparkling messages while inanities tumbled from their lips.

Gowan was no fool. He recognized that life had just presented him with a fait accompli. Everything about Edith was exquisite: her easy silence; her serenity; her enchanting face; the way she danced, as if her toes scarcely touched the ground.

She would make a perfect Duchess of Kinross. Already he could envision the portraits he would commission: one of the duchess alone, and, later, another of the four of them—or five; he would leave the number of children to her—to hang over the mantelpiece in the great drawing room.

The dance ended, and the strains of a waltz began.

Lady Edith curtsied before him.

"Will you dance with me again?" His voice tumbled out absent its usual measured tones.

She looked up at him and spoke for the first time since they'd begun dancing. "I'm afraid that this dance is promised to Lord Beckwith—"

"No," he stated, though he'd never done such an impolite thing in this life.

"No?" Her eyes widened slightly.

"Waltz with me."

He held out his hand. She paused very briefly, and then once again put her hand into his. Carefully, as if he were taming a bird, he placed his other hand on her waist.

Who would have thought that all the romantic tripe about being burned by a lover's touch was true?

As they danced, Gowan was vaguely aware that the entire assembly was watching them. The Duke of Kinross was dancing twice in a row with Gilchrist's daughter. The news would be all over London by morning.

He didn't care. His heart was thudding in time with the music as he studied her minutely, feature by feature. She was utterly delicious. Her lips held a natural curve, as if she had a kiss or a smile in reserve, one that she had never given away.

Her feet and his moved in perfect harmony with the music. Gowan had never danced better in his life. They swept through the waltz like sparks thrown from a fire, neither uttering a word.

It occurred to him that words weren't necessary. They were speaking through the dance itself.

Another thought came to him: he had never realized that he was lonely. Not until now.

As the final strains of the waltz died, he bowed to his dancing partner, and straightened again to find Lord Beckwith just there, waiting.

"Duke," Beckwith said, a distinct chill in his voice. "I believe you mistook my dance for yours." He jutted his elbow toward Lady Edith with the air of a man ill-used.

She turned to Gowan with a polite smile of

farewell, and slipped her hand through Beckwith's arm.

Gowan burned with impatience. He was a Scot: he didn't trade in that sort of politeness, not between a man and a woman. He wanted to show her what he felt, snatch her behind a pillar, wind her in his arms, and kiss her.

But she wasn't his wife . . . *yet*. Until she was, he had to follow the rules. He watched his future wife move into the next dance on the viscount's arm.

Gowan was wealthier than Beckwith. And he was better-looking than the viscount. Unless Edith preferred slender, twig-like men. He couldn't honestly say that she had looked at him with desire.

But of course, one wouldn't want a flagrantly lustful wife. His grandfather had met his grandmother at a formal dinner and had known instantly that she would be the next duchess, even though she had been only fifteen at the time, and shy for her age. One certainly didn't want one's future— let alone one's current—duchess to crave strange men.

Gowan decided he would return in the morning to pay a call. That was part of the courtship rituals in England: visit the house of the intended three or four times, take her for a drive, and then ask the father for his daughter's hand.

Once that was settled in his mind, he searched

out the earl and broached the subject of pound notes. Their work concluded, Gowan said, "I'll stop by on the morrow to pay a call on your daughter before I continue on to Brighton to discuss our conclusions with Pomfrey's Bank."

He saw approval in the earl's eyes. Obviously the man had invited him to this ball for reasons that had nothing to do with whether the government reimbursed its banknotes with gold sovereigns.

Gowan did not dance with any other women that night. He had no inclination to, and he certainly didn't want to lounge at the side of the room and watch Edith dance with other men. The very thought made his jaw clench.

Jealousy was the downfall of his countrymen. It was the dark side of their greatest virtue—loyalty. A Scotsman is loyal until death; unlike fickle English husbands, he would never turn from his chosen bride to seek other beds.

Still, Gowan knew he was a damned possessive bastard, who put loyalty above all else. It would eat him alive to watch Edith moving from man to man before he had a ring on her finger that told the world she was his.

Though his imprint on her heart would be even better.

It would be a waste of time to stand about snarling at Edith's suitors, and Gowan was not a time waster. Instead, he went home and composed a message to his London solicitor, Jelves. In it, he noted that he planned to marry in the near future, and directed Jelves to draw up a suggested settlement and bring it to his door in the early morning.

The task would probably keep the man up all night; Gowan made a mental note to send him a bonus.

He rose at dawn and spent several hours working. A night's sleep hadn't changed his mind about Lady Edith—not that he could recall ever changing his mind about something important, once he'd made it up. When a haggard-looking Jelves arrived, he gave a concentrated hour to the question of marital settlements. He and the solicitor drew up a document that Jelves somewhat nervously suggested might be overly generous.

"Lady Edith will be my duchess," Gowan told him, aware his eyes had gone wintry. "She will be my better half. Why would I stint what she will inherit after my death, or enjoy during my life? We Scots don't treat our women with the disrespect you do in this country. Even if she and I have naught but a single daughter, that daughter will inherit the majority of my estate."

He must have come close to baring his teeth, because Jelves swallowed and bobbed his head.

By now Gowan was tardy, damn it. He had to be on the coach road out of London in a matter of two hours at the very most, since a table full of bankers would be waiting for him in Brighton. Instructing his retinue to follow in a second coach, he directed his coachman to return to Gilchrist's house in Curzon Street.

The Gilchrists' butler took his cloak, informed him that the countess and Lady Edith would shortly join their guests, and opened the door to a large and gracious drawing room that—at present—resembled nothing so much as a gentlemen's club.

Men were everywhere, posies and bouquets by their side, laughing amongst themselves. Incredibly, a discreet game of piquet was going on in one corner. He recognized only the half of them. Beckwith was there, decked out in an orange coat with garish buttons. Lord Pimrose-Finsbury was there as well. Pimrose-Finsbury held only a life title, but he owned a good share of Marylebone. He clutched a delicate little violet nosegay.

Gowan felt a prick of chagrin; it hadn't occurred to him to send someone to Covent Garden to procure roses or something of that nature.

"If you would join the morning callers, Your Grace," the butler said, "I will serve refreshments very shortly."

Instead, Gowan turned on his heel and strode back to the entry.

"Would Your Grace prefer to leave a card?" the butler asked, following him.

"I would prefer to speak to Lord Gilchrist. When did Lady Edith debut?" he asked bluntly.

The butler's eyebrow twitched, but he controlled himself. "Last night," he said. "Last night was her first appearance in society."

Gowan wasn't the only man who had taken one look at Edith and pictured her by his side.

But he now knew precisely why Gilchrist had asked him to attend his ball: the invitation had included the gift of his daughter's hand. There would be no further competition if he chose to take up the earl's silent offer.

"I should like to speak to His Lordship, if he is free." He did not ask. Gowan never asked; he stated. It made no difference, because he always got what he wanted. And there was something undignified about *asking*.

Dukes, in his opinion, did not ask.

They stated.

He had a feeling that there would be no *asking* with regard to Lady Edith's hand, either.

Two

It was a fever that had turned Lady Edith Gilchrist into the greatest success of the season, winning her the hand (and presumably, the heart) of the Duke of Kinross. If Edie hadn't been dreadfully ill at her own debut ball, she might well have been less popular. But as her head felt like an empty gourd, all she did was drift about the ballroom and smile. And smile.

That turned out to be a formula for extraordinary success.

By halfway through the evening, she'd danced with every eligible bachelor on the market, and twice with the Duke of Kinross, Lord Beckwith, and Lord Mendelson. Her stepmother, Layla, caught her arm at one point and said that Lady Jersey had declared her the most enchanting debutante of the season. Apparently, the queen of Almack's patronesses would overlook the fact that at nineteen, Edie was unfashionably old.

Edie had just smiled. She was trying to maintain her balance.

By the time she appeared in her father's library late the next morning, her cheeks as white as her gown, the negotiations surrounding her marital future had already been concluded.

She kept her eyes lowered (to hide the fact they were bloodshot), smiled when spoken to, and said only: "Of course, Father." And: "I would be honored to marry you, Your Grace."

"The truth is, Edie," Layla declared five minutes after Kinross had departed and she'd brought Edie back to her bedchamber, "your fever was sent by a fairy godmother whom your father forgot to mention. Who would have thought you'd catch a duke?"

This particular duke was Scottish, which was a

23

mark against him—but according to Layla, the fact that Kinross owned the grandest estate in all Scotland made him an honorary Englishman and the most desirable man on the marriage market.

Edie just moaned and fell face down onto her bed. Her head was throbbing, she felt faint, and frankly, she wasn't even quite sure what her fiancé looked like. He had lovely voice, but he was too tall, she thought. Big. At least he didn't have red hair. She didn't like red-haired men. "That's not very kind," she said into her pillow.

"You know what I mean. You looked so lovely and pale. The way Mary wove pearls into all that hair of yours was quite fetching. And you just smiled instead of talking. That's very attractive. To men, anyway."

"Don't you think that he's a little impulsive?" Edie mumbled.

Layla pulled back the curtains and pushed the window open. Edie loved her bedchamber, which was large and airy, with a windowsill that overlooked the back garden. But she loathed the fact that Layla perched on that windowsill to smoke cheroots.

"You can't smoke one of those foul things in here," she said quickly. "I hate the smell and I'm *sick!*"

Even face down in the bed, she knew perfectly well that Layla was paying no attention to her. Edie could hear her settling in her favorite perch and lighting her cheroot at the candle so that she could blow the smoke into the garden. Which she thought kept it out of the room, but it didn't.

"I might throw up," Edie pointed out, moving her cheek to a cooler patch of pillowcase.

"No, you won't. You have a fever, not a stomach upset."

Edie gave up. "My future husband is either impulsive or stupid. I only met him last night, and I can hardly remember what he looks like."

"Not impulsive, manly," Layla said. "Decisive."

"Idiotic."

"You are beautiful, Edie. You know that. For heaven's sake, the whole *ton* knows that. He probably heard about you long before yesterday night. Everyone has been talking about Exquisite Edith, who is finally making her bow before society."

"Don't forget my Delightful Dowry," Edie said sourly. "It's more important than the shape of my nose."

"He doesn't need your dowry. You clearly have no idea how many young ladies have tried to snag the duke. He used to be betrothed to a girl from a Scottish family—the Capons? the Partridges?—some sort of fowl. She died a year ago and no one has succeeded in catching his eye since. Of course, he was in mourning for some months."

"That's so sad. Perhaps he's been nursing a broken heart."

"From what I've heard, they were betrothed in the cradle or some such and no one, including the duke, knew her very well."

"I still think it's sad."

"Don't be so tenderhearted, Edie. The duke has obviously put it behind him, since he walked into the ballroom, waltzed with you, and lost his heart." Layla paused, almost certainly to blow a smoke ring out the window. "That's rather romantic, don't you think?"

"Did the duke actually say that he lost his heart? Because he didn't seem heartsick to me, though my eyesight was so blurry that I wouldn't know."

"His face spoke volumes."

"It had better, since we were completely silent while dancing last night." Edie wiggled a fraction of an inch in order to cool her burning cheek against yet another section of sheet. "Don't wave that cheroot around. Smoke is coming into the room."

"Sorry."

There was a second of silence while Edie contemplated whether it would be worse to die of influenza, or to marry a man whose face she'd never seen clearly.

"What does he look like?" she asked. "And could you please ring for Mary? My head is pounding."

"I'll make you a cold compress."

26

"No, you can't move from the window until you've finished that vile thing."

"Then how on earth can I ring for Mary?"

Even face down, Edie could tell that Layla was staying right where she was on the window seat. "You don't have proper maternal instincts," she complained.

"That's true," Layla replied dryly. "Just as well, under the circumstances."

After the death of Edie's mother, Lord Gilchrist had remained unwed for years—until he'd lost his head at age thirty-six and fallen in love with Layla. Edie hadn't much liked her new stepmother, who had a seductive air that Edie did not appreciate at thirteen years old. In fact, Edie had been rather revolted by the fact that her father had married a mere twenty-year-old, let alone one whose crimson lips and shapely figure flaunted her sensuality.

But a couple of years later she had come upon Layla crying, and had learned just how heartbreaking it is to be unable to give one's husband an heir. They had become fast friends over the subsequent years. Alas, no children ever arrived; lately Layla had taken up smoking and developed a bit of a reckless edge.

"I shouldn't have said that," Edie said. "I'm sorry."

"It's all right. I probably would have made a bloody horrible mother anyway."

"No, you wouldn't. You're funny and sweet, and if you would throw away that cheroot and make me a cool compress I'd love you forever."

Layla sighed.

"Did you put it out?"

"Yes." A moment later fingers touched Edie's shoulder. "You have to turn over so I can put this compress on."

Edie obediently shifted onto her back. "You looked wonderful last night, too, Layla." She squinted at her stepmother. Layla was forever going on slimming regimes, but Edie thought her luscious shape was perfect as it was.

Layla smiled. "Thank you, darling. Do you want me to ring for Mary so you can change your clothes and get under the covers?"

"No, I'm too tired."

Layla being Layla—and lacking a maternal instinct—she didn't insist, but simply put the damp cloth on Edie's head and walked back across the room.

"Are you lighting another one?"

"No, I am not. I'm sitting before your fireplace like a good stepmother. Maybe I'll learn knotting so I can do a better impersonation of one. I'm not quite certain your new husband will appreciate my more eccentric qualities; I must develop some respectable traits so I'll be allowed to visit."

"Why do you say so? Is he a thoroughgoing stick?"

"I don't know him any better than you do."

"But at least you saw him clearly, *and* you weren't feverish."

"Perhaps a bit stickish," Layla said. "But nothing you're not used to, given your father."

A trickle of water ran down Edie's neck; she was so hot that it felt quite agreeable. "I was hoping to avoid marrying someone like Father."

"Your father is not so bad."

"Yes, he is. He's out of the house all the time, and he hardly ever takes you anywhere. I know that you say that it's different when you two are alone, but all he does at dinner is lecture me. Which is quite unfair, inasmuch as I've never given him the least cause for anxiety. He should be more grateful. Last time I saw her, your mother told me all about Juliet Fallesbury, who ran away with a footman."

Layla had a wicked chuckle. "My mother loves that story, mostly because the man was nicknamed Longfellow. You know, Edie, it might be good for you to rebel a little. It's not natural to cheerfully agree to marry a complete stranger."

"I am not cheerful," Edie pointed out.

"But you're not rebellious, either. I'm worried you'll let your husband have his own way all the time and he'll become a monstrous dictator."

There was something about Layla's tone that sounded a warning note in Edie's mind, but she felt too sick to figure out the problem, if there was one other than her father's dictatorial habits. "Perhaps I will run away, disguise myself as a man, and join an orchestra. Imagine it, Layla. Some people have nothing to do but play music, all day long. And then at night they play some more, but with an audience." A few notes of the prelude of Bach's Cello Suite no. 1 in G Major slid through her mind. The fever made the arpeggio shimmer in her head, as if the music floated like oil on top of water.

"What I'm saying is that you should assert yourself more, Edie. Men are not easy to live with."

"Father has never refused me anything I truly wanted."

"It's true that he's allowed you to remain home and play the cello, far past the age when you should have made your bow to society."

The notes sneaked into Edie's mind again, luring her into thinking about the broken chords in Bach's prelude. They should be easy, like a basic exercise, and yet somehow . . .

Her stepmother's voice intervened. "The fact is that your father is terrified to let you go. Who will play duets with him? Who will talk endlessly of music? Take pity on me, why don't you? I haven't the faintest interest in discussing the cello. I don't mind hearing it, but I find talk of it tedious. And yet I am facing a lifetime of your father's harangues about bowing and tuning."

"The cello is the only thing my father and I have in common. I can hardly remember talking to him of anything else. And now I'm to marry someone like that, but who likely knows nothing about music?"

Really, if Edie weren't so sick, she would feel righteous indignation, but she was already so sorry for herself that there wasn't any room to moan about marriage to a philistine. "My eyes feel like boiled eggs," she added.

"I'm sorry, darling. Do you want me to send for the doctor?"

"No. He'll give me laudanum, which won't help. Fevers can't be cured by a narcotic."

"I like laudanum," Layla said. "I had it only once, but I've never forgotten the way it made me feel all floaty and free, as if nothing in the world was worth worrying about."

"I'll have to make sure no one ever gives you any. You'd probably develop a habit, the way Mrs. Fitzhugh has. *Bell's Messenger* said that she collapsed on the ballroom floor the other day, and her husband had to carry her out."

"Reason enough to avoid it. I'm not absolutely certain your father could hoist me from the ground without staggering."

"Would you mind dipping my cloth in the basin again?"

Layla did it while Edie thought about her impending marriage. "Did Kinross give any reason for making such a precipitous proposal?"

"It was because he fell in love with you," Layla said promptly, putting the compress on Edie's forehead. "He took one look at your golden tresses, not to mention the delectable rest of you, and decided to ward off the competition." But there was something about her voice . . .

"The truth, Layla."

"And I gather he had important things to do. He left for Brighton directly after speaking with your father."

" 'Things to do,' " Edie repeated. "What sort of things?"

"Problems with the pound note. Don't think about it too closely, darling," Layla advised. Edie heard her opening the little tin box in which she kept her cheroots.

"What did he say, exactly?"

"Oh please, let's talk about something more interesting! Kinross has one of the biggest estates in Scotland. You can only imagine, Edie. He arrived in two carriages, with eight grooms, all in livery; I saw it out the window. I expect you'll live like a queen. Your father says he lives in a *castle.*"

"A castle?" Edie digested that. "But he couldn't be bothered to take me for a drive before making me chatelaine of that castle? You'd think he'd be interested in waiting until we'd eaten a meal together. What if I slurped my soup or sucked on chicken bones? Do you suppose he has illegitimate children waiting at home?"

"I doubt it. More importantly, since his parents have both passed away, you won't have to cope with a ferocious Scottish mama."

"Then what could be more important than wooing his future wife?"

"You have to look at it from a man's point of view, Edie."

"Play the man and enlighten me."

Layla's voice dropped into a deeper register and she said, "I am the top catch on the marriage market. After I have selected an appropriate consort, I shall inform the young lady's father of his good fortune."

"It's not entirely illogical."

"Your father likes the duke very much."

"That's no recommendation. Do you suppose Kinross will deign to return to London before we marry?"

"He'll travel from Brighton to the Earl of Chatteris's wedding, so we'll see him there."

Edie groaned. "One of the Smythe-Smith girls, isn't it?"

"Honoria. She's quite lovely. I know you think she's not a good musician—"

"There's no *thinking* about it. She's terrible."

"That's as may be, but she's also extremely nice."

"I don't like house parties. I can never find the time to practice."

"Your father said he expects you to behave like a proper lady now that you've made your debut, Edie. That means very little practicing when you're not at home."

Edie made a rude noise. She hadn't been able to play her cello yesterday owing to her fever, not to mention preparations for the ball. She rarely practiced fewer than five hours in a given day, and she had no intention of altering her habits. "What if my marriage ends up like yours?"

"There's nothing wrong with my marriage," Layla said. Edie could hear her blowing a smoke ring out the window.

"You sleep in separate rooms."

"Everyone in polite society sleeps in separate rooms."

"You didn't when you were first married," Edie persisted. "I often saw Father kissing you, and once I saw him pick you up and throw you over his shoulder and practically run up the stairs."

A silence ensued. "You shouldn't have seen that."

"Why not? I was a beast to you, but inside I was glad to see Father so happy. Giddy, almost."

"Well, that's marriage for you," Layla said. "Giddy one moment, indifferent the next."

"I can't imagine Kinross being giddy, can you?"

"Could you have imagined your father giddy, if you hadn't seen the evidence with your own eyes?"

"No."

"Temporary madness," Layla said sadly. "Jonas came to his senses and realized that I'm a light-headed fool, and that was that."

"You are *not* a light-headed fool!"

"I had it from the horse's mouth, just last night."

"Father said that?" Edie pulled off the cloth, pushed herself up against the pillows, and squinted blearily at Layla. Her head was throbbing, but there was no mistaking the downcast expression on her stepmother's face.

Layla stubbed out her cheroot and returned her pink glass holder to its tin box. "I shall ring for Mary so you can take off that corset and crawl into bed. Would you like a cool bath?"

"Yes," Edie said. "But are you truly miserable, Layla?"

"It's only a fit of the dismals," she replied, coming over to perch on the side of the bed. "I shall miss you, and the thought makes me fidgety. Here, let me feel your head."

"Now that I'm almost a married woman, will you tell me exactly where Father goes at night? What I'm getting at is, does he have a mistress?"

"I haven't actually asked him." Layla bit her bottom lip, and then she said: "I don't want to know. Goodness, but your head is warm. We have to cool you down." She reached over to pull the cord that summoned Mary.

Edie couldn't seem to keep her mind focused on

any particular subject. "What does Kinross look like—up close, I mean?"

"Ferociously masculine. Beautiful in that male way. Shoulders as broad as a plow horse's, with muscled thighs. I'd like to see him in a kilt. Do you suppose he'll wear one at your wedding?"

"Do you think he has a sense of humor?" And then Edie held her breath because, to her mind, that was the most important feature one could possess. Having been called beautiful all her life, she knew just how meaningless that attribute could be.

Silence.

"Oh no," she moaned.

"It was a very formal occasion," Layla offered. "I could scarcely tell him a joke about a Welshman and wait for his reaction."

"I'm to marry a Scotsman the size of a bloody tree, with no sense of humor and an impulsive bent."

Layla shrugged. "You'll have to stop swearing, at least in his presence, darling."

"Why?"

"He seemed a bit formal."

Edie groaned. "I'm marrying my bloody father."

"That makes two of us."

Three

En route to the New Steine Hotel
Brighton

At the very moment his betrothed labeled him impulsive, Gowan was saying the same to himself. He had never done anything so reckless in his life. Never.

In fact, Gowan couldn't remember doing *anything* impulsive, let alone jumping into one of the most important acquisitions of his life, without doing diligent research beforehand.

The truth was that he never made direct purchases of any kind. He had people to do that sort of thing. He didn't care to shop. The only things he bought directly were his horses.

But—and it was a reassuring thought—he had bought most of his horseflesh without fuss. He saw the right mare, and recognized instantly where she would fit into his breeding program.

Obviously, that wasn't a flattering way to think about his future wife, but it was true. He had taken one look at Lady Edith and knew immediately that he wanted her. And her children.

The idea of bedding her was entirely pleasing. For all her modesty in gaze and demeanor, her body was delightfully rounded. Other young ladies looked like skeletons swathed in a yard or two of fabric. Whole rows of skeletons, with their ringlets bouncing off the sharp edges of their bony shoulders.

Not a kind thought, he reminded himself. He was trying to curb his descriptive instincts: they might be silently expressed, but he could hardly ignore the fact that they were often critical. *Always* critical, his conscience insisted.

But he hadn't come up a single negative aspect to Lady Edith, other than the fact that he didn't care for her name. Who could? She was an angel, not an Edith.

His first fiancée's name had been Rosaline, which had a romantic sound to it. The two of them had been matched as children. Indeed, they hadn't even met until she was sixteen and he nineteen. After that, they settled into waiting for her to reach her majority—except she died a few days before her birthday. He'd only met her twice in the intervening two years. So theirs could hardly be termed a romantic pairing.

"Your Grace?"

His factor, Bardolph, was seated on the opposite carriage seat, looking annoyed. Bardolph had been Gowan's father's agent, and had been passed on to Gowan precisely as the wines in the cellars were, except that, unlike the wine, Bardolph was not improving with age. His beard came to a point in a manner that was distinctly goatlike. Goatish. Goat-reminiscent. Goat—

38

Gowan wrenched his mind back to the subject at hand. "Yes?"

"The head bailiff and the mine manager are in disagreement owing to silt carried from the diggings at the Currie tin mine, which is choking the fish in the Glaschorrie River," Bardolph said, in the painstaking way that people do when you've ignored their question the first time around.

"Halt the mining," Gowan said. "Unless the mine can control the drainage, we'll have to close. There are six villages dependent on fish from that river."

Bardolph went back to his ledger, and Gowan went back to thinking.

Gilchrist had suggested a five-month-long betrothal, which sounded fine. He was in no rush to begin married life. One had to expect that accommodating a wife would entail a certain level of fuss, and he didn't like fuss.

But then he thought about the creaminess of Lady Edith's skin. Creamy wasn't the right word. He'd never seen skin so white, like the finest parchment. He had decided that the loch was darker than her eyes, which were closer to the green of a juniper tree.

This line of thought made him feel a surge of possessiveness. She would be his soon: the dreamy eyes, white skin, rosy mouth, and all . . . He had bartered for her with a settlement that would make Bardolph turn faint.

He had given Gilchrist every single item the man requested. One didn't haggle when it came to a wife. That would be most ill-bred.

Bardolph raised his head again. "Your Grace, would you care to discuss the provisions of the contract with Mr. Stickney-Ellis as regards the bridge to be built over the Glaschorrie? I have the provisions as established by the builders."

Gowan nodded, and settled more comfortably into his seat. No more thinking about Lady Edith: it was detrimental to his concentration, which was unacceptable. In fact, once he had her in the castle, he would have to make very certain that she didn't disrupt his attention.

He wasn't entirely sure what his grandmother had done from morning to night—women's work—but it had to do with linens, and the sick, and the crofters . . . Gilchrist would have made certain that his daughter was well trained.

He was a bit stiff, Gilchrist, but a decent fellow.

Bardolph's voice filtered through one part of his mind. He held up his hand. "I'd prefer three arches rather than two."

The factor made a note and droned his way through the rest of the page.

Gowan cleared his throat.

"Yes, Your Grace?"

"Tomorrow morning, there will be an announcement in the *Morning Post* of my betrothal. Jelves is finishing the agreed-upon settlements."

Bardolph's mouth fell open. "Your Grace, you—"

"I am betrothed to Lady Edith Gilchrist. Lord Gilchrist offered to send the announcement to the papers."

Bardolph bowed his head. "May I offer my sincerest congratulations, Your Grace?"

Gowan inclined his head in acknowledgment. "The earl has suggested a betrothal of five months or thereabouts. I expect you to see to all arrangements. You may be in touch with Lord Gilchrist's representative."

The factor nodded again. "Yes, certainly, Your Grace."

"Reconstruction of the water closet between my chamber and the future duchess's must be completed."

"Of course," Bardolph said.

Then his factor pulled forward a bound volume. "Next I would like to review the estate agent's breeding provisions for the Dorbie farm. I brought the stock book with me for that purpose." He began to read aloud.

Gowan was rather surprised at how hard he had to work to keep his mind attentive. It was probably the novelty of the whole affair. It stood to reason that a new experience would be distracting.

The most surprising thing of all was the deep strain of satisfaction he felt. It threaded through all his thoughts like the awareness of a coming rainstorm: silent, but leaving its mark. Edith was *his* now. He would bring that lovely, delectable woman home.

He had been missing that calm warmth in his life, and he hadn't even known it. He felt something bigger and more profound than desire. He wasn't certain what it was.

Acquisitiveness, perhaps. Satisfaction. None of those words were right.

Bardolph cleared his throat.

"Yes?"

"As I was saying . . ."

Four

Two more days passed before Edie felt well enough to drag herself out of bed. Layla had finally insisted on a doctor's visit; the man had simply confirmed what Edie's common sense had already told her: She should remain in bed in the dark. She was not to play her cello.

"Has Father inquired how I am?" she asked on the morning she felt well enough to join her stepmother for breakfast in Layla's chamber. Layla was wearing a robe that fell open in a cascade of silk ruffles. She looked as delectable as a peach tart.

"He has not," Layla said, choosing another grape with all the seriousness of someone selecting a diamond ring. She must have started on another slimming regime.

Edie sat down opposite, picked up three pieces of cheese, and popped them in her mouth. "Beast," she said, without much rancor. "His only child could have died of the influenza, and he wouldn't have noticed my passing."

"He would have noticed," Layla said, inspecting the grapes once again. "He may not notice if I expired, but if he had no one to play the cello with, that would probably make an impression."

"Just eat some!" Edie snatched up a handful and dropped them into Layla's lap.

There was nothing that Edie could do for Layla's marriage, but the whole situation did get her thinking after she found her way back to her room and into a hot bath.

She was betrothed to a duke whom she wouldn't be able to pick out from a crowd. That fact didn't actually bother her much.

It had been impressed upon her from the age of five that her thirty-thousand-pound dowry and her blue blood ensured that her marriage would be a matter of dynastic lines, a way to create children and to concentrate wealth. She had never conceived of marriage as more than a meeting of (hopefully) compatible minds.

However, she definitely wouldn't want to live through the kind of drama that accompanied Layla and her father's marriage. Hopefully, the man

43

with the enchanting Scottish burr in his voice would be a reasonable fellow, with as little nonsense about him as there was about her.

In fact, despite her irritation with his lack of courtship, the truth was that Kinross's swift proposal was a point in his favor, as it indicated that nothing about her person had entered into his decision. He had likely decided to marry her before attending the ball, and he had danced with her merely to ascertain that she didn't have a hump or a wooden leg.

Edie sank lower into her bath, letting the water lap at her chin. She found this explanation of her fiancé's brisk proposal very reassuring. She wouldn't care for an impulsive man. She much preferred to think of Kinross as having made a reasoned decision.

She *never* wanted to face the sort of emotional storm that surrounded her father and Layla. Never.

When she finally rose from the bath, pink and wrinkly, her natural optimism was restored for the first time since she had fallen ill. She could handle a man like her father.

Her stepmother had made the mistake of falling in love, probably because the earl had wooed her with such unexpected ardor. If Layla didn't care so much, she wouldn't flirt with other men to try to get her husband's attention. And if he didn't care so much, he wouldn't get so angry. Surely Edie and Kinross could avoid that vicious circle by establishing some ground rules for suitably mature discourse.

In fact, why wait until they met again? It might be a good idea to express her ideas in writing.

The more she thought about it, the more she liked the sound of an exchange of letters. She would write her betrothed, and lay out what she considered to be the features of a successful marriage. He was in Brighton; very well, she would send a groom there with a letter in hand. It would take the man only a day if he went by mail coach. A duke who traveled with two carriages and eight footmen shouldn't be difficult to locate.

Pulling on her wrapper, she waited until her maid left before she sat down at her writing desk. Her demands must be tactfully phrased. Mutual respect was an obvious requirement. And plenty of time alone: she didn't want a husband who trailed her about and interrupted her cello practice.

The most delicate issue was that of mistresses. As she understood it, a gentleman generally had a mistress. She didn't have a strong objection; one could hardly claim that a vow between strangers, motivated by power and money, was sacrosanct. On the other hand, she did not want her husband to treat her with the cavalier disdain that her father demonstrated toward Layla, staying out all night, and so on.

And she definitely didn't wish to catch a disease from a woman in her husband's employ, if that was the right terminology for such an arrangement. Edie pulled out a sheet of letter paper and paused. Should she specify that such a disease would be grounds to break their betrothal?

Surely her father would have asked that question.

She made a mental note to check, and began to write. At the end of an hour, she had filled two pages. She read them over and found them quite satisfactory.

The letter was respectful, but candid.

To her mind, honesty was the most important thing between a husband and wife. If only her father would tell Layla that he loved her desperately, and felt hurt every time she played the coquette with other men, and if only Layla would tell her husband that she was starved for affection and felt wretched about her inability to bear a child . . .

Well, then they would have a *marriage,* instead of this unending series of battles cobbled together by a wedding ring.

She rang a bell and gave the missive to the butler, Willikins, with instructions that it be taken to Brighton without delay.

By the next morning at breakfast it seemed that her father's marriage had taken another turn for the worse. "Did he not come home last night, either?" Edie inquired, realizing that Layla had been crying.

A tear rolled down Layla's cheek and she scrubbed it away. "He only married me because I was young and presumably fertile. And now I'm not, he sees no reason to be with me."

"That doesn't make sense. He'd never been very fussed about a male heir; he likes my cousin Magnus." Edie handed her a handkerchief.

"You're wrong. He hates me because I haven't had a baby."

"He doesn't hate you, Layla. He truly doesn't."

"*And* he has decided that I have been unfaithful to him with Lord Gryphus."

"Gryphus? Why on earth does Father think that? Mind you, Gryphus is very pretty and I can see why his face would inspire jealousy."

"I don't care how pretty he is; I haven't broken my wed-wedding vows," Layla said, her voice cracking. "All I did was allow Lord Gryphus to take me in to supper two or three times, when your father didn't accompany me to a ball. I had no idea people were gossiping!"

"I expect Father is jealous because Gryphus is your age. How unpleasant it is to think that someone must have tattled."

"Jonas believed that horrid gossip, without even asking me! And now he won't—he won't have anything to do with me, and he says that I should go to the country and direct my lover to follow

47

me, except that I don't *have* a lover!" The sentence ended with a huge sob. "He says I should be more discreet."

"That's absurd, and I shall tell him so."

Layla reached over and caught her wrist. "You mustn't. It wouldn't be right. You're his daughter."

Edie frowned. "Who else can set him straight? It's a consequence of our relationship. Like *Hamlet*, you know. My governess tried to beat that play into my head for ages. Not much stayed with me, but I remember Hamlet moaning, 'Oh woe, that I was born to set it straight.' Or something along those lines."

"Jonas would be horribly offended if you mentioned it," Layla said with a hiccup. "Besides, he won't believe what you say, any more than he believes me."

Edie got up and sat down beside her, wrapping her arms around Layla's shoulders. "Oh, sweetheart, he's such a fool. He loves you. I know he does."

"No, he doesn't. I caught him in the hall last night and he—he said he wished he had never married a goose like myself. I expect that he's found someone else," Layla said, her voice cracking again. "I'm sure of it, because he went out and didn't come back home."

After a while, when Layla had pretty much stopped crying, Edie said, "Just wait a moment, dearest. I'll be right back."

She ran from the room and darted down the passage. Her cello was resting in an upright stand in the spare bedchamber that she used for practice; she picked it up and carried it, walking more slowly, back to Layla's room.

Layla was curled up in the corner of her couch, an occasional sob still shaking her.

Edie sat down in a straight-backed chair and adjusted her skirts so that she could position the cello between her legs. This position was by far the best for her bow hand, but of course it could be assumed only in private. Or in front of Layla, which was practically the same.

She made certain that the endpin of her cello was firmly set into the floor, and then drew her bow across the strings. After not having played in four days, the sound was like a blessing. She tuned it and then began, two eighth notes and a half note ringing in the air.

Layla asked in a choked voice, "Is that my favorite?"

"Yes. *Dona Nobis Pacem.*" *Give Us Peace* poured from her strings like the balm of Gilead, always stately, always measured, joy kept in check.

Maybe it was the days of enforced rest, but her fingers didn't stumble once, and her bow slid across the strings at the perfect angle, the music calibrated to make the listener's heart sing.

At the end of the hymn, she heard Layla take a

deep breath. Edie smiled at her, bent her head again, and swept straight into the "Winter" concerto of Vivaldi's *Four Seasons*, the piece she had been working on before becoming ill.

As she neared the end of the piece, and had (to be quite honest) forgotten about Layla altogether, the door opened. When she glanced up, her father stood in the door.

He was staring at his wife. Tumbled gold hair covered Layla's face, but the handkerchief clutched in her hand told its own story.

Edie almost felt a pulse of sympathy for her father. He was tall and broad-shouldered and handsome, though he'd hate to hear that. He liked to think of himself as a statesman, rather than an ordinary mortal.

That was the real trouble. Logic mattered to him above any sort of emotion, even though when it came to Layla, he was often quite illogical. "That was well played," he said, shifting his eyes to Edie. "Not perfectly, as the last movement is marked allegro. Your playing was not quite nimble enough."

Edie looked at Layla, but her only response to her husband's voice was to curl up more tightly.

"May I request a moment with my wife?" he asked, his voice as flat as his expression. At that moment his eyes fell to Edie's legs, one on either side of her instrument, her skirts barely covering her knees. "Daughter!"

"Father." She moved the cello forward and came to her feet, her skirts spilling back down to the floor. Then she tucked her bow under her arm and picked up the cello, turning to her stepmother. "Layla, darling, I shall be ready whenever you decide to retire to the country and commence on a life of unending debauchery."

Her father narrowed his eyes, but she marched past him and out the door. A half hour later, after she had requested and eaten breakfast—another breakfast, as her first had been left untouched back in Layla's chamber—she began work on Bach's cello suites.

Irritation wasn't good for music. She believed that it soured the notes. She had to start over three or four times until the notes finally carried the emotion Bach had written into the piece, rather than her own.

At some point, she stopped just long enough to eat the luncheon her maid brought her. By then she was working on a cello sonata by Boccherini that was so difficult that she had to stop over and over to look at the score.

Her right arm was aching by four o'clock in the afternoon, but she was suffused with a sense of deep satisfaction.

In spite of Layla's tears, it was her favorite kind of day.

Five

Gowan stared in total disbelief at the pages before him. The letter was written in a strong hand, too strong for a woman. His grandmother had written in a delicate script, which she ornamented now and then with flourishes. There were no flourishes to this letter.

There was nothing feminine about it.

In fact . . .

His eyes narrowed. He almost didn't believe it had been written by a woman. It was altogether too direct, too demanding.

Not the sort of letter that could have come from the delicate flower with whom he had danced, nor from the woman who had kept her eyes demurely lowered when her father announced that he had accepted an offer of marriage on her behalf. There hadn't been a flicker of dissent or rebellion on Lady Edith's face.

He picked up the letter again. In fact, it wasn't rebellious, precisely.

It was . . .

It was contractual, that's what it was. She used the phrase "I would request" when what she clearly meant was "I demand."

I would request that you do not keep a mistress, nor engage in such frolicsome activities, until such time as we have produced the requisite number of heirs (such number to be decided amicably between us) and have ceased marital relations, as will happen in due course. I am most reluctant to contract a disease of an intimate nature.

He had already read that paragraph four times, but he read it again. Frolicsome activities? Mistress? *Cease marital relations?* When he was dead, perhaps. The fact that he hadn't yet engaged in relations didn't mean that he had no interest in doing so. He had a keen interest.

In fact, he had a running tally of things he was looking forward to trying. With his wife. Who apparently thought she would make love to him on a schedule, and a limited schedule at that.

As I have very little interest in pursuits of the flesh, I shall give you no reason for anxiety in that regard.

She sounded like a nun. All right, he didn't mind that particular statement so much. He could tempt her into interest in pursuits of the flesh. Or he could spend his life trying.

But her next suggestion was a great deal more irritating.

I propose that we do not engage to produce an heir for three years, although five might be better. We are both young, and need not worry about age as a factor in procreation. I am not ready for that burden. To be frank, I simply don't have the time.

He stared at that for a long time. She didn't want children? What in the bloody hell was she doing all day that she didn't have time for children? He was ready to have children now. His half sister, Susannah, was five years old and she would do better with siblings.

What's more, the work of running the estate wouldn't be any easier in five years.

On the other hand, he did like the next paragraph:

I am certain that your responsibilities are many and burdensome; I propose that we agree not to interrupt each other during the day. I have noticed that considerable unhappiness stems from the needful behavior of a spouse. I trust you do not take my suggestion here as an insult: as we have no knowledge whatsoever of each other, you will understand that I speak merely as a proponent of a wish for a happy marriage.

He agreed with her.

But it was a bit stuffy. No, more than a bit stuffy.

Still, if he had thought to write something down—which he never would, because there was something unsettling about putting all this on paper—he might well have shaped that very paragraph himself.

Or something like it.

It was the final part of the letter that made him want to bare his teeth and growl at the page like some sort of madman.

> Finally, I wanted to note that I much appreciate the way by which you dispensed with courtship. Although I was surprised at first, on further examination, I respect your good judgment in this matter. I assume that you hold the same understanding of marriage that I do: it is a contract enacted for the good of one's lineage, and the general good of society. It is a celebration to be respected and mutually enjoyed. It is not a relationship that should provoke displays of inordinate emotion. I myself greatly dislike conflict in the household. I trust that we can avoid all manner of unpleasant scenes by making ourselves quite clear before we say our vows.

In short, she didn't love him, she didn't care to ever love him, and she thought love within marriage was rot.

The rage he felt was completely inappropriate, and he knew it. He was the one who had eschewed the idea of courtship, closed the door on a drawing room full of men, and essentially bribed her father into giving her hand to him.

But he felt insulted, nevertheless.

No: not insulted, enraged. Insult was something felt by paltry people whose feelings bruised easily. His feelings never bruised.

And she wasn't even finished:

> I would be most grateful if you would write me back. I am certain that you have requests of your own, and I am most willing to take them under advisement.

Take them under advisement?

A great swell of rage swept up his chest. She thought he would disgrace his own marriage vows by taking a mistress? She planned to take his wishes *under advisement?*

And she thought he would make *requests?* He was a bloody duke. He issued orders, not requests.

Gowan almost never lost his temper. A raised eyebrow was more than enough to cow a man aware that a duke held the power of ruination in his hands. One word, and Gowan could have anyone thrown in jail. Not that he had or would. But he held the power in abeyance.

Expression of rage was a blunt weapon, as

clumsy as it was unneeded. And he was well aware that on those rare occasions when he lost his temper, he tended to say a good many hotheaded things that he regretted later.

Unfortunately, just now anger swept straight from his gut to his head. Lady Edith's letter was disrespectful: of his person, of his title, *and* of his offer of marriage. He sat down at his desk and snatched a piece of letter paper. His quill stabbed the paper, tearing it.

He had offered to make her a *duchess*. Not just any duchess, either: the Duchess of Kinross. One of the oldest, most respected titles in all Scotland. Never held by an Englishwoman. *Never.*

Maybe there was a reason for that.

He started a fresh sheet.

Lady Edith:
Perhaps it is the Scotsman in me—

No. He didn't want her to feel uncomfortable owing to her unfortunate nationality. It wasn't her fault. And since it had been his idea to align himself with a noble English family, he shouldn't cavil about her birth.

He took a deep breath. He had to keep a sense of humor. His fiancée seemed to be a practical sort with all the humor of a dormouse, but he had never asked her if she enjoyed life. He had just taken one look at her deep green eyes and promised her father a settlement worthy of a princess.

That might have been a mistake, but it was too late now. He'd apparently got himself betrothed to a dour, child-loathing bureaucrat.

Then an image of her curves—and those eyes—drifted through his mind, and his whole being sprang to alert. Maybe they could stay away from each other except when they were in bed.

That in mind, he took up his quill again.

> Lady Edith:
> Thank you for your letter. You honor me with your candor; I hope you will forgive my bold speech. Herewith please find my expectations for this marriage.
>
> 1. I mean to husband your bed every night until we're ninety, or at the very least, eighty-five.
> 2. For a Scotsman, the bawdy hand of the dial is always upon the prick of noon. In short, I would interrupt the activities of the day for one thing only.
> 3. I'll take a mistress when you take a lover and not before.
> 4. Children come as God wills them. I've no mind to wear pig's gut on my private parts, if that's what you're suggesting.

5. Are you deranged? I'm curious. The betrothal papers are signed, so my statement is not a plea for freedom. However, you may take it as an expression of genuine curiosity.

He'd never written anything so sarcastic before; a duke has no occasion to write ironic notes to anyone except his intimates. And as it happened, he hadn't many intimates.

In fact, the Earl of Chatteris, whose wedding he would soon attend, was one of few who addressed him as Gowan. He and Chatteris were friends mostly because neither of them liked to attract attention. Years ago, when his father was alive and used to drag him to house parties in the summer, at which the children were forced to put on performances for the delectation of the adults, he and Chatteris had played the trees that moved to Dunsinane Castle and frightened Macbeth. Ever since, they had silently agreed that they found each other tolerable.

He signed the letter with his full title: Gowan Stoughton of Craigievar, Duke of Kinross, Chief of Clan MacAulay.

And then he took out the wax that he almost never used and sealed the letter with his ducal signet.

It was impressive.

Ducal.

Good.

Six

Edie's father and stepmother had apparently patched things up, but only to the extent that meals were cool rather than frosty.

"He still won't bed me," Layla confided over luncheon, a few days later. The earl had been expected to join them, but had not appeared.

Edie sighed. She disliked monitoring her father's marital folly, but whom else could poor Layla confide in? "The same problem? He thinks that you're shagging Gryphus in your spare moments?"

"He says he believes me about Gryphus. But as you will have noticed, that fact doesn't lead him to sleep at home."

Just then Willikins entered, bearing a small silver tray in his gloved hand. "Oh good," Layla said. "I expect it's an invitation to General Rutland's revue. Mrs. Blossom said that she would invite me to join her box."

"A letter for Lady Edith," the butler said, heading around the table to deliver it. "A groom will return for your response on the morrow."

Edie took the letter. Sure enough, it was a missive fit for a duke, written on thick paper that smelled like sovereigns and sealed with a fat blob of red wax.

"Is that from Kinross?" Layla asked. She put

down her fork. "I suppose it's acceptable for a betrothed couple to correspond, but my mother would have . . ."

She kept talking while Edie ripped open the letter and read it.

And then read it once more. "Husband your bed" seemed clear enough, though the man had delusions of grandeur. Ninety years old? She snorted. Look at her father, and he was only forty or thereabouts.

Kinross's answer to her point about a mistress was precisely what any woman would want to hear. But "pig's gut"? How would that prevent conception?

It was the fifth and final paragraph that she read over and over. Her future spouse *did* have a sense of humor. She appreciated his sarcasm. In fact, it gave her a startlingly different view of her impending marriage.

"What does he have to say?" Layla asked. Her head was propped on her hand. "I have a terrible headache, and I'm not capable of reading, so just tell me."

"He's boasting that we'll dance in the sheets until we're ninety."

"He can't be as stickish as he appeared, then. In fact, he sounds perfect. As unlike your father as can be."

Edie folded the letter and put it to the side. It wasn't precisely a declaration of love, but since it was the first letter from her future spouse, she meant to keep it. And to answer it. "Do you suppose that perhaps you and Father could have a rational conversation to determine the points of discord in your marriage, with consideration how to avoid them from here on out?"

Layla raised her head just enough to squint at her and then dropped it again. "You sounded just as priggish as your father when you said that."

"Really?" It wasn't a pleasant thought. "I'm sorry."

"Talking doesn't work for us. We communicate on a more intimate level. Which means we don't communicate at all, these days."

"On that front, do you have any idea what the 'bawdy hand of the dial' might signify?"

"Absolutely not. Your father would be unhappy to think that your fiancé has written you a coarse letter. Kinross didn't allude to anything improper, did he?"

Edie grinned. "Are you saying that I shouldn't tell Father that the duke is promising that the said dial is always set to the prick of noon?"

Layla picked up her head again. "He wrote the word *prick?* He wrote it down? In black and white? The *prick of noon?*"

"He did." Edie opened her letter and read it again. She was starting to like it more and more. If only she hadn't had that fever, she might have actually enjoyed meeting the duke. Now that she was perfectly well, it was vexing to think she might have charmed her future husband by being silent when that was decidedly not her normal state.

At that moment the door opened and her father walked in.

"I apologize for my tardiness," he stated. "Lady Gilchrist," he said, allowing a footman to place a linen cloth in his lap, "are you feeling quite well?"

"I have a headache," Layla replied. "Jonas, that fiancé you chose for Edie has sent her a rather lewd letter. I think he might be—"

"Not at all," Edie cut in. "The Duke of Kinross has written an entirely suitable response to a letter I sent him."

Her father narrowed his eyes. "It was inappropriate for you to write His Grace. If you desired information, I would have communicated your request."

"Yes, but Jonas, would he have written to *you* about pricks and bawdy clocks?" Layla asked.

"What?"

Really, her father was very good at thundering that sort of question. "Kinross was making a point about his nationality," Edie explained. "He writes that in Scotland the bawdy hand of the dial is always upon the prick of noon."

To her surprise, the indignation drained from her father's face. "He's quoting Shakespeare," he said, picking up his fork. "A distasteful sentence spoken by a disreputable character, but Shakespeare, nonetheless."

"I don't understand the meaning," Edie said.

"Naturally not. Such idioms are not within the purview of a gently-bred young lady." He put down his fork. "I had in mind to mention to you, daughter, that you are likely to encounter a more boisterous atmosphere amongst the Scots than you are accustomed to."

"So *prick* is a boisterous word?" That wasn't precisely the adjective that Edie would have attached to it, but she was aware that she was lacking all sorts of important knowledge when it came to bedding.

"Don't repeat that word!" her father barked. "It should never pass a lady's lips."

Layla raised her head. There was a touch of the mischievous about her eyes, the way there used to be in the early days of her marriage. "You'll be disappointed to hear this, Jonas, but women quite regularly discuss that particular organ. Depending on the size of the organ under discussion, you might call it a dart, or a needle. Then there's a pin: used only in truly unfortunate circumstances, of course. But one might discuss a lance." She swept her hair out of her eyes, the better to see whether she was getting a rise out of her husband.

And she was.

"This conversation is unforgivably vulgar," the earl said, his voice grating.

"Sword, tool, poleax," Layla added, looking even more cheerful. "Edie is to be a married woman now, Jonas. We can't treat her like a child."

Edie groaned silently. They were spiraling right back to the same emotional morass. Her father should have married a Puritan.

Luckily, there were signs of life in her fiancé. If she ventured into a spate of jokes about lances, she had the idea that he would laugh. Unfortunately, she might not understand his jokes, especially if he borrowed them from Shakespeare. She didn't know much literature. She hadn't had time for it.

"What play is that quote from?" she asked.

"*Romeo and Juliet*," her father said.

Perhaps she could take a quick look at the play before replying to Kinross. She wasn't much of a reader, if the truth be told.

"Let's change the subject. I feel truly ill. Do you suppose I've caught a wasting illness?" Layla asked. "Perhaps just a small one, something that would make me faint at the sight of a crumpet?"

"You—" The earl caught himself.

Edie nimbly took up the conversation before her father said something he should regret, even though he likely wouldn't. "I'm quite looking forward to meeting Kinross again." She could have sworn she saw stark longing in her father's eyes when he looked at Layla. But how could that be? He was always criticizing his wife, picking at her for the kind of unguarded and impulsive comments Layla couldn't help making.

"Naturally, I hope that you and the duke will be happy together," her father said.

"And I hope you have babies!" Layla said. "Lots of babies."

The silence that followed that sentence was so desperately tense that Edie found herself leaping to her feet and fleeing the room with little more than a mumbled apology.

Layla and her father had certainly loved each other when they married, but then he had begun to criticize the very qualities he once adored. The worst of it was the sense of disappointment that hung in the air around them.

Above all, she and Kinross had to avoid that sort of situation. A modicum—perhaps even an excess—of rational conversation was necessary.

Seven

Gowan did not spend his time waiting for the post from London to arrive. That would be petty and beneath him. Besides, he had sent his letter by one of his most trusted grooms, instructing him to wait for a response. Since he knew the precise length of the journey from London to Brighton, there was no need to consider the matter further.

Except . . .

He had easily checked that ungainly emotion, lust, for the first twenty-two years of his life. He scorned the idea of paying coin for intimacy, and a mixture of fastidiousness and honor had kept him from accepting cheerful invitations from married women. What's more, he had been betrothed at the time, although waiting for Rosaline to reach her majority. He had certainly felt desire, but it had never got the better of him.

That was before he saw Lady Edith.

Now he'd dropped the reins, his sensual appetite was proving to be ferocious. He could hardly sleep for dreaming of plump limbs tangled with his. His mind was constantly straying into imagery that would turn a priest pale.

He couldn't stop himself, even during occasions that demanded rational thought, such as now. He and Bardolph were working in the private parlor at the New Steine Hotel, waiting for the conference of bankers to reconvene at Pomfrey's Bank; he was reading letters and signing them while Bardolph read aloud the report of one of his bailiffs.

He signed whatever Bardolph put in front of him, and imagined that he'd taken his wife to his castle at Craigievar, where clan chiefs had slept for generations. To the bed where his ancestors had consummated their marriages.

Edith lay beneath him, her hair flung across the bed like rumpled, ancient Chinese silk. He leaned down to caress her, his hand running down her bare shoulder, over skin like cream, and then he kissed her like a man possessed, and her eyes opened, heavy-lidded with desire. Everything in him roared: *You're mine,* and she—

He was brought back to the near side of sanity by the sound of Bardolph coughing.

Gowan froze, uncomfortably aware that his breeches were stretched to the utmost by one of the hardest erections he'd had in his life. Thank God for the desk between them.

Slowly he reached out and took the letter that was waiting for his signature.

"The Chatteris wedding," he said, glancing down at the page, gratified to find that his voice was steady, if rather guttural.

Bardolph nodded. "Your gift of a rack of venison and twelve geese has already been dispatched from the estate. This note accepts the invitation the family extended to stay at Fensmore itself. I gather that the guest list is so long that many of them will be housed in nearby inns."

Gowan dipped his pen into his inkwell. He held it a second too long, and a large drop rolled from the quill and splashed on the letter. His secretary made a noise that sounded like a dry twig snapping underfoot.

"I'll travel with a small retinue: you, Sandleford, and Hendrich," Gowan said, pushing the letter back so it could be rewritten. "I finished reading

Hendrich's research into the textile factory in West Riding last night, so we'll discuss. When we reach Cambridge, the three of you can return to London. Sandleford can return to the Royal Exchange, but first I'd like to hear his opinion about acquiring shares in that glass lighting utility in Birmingham."

"A full complement of grooms," Bardolph said to himself, making a note. "Three carriages rather than four, I would think. The sheets and china must go with you for the journey, though not, obviously, for use in Fensmore."

Gowan stood up. "I'm going for a ride."

Bardolph summoned up one of his ready frowns. "We have yet fourteen letters to review, Your Grace."

Gowan did not care for dissension; he strode from the room without answering. Perhaps the Scot in him had taken over. He felt stronger and more alive than ever before, and his mind raced with tender words and wild images. He wanted to take his wife into the woods and lay her on a white cloth in a field of violets. He wanted to hear her voice in the open air, the cry of a pleasured woman, like that of a bird. He wanted . . .

He didn't want to be sane any longer, or to sit in that airless room reading fourteen more letters before he affirmed each with his long and tedious signature.

He told himself in vain that Edith was a

humorless dormouse. Frankly, humor did not come into many of the plans he had regarding her. Images blossomed in his heart like roses, each one in feverish counterpoint to the solemn intelligence of her letter.

He wanted to shower her with gifts, yet nothing he could conjure up seemed good enough. If he had the heavens embroidered on a cloth, wrought with gold and silver light, he would lay it at her feet . . .

Nay, he would lay her on top of it, as tenderly as if she were Helen of Troy, and then he would make slow love to her.

He had lost his mind.

His imagination bloomed with metaphors describing a woman whom he'd seen for scarcely an hour. Later, that night, he woke from a dream in which Edith raised her arms to him, the liquid gold of her hair tumbling almost to her waist.

"Ah, darling," he had been telling her, "I am looped in the loops of your hair." Had he said that aloud? He would never do something so imbecilic.

He really had lost his mind.

He knew why, too. Obviously, he had kept himself away from women too long, and now he was deranged as a result. Abstinence wasn't advisable for a man. It had enfeebled his brain. What's more, although he'd never before thought twice about performance, he suddenly had an image of himself fumbling about in the act, not knowing what he was doing, being foolish.

Damn.

Then the letter arrived.

Your Grace,

I was happy to read your response to my query about extra-matrimonial cavorting. It is gratifying to know that although Nature pricked thee out for woman's pleasure, you intend to reserve some sixty years' worth of said activity for myself.

Gowan read that paragraph three times and then broke into a crack of laughter. She'd picked up his Shakespeare reference and tossed another back at him.

I write with the worry that you have formed a false impression of me. I smiled a great deal on the night of my debut ball . . . because I was so ill that night that I could not bring myself to speak.

I mentioned this concern to my stepmother, Lady Gilchrist, who is firmly of the belief that it is inadvisable for a couple to learn of each other's character before marriage. But as she is not on speaking terms with my father, I consider her a less than reliable source of advice about marital happiness.

If Gilchrist hadn't been able to ascertain his wife's disposition by a quick glance at her, Gowan didn't think that all the time in the world would have helped them to a greater understanding of each other's characters. He was sorry to hear that Edith had been ill, though.

I also write to assure you that I am not mad, although my claim is of dubious value because I would likely insist upon my sanity regardless. We shall have to leave the question of my judgment or lack thereof to our next meeting, at the Chatteris wedding. You shall find me sane, but, alas, not as winsomely silent as I was during our dances.

The words were so lively that Gowan could hear a woman saying them, except he couldn't remember what Edith's voice sounded like. He was burning to meet her when she wasn't ill.

For a moment the serene angel with whom he had danced wavered in his imagination, but he pushed her away. He had much rather be married to a woman who considered him pricked out for her pleasure. A thousand times better than being married to a placable dormouse, no matter how peaceful.

I should also confess to finding Edith a name without music. I prefer Edie to Edith.

With all best wishes from your future wife, who has good reason to pray for your continued health . . . given my expectations of sixty-five (seventy!) years of marital bliss,
Edie

Eight

Fensmore
Home of the Earl of Chatteris
Cambridgeshire

Edie was aware that she wasn't acting in a normal fashion. She was accustomed to feeling strong emotion only in response to a musical score or a battle with her father. She prided herself on maintaining tight control over her sensibilities.

But now, with less than an hour remaining before she was due to join the Earl of Chatteris, his fiancée, and their guests in the drawing room before dinner, she was overwrought, for lack of a better word. She felt as if she were about to burst out of her skin, too edgy to settle down.

She found herself pacing the floor of her guest chamber, rejecting out of hand every gown Mary offered her. Edie was not the sort of woman who spent time worrying about her attire. But that did not mean she was ignorant the power of clothing to wreak havoc on the minds of men.

She hadn't paid much attention yesterday when Mary had packed her trunk for a few days at Fensmore and the Earl of Chatteris's wedding; her attention had been fixed on the Boccherini score. But now that she was here, and Lady Honoria Smythe-Smith (soon to be the Countess of Chatteris) had just informed her that the Duke of Kinross was already in residence, she felt vastly different about what she would wear.

The duke would be at the evening meal, and she would see him for the first time since his proposal. The very idea made her feel feverish all over again.

Any woman in her right mind would dislike the idea of meeting her fiancé garbed as a vestal virgin missing only a lamp—and obviously a white dress with a modest ruffle at the hem confirmed that particular illusion.

After their exchange of letters, she was fairly certain that Kinross wanted to marry someone boldly sensual. Someone who could bandy about words like *prick,* words that Edie barely understood. She wanted more than anything to look into his eyes and see desire. Lust, even. If he looked at her and his prick wasn't on the dial of noon, to put it in a lyrical but earthy fashion, she would be humiliated.

She wanted to dazzle him.

The stupid thing was that she wasn't even certain she would recognize him. She was betrothed to a tall man with a Scottish burr, but she couldn't recall his face at all.

Still, his letter—*that* letter—had given her just enough that she had decided he had a pair of laughing eyes. Not dissolute eyes or a rakish expression. But desirous.

Only after Mary had offered every single gown she'd packed, and Edie had rejected each and every one as unbearably lackluster, did she give in to the inevitable and send her maid to find Layla.

"May I wear one of your gowns instead of mine?" Edie asked, when Layla appeared in the doorway. "I loathe my frocks. They make me look like an insipid fool."

"You know perfectly well that a young unmarried lady should wear only pale fabrics." Layla strolled across the room and pushed open the window.

"No smoking!" Edie ordered, pointing at a chair.

Layla sighed, and sat down.

"I am practically married. Kinross is here, and I simply cannot wear one of these dreary gowns." She didn't know how to put it differently, but if she didn't see desire in his eyes, she might break off the betrothal out of pure embarrassment. She couldn't stop feeling that perhaps he had offered his hand due to her silence.

"Darling, you're a willow compared to me," Layla objected. "It's not that I don't understand, because, truly, I do. Your coloring has never been flattered by soft tints. Still, we don't have time to miraculously remake one of my dresses."

"We are the same height. I may be a little slimmer in the hip area, but our bosoms are the same."

"My bosom is as unfashionably large as my hips."

"You can call your bosom unfashionable if you wish, but I like mine. And it is nearly the same size. Any gown will work," Edie insisted. "Don't you see, Layla? Kinross has never really seen me, though I appreciate the fact that he chose a wife on the basis of rational analysis. I truly do. I approve."

Layla rolled her eyes. "Rational analysis is an absurd reason for marriage. Your father once told me that after your mother died he made a six-point list of attributes for his next countess, and I met five of them. Look how well that's turned out."

"What was the sixth one?"

Layla got up again and went over to the pile of dresses. "Fertility, of course," she said, turning over the gowns. "The ability to turn out baby earls

76

by the yard, if not by the dozen. What about this green one? It's not as bland as the white ones."

"You and Father love each other," Edie said, ignoring the fact that Layla was trying to rearrange the neckline of her green gown into something sensual that it could never be. "You just don't—"

"*Like* each other," Layla said, completing the sentence. With a quick jerk, she ripped out the lace trim around the gown's neck.

"I don't believe that. I believe you do like each other. I just think you need to talk more. But never mind your lamentable marriage for the moment. I'm trying to ensure that mine works out happily. I don't want Kinross to think that I'm some sort of insipid lily."

"He's unlikely to think that after reading your letter," Layla observed. "Thank goodness your father had that book of Shakespeare quotes. Do you suppose Kinross imagines you a bluestocking who's actually read all those plays?"

"He'll soon find out differently," Edie said. "You're destroying that dress, Layla!"

Her stepmother held up the green dress, now relieved of its white lace. "If you pulled down the sleeves to bare your shoulders, this one could be very appealing."

"I don't want to be 'appealing.' I want to be the sort of woman who tosses about bawdy jokes."

"That woman would definitely love this dress.

Perhaps I shall run away from your father and open my own dress shop."

Edie went over and picked up the gown. "I can't wear this: look, you've torn the shoulder seam. I just don't want to play the part of a virginal swan."

"You *are* a virgin," Layla said, sighing. "Think of it as an unavoidable stage of life, like getting old and toothless and having to drink soup. Unfortunately, men seem to think that women are like new wine, good only before being uncorked."

Edie tried, and failed, to work that one out.

"Thus the fact that women well into their thirties—and married—still wear nothing but white. I view ladies mired in that delusion as nothing short of pitiable." Anyone could guess at that scorn by measuring the distance between a white gown and Layla's daring—and colorful— concoctions.

"I'm not denying my virginity," Edie said, returning to the stool before her dressing table. "I just don't want to play the demurely chaste Lady Edith, the way I did when I was ill—indeed, as I've done all my life."

"Your father won't like it."

"My father divested his authority over me when he signed those betrothal papers. Now I need to make absolutely certain that my husband doesn't think he's been invited to play the role of father."

"Good point," Layla said. "Do you suppose that

the age difference between myself and your father has led him to consider me a child?"

Edie rolled her eyes. "Has it never occurred to you?"

That seemed to penetrate. Layla tossed the green dress back onto the bed. "I have just the gown for you. Mary, please return to my chamber and ask Trotter to give you the claret silk. This is a sacrifice, darling," she said, turning back to Edie. "I thought to wear it myself tomorrow evening, but I think you have the greater need."

She walked over to the window.

"Don't you dare take out a cheroot," Edie ordered.

"That tone must have been a direct inheritance from your father. Just as well, since you'll need to give an order now and then when you're running a castle."

"I'm practicing on you. No more smoking anywhere in my vicinity."

"I'm trying to give them up," Layla said, leaning against the frame and staring out the window. "Your father doesn't like it, and we're sharing a room while we're here."

Edie considered asking how that unaccustomed proximity was working out, but just then Mary reappeared with a pile of iridescent silk in her arms.

"Here it is!" Layla crowed, turning about as the door opened. "That color is called China rose.

Isn't it the most delicious thing you ever saw? Darker than cinnabar, more saturated than claret . . . well, close to claret."

Within a moment, Mary had stripped Edie to her chemise.

"It's designed for a chemise, but no corset," Layla noted, wandering over.

Mary dropped a waterfall of claret-colored silk over Edie's head. It felt marvelous against her skin.

Layla adjusted the bodice herself. "You look beautiful. Ravishing. Do you see all the ruching here, just under the bodice?"

Edie turned to look in the glass. The silk fell in just the right folds to reveal most of her cleavage. A narrow set of pleats came across each shoulder, gesturing toward a sleeve without bothering to form one.

She looked lusciously uncovered on top, and then the silk fell in pleats and ruching from the waist, and was tied with a bow in the back.

Mary knelt and guided Edie's feet into Layla's matching high-heeled slippers.

"It doesn't seem fair that our feet are the same and our hips so different," Layla remarked.

Edie turned to look at herself in side view. This gown had sent her entirely in another direction, from Classic Virgin to Classic Layla. It made her breasts large and her legs long. It wasn't a bad combination. "Do you think he'll like this?"

"Any man would like that," Layla said, her tone brooking no argument. "You are ravishing. Now, lip color to match. Come back over here to your dressing table."

The unaccustomed heels on Layla's slippers did something to Edie's balance. When she'd been ill, she had drifted across the floor. Tonight she wouldn't drift; she would wiggle. She looked as if she were swaying from side to side, like a moored boat in a gale.

The effect was quite feminine, not an attribute that Edie often achieved. It certainly wasn't feminine to cradle a big stringed instrument between one's legs and coax music out of it. If a true lady insisted on doing something as outré as to play the cello, she turned her legs to the side, balanced on one hip, and played sidesaddle.

Edie could do that, but she never saw the point. She wasn't stupid enough to think that she could have a career. As the daughter of an earl, Edie played solely for her own pleasure, which meant she might as well sit in the most natural position.

The fact that her father loved the cello, and that she had inherited his child-sized instrument, and then that he had bought her a Ruggieri for her sixteenth birthday . . . none of that overcame the fact that she was a lady.

There was something of an unspoken bargain between herself and her father. Edie had delayed her debut as long as possible, but they both knew that she would marry whomever he selected. It was a promise, and Edie always kept her promises, spoken or unspoken.

Now she wiggle-waggled her way back over to her dressing table and sat down. Earlier that afternoon Mary had curled her hair into the proper kind of ringlets, the ladylike kind that weren't as untidy as hers naturally were.

Layla darted forward and began playing with her curls, tousling them into a studied disarrangement.

"You're ruining all of Mary's hard work," Edie protested, as Layla adjusted another ringlet.

"No, I'm making you look a little less perfect. Men are terrified by perfection. Now a touch of lip pomade."

Painted red, Edie's mouth looked twice as large, especially her bottom lip. "Doesn't this look a trifle vulgar? I'm fairly certain that Father won't approve." She looked disturbingly unlike herself. In fact, she felt as if she'd veered from feverish saint to feverish courtesan.

"That's exactly right. Your father has never understood that a little vulgarity is a good thing."

"Why is it?"

"It wouldn't be if you were still looking for a husband," Layla explained. "But now you need to impress upon Kinross the fact that while he may have married you—or rather, he will marry you—he will never own you."

Edie turned, caught Mary's eye, and nodded toward the door. As the door closed behind her, Edie said, "Layla, darling, isn't that technique you just recommended rather a failure when it comes to you and Father?"

"What technique?" Layla had her hair up in an artful nest of curls threaded with emeralds. She stood before the glass, coaxing a lock to fall with disheveled grace over one shoulder.

"Making certain that a man feels he will never own you, or at least own your loyalty. I think it may have led to some of your marital difficulties."

Layla frowned. "I would never be unfaithful to your father. He should know that because he knows *me*."

"But if you are constantly telling him, albeit silently, that you will never belong to him . . . It just strikes me from watching the two of you that men are rather primitive, at least Father is. He looks at you with pain and possessiveness, all mixed up together."

"But I've assured him that I didn't sleep with Gryphus. He should believe me unconditionally. I am his wife."

"Perhaps he needs you to assure him that you have no interest in sleeping with any other man."

"That would be to give him too much power," Layla said instantly. "He already thinks he owns me. Last night he demanded that I give up smoking cheroots!"

That didn't surprise Edie. "What did you say?"

"I refused, of course. Although I haven't smoked any today." Layla's mouth drooped. "Marriage is more difficult than you think, Edie. If you do nothing but try to keep your husband happy, you'll drive yourself mad."

Edie gave her a kiss. "Forgive me if I say that I'll be in good company? You are far too kind to my grumpy parent." She picked up her gloves and a wrap of gossamer taffeta. "Let's go down to dinner. I'm quite curious to know what my fiancé looks like."

Nine

Gowan entered the drawing room early and stood about talking to a crowd of Smythe-Smith relations, trying to appear as if he wasn't bored to tears.

When he'd attended the Gilchrist ball, and indeed most of the time, he'd worn English attire: an embroidered coat, a starched neck cloth, silk pantaloons. But after that sparring exchange with Edie, he wanted to reveal himself to her as *himself,* not as a pretend Englishman.

He wore the Kinross kilt, in the tartan of the Chief of Clan MacAulay. It felt right. Surrounded by these sleek and silly Englishmen with covered knees, his bare legs felt twice as strong for being free of the hindrance of breeches.

Marcus Holroyd, the Earl of Chatteris, paused at his side. "Kinross, it's a pleasure to see you here. My fiancée has just informed me that you are newly betrothed."

Gowan inclined his head. "Yes, to Lady Edith Gilchrist."

"My very best wishes. I understand that she is a gifted musician. Do you play as well?"

Gowan felt not a little embarrassment that he had no idea of Lady Edith's interests, let alone her gifts. "A musician along the lines of your inestimable fiancée?" Gowan had sat through a Smythe-Smith recital once, and he hoped never to be in the presence of such dissonant cacophony again. If his wife was a musician of that caliber, he would implore her not to play.

"I have not had the pleasure of hearing Lady Edith play," Chatteris replied, not revealing by so much as the twitch of eyebrow less than complete support for his fiancée's musical talents.

There was a stir by the door, and they turned. "There's Honoria," Chatteris said. Gowan glanced at him. The man had a look of quiet longing in his eyes.

Odd. Weddings among the aristocracy weren't usually arranged for amorous reasons. As Gowan watched, Chatteris went straight to Honoria's side.

Where was Lady Edith, damn it? He was getting sick of deflecting lascivious glances from women who appreciated his kilt for all the wrong reasons—and appeared curious about what he wore under it.

The Earl of Gilchrist entered the drawing room, and approached Gowan with his slightly awkward, rigid gait, then bent his head. "Your Grace."

"We are to be kin," Gowan responded cordially, extending his hand. "It's good to see you, Gilchrist."

The earl clasped it briefly. "I expect that you will be pleased to see my daughter after this separation. It is well that you come to know each other better before your wedding."

"In fact, we should discuss dates for the ceremony. I would like to reconsider the length of our betrothal."

"I do not approve of hasty marriages," Gilchrist stated. "A year's betrothal would not be untoward, in my estimation."

Gowan wouldn't have minded before he and Edie had exchanged those letters. But now . . . "I did mention my orphaned half sister," he reminded the earl. "I would be reluctant to leave her motherless for a year."

Lady Gilchrist now joined them; Gowan turned and bowed to her, straightening in time to catch Gilchrist's unguarded look at his wife. It was embarrassing. The man was at his wife's feet, figuratively speaking.

"Lady Gilchrist," Gowan said. "It's a pleasure to meet you again."

"You must be so eager to see our daughter," she said, an unexpected dimple appearing in one cheek. When she looked like that—a bit naughty—the combination of her beauty, sensuality, and wit was dazzling.

He kissed her hand, returning her smile.

Then he noticed that Gilchrist's eyes had gone black. He was startled until he realized that blank rage could mean only one thing: Gilchrist believed his wife would stray, even to her own son-in-law. Gowan felt sorry for him.

A trace of that pity must have appeared on his face, because Gilchrist's eyes narrowed, and he raised his chin. "Lady Gilchrist," he said, his voice as hard as a piece of granite, "where is my daughter?"

Lady Gilchrist didn't show the slightest reaction to his tone, though Gowan thought his tone was harsh in the extreme, never mind that he'd changed her "our daughter" to the decidedly proprietary "my daughter."

"Edie entered with me," she said, "but she met that lovely young lady Iris, who also plays the cello. One of the Smythe-Smith girls."

She turned, surveying the room. "Ah, there she is."

Young ladies were everywhere, looking like little drifts of snow in their white frocks. Gowan's eyes moved from one to the next, rejecting each. Not . . . not . . . not . . . He frowned, looking again from white gown to white gown.

He had been certain that he would recognize Lady Edith's sweet countenance. After all, he had stared at it for two dances in a row. He knew the tilt of her nose, her green eyes, the slant of her cheekbone.

"Perhaps," Lady Gilchrist said, amusement curling through her voice like smoke, "you are not taking into account the fact that Edie is not fond of white gowns, although she does wear them when she must."

"I would hope that my daughter is recognizable to her future spouse no matter her gown," Gilchrist said, his words sharply clipped.

Gowan ignored him and began to look at each and every woman in the room, not only those wearing white. Beside him, Lady Gilchrist's chuckle was like the drowsy call of a bird at dusk.

Then he saw her.

His fiancée . . . His future wife.

Edie.

His heart thundered. He recognized every angle of her face, lush lips, hair . . . who could forget that hair? It looked as if old Roman coins had melted into canary wine, leaving strands of darker gold woven with sunlight.

At the same time, she was not precisely the woman he had chosen to marry.

This woman was utterly sensual. Her body was

shaped for a man's caress; her breasts were soft and full, alabaster skin framed by red silk. She was talking to someone and laughing . . . her laughing lips matched her gown. Her hair shone with the deep luster of jasmine honey. It was pulled up in ringlets that flowed with slight variations in color.

He heard Gilchrist say something, but he didn't listen. Blood pounded in his ears. When he'd first met her, Edie's eyes had been placid pools of sweet water. Now they were deep, filled with laughter and intelligence. There was nothing placid there. Nor in the scarlet lips, nor the rounded bosom.

"I see why you did not recognize her immediately," Gilchrist was saying, his tone pinched and disapproving. "That gown is most inappropriate. I can only think this is your influence, Lady Gilchrist."

"It is not merely my influence, but indeed my gown," his wife replied. "As a betrothed woman, she need not rigidly adhere to the conventions regarding dress which govern unmarried ladies."

"If you will excuse me," Gowan said, bowing. "I will greet Lady Edith."

"Do call her Edie," Lady Gilchrist said gaily, seemingly untouched by her husband's dour judgments. "She prefers informality among family members."

Gowan had the same edgy, intense feeling as

when he embarked on a hunt. This was the woman who had written him that letter. She was to marry him. She had written of dancing in the sheets with him.

As he moved across the room, his eyes fixed on his betrothed, his kilt brushed against his legs, reminding him of other body parts that were hardening as he walked. He sensed a kind of erotic surprise such as he'd never felt—never dreamed he would feel—before.

As if conscious of his gaze, she turned and met his eyes.

How in the world had he believed her to be chaste, quiet, and submissive? Her eyes were brilliant, her mouth mobile and utterly sensual. It was as if he were encountering a complete stranger.

Desire flamed through his body. Her lips parted slightly, and he knew that she, too, recognized him.

He had thought she was like a drink of clear water. But now, meeting her gaze, she was a river that tumbled with life and danger. She would change his life. She would change everything about him.

Instinctively, he responded as the men of the Highlands always had before the woman they honored above all others. Dimly aware that the room had gone still, he stopped just before his fiancée, sank onto one knee, and took the hand that she extended to him.

"My lady," he said, his voice deep and sure. He saw no one but her, knew she saw only him. With one swift, sure tug, he peeled off her glove. A sigh came from behind him, but he paid no mind.

This was no performance for an audience; it was for the two of them alone.

He raised her hand to his lips, and carefully placed a kiss on her naked fingers. It was a brazen, outrageous gesture.

He didn't care.

Ten

Edie felt as if she were caught up in a play . . . something larger than herself. Nothing dramatic had ever happened to *her*, to Lady Edith Gilchrist. The most excitement she'd had was when her father invited a cellist to their house so that she could play for him.

Walking into the room she had been pleased to see Iris Smythe-Smith, who was quite good at the cello, having somehow succeeded in avoiding the influence of her family's quartet. And then she had felt an odd prickling in her shoulder blades, so she had turned her head. And there, walking toward her, was her future husband.

It was as if her eyes grabbed the image of him and gobbled it up. He had muscled legs, beautiful legs, twice the size of the Englishmen's in the room. His chest was wide and his shoulders looked even wider thanks to the plaid thrown over one shoulder.

And his face . . .

It was rough-hewn, not beautiful, a warrior's face with a strong chin. But his eyes were most astonishing. There was no polite emotion in them: just blazing possessiveness.

She felt, suddenly, as if he were looking straight at her, and as if he were the first to do so in her whole life. As if he looked into her soul and saw the real woman. Her heartbeat thudded in her throat.

The duke went on one knee before her. He took her hand, peeled off her glove, and kissed her fingers.

For a moment, Edie felt dizzy. The mere touch of his lips was a voluptuous promise. This was the kiss that a knight errant gives his lady before he gallops off in her defense. The kiss that a courtier gives the queen of his heart. Kinross had abased himself before her. And yet, in the act of kneeling at her feet, he had only asserted himself as a man born to command.

Then he rose, towering over her. How could she have not noticed that the man was the size of a Scots pine? Perhaps she did notice. But not really. She hadn't seen that he was so big in every way. And ruthless.

He looked like the sort of man who saw a

woman and decided on the spot to marry her. And not for practical reasons, either.

That idea was utterly shocking—and delightful.

"Lady Edith," he said, and she remembered that Highlands burr. It rolled over her skin like a love song.

"I prefer to be called Edie," she said, forgetting to draw her ungloved hand out of his. And then: "Your hair is *red!*"

His right eyebrow flew up. "It always has been. Though nothing compared to that of most Scotsmen, my lady."

"I have never liked red hair," she said, stunned because this hair . . . this hair she *did* like. It was the color of blackened steel with fire burning in its depths. It was the red of a banked kiln at night, of a coal.

His laughter rumbled through the room and as if by a signal, the people around them turned away, judging that the drama had come to an end.

"You didn't know that my hair is red, and I had no idea that you are a musician."

"I play the cello," she said lamely.

"Which instrument is that?" he said, his forehead creasing in a frown.

"What? Which instrument? You don't know?"

His eyes searched hers, and then his laughter enfolded her again. "I suspect that you have a great deal to teach me, Lady Edie."

Edie frowned at him. "Are you jesting, or do you truly not know what a cello is?"

"I know very little about music in general. My grandmother did not approve of frivolities, and I'm afraid that she put music into that category."

"Music is not a frivolity!"

"She found it unnecessary to daily life in the way that shelter and meat are."

Edie debated whether to inform her future husband just how far ahead of bread music came for her. It didn't seem like a point she had to make at the moment. He had great composure, this duke of hers. She saw flashes of deep emotion in his eyes, but at the same time, he was so ducal.

And *male*.

And in that moment, she realized that she didn't really care what he thought of music. She was more interested in what he thought of the claret dress. Some female part of her purred with satisfaction at the way he still held her hand.

He smiled down at her, his gaze so potent that her heart sped up once again. "I believe that it is time to repair to the dining room." He drew her hand into the crook of his arm. She hadn't even heard the butler announce the meal, but the other guests were arranging themselves to proceed to dinner.

Kinross looked at her with all the fierce interest of a musician with a new sheet of music, a score never played. And she felt the same.

It was very strange.

The smile that curled her lips came from her heart. The duke—Kinross—was the epitome of imperturbability, and yet, for a moment, she had caught sight of a flash of vulnerability in his eyes.

She was not alone in this whirlpool fever of desire and curiosity.

They moved toward the other guests, who were forming themselves into a procession, according to the customary rules of rank. Her father and Layla had taken their places toward the front; Kinross, as duke, moved ahead of them. They ended up just behind the bride and groom, Lady Honoria Smythe-Smith and the Earl of Chatteris.

Kinross leaned close; his breath was warm on her ear. "Are you as musical as the bride and her relatives?"

Laughter bubbled out of Edie's mouth. "No!"

The touch of his arm sent a shock down her body. "Better or worse?"

That made her laugh even more. "What if I were to say worse?" She looked up at him from under her lashes, enjoying the flirtation.

A slow smile grew in his eyes. "Could I bribe you not to play?"

"Never. Playing the cello is the thing I love most in the world." She added, "You might as well know that it's the only thing I do truly well."

"You dance very well."

"That's part of being a musician. I was terribly ill the night we met; did you guess?"

He shook his head. "I had no idea until you wrote me about it."

"I had a high fever. I felt as if I were floating from place to place."

"I think dancers are sometimes described as levitating." His eyes crinkled with laughter. "I did think that you were marvelously graceful."

"I was afraid I might topple over," she confessed. And then: "I think the only part of the evening I truly enjoyed was our waltz. You waltz very well."

"As do you, my lady."

He was manifestly a duke. It showed in every lineament of his countenance, the unconscious grace of his every movement, in his air of authority. But at the same time . . . there was something else about Kinross as well. She cocked her head, trying to work out what it was, but the doors to the dining room were pulled open and the line began moving forward.

The meal passed in a tumble of conversation—with an older gentleman to her left, with Kinross to her right, then back to the man on her left.

When they weren't speaking, Edie kept stealing glances at her fiancé. He appeared dispassionate, as if one could never read his feelings in his face. Yet she thought she'd glimpsed a vulnerability. It made her wild to talk at great length, and see if she could tease it out again.

Kinross's face was harsh in repose. But when his eyes met hers, the ferocity in them disappeared. She didn't know what *was* there, but it felt untamed and new. No one had ever looked at her that way.

Of course, he was not truly looking at plain Edie, who played the cello. He was seeing Edie dressed up as Layla.

The duke moved his leg, and his thigh brushed up against hers and remained there. It had to be accidental; a gentleman would never do such a thing. He glanced at her, his eyes wickedly suggestive, and turned back to his conversation. It wasn't an accident.

Every inch of her skin instantly awoke. Improper though it was, Edie loved it. She'd never felt this sort of racing desire—or, if she were truthful, any desire, other than for a cello made by Stradivarius. She reached for her wineglass, discovering that her fingers were trembling. She could feel heat rising in her cheeks.

Finally, he moved his leg, turned back to her, and said, "Have you ever read *Romeo and Juliet*?"

Edie shook her head. She had given it a try after receiving his letter, but she had been unable to make head or tail of the play. It was her own fault, because she'd always disobeyed her governess and avoided her lessons. She hadn't had time for reading. All she had ever wanted to do was play the cello. It had made her a bit of a dunce.

Something hungry in his eyes made her shift in her chair. "I'm not very well read," she confessed. "I gather that you are my opposite in that respect."

"My grandmother, who raised me, disparaged reading for pleasure, but considered Shakespeare to be an exception. Generally speaking, my tutors were busy teaching me double-sided accounting and animal husbandry, and I was unable to go to university. So, believe me, I am far less learned than you might think."

She laughed. "That's impossible. I know almost everything about the cello, and almost nothing about anything else."

"I know quite a lot about being a duke and a landowner, and next to nothing about music or literature. But I do remember this: when Romeo first saw Juliet at the ball, he described her as so beautiful that she taught the torches to burn bright."

"You can't have thought that of me. I was dreadfully ill."

"You were something of a torch, from what I remember. I thought your touch was burning me." She couldn't imagine him allowing many people to hear that thread of sharp wit.

Edie was starting to feel slightly unbalanced. His eyelashes were so beautiful: thick and straight. And his eyes fascinated her. One moment they were all ducal arrogance, the next a brazen rake was looking at her with such lust and desire that it sent flames down her legs. And then there was that elusive touch of humor, a private wit that made her want to laugh with startled pleasure.

"What does Juliet think of Romeo on first seeing him?" she asked, pulling herself together. "Does she think he's burning like a torch as well?"

"Oh, she likes him well enough," Kinross said. "She probably didn't find the moment as shocking as he did."

"Why not?" Edie asked. "What did Romeo feel?"

"The man is utterly changed forever," Kinross said. "He arrives at the ball in love with another lady—"

Edie's brows drew together. "He *is?*"

"He was, but I was not," the duke said bluntly.

Edie couldn't stop herself from smiling, even as she realized that she had never smiled in quite this way before. It was a Layla smile.

"Romeo believes himself in love, but then he sees Juliet."

"She burns with a torchlike fever, so he forgets about his previous love?" Edie asked, laughing.

"Something like that." A twist of husky laughter sounded in his voice, too. She already knew that he didn't laugh much. Life was serious for the duke; she knew it instinctively. He was as driven as she was, though she wasn't entirely sure in what direction.

"He falls prey to lust. He risks kissing her, behind

a pillar, when that kiss might mean his death."

"That seems extreme," Edie remarked. She couldn't stop looking at him, at his eyes, his cheekbones, his nose, his jaw. She was quite aware that if anyone had fallen prey to lust, it was she. But somehow she wasn't even embarrassed.

"He throws everything away for the chance to kiss her hand."

"He would have been killed merely for kissing Juliet's hand?"

"Their families were enemies. But he doesn't stop with her hand." A glow in the duke's eyes lit an answering fire in Edie's belly.

"He whisks her behind a pillar and kisses her on her lips."

Edie swallowed.

"And then kisses her again."

"Very . . ." Edie couldn't think of a word.

"He would keep kissing her all evening, but she is called away. He doesn't even know who she is. But he knows that she is *his*." The duke's eyes were hot and possessive. "So later that night, Romeo leaps the walls of the orchard around her house and risks death again to find her balcony window."

"Oh, I've heard about the balcony," Edie said, making herself break the spell of his voice. At this rate, she'd find herself begging him to kiss her in front of the whole table. "Juliet asks him to marry her."

The duke shook his head. Under the table, his fingers curled around hers.

She jumped, and another wave of hot blood rose in her cheeks.

"No," Kinross said, as if he weren't doing anything so boldly scandalous, "that's putting the emphasis in the wrong place. Everyone assumes that Juliet was a brazen minx because she asked if he planned to marry her. But the two of them knew the truth."

His thumb was rubbing over her palm. Edie discovered she was trembling a little. "She knew, and he knew," the duke said, his voice low and sure. "Romeo leapt that wall because he wanted to kiss Juliet more than he wanted to live. He climbed her balcony; he offered his vows. Marriage is nothing more than a formality in that situation."

Edie could hear Layla's laughter and the click of tableware. She should have read the damned play. She should have spent hours reading Shakespeare. The duke was making literature sound a good deal more interesting than her governess had ever done.

"Without Juliet, life was not worth living," the duke continued. "So when he believed she was dead, he killed himself."

"His reaction was rather extreme," she managed. Surely someone would notice that her fiancé was holding her hand. Down the table, Layla was flirting madly with a man who wasn't Edie's father.

"Indeed, I used to think Romeo might have been a bit mad."

A shiver went straight down Edie's spine. The duke looked . . . He looked as if he had decided that Romeo was entirely sane. Mind you, *he* didn't look entirely sane. He looked ravenous.

"Stop that," she whispered. "You mustn't act like this." She pulled her hand away.

He smiled at her, a kind of happily mad look. "I'm a Scot."

"What does that have to do with it?"

"There are those who say that Romeo had Scottish blood."

"Wasn't he Italian? He sounds like a hot-blooded Italian to me."

Kinross's eyes narrowed slightly. "What do you know of hot-blooded Italians?"

"Nothing," Edie said, surprised. "Why?"

"Italians are a jealous people." He picked up his glass and took a drink of red wine.

"So I've heard," Edie said, sipping from her own glass.

His eyes had a glint of ice. "Italians are nothing compared to Scotsmen."

Edie glanced around them again. Conversations swirled around the table, and still no one had noticed that she and the duke were breaking the rules of polite dinner conversation by remaining absorbed in each other. Not to mention the fact he had just snatched her hand again and was caressing it with his thumb.

She managed to drag her mind away from the whispering touch of his fingers. "Let's drop literature for a moment, and try for rational conversation. Are you informing me that you intend to be one of those husbands who routinely accuses his wife of unfaithfulness?"

"No." He gave her a wry smile. "I'm talking bilge, aren't I?"

"Perhaps a bit," Edie acknowledged.

"We Scots are pigheaded fools," he admitted, altogether too cheerfully to her mind.

She nodded toward Layla, who was bending toward her dinner companion, her bosom brushing his sleeve. "I am not amused by that sort of accusation. For obvious reasons."

Kinross's eyes followed hers. "In my estimation, your stepmother is unlikely to be unfaithful. I would guess that she is engaging in that flamboyant display in an ill-judged effort to gain her husband's attention."

Edie felt a surge of something like joy. He was not only rational, but intuitive. She found herself grinning at him. "Exactly."

"Just because I may experience jealousy does not mean that I intend to act on it."

"Ah." She couldn't stop smiling. But they had to be clear about this, because she refused to spend her life with a man who glowered at her every time she chatted with a neighbor. She dropped her voice again, even though no one was paying attention. "I shall never be unfaithful to my husband . . . to you."

She had never realized that a man's eyes could glow like a banked fire. "Nor shall I to you."

"So if a hot-blooded Italian shows up at your castle—do you really have a castle, by the way?"

"Yes."

"And if that Italian decides he would like to flutter his eyelashes at me throughout the meal—"

"I might boot him into the next county," the duke said flatly.

Edie studied him closely. "Are you like this as a matter of course? Because I was under the impression that you ran a large estate. I can't imagine how you could do so if you have a penchant for violence."

"Five estates, as a matter of fact. I am justice of the peace in two counties. I would say that I am known for rational thought, prudence, and careful consideration of all sides of a question."

Edie raised an eyebrow.

He leaned closer, and his hand gripped hers a bit tighter. "I expect it's only because I don't *have* you yet. Not to harp on Shakespeare, but Juliet does say that she has bought the mansion of a love, but not yet possessed it." His voice dropped, too, and Edie had that peculiar feeling again, as if she were drowning in his eyes.

Then his words sank in. "Did you just imply that you *bought* me?" And: "Ow," she said, shaking free of his hand. "Your grip is very strong."

"I did not imply that I paid for you, but quite the opposite: Juliet says that she has purchased Romeo."

"So *I* bought *you?*" Edie quite liked that notion.

"But you have not yet taken possession." His voice was throaty and deep, the sound of a man who was taking pleasure in the reversal of their roles, who had utter confidence in his own masculinity. The erotic heat of his voice slipped into her blood like an intoxicating drink.

"I like Juliet. Do you know, I have always wanted to own a puppy, but I suppose a man will do just as well." She laughed. "My room here at Fensmore even has a balcony."

The look in his eyes when she said that made her color again. "I wasn't saying it for that reason!"

"The question of being owned works both ways. Juliet also says that she is sold, but not yet enjoyed."

"I had no idea Shakespeare plays were so . . ."

"So what?" The duke took another drink of wine. Somehow he managed to look calm, even serene, although he was caressing her wrist.

"Sensual," she said, clearing her throat.

"Yes, well," he said, his smile widening. "In the

right circumstances, Lady Edith, anything is erotic."

Edie started wondering how many lovers he'd had. He had probably whispered love verses into the ears of Scottish lasses from the time he was sixteen. She almost opened her mouth to ask, and then realized that there were some questions better left unanswered.

It gave her a bit of a qualm. No one had ever bothered to write her a verse. She was a naïve dunce when it came to this sort of thing.

"You've told me you prefer to be called Edie," he said.

She nodded.

"I would be honored if you would address me as Gowan."

Edie nodded again, and then caught a glimpse of the young lady seated across from her. She was staring at the two of them with stark envy, and when Edie met her eye, she whispered, "You're so lucky."

Edie smiled her thanks, and looked sideways at Gowan again. He had, finally, turned to talk to the lady on his right side.

His skin gleamed like honey in the candlelight. His hair tumbled behind his ear, the touch of red matching the dark cherry of his lips. He looked as if he came from a long line of warriors that had bred true.

Edie was starting to feel peculiar. Things like

this didn't happen to *her*. She spent her days playing an indecorous musical instrument and squabbling with her father. Yes, she was pretty, but not particularly sensual. She never thought a man like this, a man who simmered with erotic confidence, would look to her, because she wasn't one of those girls who flirted and threw seductive glances. She didn't even really know how.

Could it be that the duke greeted every woman—or at least, those he was determined to seduce—with this sort of intensely seductive poetry? How many women had found themselves compared to Juliet?

She waited until he finished his conversation; she herself was shamefully neglecting the man to her left. "I don't look like this most of the time," she told him.

Gowan broke into laughter.

"I feel as if you keep seeing me in masquerade. First, I was quiet and peaceful and all in white—"

"Like an angel," he said, and his voice had that throb again that made her feel hot.

"But I am not an angel," she forced herself to say. "I'm not even particularly quiet, though I do have a deep aversion to conflict. And now, tonight . . ." She indicated her gown. "This is not me, either."

"Seductive?" he asked. "I am seduced."

Edie now understood how Casanova got his reputation: he must have had this ability to look at a woman with melting desire in his eyes and, of course, she collapsed into his bed.

She pulled herself back together. "Queen of Babylon–ish. Truly, I am a great deal more ordinary than this."

"I don't wear a kilt often, either. I like to wear the colors of my clan, but the wind can be bloody cold on one's legs."

Edie smiled at that. "Your kilt becomes you." No woman in her right mind would dislike it when worn by this particular man.

"And that red gown becomes you."

There was a moment of charged silence between them.

He dropped his voice. "I would like to pull down the sleeves."

Edie bit her lip, her breath caught in her chest.

"I would like to lick you from your mouth to—"

"You mustn't speak like that!" Edie hissed. "What if someone hears you?"

"There would be a scandal. Perhaps we would be forced to marry immediately. Shall I create a scandal, my lady?"

His eyes were alight with something fiercer, hotter than glee. She froze, stunned by the ferocity of the emotion she saw in them. How had this happened . . . between the two of them? What *was* it?

Did people really fall in love like this, with no more than a few moments of conversation? Could *she* fall in love with a man merely because he was beautiful and looked well in a kilt? Of course, he was also intelligent, and then there was his voice, and that secret laughter, and he was funny . . . And he wanted her. He wanted her more than she could ever have imagined.

Yes.

Yes, she could.

Their hostess came to her feet; the meal was over. The gentlemen would take port in the library, while the ladies retired to the music room for tea.

She hadn't answered his question. The duke stretched out his hand and brought her to her feet. "I don't want to wait four more months to marry you," he said, taking both her hands and looking as though he might throw responsibility to the winds and kiss her right there. That *would* be a scandal.

"My father has often said that he does not approve of short betrothals." Edie was appalled to find that her voice was as breathless as that of any silly child of sixteen.

She drank in the expression on his face, feeling as if music reeled through her veins. "Perhaps I could convince him to change his mind."

A great crescendo of musical notes flowed over her and danced between them. "All right," she whispered. "All right."

She wasn't sure what she agreed to: but there was a flare of joy in his eyes, and that was enough.

Eleven

Gowan followed the other gentlemen into the library, quite aware that he was incapable of speech. He felt as if he'd been knocked unconscious and had reawakened in a different world.

As if he'd woken up in a play.

Maybe he *was* Romeo. Maybe this would end in both of their deaths.

The most shocking thing was that he could actually contemplate that without much turmoil. If Edie died . . .

What in the hell was he thinking? They weren't even married yet. He hardly knew her. Edie's father was standing by himself, staring down into the fireplace, so Gowan accepted a glass of port and joined him.

"Lord Gilchrist."

"I'm no longer sure you're the right man for my daughter," the earl said abruptly.

"It grieves me to hear you say it, but I'm afraid it's too late for second thoughts. I will marry Lady Edith." The force of his ancient dukedom spoke through his tone.

But behind a flash of entitled aristocratic irritation—who was the earl to question his betrothal?—was something more primitive: Edie was *his,* and if he had to revert to the practices of the ancient Picts, steal her from England and carry her to Scotland on the back of his horse . . . he would.

The earl looked sharply at him, and then back at the fire. "That's what I mean."

"What?"

"You're consumed by desire for her, aren't you? She put on that red dress belonging to my wife, and now you've lost your head altogether."

"Something like that," Gowan agreed.

"It is a disaster," Gilchrist said, his voice heavy. "A disaster."

Gowan opened his mouth to contest his prediction, but Gilchrist continued. "I chose you precisely because I judged you unlikely to succumb to passion. I can tell you from my own experience that the passions of the flesh are no basis for marriage."

"Ah." Gowan was still trying to sort out how he could respond to that savage comment, when the earl launched into speech again.

"My daughter is a true musician. I wanted a marriage of the rational sort for her. One in which her husband would respect her talent—nay, *genius*."

"Genius?" Gowan put his glass onto the mantelpiece.

"She plays the cello like no other woman in this country, and very few men."

Gowan had never known any woman who played the cello—or indeed, any man, either—but he knew better than to point that out to a man whose face was alight with a combination of pride and rage.

"She plays better than I do, and I fancy that I could have had an excellent career had I been born outside the peerage. Were she not my daughter, she would be playing in the world's greatest concert halls. Do you know who told me that?" His eyes were as ferocious as his tone.

Gowan shook his head. How in the devil could he know? He scarcely knew what a cello was.

"Robert Lindley!"

His expression must have betrayed his ignorance. "The greatest cellist in England," Gilchrist said flatly. "Edith played for him—in private, of course—and he told me that were she not a woman, she would rival his own son. In my opinion, she would rival *him,* not just his son."

"I know little about music," Gowan said, clearing his throat, "but I am delighted to hear that my future duchess possesses such a gift."

The earl opened his mouth, then clamped it shut again. "There was nothing else I could do," he said, his voice despairing. "She is the one child of my lineage. She had to marry."

The man's face was twisted with regret. What in the hell did he think Gowan would do? Throw Edie's cello out the window?—not that he had figured out what it was. Some sort of stringed instrument, he assumed. The only one he knew of was the fiddle.

Gowan didn't feel like drinking port, nor did he particularly want to spend more time with Gilchrist, who was growing distraught in a way that he did not admire.

There was an undercurrent here, he thought, that had to do with the unruly relationship between the earl and his countess, and nothing to do with Edie. In fact, based on Edie's measured and intelligent letters, he was marrying just the right woman. She had undoubtedly come to value rational communication precisely owing to her intimate view of her father's marriage.

He bowed. "If you would excuse me, Lord Gilchrist, I believe I shall take a walk in the gardens."

The earl nodded, without taking his eyes from the fire.

Gowan exited the library through a side door and found his way outside, where he embarked on a slow, careful inspection of Fensmore. The seat of the Earls of Chatteris was a great pile of brick and stone, added to by ancestors who were intelligent and by those who were fools.

By an hour later, he had formed a good sense of its two courtyards, its great back lawn, its tennis court and hedge maze . . . and its balconies.

There were six of these. Two looked over the inner courtyard, and four over the great lawn. They were all accessible, though he wouldn't be foolhardy enough to risk his life climbing the ivy. Those overlooking the courtyard, he reckoned, had probably been added in relatively recent years; the four in the back were far more ancient and likely belonged to the house in its first incarnation, or shortly thereafter. Truly, Juliet's balconies.

But he had a shrewd idea that the old balconies corresponded to the bedchambers assigned to the master and mistress, as well as the two largest and grandest guest rooms. Edie would not have been assigned one of those, as she was neither family nor a particular friend of Lady Honoria.

He returned to the courtyard and once again surveyed the two inner balconies, which were formed by marble balustrades. They were, he determined, strong enough to support a rope.

Then he strolled back into the gardens, his mind busy. He would never dishonor his future duchess. But that didn't mean he was content to sleep under the same roof and not kiss her good night. Chastely and tenderly, naturally.

It was bewildering, this thing that had happened between him and Edie. Like being caught in a whirlwind. Even the thought of her brought a stab of raw hunger that made his stomach clench. When her fingers had brushed his hand, a sensual fleeting touch that shied away like a frightened deer, it ignited a fire in him. He was ravenous. Out of control.

He made himself walk around the gardens for another half hour, using the chill evening air to force his body into quiescence. Then he rejoined the gentlemen. Chatteris called over to him, and they retired to his study for a game of billiards, another friend of theirs from childhood, Daniel Smythe-Smith, wandering after them.

They played silently, until, after successfully pocketing a ball, Chatteris straightened and said, rather abruptly, "I watched you speaking to your fiancée during supper."

Gowan glanced at him. "I was seated beside Lady Edith. Naturally I spoke to her."

"Congratulations," Chatteris said. "Lady Edith is truly lovely."

Chatteris lined up his cue and neatly sank another ball into the bag hanging on one of the far corners. "When do you plan to marry?"

"In four months," Gowan replied. But that idea was no longer palatable. "Or perhaps somewhat sooner."

"I was not the only one watching you. The lady's father did not seem pleased."

Gowan shrugged. "The papers are signed, though the earl would rather his daughter's marriage remained a matter of cool practicality."

Chatteris sank yet another ball. Then: "Your conversation did not appear to be, shall we say, emotionless."

Gowan refused to pretend that his marriage was

a matter of convenience; that would tarnish the growing feeling between himself and Edie. He contented himself by retorting, "Yours is merely practical as well, as I noticed earlier this evening."

Chatteris's smile revealed that he knew precisely what Gowan meant. "We are both lucky men." His ball ricocheted and spun to a stop. "As are you," he added, nodding at Smythe-Smith, whose own marriage would take place in a week or so.

Gowan lined up a ball. "My fiancée tells me that she has a room with a balcony." He glanced up at Chatteris. "I am guessing her chamber faces your inner courtyard."

The earl frowned. "I couldn't say."

"Oh for God's sake," Smythe-Smith put in. "If Lady Edith has a balcony, it must be facing the inner courtyard, since my parents have rooms facing the back gardens. You do *not* want to make a mistake and climb to my mother's balcony, Kinross."

Chatteris leaned against the table, ignoring his soon-to-be brother-in-law. "I believe I've known you my whole life, Kinross."

"We met at eight years old." Gowan sank the ball. "A party in this very house, as I recall."

"That makes it a particular pleasure to see you falling victim to an arrow shot by a blindfolded child."

Did he mean Cupid? It wasn't an unreasonable

supposition. "Pot. Kettle," he retorted. "So is Smythe-Smith correct about the balcony?"

"It's just a thought," Chatteris said, "but why not follow the path of least resistance—in short, the stairs?"

Gowan looked up, knowing that his eyes were alive with a wild mischief that his friend would never before have seen in them. "I would prefer to surprise her. We were discussing plays at dinner."

"Oh, was *that* what you were discussing?" The earl broke into laughter. "I'll warrant over half the company thought there was nothing literary about the conversation."

"It was bookish, I assure you. *Romeo and Juliet.*"

"Ah. Dangerous things, balconies."

Gowan pocketed another ball. "I'm fairly fit."

"I'd guess the old ladder in the carriage house that we used to play with as kids is still there," Smythe-Smith said, laughing.

"Surely a ladder would not reach that height," Gowan said.

"It's a rope ladder," Smythe-Smith explained. "Woven from horsehair, as a matter of fact. Could have been made for that purpose."

"I find that suggestion highly inadvisable," Chatteris said.

"Nonsense!" Smythe-Smith retorted, poking his friend in the side. "You'll be married by tomorrow, and I've only a week or so to wait, and poor Kinross is looking at months, if not longer." He turned back to Gowan, his eyes alight with mischief. "I'll send someone to fetch it. My man will attend to it without the lady's maid knowing aught of the matter."

Gowan took care of the last ball, straightened, met Smythe-Smith's eyes, and burst out laughing. "You've used that ladder yourself!"

"I couldn't possibly comment on such an assumption," the man said, his eyes dancing. He turned. "The ladies won't retire for an hour or so. Consider it my wedding gift."

Gowan watched Smythe-Smith weave his way out of the room, followed by the earl. They were both damned handsome men.

He felt a sudden flash of gladness that Edie hadn't debuted last year, or the year before. What if he'd only met her as Lady Chatteris?

Inconceivable.

Once they married, he could kiss her at the dining room table if he wished. At Craigievar, there was no one to say nay if he commanded the footmen to leave so he could tup his wife on the table itself.

With a silent groan, he realized that the calming effect of the gardens had been utterly lost.

Twelve

Edie prepared for bed in something of a dreamlike state. She bathed and put on a night-dress and a wrapper, then sat on a stool as Mary took the pins from her hair and brushed it out.

Gowan was such an odd mixture: grave and intense, with just the faintest strain of sardonic humor. His heart was true. But he was a complex man who, in her estimation, revealed almost nothing to anyone.

"Would you like to slip into bed now, my lady?" Mary asked.

"Not just yet," Edie said, smiling at her. "I must practice first. Thank you; that will be all."

After Mary slipped away, Edie took her cello from its stand by the wall and began to tighten the bridge. Even weary as she now was, she had to play for at least an hour. Tomorrow, the day of the wedding, would be entirely lost.

Years ago, when she had begun to refuse to travel without her cello, her father had had a special case constructed, padded and lined in velvet, a near duplicate of his own. Now their instruments traveled in a separate carriage, their protective cases so heavy that they needed two grooms to carry them between house and vehicle.

She began with Vivaldi. The "Winter" section wasn't going well. A half hour later, she was working hard on her bowing, playing two phrases again and again until she was satisfied.

With that, she started again from the beginning, intending to play the piece all the way through before allowing herself to retire at last. She was concentrating so hard on her music that she started when a sudden gust from the French door leading to her balcony ruffled her score and blew a few pages to the floor. Her fingers slipped, and with a muttered curse she started over.

She didn't need the score by now: the music swept through her mind a half note ahead of her bowing. The notes slid like water from her cello.

A breeze stirred the pages again, but this time her concentration didn't break. She was almost at the end when the door to the corridor opened without notice. She jerked her head up with a scowl. Mary knew just how much she hated to be interrupted during practice.

But it wasn't Mary; it was her father, carrying his cello. His face was drawn, his eyes dark.

She lifted the bow from the strings and nodded to the chair on the other side of the fire, near the window. As he carried his instrument across the room, she tugged at her gown so it covered her legs again. Because she often played before bedtime, all her nightdresses were made with a very high slit, which freed her legs while allowing her to be decently covered.

Her father understood the limitations of playing

sideways. No serious cellist could tolerate the restriction of her arm movement.

Now he sat down and drew his bow across the strings, tuning his instrument to hers.

"The new arrangement of Bach's Italian Concerto?" she suggested. Playing duets was the heart of their relationship. From the time she was a very small girl, she treasured his evening visits to the nursery. She had begun working hard at music in order to earn a smile from him . . . but she kept working once it got into her blood.

The earl was never very good at demonstrations of affection. But he had come to the nursery every single evening, without fail, and had taught her to play. The time had come when there was nothing left to teach her, but still they practiced together.

He nodded now in silent agreement to the Bach. They drew their bows at the same moment, having played together for so long that they followed each other without conscious thought. The piece she had suggested was powerful and rich, the notes deep and nearly sobbing from their strings.

She played the counterpoint, her notes dancing around his, picking up the severe bass line, blending it with the melody, weaving a strand of sunlight into midnight. Her father sat facing her, his expression a mix of joy and fierce concentration.

Halfway through, the wind stirred again and she

glanced up. Her bow nearly faltered even as the arrangement sent her notes soaring above her father's strong bowing. His utter absorption was fortunate, because to her complete astonishment, Gowan was standing just outside the open French door behind her father, on the balcony.

Her left hand flew up and down the fingerboard automatically as she stared at the Duke of Kinross. Then her father lifted his bow and the music stopped abruptly, leaving her notes to fall into the air like thin versions of what they should be. Had he heard something? She lifted her bow as well, scarcely breathing.

"*Da capo*?" he said. To her relief, there was no suspicion in her father's voice, merely an acknowledgment that she was no longer *in* the music. Little wonder: it was impossible to maintain the intense concentration needed for a piece like this when one's fiancé materializes like a Scottish specter on a tiny balcony, twenty feet above the ground, outside one's bedroom. How on earth had he got there?

If her father were to turn around . . .

The vain part of her wanted Gowan to believe she was a sensuous woman whose crimson lip color advertised her inner self. She twitched her nightdress and it fell open, exposing her left leg. Her father would never notice; no musician looked at another while playing. Indeed, he often closed his eyes while he played.

"Yes," she replied. "Or rather, *no;* instead, let's play the Largo from Vivaldi's Concerto in G Major. I was working on Melchett's cello arrangement earlier."

"Do you need the score?"

"No. I worked on it quite a lot in the month before I became ill. I've been playing the second cello, if you would take the first."

Her father nodded. "Remember the lyricism in the music, Edie. Last time, you were concentrating too much on the fingering and not listening to what the music meant." The weariness had fallen from his voice.

Reassured that her father was oblivious to Gowan's presence on her balcony, Edie relaxed a bit and let herself glance at the duke again. He was still leaning there, silent, outlined against the sky. The feeling she had for him was so odd.

Meeting his eyes, seeing a glint in them that was surely lent by the devil . . . she felt as great a pull inside her heart and body as she had upon hearing the cello for the first time.

Her father bent his head and repositioned his bow. Edie drew her bow long and slow in the first section, and fell into the music.

She wanted Gowan to understand this passion of hers, to see that it wasn't a mere pastime. So she pushed him out of her mind, and moved back into the music with the weight of years of experience behind her, her bow now playing an elegant flurry of notes above her father's melody, now providing a stately counterpoint.

Slowly the music swelled around them, taking the air and distilling it into sounds so sweet that they were emotions become audible. Her body swayed in unison with her bowing. They neared the most difficult part of the piece. Edie bent her head, making absolutely certain that her fingers leapt flawlessly from note to note.

She did not stumble. Her bowing had never been better. Her father didn't look at her, but with a musician's perception she knew there was the deep joy spreading through his body. His taut despair was gone now as he breathed music, created music. The last measures were slow breaths, music and air winding together.

As the final note floated across the evening air, her father at last raised his head. Edie twitched her gown so it fell back over her leg, while keeping her eyes from straying to the balcony behind him.

"You were right," he said, rising. "You have indeed learned the piece." That was high praise.

Edie smiled at him. They were often at odds, but she loved him deeply. And under all his stiff demeanor she knew he loved her. "Thank you," she said softly. "Good night, Father."

He inclined his head, one musician paying respect to another. "Daughter. Good night."

He collected his instrument, crossed the room, and left without another word.

Edie closed the door behind him and turned. Gowan had melted into the darkness. She could just see him, silhouetted against the starry sky. Rather than move toward him, she leaned back against the door and, like a wanton, let her leg slip through her nightdress. "Your Grace," she said. "I am surprised to have a visitor at this hour of night."

Gowan moved into the room. "I, too, am surprised."

"What surprises you?" She remained where she was, willing him to come to her. Music exhilarated Edie; she had always known that. But she had never realized that it could drive a deeper intoxication, singing in her veins. This new, deeper one made her want to play the man before her like an instrument. Or let him play her . . . she wasn't certain. It was an unfamiliar kind of madness, but just as all-encompassing.

Like the blood in her body, like the music in her soul.

Madness.

"Your father says that you rival the greatest player in all England."

"He's my father. He exaggerates."

"I gather from what I heard tonight that he himself is one of the great players as well." He had cut in half the distance between them.

"That's true." A thrilling sense of power was flowing through Edie's veins. It was the feeling of a woman's power, something she had never bothered to learn about. No wonder Layla flirted with other men . . .

Gowan frowned. "There is no one who plays the cello in all Scotland, I should think."

"Hmmm." Edie didn't care. She enjoyed playing with her father, but she also loved playing solo, and happily did so for hours at a time. "How on earth did you reach my balcony?"

"I climbed. I thought to play Romeo to your Juliet and call you outside, but when I heard you playing I was drawn up, as if by music from a fairy mound."

"A fairy mound? What is that?"

"In Scotland music leaks on occasion from the land of the fairies, which is located under a grassy hillock." He came a few steps closer.

Edie smiled at him. She did not move. "So I lured you, as if 'twas magic from my strings?"

"Yes."

"We were playing a Vivaldi concerto."

He was silent a moment. "There is a great deal I do not know of music, my lady."

"So I gather, if you had never heard of a cello."

"In truth, I have never heard of a woman musician. Singers, yes. And certainly ladies play the pianoforte."

Edie nodded, at peace with that. Public performance had never been a dream of hers. "I do not wish to play for an audience. Though I rather liked having one this night."

"Will you play for me again?"

"Of course."

He came closer still, close enough that his breath stirred the tiny curls on her forehead. "I arrived before your father entered the room."

That look in his eyes . . . Hot color flooded Edie's cheeks.

"You, playing a cello, is the most erotic thing I ever saw in my life," he whispered. Then his mouth closed over hers.

Her first kiss.

His lips were sweet on hers, tender somehow, even though they hardly knew each other. Yet it was possible he knew her better than anyone else.

His first kiss.

Her lips were like the sweetness at the heart of a honeysuckle blossom. For a second Gowan couldn't believe that he was actually kissing her. Their lips brushed together once, twice . . . his tongue dipped inside her mouth.

She opened her lips to his with a surprised little sound. He leaned closer, bracing his forearms on the door. Their tongues tangled for a moment, then Gowan kissed her eyes and her cheeks and then, powerless to resist, returned to her mouth. They kissed until Gowan's head was filled with images of Edie's pale legs twisted with his, her body arched on the bed, a cry bursting from her throat . . .

No.

He would not dishonor his bride-to-be, no matter the fact that she had her arms wound around his neck and was kissing him feverishly, her tongue as bold and sensual as his.

No matter the fact that her slender fingers were playing in his hair, leaving little tingling reminders of her touch.

No matter that his heart was pounding as hard as hers. He could feel it through the insubstantial fabric of her nightdress, just as he could feel her breasts, soft and tremulous against his chest.

He turned his head away, hearing his own breath coming harsh from his chest. She murmured something and her lips skated across his jaw. He felt her lips touch his ear; a groan escaped his mouth.

"We cannot do this," he whispered, putting his forehead against the cool wood of the door. "We must not."

"Gowan," she breathed, and Lord help him, her hands slid from his neck and down his chest.

"Edie. I will not dishonor you. My bride. My duchess."

Her eyes were slightly glazed, her mouth pouty with his kisses. But she cocked her head, that formidable intelligence of hers snapping into place almost audibly. "How honorable of you."

They stared at each other. She was a sonnet sprung to full life, but none of that mattered.

The little lopsided smile she had, with the kiss that she had never given to anyone, *that* was what caught his heart and put the groan in his throat.

"I must go back down the ladder," he said hoarsely.

Her smile strengthened. "I find myself very glad to be marrying you, Duke."

"I'm very happy to hear it, lass. In the circumstances." He couldn't help touching her, curving his hand around her neck and bringing her mouth to his again.

"I don't believe that this is customary among—among the nobility," she said with a little gasp, a while later.

Gowan shook his head. He couldn't bring to mind a pairing that had erupted like theirs, in a burst of flame. He cupped her face in his hands. "We must be certain," he said, the words growling out like a vow, "that we are not *quick bright things* that come to naught."

Edie's hands came over his. "I feel as if I should engage a governess and bring her along with me to Scotland. Was that Shakespeare again?"

He nodded.

"I never did like poetry all that much," she said, turning her face so that she kissed his palm. "Although you might be able to change my mind."

"I am fond of verse."

"Any woman could tell that you're fairly swelling with your seductive prowess."

He fell back a step and broke into a crack of laughter at that. "Swelling? *Swelling?*"

Edie's already flushed cheeks turned rosier still. "You know what I mean!" she said. "You're—you know everything and I don't."

Should he be honest?

She put her hands on her hips—and she had luscious hips, perfect hips. The action pulled her nightdress taut across her equally perfect breasts. Her gaze was so sincere and direct that he confessed the truth. "I don't know about it, either, Edie."

"I'm not talking about marriage," she said instantly, her cheeks turning even brighter red.

"What, then?" he asked. He was really enjoying himself.

"The bedding part!" she cried. "*That* part. You know it, and I don't." Her eyes narrowed. "Though if you laugh at me again, perhaps I'll see if I can gain a bit of experience in the next few months before we marry."

He backed her against the door in a flash, caught her hands over her head in one of his, felt her body hot against his. "Absolutely not."

Laughter shone in her eyes and she batted her eyelashes at him deliberately. "I'm sure you'd be grateful to find that you didn't have an ignorant chit like myself in your bed on your wedding night."

"No." He bent his head and drank her in, deep and fierce.

When he drew his lips away from her again, she said in a ragged voice, "You have all those love poems and lines of Shakespeare and the rest. I have none of that, Gowan. I can't read a play to save my life. I tried, and I couldn't make head or tail of it."

"I don't care. Let me teach you to love poetry." He traced the curve of her bottom lip with his finger. "You're mine, Edie."

"That is hardly the point," she said, her voice darkening. "I'm . . . And you're . . ."

"As untouched as you are," he said, fascinated by the way thick lashes framed her eyes.

Her brow furrowed.

"A virgin," he said, growling it because, after all, a man isn't supposed to be a virgin. Ever.

He released her hands and swung her into his arms. She was a snug weight, a soft female weight that sent a flame right down his limbs. But he made himself walk to a chair rather than topple her onto the bed.

"You?" She was stunned.

"Aye." He sat down, relishing the way her bottom settled onto his lap. "I was betrothed from the time I was quite young, so I could not sleep with a woman who might have expectations—or dreams—of becoming a duchess. Paying coin for the act would be distasteful; I would have dishonored my fiancée at the same time as myself."

Edie sat still as a mouse; he drew his arm tighter around her back. Her eyes searched his, wide and surprised.

"So I am quite certain that I do not have 'a disease of an intimate nature,'" he told her.

"Ah, my letter." She recognized her own words. "No, I suppose you do not."

He gave her another fierce, lingering kiss. They broke off with a new wildness between them, all but visible in the air. And they met each other's eyes now with that between them like a glimmering possibility.

"Together," she whispered, awed. "It's nothing I would have expected. I always thought that a woman brought such a thing to her marriage, but a man . . ."

"Is supposed to have slept first with a chambermaid or a barmaid," Gowan said. "That would be to abase myself as well as a woman in my employ."

A choked laugh escaped from Edie's mouth. "You're a man of principle, Your Grace."

"Is that not a good thing?"

Thirteen

Laughter was fighting with an aching, twisting *need* in Edie's heart. She couldn't look at Gowan any longer without leaning in to kiss him. She closed her eyes and put her cheek against his shoulder. "It's a very good thing to have principles," she said, the words coming soft and low. "You must have laughed when I wrote you about mistresses, let alone diseases."

"I didn't laugh. It was a fair question. There's many a man has a mistress in addition to his wife. But I always hoped that I'd find a wife who would want to carry my children, and how could I dishonor that wife by pouring gold into the lap of a woman whom I had no intention of marrying?"

Edie turned and kissed Gowan's neck. It was a strong column, that neck. "You are a complicated man."

"These are not complicated things. There's an old Scottish saying that 'your present is your future.' I choose not to tarnish what may come. Besides, my father . . ." He trailed off.

"Had mistresses?" Edie asked.

"Many."

She dropped another kiss under his jaw, where his pulse was beating. "I thought my father had a mistress, but now I'm not so sure. Layla fears that's why he doesn't come home at night."

"I doubt it," Gowan said. "'Twould shame him to do so, and your father is not a man who would bring shame upon himself."

Edie smiled, knowing he couldn't see it. Her father was a bit stiff, but at heart, he and Gowan were both the sort of man whom a woman is lucky to find at her side. "Did your mother know of your father's affairs?"

"Aye, she did." The burr of his Scottish ancestry grew more pronounced. "But her behavior matched his. She would have had no right to make complaints."

"I'm sorry," Edie murmured, and leaned back against his arm in order to see his face. "That must be a difficult thing to find out about one's parents."

"My mother was notorious for her dalliances, so I learned it as a young boy." There was a bleak acceptance in his voice. "Did your father tell you that I have a half sister, called Susannah?"

"Really? No, he didn't mention it. Does she live in Scotland?"

"She lives with me, and she is five years old, or so we think."

"*What?*" Edie sat up straight. "You have a half sister who lives with you and is five, '*you think*'?"

"My mother left us when I was eight, and she died a few months ago, leaving a child. Presumably, she remarried after my father died, though I had no knowledge of it. We have not yet found a baptismal record for my sister."

"Oh my goodness." Edie sprang from his lap and walked across the room before turning to face him. "Do I collect that you are marrying partly in order to provide a mother for your sister? I must tell you that I have no experience of children whatsoever."

He had stood, of course. "Neither have I. But I engaged three nursemaids and a nanny."

"I'm sorry; I didn't mean to make you rise." She came back and sat down opposite him. "I don't even know how big a five-year-old child is. Has she adult teeth yet? Can she speak? What am I saying? Of course she speaks!"

"Oh, Susannah speaks," Gowan said, with feeling. "All the time. And she has teeth, too; she bit me the first day she came to Craigievar. So I would advise you to be careful when approaching her." He sat again and reached out to take her hand.

"Oh my," Edie breathed. Without really noticing, she watched as he traced a pattern on her palm with one finger. Her mind was reeling. She was not only marrying and moving to Scotland; she was evidently taking on an orphaned child. Really, her father could have mentioned that detail.

"I do remember that you expressed the wish to have children only after a few years. I was not

135

prevaricating by neglecting to mention Susannah in my letter; I must confess that, because I wasn't in Scotland, I actually forgot about her."

He didn't look guilty in the least.

"Have you any family members who are helping raise her?" Edie asked hopefully. "An aunt, perhaps?" She couldn't possibly become a mother to a five-year-old, overnight. She wasn't sure she had even *seen* a five-year-old before.

"Unfortunately, no. I have some aunts, but they haven't yet met Susannah. They are my father's sisters," he explained. "They live in the Orkney Islands."

"She is in the castle alone?"

"There are one hundred and thirteen servants in residence, including the four who are dedicated exclusively to her care."

Her own mother had died when she was still a child, and so Edie was well aware that even one hundred servants couldn't make up for a lost parent. "Perhaps there are books about this sort of thing," she muttered. "Is the poor child terribly grieved? How did your mother die, if I might ask?"

"She drowned in a loch after imbibing more whisky than advisable." There was a pause, and then he added, "My father died years earlier, after drinking two bottles of whisky. On a bet, you understand."

Edie began sorting through the standard

expressions of sympathy she had been taught; none seemed adequate.

"Still, my father died triumphant in his ill-advised wager, which would undoubtedly be a consolation to him. I do not drink spirits, in case you are concerned about the possibility that I have inherited the family susceptibility." Gowan delivered these facts in an utterly even tone, as if he were recounting no more than a change in the weather.

"And Susannah's father . . . your stepfather?"

"My mother referred to herself as a widow, though no one in her household knew much about her life before she moved to Edinburgh last year. She may have concealed her marriage from me in order to protect her allowance. Or it may be that Susannah is illegitimate. I have hired Bow Street Runners to find out." He folded his arms over his chest. "There are those who would maintain that I offer you a tarnished name."

"Don't be ridiculous." Edie frowned at him. "Your parents' foolishness does not reflect on you."

"That is very generous of you." He hesitated, then said, "I must add that Susannah appears to be fairly unmanageable. I'm not the only person she's bitten: I gather the nursemaids consider themselves in danger as well."

Wonderful. Edie was already unnerved by the idea of caring for a child, let alone a difficult one.

"Did she have any idea that you existed before she arrived on your doorstep? What is she like?"

"Small. Puny, in fact. I think she is remarkably articulate for someone so young, though her governess assures me female children are often so. And no, she seems to have had no idea she had family at all."

"Does she look like you?"

"Her hair is a much brighter red. Other than that, I cannot say. I have not yet spent much time with her."

"She must be miserable, what with losing her mother and then meeting a strange brother."

"There is no reason for her to be miserable. It is my impression that she knew little of our mother."

Edie had the distinct feeling that the Duke of Kinross was of the opinion that there were only narrow circumstances under which someone might be allowed an emotion as powerful as misery. "Even if Susannah was not close to her mother, she lost everyone who was familiar to her," she pointed out.

"I receive a complete report every day of all events of significance, and the nursery has not been mentioned since a biting episode last week, so I am confident she is happy."

Edie jumped up from her chair again. All that tingling awareness of Gowan she had felt earlier had been swallowed by a storm of nerves. She went over to the mantelpiece and picked up a pretty little porcelain Madonna holding the infant Jesus, fiddled with it briefly, then put it back down. Likely Mary had known perfectly well how to raise her son. Whereas Edie felt a dawning terror at the thought. Why hadn't her father mentioned the child when he announced that she was marrying Gowan? She might have launched a protest.

Not that her father would have paid the slightest attention to her qualms, given that the alliance would make her a duchess.

"How on earth do you receive daily reports if you are here, and Susannah is in Scotland?" she asked Gowan.

"A groom leaves the castle every morning with a full report." He, too, had risen, and stood at the opposite end of the mantelpiece. "I find that managing a large estate is significantly easier with a constant flow of communication. My more remote estates send messages to the castle every two to three days."

"That must require a great many servants," she said, awed at the idea. "And coaches, and horses."

He shrugged. "I have a great many."

Then, in an instant, a taut desire came back into his eyes, making her pricklingly aware of her body again. He took a step toward her. "Don't worry about my sister," he said. "If you don't like her, I'll find someone else to care for her."

"Absolutely not!" Edie exclaimed. "I'm merely

unused to children. But I shall manage." Gowan's smile was pure temptation—and had nothing to do with her reassurance as regards his sister. "This is terribly risky," she said, remembering suddenly that they were alone in her bedchamber in a strange house in the middle of the night. "You must leave. I wouldn't want to ruin Honoria's wedding by creating a scandal."

"Yes, I must." His deep voice caressed her skin like velvet. She shivered and heard a strand of music in her head. And he didn't move.

"If you are caught, it will cause a terrible uproar," she said, and then added, "You're rather large. Wide, I mean. Broad."

"I swim in the loch every day."

Apparently it was swimming that had given him the chest she longed to touch again. He bowed, and then started toward the balcony. She followed him as if drawn by a string.

"What did you think of my playing?" she asked, just when Gowan had one hand on the balustrade and was about to swing down a rope ladder that had been tied to the corner baluster.

His face was in shadow; the courtyard below him was illuminated only by moonlight. "I thought you were a genius," he said. "Just as your father said. Will you teach Susannah the cello?"

"Yes," she said, realizing for the first time that of course she would teach the child, just as her father had taught her.

"Then we must make it possible for Susannah, and any children of our own, to play for an audience if they so wish." He began his descent.

His head disappeared below the marble parapet while she was still digesting that sentence. She leaned over and watched him as he climbed, making it look as easy as descending a flight of stairs.

Once on the ground, he threw back his head and looked up at her. Her heart gave a great thump at the sight of him. But she was also experiencing a toe-curling sense of embarrassment. Perhaps she should have been more standoffish. What if, after what had just occurred between them, he thought she was a wanton?

"Perhaps you're right," she called softly, staring down. "We are 'quick bright things' . . . too rash, too sudden, too ill-advised."

"I can woo you tomorrow as if we'd never met, but I'm afraid that everyone in the drawing room already knows how I feel. And the notice is already in the papers."

"Things like this don't happen to people like me," Edie said.

"Your voice is like music," Gowan said, staring up at her. "What time do you rise?"

"Why do you ask?"

"I want more of you, and not just while staring across the pews during the wedding."

He said it matter-of-factly, but her heart soared.

"Nine o'clock in the morning. Good night," she called.

"Good night," he said, too softly for her to hear.

But somehow she heard anyway.

She stood gripping the cold marble, watching as Gowan strode across the courtyard and disappeared under the portico.

And then she stood a little longer, hearing music tumbling through her mind, even deeper and sweeter than she made on her cello.

Fourteen

No. 20 Curzon Street, London
The Earl of Gilchrist's town house

"Your fiancé," said the earl, with icy precision, "initially agreed to a five-month betrothal, but now he wishes to reduce that period. As I believe I mentioned to you, he has recently come into guardianship of an orphaned sister, a very young child. I gather he is worried that she will remain motherless during the interval, though he expressed no pressing concern when he asked for your hand in marriage."

The Gilchrists had returned to London directly after the wedding, and Gowan had gone back to Brighton to talk to those bankers. Edie was secretly counting the days until the conference of bankers concluded. Tomorrow, she thought, or even tonight.

"I would be pleased to agree," she said, shaping her tone to docile compliance. The last thing she wanted was to spur her father to a fit of righteous rage by pointing out the fact that he had neglected to mention Susannah to her altogether.

"I do not like it," he said abruptly. He wheeled around and put his glass back on a table.

"May I inquire why not?"

"The duke isn't the man I believed him to be."

"That is not true," Edie protested. "Gowan is precisely—"

"*Gowan?* You address him by his given name? That is outrageous." Her father's mouth flattened into a thin line.

She wanted to snap back at him, but it would only hurt her cause. "I did not mean it in that fashion," she offered.

"I am expected in Parliament," her father stated. He bowed, and left.

He did not come home that night for supper. "You know," Edie said at the table, "I think you treat my father altogether too kindly, Layla. Here you are in the house whereas your husband is out gallivanting, doing whatever he pleases."

"What would you have me do? Flirt with Gryphus? I don't even like the man. He's too young."

"Of course not." Edie put down her fork. "But

why should your life be so miserable? I'm not saying that you should flirt, Layla. I'm just saying that perhaps you should build a routine so that you aren't so gloomy when Father fails to return home."

Layla looked dubious.

"I know that I gave you something of an excuse, since I didn't debut until this year, but there is no reason for you to stay at home these days. Yet you rarely leave the house."

"That's what a wife is supposed to do."

"But her husband is supposed to join her at home. Not to mention the fact that he is supposed to escort her to balls and plays. My father is rarely here, and when he is, he's so cold you could chill an ice by him. Where would we be going tonight, if Father hadn't accepted Kinross's offer? If I were still searching for a husband, in other words?"

"Almack's, I suppose," Layla said. "It's a Wednesday night and you were sent a voucher after your debut."

"Right," Edie said. "That's where we'll go tonight."

"But why? Your father won't know where I am, nor will he care. What if he doesn't come home all night, as he didn't last night? He maintains that he sleeps in his chambers at the House of Lords." She said the last with a patent lack of belief.

"Then you will have had a lovely time dancing, which is important, too. There is no reason for you to sit about twiddling your fingers while I bore you silly playing the cello." Edie stood up. "I will ask Mary to dress me for dancing."

"All right."

Edie pointed at her. "*You*, Mistress Stepmother, shall be happy tonight."

"I suppose." Layla looked willing but incapable, her smile wobbly.

"Tell Willikins that we want champagne before going out. We'll both get bosky and then dance with anyone who puts a hand in our direction. Let the gossips tell Father that!"

Edie came down the stairs a while later looking somewhere between maidenly and seductive. She'd had no word from Gowan indicating that he had returned to London, but of course one didn't dress merely to please a man.

Though that was what she had done.

Mary had used the curling iron to straighten her hair, and then had managed to make most of it stay above her shoulders.

Layla gasped. "Oh, Edie, darling, you look utterly delicious!" She looked down at herself. "You're so slender, and I'm getting fat."

"You are not fat. You are delightfully curved, Layla. There's a difference. And I am not slender, either."

"You're slender in comparison to me, probably because you don't take afternoon tea. Every one of these curves is made from crumpets. Your champagne awaits." Layla waved a glass in her direction. "Perhaps I have too many curves for your father's liking."

"Layla, dearest, are you bosky already?" Edie accepted a glass from Willikins, who bowed and left.

"I believe I am a bit tipsy. It's my new slimming regime; I've decided to eat only grapes after three in the afternoon. No more tea. It's my downfall."

"Absurd!"

"If I manage to stay on this regime, I might be able to win your father back from Winifred."

"Winifred? Who's she?" Edie sat down opposite her stepmother and took a sip of her champagne. Then, after another look at Layla, she took a proper gulp. She might as well get in the spirit of things. "Are you saying that you have found out the name of Father's mistress?"

"No, but I've named her Winifred. It's a name I've always loathed, so that makes it easier."

"Makes what easier?"

"Loathing her, of course," Layla said. "For wrecking my less-than-happy home. I also consider her responsible for the fact that I have eaten too many crumpets. *And* for the fact that the only reason my husband gets up in the night is to use the chamber pot."

"Ha," Edie said, giving that jest precisely its due and no more.

"What I need is inspiration. I shall use Winifred

as a spur to reduce. I'm sure she's slender and sylphlike and utterly gorgeous."

"*You* are utterly gorgeous," Edie said, watching as Layla quaffed half her glass of champagne.

"More importantly, the time has come," Layla said, pausing dramatically, "to tell you the secrets of the marital bed."

"I know them," Edie assured her hastily.

"No, no, not the basics. What I'm about to tell you are secrets that are passed from mother to daughter." Layla paused and then frowned. "Do you know about the *petit mort*?"

Edie was pretty sure she did, so she nodded.

"It's just like us to have no word for it ourselves," Layla said a bit crossly. "We have to resort to French, as if Frenchmen were the only ones able to give a woman pleasure. I could tell you—" She caught herself. "You wouldn't appreciate the details, as it's your father in question."

"No," Edie said. "I would not."

"Well, the most important thing to remember is that anything a man asks you to do for him can and should be reciprocated."

Edie frowned. Granted, her understanding of intercourse was at a rudimentary level, but she couldn't imagine any reciprocity.

"No, not that," Layla said, waving her hands. "You'll know it when you see it. I mean, when you are asked to do it. Just take my word for it."

"All right."

"I have to say that I consider this extremely unlikely, but should Kinross prove to be able to maintain his tool for only a few minutes, or if he can't get it up at all, I can help. There are potions for that! So just tell me, darling, and I'll get my hands on the right medicine. I could even send one to you by post."

"Thank you," Edie said, wondering whether women informed their husbands of the potion's effects or administered it secretly.

"And here's the big secret, though I never thought I'd need such a thing." Layla's eyes filled with tears. "But I have."

Edie was starting to feel bewildered. "Does it have to do with virginity?"

"That? Oh no. That didn't hurt much at all. Don't let those old wives' tales frighten you. There may be a few drops of blood, which will make your Scotsman happy. Men are absurdly proud to think they're plowing a virgin field."

"A *field?*"

"You're the field, darling, and he has the plow, if you follow me. Though perhaps a hoe would be a better comparison. No, the real secret has to do with leading your husband to believe that you are experiencing pleasure when you aren't."

"Oh dear," Edie said. The more she heard about her father's marriage, the more broken it seemed.

A tear slid down Layla's cheek. "We never had any trouble before everything turned to having a baby. It's just so distressing." She sniffled. "But that won't happen to you. Did I tell you how envious I am that you have a child ready-made and waiting for you in Scotland?"

Edie kept silent. She could hardly tell Layla that she had lain awake the night before worrying that little Susannah wouldn't like her.

"Some women never have to fret about these matters, because their husbands don't care if they experience pleasure or not. But good husbands *do* care. And there are times when, if you don't bring it to a close, he'll just keep trying until you want to scream. What men do not understand is that a woman may be so fatigued or miserable that she simply can't feel all that he might wish her to feel. Are you following, Edie?"

"More or less."

"So in that case, she has only one recourse: she acts the part."

"Sorry?"

"Acts," Layla said. "Performs. Pretends."

"Performs what?"

"*Le petit mort.*"

"Oh."

"You're not following, are you?"

"Not really."

"Making love is a noisy business," Layla said.

"It *is?*" Edie was growing more and more fascinated, if still confused. She hadn't quite imagined it that way.

Layla put down her glass, now empty, and tipped back her head. A husky, sensual moan poured from her lips. She slipped her hands into her hair and tossed her head back and forth. "Yes, *yes,* just like that, *more,* more!"

The door opened and Willikins appeared behind Layla's shoulder.

"Ahhh, like that, *mon cher*, harder, harder! You . . . you are so . . . so . . ." She tossed her head again and her voice rose. "You make me mad. You make me delirious. I'm beside myself. I'm—I'm *coming!*"

Willikins was frozen in place.

Layla snapped upright, patted her hair back into place, and said, "Willikins, we should both like our glasses refilled."

"I can imagine that you're thirsty," Edie said, giggling madly.

"That is the secret to a happy marriage."

Edie reserved judgment; it didn't seem to be working for Layla. Willikins, meanwhile, began to pour champagne without visible signs of shock. He was worth every ha'penny her father paid him.

Layla downed half the contents of her glass at one go.

They were flute glasses, but still . . . Was it her third? "Time to leave," Edie said, putting her own glass down. "Almack's awaits."

"Almack's," Layla said, with just the tiniest slur to her voice, "is not a place where an adulterous

150

woman can spy on her husband's mistress. Did I tell you that I've decided to remake myself? I'm tired of being Layla. It's such a tiresome name. Impossible to spell."

"Just be grateful you're not named Edith. And you are *not* adulterous."

"I'm aging, which is worse."

"I don't think the archbishop would agree with your estimation of relative evils."

"Prematurely aging," Layla said, sighing. "That's what happens to women like me. We sit around getting old, while the Winifreds of the world steal our husbands. If I had been called Joséphine, it would all be different. No man would cheat if he were married to a Joséphine."

"We really should call for the carriage."

"I believe I'll start speaking French," Layla said, ignoring the question of Almack's while picking up Edie's glass and disposing of her remaining champagne. "It will be good practice. I could move to France rather than retire to the country."

"*C'est la vie,*" Edie said. "That's all I know, so our conversations will be short."

"Darling, everyone can speak French if they just apply themselves. Here's a good phrase: *Évacuez les lieux!*"

"What does that mean?"

"Evacuate the area!" Layla cried, waving her arm. "You never know when you might need to scream that in a crowded place. My governess taught me all sorts of useful phrases. *Êtes-vous enceinte?* That turned out to be not so useful. No, I am not pregnant." She reached out and rang the bell. "I need more champagne before we leave."

"We should go to Almack's now," Edie repeated. "Don't they lock the doors and keep you out if you arrive even a moment too late?"

"You know I could *be* pregnant by now if your father wasn't so stubborn," Layla said, continuing to ignore her. "You do know why rabbits have so many baby bunnies, don't you?"

Edie hauled her stepmother to her feet. Tipsy or not, Layla was delectable, like the prettiest cream pastry a man could hope to eat. The bodice of her sky-blue gown seemed to indicate there was a severe shortage of silkworms in the world, but Layla definitely had the bosom for such a frugal use of cloth. "That dress is absurdly flattering on you."

"I have to remember to hold in my stomach," Layla said, heading for the door, Edie's empty glass still clutched in one hand. "Oh, there you are, Willikins. Why don't you pour me another glass, and I'll drink it while I think about a cloak."

Edie took the glass from her and handed it to a footman. "Our carriage, please, Willikins. Almack's awaits."

"As does the carriage, Lady Edith," the butler replied, bowing. He turned to the footman and took Layla's cloak in his hands. "My lady, if you will allow me."

"Those rabbits, the ones with baby bunnies, know what they're about," Layla said, as Willikins draped the cloak about her shoulders. "Besides, Edie, I've changed my mind. We're not going to Almack's. They don't have any champagne there. We shall go to Lady Chuttle's instead."

"Who is Lady Chuttle?"

"A remote acquaintance. Ordinarily I would dismiss a ball of hers as a trifle vulgar, but that was before I received *this*." She pulled a crumpled note from her reticule. "I sent a note to your father requesting that he accompany us to Almack's. This is his reply."

Edie flattened it out. Only two lines long, his note expressed regret at being unable to attend them at Almack's, as he had accepted a prior invitation. "How did you know that he plans to attend Lady Chuttle's ball instead?"

"I didn't have to be told. I was quite aware that a man in his situation would visit that particular event, so I simply replied, informing him that we would meet him there."

"What if he has an entirely different appointment?"

"Where else would he be going?" Layla demanded, with magnificent disregard for the presence of the butler and two footmen. "He'll be escorting Winifred, no doubt. I might just mention rabbits to your father if I see him. Just drop the word into the conversation and see whether it gives him any ideas."

Edie glanced at the butler's impassive face. "Right. Inform the coachman we're going to Lady Chuttle's, if you please, Willikins."

And so he did, and a minute later they were under way. Unfortunately, the lady's house was but a fifteen-minute drive, which meant that Layla was only slightly less tipsy by the time they arrived. "I shall know instantly who she is," she said chattily, as they descended from the carriage in front of a large town house.

"Are you implying that there will be courtesans in attendance?" Edie asked, feeling rather more interested in the Chuttle ball than she had been in visiting Almack's.

"Undoubtedly," Layla said. "That's why your father will be here. As I was saying, I shall recognize Winifred. I know the sort Jonas favors. I'm sure she's one of those women who rush up and tell you that no matter what they eat, they simply *cannot* gain weight. He told me once that I had a flat stomach, you know. That was back when I *had* a flat stomach."

"Layla," Edie said. "I am bored by Winifred, and I haven't even met her. Follow the nice groom and let's get out of the chill."

"I am the daughter of a marquess!" Layla announced.

"That's right," Edie said encouragingly. "Winifred probably sprang from a cabbage patch. And I bet she has to stuff her corset in order to achieve any curve in the front."

"I need not resort to such sorry tactics," Layla said, tossing her cloak behind her shoulders, and thereby revealing her quite magnificent bosom.

"Winifred would have to put a cabbage down her corset in order to look anything like you," Edie said. "Two cabbages, one for each side."

Layla nodded sharply and swept into the house.

As far as Edie could see, there was nothing about the entryway that signaled the possible presence of courtesans. The butler bowed, precisely as butlers did, handed their cloaks to footmen lounging by the wall, then led them down a hallway to the ballroom, where he announced them.

"Oh, look," Layla cried with delight, plunging down the stairs and knocking the butler to the side as she did so. "There's Betsy!"

"Who is Betsy?" Edie asked, trotting down the steps, braced to catch Layla if she stumbled.

"A dear friend of my mother's. Lady Runcible, she must be now. I believe she was widowed last summer, the poor woman. That would have been her third—no, her fourth husband."

"Quite a tragedy. Or perhaps *triumph* is a better word."

Layla dove into the crowd, towing Edie behind her. "It's not her fault. They just drop off after a year or two. But she's managed to keep her hair yellow through all of it, and you have to admit . . . *that* is a true triumph."

A second later she plunged into conversation with a woman whose hair did, indeed, have a touch of the victorious about it: time had apparently stood still for Lady Runcible. Edie smiled politely and glanced about for her father. She was certain that he wouldn't be able to resist following Layla to the ball.

She heard a deep voice, and someone touched her elbow. She turned to find Lord Beckwith standing beside her. "Lady Edith." He glanced at her gown—pale pink but without any trim to disguise her bosom—and his face came alive with admiration. "What a pleasure to meet you here."

Edie curtsied. "Lord Beckwith, I am very glad to see you."

"*Au contraire*," Layla was saying nearby. "I have been out of society far too long. I have decided to turn over a new leaf. *J'arrive, ma chère, j'arrive!*"

Lord Beckwith bowed, took Edie's hand and kissed it, then didn't release it when he ought. "I hope this is not inappropriate, but I know I express the feelings of many gentlemen when I say how much I regret your expeditious betrothal."

"Lady Edith won't marry for months," Layla said, nipping about suddenly and joining the conversation.

Beckwith bowed again. "Lady Gilchrist. It is a true pleasure to see you."

"My dears, shall we find some refreshment?" Layla asked. "I must admit that after that tiring coach ride, I would welcome something restorative to drink." Moments later, they were seated at a small table, champagne and small plates of *bonnes bouches* before them.

"Eat," Edie said to Layla, pushing a plate of little cakes closer to her. "You'll have a terrible head in the morning."

"*Au contraire,*" Layla said in a silvery voice. "I've always been able to handle my champagne. I believe I was born with bubbles in my blood."

Widow Runcible had towed two men along with her; candidates, Edie presumed, for the hazardous role of her fifth husband. Layla began flirting madly with one of them, Lord Grell. Edie sighed and turned back to Beckwith. "I don't suppose you've seen my father this evening?"

"Yes, he is here, Lady Edith. I gather you arrived separately?"

Layla must have heard; she stiffened and leaned even closer to her prey.

"Lady Edith, may I have the honor of this dance?" Beckwith asked.

She was about to say yes, when she saw her father stalking toward them. "Father!" she cried, popping up and curtsying. "There you are!"

Layla took a deep breath, picked up her glass so

forcefully that Edie was surprised it didn't shatter, and drained it.

"Daughter," her father said, coming to a halt. "Lady Gilchrist. Lady Runcible. Lord Beckwith. Lord Grell."

The second of Lady Runcible's followers had melted away before he could be greeted; the arrival of an incandescently angry man could do that to a conversation. Her father looked like a barbarian dressed in evening wear: though his jacket was plum velvet and his neck cloth immaculately tied, there was more than a hint of madness about his eyes.

Edie followed his gaze and saw that Layla was leaning close to Lord Grell, who was such a fool that he didn't have the sense to look alarmed.

Even after a lifetime of skirmishing with her father, Edie felt apprehension at the look on his face now. Lord Beckwith gave her an apologetic smile and sidled off into the crowd.

"Goodness me, there's my husband," Layla cried, pretending to see the earl for the first time. She bent sideways, as if she was about to fall off her chair, though Edie knew she was craning to see if Winifred stood anywhere nearby.

The earl was alight with fury; Edie truly doubted that there was a Winifred.

Lady Runcible now stood up as well and towed Lord Grell away with her, quite likely saving his life.

Edie expected her father to drag Layla to her feet and call for their carriage, but instead he dropped into the chair Beckwith had occupied until a minute earlier. Edie took her seat again as well, and for some moments the three of them sat in tense silence around the small table.

At last, Edie broke the silence. "Should I leave the two of you alone? I could stroll around the room or dance with Lord Beckwith."

"Why should you?" Layla said. "It's not as if we will have a meaningful conversation in your absence. His Lordship is likely going to accuse me of doing something unsavory with that poor man who was here a moment ago. As if I would have a chance, now that Betsy has decided to marry him."

"I had no such—"

Layla interrupted her husband. "Where is Winifred?" She looked up and caught the eye of a footman.

"Who is Winifred?" the earl asked with a frown.

Layla was busy explaining to the footman that she'd like four glasses of champagne, of which two were for her, so Edie undertook to answer. "Your mistress, Father."

"How dare you say such an impertinent thing to me? Who has been telling your stepmother lies? I don't even know a Winifred!"

"Oh?" Layla said, snapping back into the conversation. "Thin, very thin, with a corset stuffed with vegetables, too lightweight to sink: you know the type. You could throw her in the Serpentine and she would just bob to the surface, muttering about how much she envies women who are able to put on weight."

The earl was clearly lost.

"Don't try," Edie advised him. The footman arrived with the champagne, and she safeguarded hers before Layla could snatch it.

"Winifred," Layla said, a bit sadly, "is the woman who stole you away from me, Jonas. I used to please you, you know. We weren't exactly like rabbits, but *c'est la vie*." She shrugged and, with one gulp, drank half a glass of champagne.

"How long has she been like this?" The look on Edie's father's face was edging from half to three-quarters barbarian.

"Oh, about two years," Edie said, considering. "In the stages of marital harmony, I'd say the two of you are at about stage eight of ten—ten being the slough of utter despond."

"You have no right to speak to me this way, daughter!" he snapped.

Edie looked away from the mix of anger and anguish in her father's eyes . . . to see Gowan standing behind the earl.

Fifteen

The Duke of Kinross was magnificently dressed in a coat of darkest blue velvet with silver buttons. He fell back a step, moving into a bow that would have graced a prince. "Lady Edith." He straightened. "Lady and Lord Gilchrist." He bowed again.

Edie rose, well aware that she was smiling like a loon. "Your Grace, I gather you concluded your business in Brighton sooner than you thought possible."

He took her hand and raised it to his lips. "I whipped the bankers into a lather. They were glad to see the back of me."

"*I* am glad to see the front of you."

His smile was response enough.

"Good evening," Layla cried, her voice sounding more musical now that it had a faint slur. "You've returned just in time, Your Grace. I do believe that Lord Gilchrist is thinking of nullifying your betrothal. He's rather fickle these days."

It was astonishing to see how Gowan suddenly radiated pure menace, without even shifting a muscle. "I trust Lady Gilchrist is mistaken," he said, turning to the earl.

Edie's father had risen. "My wife exaggerates. As I explained to you, Your Grace, I have doubts about your marital happiness, but such worries are no grounds for breaking a contract."

"Taking a more optimistic view of our future, I have brought with me a special license," Gowan said, taking Edie's hand and drawing it into his arm. "My lord the Archbishop of Canterbury was very amiable about the matter."

"Marry in haste?" the earl said, scowling. "Cast a shadow on my daughter's reputation?"

Gowan looked down at Edie. "Being a Scot, I don't understand the intricacies of English polite society. Would it be so terrible?"

"Yes, it would," Edie replied. "We'd be pariahs for a time, though not as much as if we fled to Scotland and married in Gretna Green."

The smile in his eyes told her all she needed to know.

So she answered his unspoken question: "I am not afraid of scandal."

Layla came to her feet with a slight wobble. "It will be no more than a seven-day wonder. Dukes will be dukes. What a charming notion!" She swiveled. "Betsy, *ma chère*, where have you gone? My darling stepdaughter is to be married tomorrow morning. The tide of true love is sweeping her into the arms of a duke!"

Lady Runcible jumped up from a nearby table, looking as curious as is possible for a woman whose face paint would crack under the influence of a truly powerful emotion. "How charming," she cried. "I saw the announcement in the *Morning Post*, but I had no idea that the event itself would be so speedily effected."

"True love cannot be denied," Layla said. "You know that yourself, Betsy, given your sad experiences. Life is fleeting and one should gather rosebuds—or is it rainbows? At any rate, one should get on the stick before it's too late."

"His Grace has many important affairs to attend to in Scotland," the earl said with chilly precision. "Therefore, he has requested an immediate wedding date."

"Exactly," Gowan said, smiling at Lady Runcible. "I cannot wait to bring my beautiful bride to my castle at Craigievar." He drew Edie a little closer to him.

"I am sure that I speak for all when I wish the two of you a most happy life together," Lady Runcible pronounced.

"Love sweeps away all barriers," Layla put in, sounding a bit ragged. She sat down again.

Lady Runcible gave them a toothy smile and trotted off, undoubtedly to inform everyone of the scandalous haste with which the Duke of Kinross was to marry the daughter of the Earl of Gilchrist.

"If I am to marry on the morrow," Edie said, astonished at how calmly she said the words, "I believe I would like to go home now."

"You are not marrying on the morrow," her father said grimly. "Even if I acquiesce to this

163

notion of a special license, the ceremony will take place in a measured and prudent fashion."

Gowan bowed, looking quite pleased with himself. "I will be delighted to pay you a visit tomorrow afternoon to discuss these arrangements, my lord."

"In that case, I would prefer to stay here," Layla said, adjusting the pearl-embroidered band in her hair. "I haven't even danced, and *naturellement* . . ." The intended point of that thought seemed to elude her, so she merely added, "I refuse to return home at such an unfashionably early hour."

The last thing Edie wanted to do was remain in her father and stepmother's company. She threw Gowan a pleading look.

"I would be happy to escort my fiancée to your house," Gowan told the earl. "You can be assured that I have only the most honorable of intentions."

Edie's father's jaw was clenched, but he managed to speak. "I would be most grateful if you would escort my daughter, Your Grace. My wife and I shall return in due course."

"Not if Winifred is in the carriage as well," Layla said with great dignity. "I have standards."

Edie's father sat down at the table, an expression of confounded rage on his face. "Will you please do me the courtesy of enlightening me as to the identity of this Winifred?"

"Not until we discuss rabbits," Layla said, her jaw set as firmly as her husband's. She pushed away the empty glass and delicately took hold of the stem of her second.

"Rabbits?"

"Good evening, Layla, Father," Edie called, dragging Gowan away without waiting for a response. "I apologize for that scene," she said, when they were a safe distance away. "I believe their marriage has reached a boiling point."

"I trust that we can avoid that sort of over-wrought emotion," Gowan said.

Edie laughed. "You're quoting from my first letter to you!"

"Paraphrasing," Gowan said. "I'm afraid that I do not remember your exact words."

"I cannot imagine the two of us in that sort of tangle."

Gowan began guiding Edie toward the door, the crowd parting before a duke like minnows before a shark. "Do you have a temper?" he asked her. "I don't mean to be rude, but your father looked a trifle irritable."

"I've spent a good part of my life playing peacemaker," Edie said. "The household couldn't have survived if I'd begun indulging in fits of temper, too. What about you?"

"Regrettably, I do have a temper." They reached the entryway and he sent a footman for his carriage. "In fact, your father and I might have more in common than I thought." He didn't look entirely pleased at that idea.

"But you appear so composed!" Edie exclaimed. "In fact, I was slightly worried at first that you might never put aside your ducal calm."

"I think it's more worrisome that you have never been given free rein to lose your temper."

Edie laughed. "I did tell Layla that I would knock you over the head with my cello if you took a mistress."

Gowan gave her a wry grin. "I lose my head and say things that I don't actually mean. It has taken me twenty-two years to admit it, but I can be a hotheaded dunce."

"I would rather like to see you in a passion, I think."

"You will." His voice stroked her skin like a velvet kiss.

"I didn't mean that!"

"When I lose my temper, I shout like a madman."

Edie felt a prickle of unease. "That doesn't sound very pleasant."

"It's not. I've had to train my household to bear with me. They never obey me when I speak in a complete rage."

"What exactly does such a lack of obedience entail?"

Gowan grimaced. "Very occasionally, I throw people out of my household. And then regret it. But I can assure you that this has happened only three or four times since I inherited my title."

"Should I anticipate being tossed on the doorstep?" Edie didn't know what to think about that. Her father certainly had a temper, but he'd never threatened to disown or dismiss anyone. He just shot out some angry sentences and disappeared from the house.

The butler appeared, holding her cloak. Gowan took it from him and put it around her shoulders himself. "*Never.* Though I can't promise not to banish a man who ogles my bride."

Edie looked up at him, feeling a distinctly female thrill as she met his eyes. Still . . . much though his deep male possessiveness felt delightful, it wouldn't be so in reality. "Please don't turn into my father . . . you've seen how jealous he is. Though I should add that you've just seen my family at its worst. Most of the time we are both sober and sane."

"Unlike my family, then," Gowan stated.

Edie waited until they were seated opposite each other in the quiet luxury of his carriage before asking, "You have told me of inebriation, but what of madness?"

There was that glimmer of a smile again. "It takes a mild form. I have three aunts, each of whom is obsessed by her dog. The dogs have birthdays, jeweled leashes, and more coats than I."

"More *coats?*"

"Velvet for winter; oiled linen for summer. Their own fur is apparently inadequate for weathering Scottish winds. Various other animals periodically join their household. My aunts—the ladies Sarah, Letty, and Doris—are convinced that any animal can be trained like a dog, if only one applies oneself to the task."

"Any animal? What are they expected to learn? Can a rabbit be trained to bark?"

"A dog is not trained to bark," Gowan pointed out. "Training, with respect to animals, might be summed up as an ability to answer to a given name, control the bladder, confine any droppings to a chosen arena (*not* the drawing room carpet), and in general respond to commands."

"I suppose you might train a cat," Edie said, though she was doubtful. She had never had close contact with animals of any sort. "Though from what I understand, they do not respond readily."

Gowan shook his head. "Cats lie in the distant past. My aunts have proceeded through several species of bird, a vole, a hedgehog, three squirrels, and a whole family of rabbits. At the moment they are working with pigs. Piglets, actually."

"They're training piglets?"

"They prefer to have it be known that they are 'domesticating' them." His tone was so dry that Edie broke into giggles. "When I last paid them a visit, the piglets had learned their names—which are, by the way, Petal, Cherry, and Marigold. By now, I have to assume that the triplets have probably become mothers. Or bacon." He stretched out his long legs and his boot brushed Edie's slipper. Even that fleeting touch made her shiver, which was absurd. *Absurd.*

"For my part," she said, collecting herself, "I would think personal hygiene considerably more pressing than names."

"All three piglets were making excellent progress," Gowan said gravely. "They were paraded in front of me at dinner, looking quite pink and scrubbed and adorned with matching ribbons. Reportedly, there had been a few regrettable incidents, but far fewer than you might suppose."

"I shall be quite delighted to meet them," Edie said, with equal solemnity. And then she laughed again. "Do you know, I've never been close to any sort of animal except a horse. I do know how to ride."

Gowan waved his hand dismissively. "Horses are in the dark ages of the history of domestication."

"Where did your aunts come up with the idea?"

"Letty posited the notion as a girl, and all three picked up the challenge." His foot touched Edie's again. But his face didn't change. Perhaps his move was inadvertent? It made her toes curl.

"But what makes them think that they will succeed?"

He looked surprised at that. "Why shouldn't they? If anyone can domesticate a pig, I would put my money on Aunt Sarah, in particular. She had a squirrel eating from her hand last year."

His certainty made Edie smile. She had grown up knowing that she was a member of the peerage, and as such, had a claim to blue blood and the rest of it. But the truth was that her father only truly cared about music, and so did she. That fact had diluted the effect of upper-class breeding. In Gowan, and presumably his aunts, there had been no dilution. Hundreds of years of self-assurance had been drilled into him with the same rigor as had her musical scales.

His raised eyebrow let it be known that his aunts could certainly train a pig, if a pig was to be trained, and probably even if it wasn't. "It's something of a scientific experiment, you understand. Curiosity runs in my family. In the last few generations most of us have been obsessed with one investigation or another. Even my father's death could be put down to an unfortunate attempt to prove a point."

"And you?" Edie asked.

Gowan shrugged. "I take some interest in wheat. I am cultivating a new variety at the moment."

Cultivating wheat was certainly more useful than training piglets, so Eddie made an encouraging sound, and was about to inquire whether the aunts had had any luck with geese—having met a cheerless and aggressive goose in her girlhood—but the carriage had come to a stop. They had arrived at her family's house in Curzon Street. She was feeling about for her reticule when a rattle of wheels passed them and drew up sharply.

Edie slid over to the window on her side of the carriage and pulled open the curtain. Her father's carriage had also just drawn up. A liveried groom popped down and opened the door. "My parents have arrived."

Gowan moved to his window and peered out with as much interest as she. "Presumably your father managed to convince your stepmother that dancing while inebriated is not a good idea."

"Why aren't they coming out?" Edie said, after a moment.

"I cannot say with certainty, but I would guess your father is endeavoring to rouse the countess. I expect that drink has rendered her sleepy, if not insensible." There was a biting undertone to his voice that Edie didn't like.

She opened her mouth to defend Layla, but at that moment her father emerged from the carriage carrying his wife in his arms. Sky-blue silk rippled behind him as he walked up the front walk toward the open door, Layla's head lying on his shoulder.

"You're right; she must have fallen asleep," Edie said, instead. "I would have thought one had to imbibe something stronger than champagne."

"It's not only the quality of the drink, but the quantity. How much did she take?"

"Perhaps six glasses? But she hasn't eaten much today."

"Nearly an entire bottle," Gowan pointed out. "She's soused."

As the earl neared the front step, Layla suddenly reached up and pulled her husband's head down to her mouth. She was, definitively, awake. Edie dropped the curtain and sat back. "Goodness," she said. "I'd rather not have seen that. Nevertheless, we now know that Layla is not insensible."

"She can certainly hold her drink."

"You needn't say it like that," Edie said, frowning at him. "Layla is not an inebriate."

"In my experience, inebriates aren't nearly as unfamiliar with the bottle as they would wish their family members to believe."

"That certainly may have been true of your parents," Edie stated. "Though I am loath to insist on an unflattering distinction between our families, I see Layla almost hourly, since I have been unable to convince her not to interrupt my practice. Tonight was the first time I've seen her befuddled."

Gowan's eyes had turned sympathetic. "The most ferocious of rebuffs would not have stopped my father from interrupting my studies."

"*Gowan.* That was not my point."

After a few second, he said, "Oh?" It seemed that the duke was not accustomed to opposition. Well, one had to assume he could learn.

"While your cynical attitude arouses my sympathy," Edie continued, "I would like you to acknowledge my point. My stepmother does not drink to excess. We don't even take wine at dinner as a matter of course: only if my father is coming home, which is rare, these days."

"I understand," Gowan said, nodding. He glanced back out the window. "They're still kissing. Your father is quite passionate for a man of his years."

"He's not so very old," Edie said, switching from defending her tipsy stepmother to her irascible father. "He's only just over forty. You yourself boasted that Scotsmen are active for many years past forty."

"I thought the man had a touch of the Scots about him."

It was absurd that even a glimpse of Gowan's smile made her feel unsettlingly soft and melting, but that was the truth of it. "I thought perhaps you had mislaid your sense of humor," she observed.

"I apologize. I'm afraid that my parents left me with a distinctly unsympathetic attitude toward over-indulgence in alcohol."

"That is quite understandable," Edie said. "Do tell me when my parents are finally inside, because I should follow. There will be hysterics if Layla looks in my chamber to say good night, and I'm not there."

Gowan glanced out again. "They've entered the house."

"In that case, I must retire. We should not be sitting in a stationary carriage without a chaperone, betrothed or not."

"That doesn't seem fair," Gowan said, a wicked light rousing in his eyes. "I could take you driving alone in Hyde Park."

"Not in the dark. I really must go in." But the sentence came out in a rather husky tone.

"Not until I kiss you good night," he whispered, taking her hands and drawing her to his side of the carriage. "My nearly wife."

Edie tipped her head so she could see his eyes. They had gone sleepy and possessive.

His head came closer, and she held her breath for a moment, wondering if the kiss would be as intoxicating as their first . . . and then she didn't wonder any longer. His tongue slid into her mouth, and she stopped thinking altogether.

She was learning that there were some things that you shouldn't try to think about while you were experiencing them; you should simply feel them. So she let herself feel how thick and soft his hair was, and then, when her hands drifted down from his neck to his shoulders and below, the way his back was corded with muscle.

By then the kiss was growing more insistent, and she found herself clinging to him, hardly breathing, her body thrilling to a rhythm she didn't know but instinctively felt in her veins.

"Edie," Gowan said hoarsely, breaking off their

kiss with a muffled groan. "We have to stop before—"

"Don't stop," Edie said, pulling his mouth back to hers. "No one knows where we are."

And so he didn't stop, and the next time either of them spoke was when Gowan cupped Edie's breast, which felt so wonderful that she uttered something incoherent. He laughed low in reply, and rubbed his thumb across her nipple.

The sensation made Edie cry out and press forward into his hand. Her cloak had disappeared somehow, and even through layers of cloth she could feel the heat and power in his hands as he touched her. Each touch brought a wild surge of feeling.

He seemed fascinated, watching intently as her breasts overflowed his hands.

"They're rather large," Edie whispered, thinking of how Layla had characterized her bosom as unfashionably ample.

He glanced at her, a fleeting gleam of his eyes that made her want to curl against him and beg him for more caresses. Harder ones.

"They are perfect," he said. The sound of his voice rubbed against her skin like her cello's deepest notes. "I have dreamed of holding you, Edie."

"You have?"

"Since the night I met you. But no dream is like reality."

He did something so pleasurable with his hands that Edie could do nothing but sink back onto the seat. He followed, and then he was kissing her neck, and all the time he caressed her breasts while Edie thought about what it felt like to have the weight of a male body on her. And how nice it would be if he were touching her without the barrier of her gown and chemise.

She would have thought he'd be too heavy, even propped up on one elbow. But he wasn't. Her body loved the feeling of all that muscle and heat; it made her want to form a cradle with her legs. Which was such an outrageous idea that she shocked herself.

He'd reached the base of her neck, but instead of a kiss he gave her a little lick, which felt so good that, quite involuntarily, she whimpered and arched her back a little. It made his body settle more firmly on her.

Now he was kissing the slope of her breasts and then he dropped his thigh between her legs and pressed. She clutched his shoulders so hard that she was certain her fingernails would leave little marks.

Gowan murmured something so low she couldn't hear it, and then he pulled sharply on her gown; her bodice slipped down, and his lips closed over her nipple. Edie had literally never imagined such a feeling. She arched again with a little shriek.

Gowan was nibbling and licking and kissing in a sensual assault so overwhelming that Edie stopped thinking altogether and just let herself feel. She felt like one of the tin pots that boys blew up on Guy Fawkes Day. She was ready to explode into something bright and frightening and gorgeous, if only . . . She pushed up against his leg, feeling a fiery burn spreading through her body that left her breathless.

But just then, when she felt kindling catch fire—Gowan stopped. An unwelcome coolness replaced the warmth of his mouth. She looked down. In the dim light her breasts were pale but her nipples had turned dark pink and stood out, begging for more attention.

His gaze followed hers, but he had that look on his face again, or perhaps it was no look at all.

This was a problem, Edie thought groggily. *She* fell into melting darkness when he kissed her, and if she was truly honest, she didn't care whether they were married or not. She wanted to make love on this carriage seat. Or the ground. Or anywhere else he cared to put her.

On the other hand, *he* seemed to have retained a disconcerting amount of clarity.

"How can you be so composed?" she said, a moment later, when he had deposited her on the opposite seat, located her cloak, and begun tying it as if she were a little girl.

"I'm not composed," he said shortly. His voice

made her feel better, because there was a raw sound to it.

"I feel hot all over," she whispered, kissing his brow. It was the only part of him she could reach while he concentrated on tying a perfect bow. "I feel as if I won't be able to sleep. I feel . . ."

"I know I won't be able to sleep." His fingers paused and he met her eyes. "I never dreamed that I would share my life with such a sensual woman."

"I'm not sensual," Edie whispered. "I'm quite ordinary, really."

"You are anything but ordinary," he said, cupping her face and giving her a hard, swift kiss. He had the door open and handed her down to the pavement, almost before she knew what was happening.

"Gowan!" she protested. She lowered her voice, realizing that grooms had hopped from the carriage and were standing to attention, two on either side of the door. "Don't you think that I have a significant point, given that special license you acquired? If our reputation is to be ruined under the suspicion that we have anticipated our vows, we might as well do so!"

Gowan tucked her hand in his arm, and began walking up the path toward Willikins, who stood in the light of the open door. "I indeed take your point, but you must understand: I value my honor above my reputation." He had assumed his ducal voice again—in response, she had to suppose, to all the men standing about in livery.

Edie stopped when they were halfway up the walk and, she hoped, out of earshot of both the grooms and Willikins. "Gowan," she hissed.

He looked at her with a kind of placid tolerance, though it was hard to discern in the flickering light from the doorway. She found it so annoying that she gave his arm a shake. "You are behaving in a rather stickish manner, Duke."

"Stickish?" A flash of wry humor returned to his eyes. "Addressing me by my title is stickish as well."

She felt all hot and melting and urgent, and it was extremely vexing to see Gowan looking as calm as a vicar after his Sunday's sermon. So she came up on her toes and licked his bottom lip.

"What are you doing to me, Edie?" The sentence growled out of some deep part of his chest and flooded her with satisfaction. Perhaps he was simply better at covering up things than she was.

"I'm making certain that you will have as much trouble sleeping as I shall." Then she reached up, pulled down his head, and kissed him. It wasn't their fourth, or even their fourteenth kiss, but it was the first kiss that *she* gave *him*.

There was something about that realization that made her feel even more melting. But even though he showed satisfactory signs of enthusiasm, Gowan did not sweep her into his arms and stride back to the carriage, shouting to the coachman to take them to a bedchamber somewhere.

In fact, after a bit, he pulled his mouth away, peeled her arms from around his neck, and growled, "I'm taking you to the door now, *Edith.*"

Edie had managed to get her breath back by the time they reached the long-suffering Willikins. His countenance was expressionless, and for some reason, that made her feel even crosser. Was she to spend her life being watched by living statues?

So she curtsied good-bye to Gowan, but refused to meet his eyes. She had just turned to climb the stairs when she heard an exasperated sound and he spun her around and said, low and fierce, "Dukes don't deflower their wives-to-be in carriages, Edie."

She glanced to the side, but Willikins had shown his intuitive grasp of a butler's more sensitive duties and disappeared into the recesses of the house.

"It's not that," she said. "It's the way you lose all expression. One minute I'm kissing you, and the next I find myself being put aside by a man exhibiting all the emotion of a block of wood. One moment you make me laugh, and the next you assume the expression of a schoolmaster speaking to a naughty boy. I find it annoying. In the *extreme,*" she added, in case he thought to discount her feelings.

"A man is what he does," Gowan said. "If I

deflower my fiancée, I am not myself, but some other being, some person so overcome by lust that he forgets the rules that govern civilization."

Edie suddenly felt too weary to argue. "Yes, well, you're probably right," she said. She thought of dropping another curtsy, but it would likely be taken the wrong way. So she patted his cheek because, after all, he was a dear man, if a misguided one. And then she made her way to her room.

Sixteen

Gowan returned to his carriage, climbed in, and sat there with his arms folded during the short drive to his own town house.

Once home, he nodded to his butler, tossed off his coat, and went up to his bedchamber. All the while a kind of desperate sensuality tore at him, buffeting him with images of Edie's luscious breasts, of the way her breath had caught in her throat when he'd kissed her.

His man entered the room and asked whether, while His Grace unclothed, he would be interested in reviewing the butler's report regarding house-hold expenditures, as was customary. Gowan ordered a bath and then threw the fellow out; he had no wish to display an erection that showed little signs of softening.

Hell, it probably never would. He'd have this

arousal at the altar. And what would follow that? What would he do then?

Throw his duchess into a carriage and take her like some sort of wild animal, right on the seat? His mind duly noted that Edie wouldn't argue with it. In fact, he thought it was possible that somehow he'd been lucky enough to find a woman who would relish anything he could come up with.

And he could come up with a lot. It wasn't just his imagination; his Kinross forebears had been possessed of bawdy imaginations and had stocked the library to suit. Oddly enough, all those books' images seemed vulgar now that he'd kissed Edie and heard her little shriek. Seen the delicious curve of her neck when she gasped for air.

He wished that he could take her to Craigievar and marry there, so that he could take her directly from his own chapel to his own bedchamber. But no—Edie said that it would cause an indelible scandal if they ran off to Scotland. Frankly, he could see no real difference between marrying in haste in London and marrying in haste in Gretna Green. Any man with a few pounds could get his hands on a special license, after all, whereas a trip to Scotland was expensive, given the changes of post horses, the inns, the inevitable broken axle.

Why should that cause the greater scandal?

He looked around his bedroom in some distaste. Given that he refused the carriage seat as a substitute for the marital bed, he had to find a lodging in London that was worthy of their wedding night; this wouldn't do. The house was in the very best section of London, only three or four streets from the earl's town house. But he'd never bothered to change the furnishings after he bought it, and the previous owner had a veritable mania for outré Egyptian flourishes.

He went to sleep every night under a frieze of jackal heads. Not that he disliked jackals, precisely. From what he'd seen in the British Museum, Egyptian jackals had long muzzles and a regal expression. These jackals looked more like beagles, a breed he enjoyed. Nevertheless, he didn't want to bring his bride to a bed surrounded by panting dogs.

It would have to be Nerot's Hotel. He rang the bell and his man, Trundle, reappeared with satisfactory haste.

"Inform Bardolph that I wish him to visit Nerot's and rent the best suite."

Trundle bowed. "For how long, Your Grace?" He ushered footmen with hot water into the bathing chamber while Gowan thought about it.

The Earl of Gilchrist would resemble a beetroot if Gowan suggested a wedding on the morrow. But on the other hand, he would not—*could* not— wait much longer.

"From tomorrow until further notice," he said, when Trundle reappeared. "If the best suite is currently occupied, pay the hotel double to get them out."

One would never know that he was the most fiscally prudent duke the duchy had seen in decades.

"Would you care to undress now, Your Grace?"

"No."

"So that you could take a bath while the water is hot?" Trundle sounded a bit desperate.

"No. You may leave. Deliver the message to Bardolph. I shall undress myself."

Trundle frowned and opened his mouth.

Gowan raised an eyebrow and the man whisked himself out the door.

He went into the bathroom and stared at the steaming tub for a bit before he pulled his wits together. It was distracting to picture Edie's mouth. More than distracting. There lay madness.

He stripped naked, turned, and caught sight of himself in the glass. Would he be pleasing to Edie?

At twenty years of age, he'd stopped growing any taller. Instead, in the last two years, he had just been growing broader. His legs were huge, probably the result of hard physical labor. When he was in residence at Craigievar, he would rise at five and go to his study, then head into the fields in the afternoon to work alongside his crofters.

An English nobleman couldn't do that, but his clansmen expected him to lend a hand when he was able. They'd hand him a scythe and point to a row with considerably less amazement than if he bought them a round at the tavern. Whether they were hauling logs or making barley sheaves, he worked alongside them.

The physical work, together with years of swimming, had broadened his chest, too, making it quite unlike the lithe bodies of most English gentlemen. He didn't fool himself that they were soft and defenseless, because he knew they weren't. He'd been to Gentleman Jackson's Saloon in London and seen them boxing each other with calculated ferocity. But English physiques tended toward the sinewy.

Scottish ones just bulged.

Below his broad torso . . .

He was bigger than average; he knew it empirically, from unavoidable observation. After a hard day in the fields, his men would strip naked and plunge into the bitterly cold loch, he among them. Even at eighteen, he could see his ancestors had bequeathed him more than a castle. What if Edie didn't like that part of his body?

He reached down and palmed his balls. They were drawn up close to his body, and had been from the moment he'd caught sight of Edie that evening. It wasn't particularly pleasant to feel like a powder keg, overly tight and explosive.

Watching in the glass as he wrapped a hand around his tool, he saw it in double vision, as if

Edie were beside him, and it was her delicate, long fingers that caressed him.

She looked a perfect lady, but the fingertips of her left hand were callused from endless hours of playing. He was still trying to get his head around the idea that he was marrying a musician. Watching her play a duet with her father had been a revelation. Her body bent with the music like a willow in a high wind, her face utterly alive with joy.

He wanted her to feel that with him as well. And he wanted her to stroke him with her musical hands.

The thought led to an image of Edie kneeling at his feet, that wash of golden hair over one shoulder, her lips opening as she . . .

A hoarse noise broke from his throat and his hand tightened.

A few minutes later, he lowered himself into the tub. The water felt like a caress, causing his body to stiffen again. Still, the swiftness with which he had lost control was percolating into his brain, and not in a happy way. It was unacceptable.

He couldn't blaze up like brandy put to flame: he had a responsibility to Edie. It was more than a responsibility with regard to consummation of their marriage. He had a distinct sense that a couple's first night together determined the pattern of their marital relations for years to come.

Having inherited his dukedom at an early age,

he had long ago learned to plan out, and rehearse, any new action. A young boy tasked with leading a household can practice what needs to be said in the privacy of his bathing chamber, if that happens to be one of the few places where he's ever alone.

On another day, he can rehearse the speech he will make while taking back control of the local bench. And when joining the bank's board of governors. Over time, he can become so good at thinking through the various possible outcomes of any action that he rarely makes a mistake—because he had thought through all conceivable weaknesses beforehand.

Marriage and intimacy were just another challenge. There was a danger that, having never done the act before, he would lose control and act like a raw boy of fourteen. That would be unacceptable, but he wasn't overly worried. He had not enjoyed pulling away from Edie, even less so when he tucked those luscious breasts back into her bodice, but he'd never been in danger of losing control.

The key was to make a mental list of what needed to be done in order to ensure that Edie enjoyed her first experience, particularly given the pain that women apparently felt. That was the one eventuality for which he couldn't plan, since by all accounts the amount of pain varied from woman to woman. Some felt a sharp pang and others something more distressing. Many women, he'd been given to understand, felt no pain at all.

He had hopes that Edie would be one of those, but either way, he was responsible for her pleasure, if not rapture, during the rest of the evening. She was demonstrably responsive, so he didn't have to worry about frigidity. It didn't take long to come up with a step-by-step plan for their wedding night. Images popped straight into his head, thanks to the illustrated volumes found in the ducal library.

His mind went hazy at the memory of how Edie's breath grew choppy, and how she gave a little cry every time he suckled her. The mere thought of sinking into her hot depths, seeing her eyes widen with ecstasy, feeling her, slick and tight around him . . .

Gowan ended up with his head thrown onto the back of the tub. Damn, but he was sick of this. Once he was married, he didn't want to touch himself ever again. Ever.

He would be touched only by Edie. Her hands . . . Her body.

Seventeen

Edie dreamed about dancing with Gowan. They were sweeping through a ballroom in larger and larger circles, in perfect step together. And then she stopped in the middle of a twirl, pulled his head to hers, kissed him.

And woke up feeling happy. It turned out she had slept through breakfast, so she practiced for a few hours until it was time for luncheon. When she made her way downstairs, she found Layla seated in the dining room, looking rather the worse for wear, but more cheerful than she had been in some time.

"Darling!" she cried. "Do join me. Jonas will be here presently."

"I don't want any details," Edie stated, rounding the table.

"As if I would do something so uncouth," Layla responded, waving her hand, and then dropping it onto her forehead with a muffled groan. "I have a terrible head, darling. You can't imagine. Your father and I were up—"

"I hope you managed to have a rational conversation?"

Layla giggled. "I wouldn't remember. I don't think so. Rabbits, darling. Rabbits!"

It was Edie's considered opinion that rabbiting through the night, though it might be a good start, was not a sufficient way to heal a marital breach.

"Luckily for you," Layla continued, "I can plan a wedding even if my head does feel as if it's about to cleave in two. Not to mention going shopping: we must buy some presents for your new little daughter. Well, technically your half sister-in-law or something like that."

Edie bit her lip.

Layla's eyes softened. "You will be a wonderful mother to that poor little scrap, Edie. You'll see. The moment you see her, your heart will melt."

Layla's heart melted at the sight of any child: she stopped at every perambulator to coo and admire. But Edie tended to hang back. Children were so small and looked so fragile, and she had no idea what to do with them, or what to say.

"We'll pay a visit to Egbert's Emporium this very afternoon," Layla continued. "She'll need a doll, of course. Perhaps a toy farmyard as well, and one of those new dissected maps of England."

"A map of Scotland would be more appropriate," Edie put in.

"England, Scotland, whatever. I saw the most adorable doll a few days ago. It came with three bonnets. If only I'd known, I would have bought it, but your father hadn't mentioned Susannah to me."

Edie had a good idea why the earl hadn't told his wife. The very idea of orphaned little Susannah made tears well in Layla's eyes, and her father had obviously chosen silence over a difficult conversation. She reached across the table and squeezed her stepmother's hand. "You will visit, won't you? Please?"

"Of course! I shall be the most indulgent auntie any child has ever imagined. I'll warn you now that I intend to shower her with ribbons and slippers and all kinds of fripperies. Between us, we'll make up for the fact she lost her mother. "

At that moment the door opened and Edie's father entered. Unlike his wife, he looked groomed as ever. Edie had the greatest difficulty imagining her father less than immaculately dressed, though, of course, she didn't really care to pursue the image.

Once he was seated, and the first course was served, he announced, "I have come to a conclusion about your wedding ceremony, Edith."

Edie nodded. She had made up her mind that she would refuse to wait four more months.

"The duke hopes to force my hand by purchasing the special license. Recognizing that fact does not mean that I am necessarily unsympathetic. Besides, rumors will do the damage, whether we wait four months or not. It's most unfortunate that Lady Runcible was told of Kinross's request." He flicked a disapproving glance at his wife that told Edie she was right: rabbiting did not magically cure marital disruption.

Luckily, Layla had her head down on her arm and didn't see his silent reprimand.

"I have decided that I will allow the marriage to happen in the very near future," he pronounced. "The wedding party will be small, naturally. I shall ask the Bishop of Rochester to perform the rites; he and I were at school together."

Edie found a smile growing on her face without conscious volition.

"However, I shall insist that the duke either stay in London with you for some months, or, if he must travel back and forth to Scotland, that he do so while you remain in the city. I intend to see to it that there be no question in anyone's mind about whether the marriage had to be speedily effected due to a breach in proper behavior."

"But what if Edie finds herself *enceinte* within a week or so?" Layla asked, raising her head. "Then it will make no difference whether she stays here or goes to Scotland."

"I won't," Edie said hastily. "I'm sure that never happens."

"It happened to your mother," her father said, unforgivably.

Layla's chin stayed admirably high. "The Duke of Kinross certainly seems remarkably virile."

"I don't know where we would stay in London!" Edie babbled, her heart racing in response to the tension around the dining room table. What would happen to them once she left? She had played the role of family peacemaker for most of her father's marriage.

"The duke owns a large town house a short distance from here," her father said, his tone as measured and cool as ever. "You will have to learn your husband's holdings, Edith. He holds a castle and its accompanying lands in Scotland, and as well as two other estates at some distance from his country seat, one of which, in the Highlands, is the seat of his clan. He owns a house in Shropshire and the aforementioned town house here. And," he added punctiliously, "there was mention of a small island off the coast of Italy."

"That is so romantic," Layla exclaimed. "Please say that you will invite me to your island, Edie." In the wake of the vicious little exchange earlier, she couldn't match her husband's composure. Her voice shook a bit.

"Of course," Edie cried. "If there's a house on the island, we would love to have you join us."

She felt a bit peculiar about all those estates. It seemed she was marrying a potentate. It wasn't that she was displeased to find that her husband was wealthy, but she wasn't overjoyed, either. She'd seen her father run ragged by the responsibilities inherent in managing his estate and various houses.

Without those responsibilities, the earl could have been one of the world's most renowned musicians. She felt a prickling of sorrow for him at the thought. She'd grown up knowing that women had no chance of performing in public, but for her father, a choice must have presented itself, at some point.

Then, looking at his strong jaw, she was struck by the truth of it: there had never really been a choice. The earl would never have turned his back on his responsibilities. He was as trapped by his birth as she was by her sex.

If Gowan hadn't inherited his own set of responsibilities, he would presumably have spent his life growing wheat. The idea didn't have the same force as becoming a world-class musician, although it did have a certain bucolic charm.

"I shall inform the duke of my decision as regards the ceremony this afternoon," her father said now.

"Since there won't be enough time to have a wedding gown designed for you, you can wear mine," Layla put in. "The fashion has not changed so very much since I wore it. We'll have it taken in, a stitch or two here and there, and it will fit you perfectly."

"Oh, Layla, that is such a generous offer." Edie took her stepmother's hand again, wishing with all her heart that things had been different. Layla had been keeping the gown for her own daughter . . . but had apparently abandoned that dream.

Even in the grip of adolescent charmlessness, Edie had been in awe of her new stepmother's wedding gown. It was made of silk embroidered all over with pinpoint spangles so that it flowed like water, catching the light and lending its wearer an impossibly ethereal air. Layla had floated down the aisle, beaming at Edie's father. The memory was unbearably poignant now.

"Edith will wear her mother's wedding gown," the earl stated, brushing aside the offer.

Layla flinched.

Edie scowled at him. "I didn't know my mother left a gown."

"Her gown and her jewels are to be given to you upon your wedding."

"I see." She gave Layla's hand a squeeze under the table.

Her stepmother's eyes had grown precariously shiny. She stood up and said simply, "I do believe that I drank too much champagne last night to enjoy this meal."

Edie and her father finished eating in complete silence. She waited to see if he was going upstairs to talk to his wife, but instead he strode into the hallway calling for his cloak. A moment later, the front door opened and he was gone.

So Edie ran up the stairs and found Layla surrounded by maids—and three open trunks.

"I am leaving to pay a visit to my parents in Berwick-upon-Tweed." Her face was the color of parchment, but she wasn't crying. "Now that my father's gout precludes visits to London, I must travel to them instead."

Edie sank into a chair.

"The only thing I'm sorry about is missing your wedding," Layla continued. "But for all I know, I wouldn't be welcome in the presence of your mother's dress."

"Oh, Layla, no!" Edie cried.

Her stepmother's eyes were brimming with unshed tears. "You know how much I love you.

But the idea of standing in a church next to your father during a wedding, and pretending that he is anything other than indifferent to me . . . I can't do it."

"I understand," Edie said, getting up to give her a hug. "I truly do."

"My parents' country house is close to the Scottish border, so I'll pay you a visit before—if I return to London." She swallowed hard.

Edie pulled her closer, her heart aching. She opened her mouth to say that her father would surely fetch his wife back home, and then closed it. It seemed quite likely that the earl wouldn't bother.

"The important thing is that you, my darling, are going to be happy with that gorgeous Scotsman of yours," Layla said, giving her a kiss on the cheek.

Sure enough, when her father appeared at the dining room table that evening he remarked indifferently that there was nothing to do in a small town on the Scottish border. "My wife will find no frivolities to entertain herself, and she is sure to return posthaste. I see no reason to waste my time and energy following her."

"If you could just be kinder to her," Edie implored. "She adores you."

"You know nothing of what you are saying!" her father snapped.

"I know that you love her, and yet you treat her as if she were a veritable concubine. As if the fact that *you* conduct yourself with such a high moral tone means that everyone must genuflect as you pass. I know that she loves—"

He didn't wait for the rest of her analysis, but stood up and left the room. Edie sighed. Her father's rudeness was a sign of extreme agitation, given that he considered manners to be next to godliness, or perhaps even above it.

The house was strangely silent without Layla's husky bellow of laughter and fluting voice shouting outrageous comments.

At luncheon the following day, the earl's face was more withdrawn than ever. For the first time in Edie's memory, he shook his head when she asked if he wished to practice duets. When it was plain that he would not be persuaded, Edie retired to her room and played for hours, but the music sounded as hollow as her heart.

Gowan appeared in the late afternoon and suggested an immediate ceremony, employing a ducal tone that assumed compliance. Her father didn't bristle, as he would have earlier. And then Gowan added that, as far as he was concerned, it was absurd to stay in London merely to satisfy gossipmongers, and that anyone who wanted to believe ribald rumors could go to the blazes. The earl didn't argue over that, either. He simply capitulated to everything the duke demanded.

He managed to keep that wooden expression for days, until the morning of Edie's wedding. Edie came down the stairs wearing Layla's gown after all because, as it turned out, her mother's gown had been eaten into ribbons by moths.

Edie was not given to immodesty, but she could see that Layla's dress did her proud. All the tiny spangles caught the light and made her look as if she were wearing a gown fashioned from diamonds. Its small sleeves and form-fitting, deeply cut bodice shaped her breast, and fell into graceful folds around her hips. She wore her hair caught up with jewels, just as Layla had, though she wore her mother's opals, rather than Layla's pearls.

It was only then that her father's stony façade cracked: he flinched, and there was a flash of something like agony on his face, but he bowed and stated, "Daughter, you look extremely well," in that measured tone of his.

Even when they entered Westminster Abbey, her father showed no signs of regret that Layla was not at his side.

Edie, on the other hand, desperately wished Layla were there. What's more, she hated the idea of leaving her father alone in an echoing house with nothing more than four cellos, no matter how much consolation he derived from playing them.

They had decided to eschew a reception of any sort, given Layla's absence, so after the brief ceremony they returned to the earl's house and shared a surprisingly cordial luncheon in which all three of them carefully avoided any mention of the countess.

Instead, Gowan and Lord Gilchrist had, to Edie's mind, a very good time denouncing the British tax system, particularly efforts by certain astonishingly unsympathetic politicians to reintroduce a personal income tax—which would thereby defraud such innocent persons as the two noblemen at the table of their rightful profits. Edie found herself looking from her father to her husband and realizing that they truly had a great deal in common. It was an odd thought, and one she stored away to consider further.

In the late afternoon, after she had changed into an extremely chic new gown, and all her trunks and belongings had been whisked away by the duke's men, the time came to say good-bye. Gowan stood waiting beside the carriage, flanked by so many liveried grooms that he looked like a member of the royal family.

She took her father's hands and tried once more, "Please bring her back."

He nodded, but it was such a clipped gesture that she knew it indicated only that he'd heard her, not whether he would obey.

She could do no more. So Edie stepped up into the carriage. She was no longer Lady Edith. She was no longer the peacemaker in the Gilchrist household. She was no longer an unmarried daughter.

She was the Duchess of Kinross, and there, sitting across from her, was her *husband*.

And her husband . . .

Gowan looked entirely calm and inscrutable but she knew the truth: he had been as moved by the wedding rite as she had been.

When he had promised to "love her, comfort her, honor and keep her in sickness and in health," she had felt color creep into her cheeks at the expression in his eyes. The breath had caught in her lungs and she had clung to his hands as if they were the only things keeping her upright.

She had never dreamed that wedding vows could mean so much. Nor that she would be so lucky as to find the one man in the world who was perfect for her.

And then, when she had promised to "keep thee only unto him, as long as ye both shall live," Gowan's eyes had glowed with a joy that she had seen only a few times in the whole of her life.

Now, she was sitting opposite him in a velvet cloak trimmed with real pearls. After a moment, she allowed the cloak to slip down her shoulders so that her breasts gleamed like the opals in her hair.

A banked flame smoldered in Gowan's eyes, a fierce interest that made her shift in her seat and straighten her shoulders, which merely served to bring her bosom into further prominence. "You've got them," Layla had told her. "Flaunt them."

Edie reserved judgment about whether Layla's propensity to flaunt her bosom in public had done her marriage any good or any ill. But Layla's propensities—and Layla's bosom—aside, she was keenly aware that Gowan liked her breasts.

They had said to each other all the words that needed to be said.

The rest of the evening?

No words.

Eighteen

Nerot's Hotel
London

"I've never been inside a hotel," Edie said as they entered, looking about with a great deal of curiosity. "I still don't understand why we don't simply repair to your house, Gowan."

"My town house is not acceptable for my duchess," he replied. The very idea of bringing Edie into a room festooned with jackals offended him. Nerot's, on the other hand, offered a suitable level of luxurious privacy. If they could not spend their wedding night at his castle, Nerot's was the next best thing.

Mr. Bindle, Gowan's butler, came toward them across the entrance hall, followed by a short man with a remarkably full head of hair, which gave him the appearance of a blown dandelion. It emerged that this flowery fellow was Mr. Parnell, the manager of the establishment.

Gowan saw no compelling reason to spend time with the man—surely Bindle had seen to every detail—but he listened with controlled civility as Parnell babbled about the various arrangements for housing his entourage, including Bindle, his cook, and his personal servants.

Yes, he'd brought six footmen and grooms, his cook, his valet, and various other retainers—not to mention their trunks and the carriage bearing Edie's cello—but surely his retinue could be housed without his help.

He glanced at Bindle, who put a hand on Parnell's arm and drew him ahead of them at a brisk walk. They climbed a flight of marble stairs, where, at the end of a short corridor, they arrived at a set of tall, lavishly gilded double doors.

"How lovely," Edie exclaimed.

Mr. Parnell wiped his brow. "The Royal Suite. The doors were brought from France, where they used to hang in Le Palais-Royale in Paris, Your Graces." He turned the key in the lock and they entered the suite's great drawing room. Bindle announced that a meal, which was even now being prepared by the duke's chef, would be brought up in five minutes.

Edie drifted around the room examining the furnishings. She glanced over her shoulder at Gowan and he felt her gaze as if he'd been struck by lightning. She expected him to refuse the meal; he could see it in the sparkling naughtiness of her gaze.

But omitting the meal wasn't a part of his plan. The last thing he wanted was for her to grow weak from lack of sustenance. He nodded his assent to Bindle and sent him and Parnell out of the room. Then he prowled toward Edie, enjoying the way she stood before tall windows looking like a column of golden light. Her gown had been designed to drive a man into blithering incoherence. It resembled a mere length of fabric wrapped around her. As if a man might reach out and pluck a pin here or there, and a delectable, naked woman would stand before him.

The door opened again, and Mary, Edie's maid, bustled in, followed by his valet, Trundle.

Gowan glanced over his shoulder. "You will not enter this suite unless you are expressly summoned."

Mary dropped into a curtsy so low she almost lost her balance. She and Trundle fled.

"Was that truly necessary?" Edie asked.

"My servants are not accustomed to granting me privacy," he said, reaching out with a finger and tracing the line of her eyebrow, "because I have never before requested it. They will have to learn new ways."

"You've never requested privacy?"

"In the bathroom, of course."

"Servants come and go as they please?" Her voice was faintly disbelieving.

"Only if they have reason to enter a room, naturally."

"I am almost always alone. And no one enters my rooms without warning except Layla."

"When you were playing, the evening when your father joined you, you looked fit to murder until you knew it was he entering your room."

"It wasn't *who* he was; it was that he was carrying an instrument. I cannot abide being interrupted while playing, or being asked to stop before I am ready."

"I shall inform my people. They will not disturb you." He shifted so that he stood squarely before her, and let his finger run down her cheek and under her chin, tipping it back. "You're so beautiful, Edie. I am awed."

"Well, I don't know why you should be," she said in that endearingly practical way she had. "Awe is not what I feel when I look at you."

And indeed, he saw nothing like awe in her eyes; rather he saw a mix of mischief and lust. It made his mind blur, and he nearly lit upon her like a ravening wolf, but he forced himself to remember his plan.

Instead, he bent his head and kissed her gently. The way a gentleman kisses his wife, with reverence.

Edie wrapped her arms around his neck and

kissed him back. She seemed not to care for the reverence, because her lips were greedy and she demanded a kiss of an entirely different kind. The slightly awkward way she pushed her tongue between his lips lit a slow burn in Gowan's groin.

Then they were kissing so deeply that he came back to himself only with the realization that she was tugging at his neck cloth. He brought his hand up and stilled hers. "Our supper will arrive presently." In fact, he was surprised it wasn't there already. Bindle had said five minutes, and Gowan could usually set his clocks to Bindle's reckonings.

"Who cares?" Edie whispered. She leaned forward and pressed a kiss on his neck. He felt a pulse of desire so powerful that it nearly unmanned him.

So he did the only thing he could, and stepped back. As her hands fell away, his neck cloth dropped to the floor.

"Oh dear," she said, shaking her head. "This is not the moment to become stickish, Gowan."

The door once again swung open, and Bindle bustled in with his usual silent efficiency, followed by his wine steward, Mr. Rillings, and four footmen bearing a loaded table. The footmen set the table down in the middle of the room, placing chairs at the head and foot.

Gowan introduced his wife to those servants whom she hadn't already met. Edie's demeanor was exquisite, as befitted a young lady of her pedigree. She was respectful and courteous to all, with slightly more warmth extended to Mr. Bindle.

They took their seats at the table, which was laden with silver platters, cutlery, and chinaware painted with the ducal seal. Edie stared down at her plate in silence as Mr. Rillings explained his wine choices for the meal.

Then Bindle took over, and began to explain the delicacies that lay under the silver domes. Gowan noted absentmindedly that his servants were doing an excellent job of reproducing dinner at Craigievar, even in the unfamiliar surroundings of a hotel.

His butler was a bit long-winded; this was not news. But as with Bardolph, he had inherited Bindle, and had never thought it worth the fuss to train him to be more succinct.

But now, sometime into the recitation—just as Bindle had begun to describe the *boeuf en daube*—Edie raised her hand. He stopped.

"Mr. Bindle," she said gently, "I think I should prefer the delights of discovery this evening."

The butler gaped at her. He was not a man accustomed to interruption. The duke's household moved in a steady rhythm, as regular as the tides: everything at its expected moment, for precisely the right period of time.

Edie smiled at him, and finally the man

understood that it was time to go. He rounded up his footmen and Rillings, and they left the room.

"That was masterful," Gowan said, raising his glass and grinning at her. It felt good to recognize that he would no longer be the only power in his particular world. *She* would be there, too. Alongside him.

"I am less interested in the preparation and ingredients of food than you must be. This looks and smells like a good beef stew, which is all I need to know."

"I never listen very closely when Bindle explains the menu."

"Then why on earth does he give you such a lengthy description?"

"It's the way it's always been."

Her brows drew together. "That does not seem a reasonable explanation, Gowan."

"I think it makes him happy," he observed.

She stopped with her fork halfway to her mouth. Her green eyes surveyed him in a manner that sent a new flush of heat to his groin.

Then she brought the fork to her lips, and he desperately longed to throw the table to the side and be damned if the crash of crockery disturbed all of London. He would carry her to the bed and—

He took a deep breath.

One did not lose control and ravage one's wife. It was beneath one's dignity.

"It's very thoughtful of you to consider your butler's pleasure, Gowan," Edie observed, swallowing. Her lips glistened, and he wanted to throw back his head and howl. He didn't want this damn food.

Instead he sipped his wine and tried to turn his attention to its complexion, made from grapes that grew only in the mountains, of a ripe sweetness, whose color was gold . . . as recounted by Rillings.

And failed.

Edie ate two more bites while he watched her lips from beneath his lashes and reviewed his list.

"I am sorry that your aunts missed our wedding. Will they be distressed, do you think?"

"I doubt that very much. They will be happy to meet you, but they would consider it a betrayal of the scientific temperament to grow excited about a wedding. They have not yet traveled to Craigievar to meet Susannah, for example. That would interrupt the training program of the moment."

"How much must I eat?" she asked, swallowing another bite.

"What do you mean?"

"I gather that you have decided that I need to fortify myself for the strenuous exercise that lies ahead? It must be I who is in need of food, insofar as you haven't touched yours."

"You are my wife," he said, a little apologetically. "I'm responsible for making sure that you are clothed and well-fed." Even as he said it, he wondered if it sounded as stupid to her as it did to him.

But if it did, Edie had the tact to ignore it. She rose with the grace that was inherent to her every move, from the slide of her bowing to her walk. Perhaps she did everything to a rhythm only she could hear. He came to his feet, and watched hungrily as she walked from the table toward the bedchamber door.

He stood there, frozen, drinking in the generous swell of her hips.

She looked back at him and smiled. "Gowan."

He was at her side in a moment. She was a witch, this bride of his. She had but to smile and he knew he'd follow. He probably always would if she looked at him with that hunger in her eyes.

Then he pulled her into his arms, and he was drinking her down, deep and fierce, knowing that she was *his,* finally his. His wife. His lover. His Edie.

He ran his hands down her back and pulled her against his body. They could do that now, fit their bodies together like puzzle pieces. They fit together perfectly, his hardness cradled by her softness.

"Now, Gowan," she whispered.

So he picked her up and carried her into the bed-chamber. Nerot—whoever he was—had installed a bed the size of a small granary. It was as long as it was wide, and hung with pale pink silk embroidered with silver thread and pearls.

It was a bed made for a duchess.

He jerked back the coverlet and then laid Edie on the sheets. She smiled up at him, all her glorious hair swirled at one side. "My wife," Gowan whispered, dropping a kiss on her brow, another on her nose, another on her lips. "You're exquisite. May I remove your gown?"

Edie twisted to the side, showing him a line of seemingly infinite tiny buttons running down her back.

So he concentrated on the buttons, trying to ignore the fact that they ended just above a lusciously rounded bottom.

The final button surrendered only to reveal a corset underneath. Edie watched him unlace it without saying anything. Under the corset was a chemise, made of a fabric so diaphanous that he could see the shadow of her nipples beneath it.

"Are you going to remove your clothing?" she asked. He stepped back, thinking that perhaps she felt shy at the idea of being unclothed while he was dressed. "Yes. But there is no need to feel embarrassment, Edie."

"I don't feel embarrassed," she said, smiling at him.

He believed her. There was something about

Edie's straightforward manner that made him think he could trust whatever she said.

"Is that your clan colors?" she asked.

"Aye." He bent, unlaced his brogues, threw them to the side. "I'm wearing a philabeg or, in Gaelic, *feileadh beag*." He removed his hose, and unbuckled his sporran.

Edie seemed fascinated. "What's that little packet for?"

"A few coins." The kilt was made to be unwrapped with speed—but suddenly Gowan realized that Edie was examining him, every inch of him. He had the feeling that she liked what she was seeing, that she wasn't hankering after a ropy Englishmen like those he'd seen in boxing saloons.

He removed his coat and pulled up his shirt rather more slowly than he ordinarily would, suppressing a grin at the silliness of it. His arm muscles flexed as he took the shirt over his head and tossed it to the side. But he figured that she might as well see it all. If Edie was put off by his body, she wouldn't have that look in her eyes.

A desirous look. The same kind of ravenous hunger that was eating him alive.

Right. Time to return to his plan. He made certain that he had each of its points in mind.

On the bed, Edie mimicked him, pulling her chemise over her head. He forgot what he was thinking about. The generous swell of her breasts rose in the air, framed by the graceful arc of her arms, and then he looked lower and saw the curve of her inner thighs, almost hiding a small triangle of golden hair.

The sight threatened to pull him into a dark place in which he would have no control. He refused to succumb. Instead, he joined her on the bed, gently adjusted her body until he had her in just the right position, and proceeded to make love to her.

First, he kissed her until her lips were plump and dark and she was making little hungry sounds in the back of her throat. Only then did he allow his hand to drift below her collarbone. While one half of his brain gloried in the weight of her truly magnificent breasts, the other catalogued the way she writhed under his touch, her arms tightening about his neck and her breath coming shallower and faster. He gave her a little bite, just a tiny one. That made her scream, and he ticked off one of the items on his list.

Heard, learned, and understood.

After a time, he slid his hand down her body, curving around her inner thighs—God, but he thought that might be what drove him over the edge, the soft curve of her legs. He wanted to bury his face there and leave bite marks all over her, and then shift a couple of inches higher and play.

But no. He had to keep his mind on the task at hand. So he ran his hands up her thighs and touched her very core. She was so much more pink than he imagined: more beautiful, softer, wetter, a fluted flower. And she was trembling all over, her hands gliding over his shoulders, stroking him wherever she could reach.

He couldn't permit himself to think about that, so he blocked out the signals coming from her caresses.

She felt wet and ready, but when he gently slid a finger inside her she was so small that he froze.

"Gowan!" He heard her voice through a fog. His mind scrambled, trying to imagine how this would possibly work.

Between the two of them, with him the size he was and her . . .

Presumably Englishwomen were simply smaller there, just the way Englishmen's biceps were smaller.

Damn.

Nineteen

Edie felt as if she were living the experience and observing it at the same time. The two of them lay on the bed, but the other version of her watched them from above.

She was spread out like a feast, trembling from little erotic pulses radiating down her legs. The logical part of her supposed she should probably roll on her side so that her legs didn't look plump.

Generally speaking, she liked her legs, but her thighs . . .

Gowan lowered his head and put out his tongue and nuzzled her, very delicately, *there,* and she lost her train of thought. A second later, her instincts overcame an initial faint feeling of horror, and she heard herself crying, *"Please,"* over and over, just as Layla had demonstrated in the drawing room.

Once he was licking her, her body ignored the odd thoughts going around in her head. The logical part of her felt a bit lonely, which was stupid, because it was Gowan kissing her, in this erotic, intimate way . . .

Her legs had just begun to feel peculiarly warm when he stopped and came up above her again. "I think you're ready, Edie."

She frowned. The word made her feel like a loaf of rising bread, and instantly dispelled the warm fuzziness, but she nodded and pulled him closer because she still felt alone.

"I want you so much," he said, his voice hoarse as he dropped a kiss on her lips. "But I'm afraid I will hurt you."

She smiled at that. Now that his face was near hers, she felt better. "I have been told it doesn't hurt very much. Layla called those rumors old wives' tales."

He reached down and put himself there, at the opening of her body. Edie stared down with some bemusement. He looked huge, like a giant pink mushroom stalk, which was accurate, though not a very romantic metaphor.

The first few seconds felt good. Odd, but nice. Gowan stopped and said, "How is it?"

It was so *intimate* that Edie could hardly bear it. His face was next to hers, closer than that of any person she could remember. Together with the fact that his body lay right on top of hers, and now part of him was actually *inside* her—it made her shiver all over. She wanted to push him away, and at the same time, pull him closer.

"It feels good," she said, her breath puffing against his face.

"May I continue?"

Edie nodded. Gowan flexed his hips, and from that moment, it was not good at all. Involuntarily, she sucked in a deep breath of air, and dug her nails into his shoulders.

"Am I hurting you?" His voice had fallen an octave.

"A little," she managed. A little? It was *agony*.

"Shall I stop, Edie? We could try again tomorrow."

Edie had lost every bit of happy sensuality she felt a few minutes ago. Her body was being torn apart. But the last thing she wanted was to have to try this again the next day. The anticipation alone would kill her. "You just have to do it," she said, her voice rasping. "Get it over with. Please."

He dropped a kiss on her lips, a sweet, tender touch.

And then he thrust, one deep, convulsive movement that seemed to take a minute, or an hour. Her mind shuddered away from the pain, from the pressure and sense of being sliced in half.

He was stuck inside her as if she were a bottle and he a cork. Edie was completely outside the experience now. A flood of curses went through her mind, things she would say to Layla next time she saw her. This pain was no more than an old wives' tale? Bloody hell.

"Are you done?" she whispered, when he still didn't move. His breath was harsh in her ear.

"No."

"Does it pain you as well?"

"Nay, it feels better than I could have imagined." He pulled out and then pushed back inside again. The sensation was terrible.

And again.

He did it four times, five times, six . . . It felt as if he were a metronome, counting off staves.

"How long does this go on?" she gasped. Seven, eight . . .

"I can go as long as you need me to," Gowan said, his voice strained but calm. "Don't worry, sweeting, it will improve. Any moment you'll start feeling a wave of pleasure."

She didn't. Her brain presented her with the opening chords of a funeral dirge put to the rhythm of Gowan's thrusts. Nine, ten, eleven . . . fourteen, fifteen. Her eyes filled with tears.

"Excuse me," she whispered, "I would truly appreciate it if you could finish now."

He paused for a moment. "I'm not coming until you are." He sounded stubborn and Scottish.

"Maybe next time, Gowan. *Please.*"

"I'm sorry it hurts so much."

"It's just the first time." Some sort of instinct came to her and she arched against him so he penetrated even deeper inside her. "Do it, Gowan. Go faster."

He pulled back and then thrust again and again. Sixteen, seventeen . . . twenty . . . twenty-seven, twenty-eight. It hurt and hurt and hurt, and she could no longer imagine a time when it wouldn't.

"Gowan!" she cried, on the very edge of informing him that if he couldn't get where he was going, they would have to try tomorrow.

"Oh, Edie," he groaned, and then she felt him pulsing deep inside her.

She actually gasped at the relief of it; it must be almost over. But it wasn't.

Twenty-nine.

Thirty.

Thirty-one.

Finally, his body slumped, and he collapsed on top of her, shuddering all over. Edie patted him on the shoulder, discovering he was positively slick with sweat, which was rather disagreeable. So she picked up a corner of the sheet and dried his shoulder with it, and then patted him again.

Then, mercifully, he braced himself on his hands and withdrew.

Even that hurt so much that she felt tears stinging the back of her throat. When Gowan rolled to the side of the bed, she lay frozen for a moment, afraid to look down.

There must be blood everywhere. It would be soaking into the mattress. At home, the maids would have whisked it away and a new mattress would appear by the evening. But they were at a hotel, and how was she to explain it? With all her heart, she wished she were home.

There must be something wrong with her, because Layla had said it wouldn't hurt. Or there was something wrong with him. Or both of them. She didn't know what to do about it. She couldn't imagine telling a doctor about something so intimate.

Then Gowan raised his head, his eyes still dazed with pleasure, and asked, "Edie, was it horribly painful?"

She swallowed and knew, in that moment, that she couldn't bear to disappoint him. And so she told her first lie, because she said, "No," when she meant, *Yes*. And when he said, tenderly, "We won't do it again tonight," she said, "All right," when she meant, *We'll never do it again*.

She looked down at that huge part of him and

blurted out an observation. "I thought you were supposed to grow soft afterwards, and smaller."

He looked down as well. "I believe I could pleasure you all night long if you wished, Edie."

She must have turned pale, because he didn't offer.

And even after she discovered that there wasn't as much blood as she'd feared—though a good deal more than Layla had described—she couldn't bring herself tell him that she might have suffered serious internal damage.

Instead, she let Gowan wash her, which he did.

When he finally fell asleep, she moved his arm from her waist and turned to face the other way. Then she curled up into the smallest possible ball and cried, very quietly, so he wouldn't wake.

And he didn't.

Twenty

When Edie woke up, she jumped out of bed, leaving Gowan sleeping, and fled into the palatial bathing chamber attached to their suite. She was feeling much better. It was over. Yes, it had been horrible, but now it would all be different. Not that she was precisely looking forward to their next encounter, but obviously, with the virginity business out of the way, things would improve.

Still, she had absolutely no inclination to return to the bedchamber and test that hypothesis, and when Gowan knocked on the door to ask if she would care to stay in London for some time, or leave for Craigievar, she chose the castle.

"After all, Susannah is waiting for us," she said, putting her head out the door.

From his expression, Gowan had forgotten all about his sister, but he nodded readily enough. "I'll send a groom ahead to reserve our rooms. We should begin our journey immediately if we are to make Stevenage in time to have luncheon at the Swan."

He stepped forward. He really did have the most beautiful eyes. "Good morning, wife," he whispered, towering over her.

Edie stayed in the doorway, feeling that her position signaled that she would not welcome a return to the bed, in case he contemplated something of that nature. He cupped her face in his hands and kissed her so sweetly that she felt ravished. "If only . . ." she said, looking up at him when he drew away.

He ran a finger down her cheek. "If only what?"

But she couldn't voice, *If only one got children from kissing,* so she went up on tiptoes and gave him a little buss by way of answer, and then retreated back into the bathing chamber.

A mere hour later, they were on their way. Edie was rather surprised when Gowan's factor, Mr. Bardolph, joined them in the magnificently appointed ducal coach and briskly wished her a good day. Given her druthers, she would have uninvited him, but the moment passed when she might have done that without seeming rude.

It certainly wasn't a matter of space. Though four service carriages had left already, the carriage that would follow theirs contained a solicitor, two estate managers, and her maid. After a bit of explanation she understood that the men would take turns consulting with Gowan. A third carriage brought her cello, under the care of Gowan's personal servant, Trundle.

She had been hoping that perhaps she and Gowan could talk in the carriage. She even thought that perhaps she would describe what it had really felt like last night. After a night's fitful sleep, she felt less frightened, but even so, she would like to talk about it.

Obviously, she could not bring up the subject in front of Bardolph. "It's like a Star Chamber," she told Gowan as he, too, entered the carriage, pushing away her hopes for the day. "As if you are the sovereign of a smallish principality."

Bardolph cleared his throat, and then, practically before the carriage had rocked its way around the first corner, he had three or four ledgers open and was droning on about a particular kind of wheat that only sprouted in winter.

What's more, Gowan acted as if this was entirely normal, this conducting of business the morning after one's wedding, and sat in his corner listening as Bardolph enumerated the acres of wheat that were sown versus those that were harvested.

"Must you really itemize these things?" Edie asked, after about an hour. London lay behind them now, and Gowan and Bardolph had moved on to baskets of butter and milk. Or lard. Something like that.

Bardolph paused. She couldn't help but notice that his nose looked like a flying buttress on a cathedral.

"Yes, we do," Gowan replied. "There was a great deal of waste on the various estates before we established a system by which to see the balance between what is put into the land and what is taken out."

"Are you trying to control theft?"

"That is one goal. But more importantly, by ascertaining whether a certain technique was successful in one field, we can make an informed decision about whether to carry it over to different locations."

Edie nodded and lapsed back into silence. Numbers flew past her ear, and Bardolph turned page after page with his whispery fingers. She started to loathe the factor's voice. It was curt and dry, and emerged from a mouth so tight that she never saw his teeth.

When he began enumerating the eel traps at one

estate and contrasting them with the eel traps at another estate, she broke in again.

"Gowan, will we stop for the midday meal?"

He had been listening to Bardolph, occasionally putting in a directive or command, even though he was perusing a different ledger at the same time. "Of course. We should be in Stevenage, our first stop, in precisely an hour and a half. We will take three-quarters of an hour for luncheon."

"His Grace makes the trip from London so frequently," Bardolph elaborated, "that we have devised a precisely timed itinerary for the entire journey."

"A *timed* itinerary?" Edie repeated.

Bardolph nodded like a nutcracker. "We take the Great North Road, rather than the Old North Road, as it is in better condition and fewer carriages have accidents there. His Grace dislikes being detained for any reason. The inns we regularly frequent stable our horses, so we will switch to fresh livestock."

"I am sorry for the tedium," Gowan said, with a paternal solicitousness in his voice that grated on her nerves. "Are you dreadfully bored?"

"Bored by the recitation of eel traps? Not I," she said. "Do go on. So one estate set their eel traps by night. Did timing have any effect on the eel harvest, if one might use the word?"

Bardolph recommenced from where he had left off, without seeming to notice the sarcasm in her voice. Edie stared out the window at the passing fields, because if she faced her fellow travelers she could not help watching Bardolph's lips shape words without seeming to open.

When they reached the Swan in Stevenage, they were escorted into a private parlor where a hot meal awaited them. Some forty minutes later, just when Edie was contemplating whether she would shock Gowan by dismissing the footmen attending them, Bardolph stepped back into the room. A moment later, the plates were whisked from the table.

"I wasn't quite finished with that trout," Edie said, but it was too late; the plates had been lifted in a beautifully synchronized motion and were gone. A tea service was being brought in.

Gowan looked concerned. "Bardolph, it seems your order was precipitous."

"Never mind," Edie said, selecting a piece of fruit.

"In future, Her Grace is to be consulted before anything is removed," Gowan pronounced.

Edie would have thought that went without saying, but it seemed she was being introduced to life in a monarchy. Where there was only a king and no consort. Bardolph's bow made that clear enough, as did his remark, some three minutes later, that in order to keep to schedule, they should return to the carriages.

She considered volunteering to ride with Gowan's

solicitor, Jelves, who seemed like a nice man, but it emerged that he was joining them in their carriage.

So Edie kept to her corner while the three men talked among themselves for the remainder of the afternoon's journey. By the time they reached the designated stop in Eaton Socon where they would be laying over for the night, she felt as if she'd been pummeled, her private parts both numb *and* sore, which was quite a feat.

Gowan took her arm to lead her into the George and Dragon, but she stopped him. "Just look at that," she breathed, pointing to the roof.

The sun was setting, and its rays spread like copper wires from the horizon, painting the shingles a dark mulberry.

"No sign of rain," Gowan remarked.

She tried again. "See how the sun is turning the roof that beautiful color and the swallows are swooping through the light as if . . ."

"As if what?" he asked.

"Well, as if they were listening to Mozart. As if the rays were staves of music. It would have to be Mozart because of the way they swoop up and down—" She tightened her grip on his arm. "There! Did you see that one? He's dancing."

She looked up. Gowan was smiling down at her rather than looking at the swallows. His eyes were dark and hungry. "You're right," he said, clearly not meaning it. "The swallows are dancing." He put a finger on her lower lip, and Edie felt that odd quiver in her middle that she felt whenever he looked at her like that, as if she were delectable. As if he wanted to lick her from head to foot, the way he had promised to do, back at the wedding.

Standing there in the fading, coppery sunshine, Edie thought it would be a fine thing to be licked by a man who looked like her husband.

She was about to say it aloud when Bardolph stepped forward, making a scratching noise in his throat. At home, Layla had always handled the servants, and Edie had had little role other than to listen to her stepmother complain about the staff. Even given years of listening, she had no idea what Layla would do in this circumstance.

If she objected to Bardolph's presence in the carriage—and in their life—it seemed likely that Gowan would simply overrule her. She didn't have a sense that the servants were *hers,* as much as she had somehow just joined the ranks of Gowan's retainers. In fact, she had an uneasy feeling that Bardolph outranked her.

So she stood there in the courtyard of the George and Dragon, staring blindly at the sunset, while Gowan listened to Bardolph's recitation of how the best rooms were already made up with ducal linen (because it seemed the duke traveled with his own linen as well as his own china).

By the time Gowan turned back and offered his arm to escort her into the inn, the swallows had swooped below the roof and flown off straight as arrows into the fields, heading into the setting sun.

In contrast to the Royal Suite at Nerot's Hotel, here they had separate rooms; presumably there was no suite grand enough for the both of them. Feeling human again after a hot bath, Edie descended to the private dining room. She could not help but feel a creeping anxiety. What if it was still painful tonight? Perhaps she should tell Gowan her fears before he even came to her bed.

As soon as she was seated, Gowan's butler launched into an interminable disquisition of something that looked to Edie exactly like a ham pie, although Mr. Bindle had a far fancier name for it. When Bindle was done, Rillings took over, describing the first wine that would be served during the meal.

The footmen standing against the wall behind her seemed to have little to do but to fill her glass, so one of them would lunge forward after she'd had two sips. It was so disconcerting that when the second course was served and Rillings solemnly opened a bottle of Tokay wine, Edie declined.

"I would prefer some water," she said.

Rillings frowned. "Water in an establishment such as this is likely to be unhealthful, Your Grace."

Edie sighed and accepted a glass of wine. It was sweeter than she liked.

"Tokay wine originates in Hungary," Rillings

was saying. "Its deep garnet color comes from the Tokaji grape that . . ."

When he finally had imparted the entire history of the Hungarian wine trade and left the room, Edie pushed her glass away. "Gowan, why must we know the origins of the wine we drink? I would rather not know that these grapes were infested with rot."

"I don't think *infested* is quite the right word," Gowan said. "The mold that forms on the outside of these grapes is referred to as 'noble rot.' "

"I don't care if it's noble or ignoble. I would prefer merely to drink the wine than listen to a lecture on the subject."

"I understand," Gowan said. "I will ask Rillings to deliver his report to me at another time."

"Another report. How many reports do you already listen to daily? Why this one?"

"We paid thirty pounds for a dozen bottles of this wine. If I make an expenditure of that sort, I should like to know precisely what I am getting."

It was disconcerting, this marriage business. She couldn't seem to stop observing her own life. On the one side, she was sitting at the table with her new husband; on the other, she was watching Lady Edith Gilchrist—no, the Duchess of Kinross—dine with the Duke of Kinross while four footmen darted around the room tending to their unspoken wishes. Bindle moved to and fro, ushering in new courses. The duchess accepted a slice of almond cake and a bite or two of syllabub. Yet another wine and a delicate elderflower mousse followed that course.

"Please give my compliments to the innkeeper," she said to Bindle. "This mousse is delicious."

"I will inform His Grace's chef of your pleasure," Bindle said, bowing as he left the room yet again.

Edie raised an eyebrow.

"My chef travels with me," Gowan explained.

"Isn't that a bit . . . well . . . excessive?"

"I instituted the practice three years ago, after we were all sickened for five days—one groom to the point of death—by an improperly prepared meal. At that point I determined that it was worth the additional expense to add another person to the entourage."

Edie nodded, looking down at her plate, which carried the ducal crest. "Is that why you travel with your own china?"

"Precisely. There is a lamentable lack of science when it comes to illnesses of this sort, but the condition of the kitchen and dishes surely figures into them."

There was a logical and unassailable reason, it seemed, for every person in the retinue, for each practice and custom. The duke needed so many grooms because one man traveled daily to Scotland, only to be replaced by a man coming from the other direction. The estate managers came and went; his solicitor might be needed at any moment; Bardolph *was* needed at every moment, apparently . . .

"I am not accustomed to being surrounded by so many people," she observed. She badly wanted to say what she meant—that she didn't like it—but she couldn't quite bring herself to do it.

Gowan was like a force of nature. His body seemed to be formed of coiled energy; no wonder he kept six men in constant motion doing his work. His mind was exploding in many directions at once. All this made sense to him. It made sense to carry a chef in order to do away with the risk of losing five days, or any days at all, to illness.

The problem was that everything was scheduled—including intimacy. She knew perfectly well that his huge body was strung tight as a bow, wanting her. He'd been that way all day, through the talk of acreage and wheat and eel traps. Every time his eyes met hers, she saw a craving, a wildness. But privacy, it was beginning to seem, was limited to the bedchamber, after the evening meal.

"I'm afraid that I am rarely alone," he said now, guessing her thoughts. "You may arrange your own schedule, of course, although running a large household may mean that you have less time to practice your cello."

She looked at him sharply to see if he was

joking, but he wasn't. There was a tinge of apology on his face, as if he were beginning to grasp the importance of music in her life . . . but clearly, he didn't yet understand.

Edie never bothered to fuss about things like servants and food; before Mary, she'd had a lady's maid who was always falling in love with the footmen and bursting into sobs when they disappointed her. It would have been a bother to replace her. She got used to lending her handkerchiefs and brushing out her own hair while she listened to the latest romantic travail. Gowan guarded every moment; she guarded only those when she was practicing.

"I play the cello every morning for three hours," she told him. "It is my habit to work through the noon hour. Sometimes I also work in the afternoon, but my bow arm grows tired and needs a rest. As you have seen, I often play before retiring as well."

He put down his fork. "In that case, you will need help running the household."

"Who does it for you now?"

"My housekeeper, Mrs. Grisle."

"I'm sure she does an excellent job." It was Edie's general practice to let people do what they did well, and to praise them after they'd done it. She could already see that Gowan and she were profoundly dissimilar. He ruled—the word seems to fit—an enormous estate, apparently keeping

231

even trifling details in his head. "Do you ever forget anything, Gowan?"

"It occurred to me the other day that I had forgotten my mother's face." He didn't sound sorry about it.

"I meant a fact or a figure."

"I'm lucky enough to have the sort of brain that catalogues detail, so very little slips by me."

No wonder people kept wheeling around him as if they were a crowd of sparrows rising from a fencepost. "Why didn't you go to university?"

"I could not because my father died when I was fourteen." He shrugged. "Tumbling maids while throwing back whisky didn't leave him a great deal of time, so his affairs were left in a tangle. The home farm took four years to recover, and some of the others have only turned a profit in the last two years." Gowan's face was so expressionless that Edie shivered.

He wore a dark gray coat, the color of fog in the early evening, trimmed in silver thread. Its buttons were marked by tasseled frogging with silver spangles. The candlelight gave a sheen to his hair and glinted on the ducal silver as Gowan cut his meat with customary economical grace.

He was the personification of civilization, culture honed to a high polish.

At the same time, he was utterly uncivilized in a fundamental, deep way.

And he was still young. If he was like this at

twenty-two, by the time he was forty he would be ruling Scotland. Or the entire British Isles, if the hereditary monarchy didn't stand in the way. He had that sort of enthralling but contained power about him. Men would follow him anywhere. Women, too, of course.

Edie sipped her wine, thinking about that. It was as if she had married a tiger. Just because a tiger keeps his claws sheathed doesn't mean they're out of reach. It was somewhat shaming to realize that she—a perfectly logical young lady who had been brought up to regard music as the epitome of civilization—thrilled all over at the touch of savagery that clung to her husband.

Even after the misery of the previous night, she had only to look at him to feel a melting softness between her legs. All the same, she thought it was very strange that two people who scarcely knew each other should be expected to sleep in the same bed, let alone engage in all those other things they were probably going to do. Again.

"Don't you think it's odd to marry a near-stranger and find oneself eating meals with her?" she asked him.

It had been a tiring day, so she put one elbow on the table—manners be damned!—and propped up her head so she could stare at Gowan without being too obvious about it. He was a gorgeous man, this husband of hers.

"I see nothing odd about it," he said. "I feel

that I know everything of importance about you."

She didn't like to think that he had summed up everything about her in a matter of minutes, but to be fair . . . "You told me about your parents," she said slowly. "And you've seen me play my cello, so perhaps we do know the most important thing about each other."

Gowan had a truly ferocious frown. Nearing the ferocity of her father's, in truth. "My parents do not define me," he stated.

Maybe he thought she'd feel rebuked by his cool tone, but she'd grown up in the boxing ring. Just because she didn't throw her weight around like Layla didn't mean that she was intimidated. "What *does* define you then? Is it your title, do you think?"

"No."

"Well, then?"

"No person is defined by a single quality." To be fair, he controlled his temper a good deal better than her father did. "You may be a musician, but that is not the sum of you."

Edie rather thought it was, but he could discover her shallowness in due time. "So what qualities define you, other than your parents and your title?" she asked, straightening up.

"This is not a proper conversation to hold in front of the servants," he said, having a stickish moment.

She raised an eyebrow. "Gowan, you eat every meal surrounded by servants. Will we never have an interesting conversation over food?"

He looked truly angry now, which was interesting. Edie smiled at him, because it was quite fun to bait a tiger. She truly liked her husband. In fact, she was embarrassingly aware that if she didn't pay close attention, she might end up in a morass of emotion that would make Layla's misery resemble marital harmony.

He hadn't answered her question, so perhaps he thought she'd simply accept a reprimand. Not so. "When *are* we to talk?" she repeated. "When you are not working, we're at the table. Or we are in bed."

His lips were pressed tightly together. Over years of living with her irascible father, she'd noticed that he often needed a day or two to arrive at acceptance of a point she'd made; likely it was the same with Gowan. She gave him a brilliant smile. "In the meantime, perhaps you could tell me more about eels."

The corner of Gowan's mouth quirked. "Am I to understand that I have a choice of dispensing with footmen or discussing eels?"

"I could discourse at length on Domenico Gabrielli's charming preludes written to highlight the melodic possibilities of the cello."

His wry smile deepened and Edie thought she had probably made her point. "We can save the

Gabrielli for tomorrow." She glanced at a footman, who stepped forward to pull out her chair.

Gowan came to his feet and walked around the table to her. "You must be exhausted."

In fact, she *was* exhausted, but she hadn't played yesterday or today, and her fingers were beginning to twitch. "I must practice," she explained. He put a hand under her arm and heat shot down her body. She actually felt a little dizzy with the power of it.

"You will practice for an hour?" he asked, as they walked from the room. There was no echo on his face of the sensual warmth that was weakening her limbs.

"Two hours," she told him, deciding that she had to make certain that she didn't neglect her instrument simply because she enjoyed her husband's kisses so much.

He nodded to Bardolph, who was hovering in the hallway. "It seems we will have time to review the plans to buy the mining concern. I will join you in the sitting room; Jelves should be there as well."

As they walked up the stairs, Edie realized that Bardolph had disappeared into their sitting room, and that they actually had a moment of privacy. "Will you come to my room tonight?" she whispered.

"Yes."

The pleasurable heat in her legs spiked at his

expression. She could see the tiger behind his dark eyes. Even though she still felt a bit fearful, hope surged.

He read her mind. "You are no longer a virgin," Gowan said, taking her hands and bringing them to his lips. "It will all be different tonight."

There was a promise in his voice and she thrilled to it. He must be right, of course. She felt as if every time she met his eyes the odd, empty feeling inside her grew more acute.

"Don't look at me like that," he growled. "Damn it, you want to play your cello, Edie."

She pouted, taking a kind of blissful female pleasure in the way his eyes clung to her bottom lip. "I do want to practice, but . . ." She came a step closer, and he dropped her hands and pulled her against his body. Edie buried her nose in his coat. "I love the way you smell." Perhaps she would get up at dawn to practice. Her cello could wait.

Gowan tipped up her chin and brushed his lips across hers, leaving a trail of fire, like stardust. "You smell like wildflowers."

But he stepped back, and she didn't have quite enough courage to take his hand and pull him into her room. Instead, she slipped through the door, picked up her cello, and sat down, pulling her skirts all the way up her thighs.

Once she began playing, her emotion slipped

into the music and she understood Vivaldi's seasons in a different way. There was "Spring" . . . the burgeoning of emotion. But "Summer"? All those joyous notes turned to wild fertility under her bow. She halted only when she realized that more than two hours had passed and she was utterly exhausted.

Mary came to help her out of her clothing after she rang the bell, good-humoredly accepting her apologies. "This schedule is daft," the maid told her. "Utterly daft! Mr. Bardolph is like a general in the army, to my mind. Thank goodness I'm your lady's maid and will be needed to dress you, my lady. Otherwise, I'd be up at three in the morning and in the carriages at four."

"That's terrible!" Edie exclaimed. "No sleep at all?"

"Oh no, that's not the trouble. His Grace is quite fair, by all accounts. You're paid more for travel, and most people have the afternoon to sleep before the duke's carriages get to the inn."

"Still, I would hate to be rising that early."

"It reminds me of when I was a chambermaid," Mary said, pulling a nightdress over Edie's head and handing her a toothbrush. "We used to have to rise at the crack of dawn and begin cleaning the grates. I was that grateful when I was promoted to downstairs maid; you can't imagine."

"Well, I'm very sorry you're up so late tonight," Edie said, hopping into bed. "Tomorrow evening I shall put on my nightdress before I begin practicing, so that you can go to bed."

Mary turned from the door. "We're all saying that you and duke are well matched," she announced.

"Really?" Edie was startled. She didn't, personally, think that she and her husband had much in common. In fact, she was a little worried that he was all about eels and she about staves, and there wasn't much of an overlap.

"You've both beautiful manners," Mary said. "They as have worked for His Grace for years don't even mind the daft schedule because they say he's always fair and he never makes a body feel like an idiot. Though he's some sort of genius, or so they say." She opened her eyes very wide.

"Therein lies a huge difference between us," Edie said. "But thank you, Mary. I hope you're right."

It was rather odd, lying in bed, waiting for a man. It made the parts of her body to which she usually paid no attention prickle all over.

The night before, Gowan had whispered in her ear that he loved her bottom. It was nice to have someone telling her how fine it was, given that she'd never thought twice about her rear. Like getting a bequest from some relative one never knew.

Now, lying in the dark and waiting, her body started waking up all over because she couldn't stop thinking of the way his big hands had slid over her hips and down the slope of her bottom. And the way he had sucked her breast, and then had actually nipped her. Her nipples stood out against her nightdress at the memory.

Still he didn't arrive, but Edie's imagination kept presenting her with images of the previous night. Gowan had kissed her fiercely, until the only thing she could hear was the thunder of his heart, or perhaps of her own. So she could see . . . she really could see how . . .

After another few minutes, she decided to check whether she was as sore down there as she had been.

She wasn't.

That was surprising. Then, without really thinking about it, she started touching herself as he had. Her private parts felt soft and complicated under her fingers, her caress sending little whorls of heat down her thighs. The area she had briskly washed once a day for nineteen years felt . . . different.

Not quite hers, yet entirely hers.

Behind the safe darkness of her closed eyes, she relived the way Gowan had removed his clothes and slowly unwound his kilt. The sparkling, hot feeling that she had had when he cast his shirt aside and she saw all the taut muscles on his abdomen and below.

And all the time the stroke of her finger was

making heat gather in her limbs until she was practically throbbing there.

It was as if she was in a safe cocoon in the dark room, tucked under the covers.

Then the door opened.

Twenty-one

When the door swung open, Edie froze, instinctively clamping her knees together. Gowan stood in the doorway, light falling over his shoulder, talking to someone who remained out of sight.

She sat up in the bed. "Gowan."

"Yes?" He turned, and for a moment the heat pulsed again, because he was so beautiful. A lock of hair fell over his brow, and his cheekbones gave him the look of a Spanish conquistador.

"I am sleeping or, rather, I was sleeping."

His brows flew together and she could practically see him formulating another rule. *Don't wake my wife.*

"I don't mind if you enter my room, but I'd prefer that you concluded your conversation before doing so."

He nodded with his usual decisiveness. Edie slipped back down under the covers while he stepped into the hallway to finish his conversation. She had that restless, burning sensation again, worse than the previous night.

Gowan walked back in, closing the door behind him. "I am truly sorry to have woken you up."

"It's not that . . . who were you speaking to?"

"Bardolph. He wanted to—"

"So Bardolph knows that you have come to my room rather than to your own?"

"Yes."

"I don't like that," Edie said. Gowan tossed his dressing gown onto a chair, and with that gesture, her next sentence evaporated. He was naked, those long-muscled legs glowing like dark honey.

He loomed over her, bracing one arm on either side of her shoulders. "Yes, wife?"

"I don't think the servants should know what we're doing," she said, alarmed at how weak her voice sounded.

"They won't know everything." He dropped a kiss on her brow. "They don't know that I intend to kiss you until you are helpless." A kiss on her nose. "They don't know that I intend to make love to you until you haven't any breath in your body." A kiss on her lips, a lingering one that promised, but didn't breach. "Bardolph thinks I was listening to him all afternoon."

"You were," she said, feeling a bit breathless. "I listened as well, at least to part of it."

He shook his head.

"No?"

"I thought about you all day. I know it was painful last night, but I intend to make up for it."

Edie smiled up at him. "Have you had a bath?" she asked, running her hands over his shoulders. He was naked and smelled of almond soap, and she was clothed. There was something quite enticing about that.

"Of course," he said, lowering himself onto the bed but holding his weight off her body.

Edie had rather like how he'd smelled earlier, like male sweat and leather. "I wouldn't mind," she murmured.

"I would never come to my lady unbathed." Well, that settled that.

Edie discovered that Gowan was as muscled below the base of his spine as he was elsewhere. "My rump is very soft," she told him, "but yours is not."

"I'm a brawny brute." He shifted onto his side, his hand curving around one of her breasts.

"If you're a brute, what am I?" Edie prompted, enjoying herself.

"Perfect."

Their kiss was like a whirlpool: it made Edie's head spin until she clung to him, her breath coming in urgent little pants. Part of her felt self-conscious about the way their tongues kept touching, but another part of her relished it. He still had a hand on her breast and he was caressing her in such a way—rough and gentle at the same time—that she kept choking back little cries. Embarrassing ones.

Then Gowan pulled back and kissed his way down her neck. He slipped lower in the bed, and his mouth was on her nipple, suckling her straight through the thin lawn. Edie's fingers dug into his shoulders and she sobbed because it felt so good. She even tried to pull him over so that his weight was on her, so that he rubbed against that part of her, so her knees could cradle him . . .

Her mind was an incoherent storm. As Gowan moved to the other breast, Edie had a brief moment of clarity. It was very odd to realize her nightdress was wet. She wouldn't want to have cotton in *her* mouth, no matter how clean.

"Would you like me to remove my nightdress?" she asked, looking down at his head and feeling another pulse of heat so deep that she almost moaned aloud.

Gowan glanced up at her, his eyes dark as a crow's feather. A moment later she was unclothed, her gown tossed by the bedside, and they were lying side by side.

Heat rushed up into Edie's cheeks. They had been naked the night before, so it shouldn't feel so awkward to have his naked body next to hers. It was, though. And then he started kissing her again.

"I really . . ." she began, loving the gleam in his eyes. But she wasn't sure what she meant. Did she love him? Was it an insult to say that she *liked* him? She did like him. She was beginning to think that he never considered himself, which was a problem. But it was like saying that hot cocoa was too dark: he was good, through and through.

"I want you," she breathed.

Gowan's eyes lit like a flame, and then he rolled her onto her back, running his hands down her body, studying her so intently that she couldn't see past his thick lashes.

"Do I look all right?" she whispered.

"I was thinking that you look like that cello you love so much. You see the curves here, and here?" His hands shaped the slopes of her breast, the inward tuck of her waist, the generous swell of her hips.

"I never thought of that," Edie said, feeling more pleased about her body than she usually did.

"You make love to that cello," he said, "but I make love to you."

She was still smiling at that when his fingers dipped between her legs and she realized that she'd grown wetter and more swollen since she'd touched herself there. It felt different when he touched her. Her fingers had been soft and tentative and coaxing. But there was nothing tentative about the way he rubbed her. His touch was a demand, on the very edge of painful, as if she was about to be scalded.

Edie twisted up against his hand, her body

turning into a flame. "That feels so good," she gasped, and then arched again, chasing the twirling sensation that turned her limbs liquid.

"This will feel even better," Gowan said, his voice thick. He lowered himself on top of her.

It didn't.

By the time Gowan had pushed all the way inside, Edie was rigid with shock. It hurt like the devil. Maybe worse than yesterday, because she felt raw inside, as if . . .

She didn't know what. She buried her face in his shoulder and sucked in a great breath as he drew back out and then a moan when he thrust back in . . .

"That's it, Edie," he said, low and fierce. "Let it come."

By the time she realized that he had taken her gasp for pleasure, it was too late. He was braced over her, thrusting into her over and over.

"You can do it, Edie," he whispered. "I can go all night if it will make the difference."

Edie hadn't realized this was a competition, though that wasn't the right word because there was no one to compete with. Still, she was clearly supposed to have an explosion of pleasure, the *petit mort*. And that was about as likely to happen as the inn falling down around their ears.

Still, Edie gave it a try. She hated the idea of disappointing Gowan. She tried bending her knees. She tried arching her back. She figured out that if she slid down a little it took off some of the pressure, but the truth of the matter was that her husband didn't fit inside her.

Her body had lost every pulse of that sweet heat she'd felt before. In fact, she was on the edge of tears, which wasn't good. Gowan's breath was growing harsher. A drop of sweat fell on her arm, and she flinched.

He was caressing her breast, and every once in a while he would kiss her again, but all she felt was a frantic need to buck him off. Anything to stop the pain and the awful sense of being suffocated. When he moved faster, a cry actually escaped her lips. "That's it," Gowan breathed, giving her a kiss that made her feel as if he was congratulating a dunce who had just sounded out her first word.

She could not do this much longer. In fact, not another minute.

If this was a competition, she was willing to lose. Gowan could be the winner. She had to get him off, out of her, *now*. There was a ferocity in his eyes that promised he would go on all night until he pleasured her.

Edie would rather die.

Layla said their joining would be noisy and loud, which it certainly wasn't on her part, unless she planned to start screaming.

"Oh!" she cried, but the word didn't come out right. She sounded dismayed, like a matron finding a vase of flowers broken on the floor.

She hadn't hit the right tone. "Ohhh," she said, a little louder. She had never felt so ridiculous in her life. Gowan had lowered his face and was kissing her neck, so she couldn't tell whether he believed her. His hand was still curved around her breast. His thumb rubbed across her nipple, which should have felt good, except that nothing felt good.

His heart was hammering in a way that proved *he* was experiencing pleasure, even if she wasn't. That made her feel a little better. She arched up against him, because that did seem to take the pressure off and made it hurt less. Then she threw back her neck, exactly as Layla had, and let go.

She would have said that she had absolutely no acting ability. But apparently she was good enough.

Gowan muttered something that sounded like a thankful curse, took a deep breath, and began going even faster. After what felt like a century, she felt tremors hit his body. A groan erupted from his lips and then a tangle of incoherent words.

She liked that part.

It was wonderful to have such a self-controlled, powerful man shatter in her arms. His face contorted as he let go, every bit of civilization stripped from his face. She was the only woman in the world who had seen that.

The others saw only the duke, whereas she got to see a primitive man who lost himself in her body. He was still there, actually, inside her. Thinking about his face made her inner parts clench around him suddenly. The pain burned away for the moment and she felt a delicious sense of fullness.

Gowan was braced on his forearms. "God, that feels good, Edie. Just give me a moment," he gasped, panting.

As his words sank in, Edie panicked. Her inner parts had been pummeled enough. She pushed at him gently, and he rolled off and to the side. Sure enough, his tool was still ready to go.

When she peered gingerly down at herself, she didn't seem to have bled any more, which had to be a miracle.

Gowan reached over and pulled her against his sweaty body. "I don't have to ask if it was good for you. You're so tight and hot . . ."

"It still hurts a little," she whispered.

He bathed her so gently that she almost started crying again.

She hated lying. And the *petit mort* that never happened was such a huge lie. But it was only a matter of time, she told herself. Tomorrow was another day. It would be better. Gowan was gently patting her with cool water, giving her that restless, twitchy feeling again.

"That's enough," she said, sitting up in case he took the fact her hips were moving under his touch as encouragement.

He gave her a kiss. "Would it be all right with you if I slept here?"

She could feel a silly blush rising in her cheeks. "All right."

It was hard not to feel resentful the next morning. Gowan's eyes glowed when he told her that the night had been better than his wildest imaginings. Edie hated the fact she'd lied to him. Hated it.

She took a deep breath, about to confess, when there was a scratch on the door. Gowan called, "Come in," and in bustled Mary, followed, to her horror, by Gowan's valet. And on their heels were maids carrying breakfast trays.

The chance was gone. She nibbled toast while Trundle laid out Gowan's dressing gown, and Mary began preparing Edie's toilet. When Gowan finished eating, he got out of bed and went to his room, where he could listen to some sort of report about paddock fencing while he dressed.

Edie told herself that marriage involved compromises.

If only she hadn't lied . . . Her stomach clenched every time she thought of it. But if she confessed, he might think she was incapable. And there was that terrible word, *frigid*. It made a woman sound like an icehouse. What if she was? What if she could never achieve all that noise Layla described?

She wasn't a very loud person ordinarily.

But if she told the truth now, would Gowan make her see a doctor about the pain? She couldn't imagine telling anyone. Well, she could tell Layla, if only they were still in London.

The whole thing was a mess.

Twenty-two

Another interminable morning passed in the carriage, more or less indistinguishable from the day before. Edie kept to her corner of the carriage all morning, ignoring the stultifying conversation Gowan was conducting with a bailiff. She certainly had nothing to contribute. Instead, she brooded over what had happened the night before. Or rather, what *hadn't* happened.

It wasn't so much that she had failed at the *petit mort* yet again; she was beginning to believe that it wasn't likely to happen for her. But she felt awful about the way she had handled it. Lying to her husband. Dissembling—

She cut herself off. It was just plain wrong, and she knew it. And—she peeked at Gowan—she was starting to *like* him. That was a good thing for a wife to feel toward her husband. The aversion she felt about the marriage bed? That was *not* a good thing.

She had to tell him the truth.

After the carriage had stopped for luncheon (served and eaten at a galloping pace), she put her hand on Gowan's arm. "I would like to speak to you." She said this in front of Bardolph and a footman, because if she didn't speak before servants, she would never speak at all.

"Certainly." Gowan had been about to escort her from the dining room, but he paused expectantly.

"In the carriage," she clarified.

"Yes, that would be more efficient." He turned to leave, nodding to his entourage to follow, thus displaying a deafness to nuance that was, to Edie's mind, the distinguishing trait of his sex. She didn't budge.

"*Alone,* Gowan." If her husband consulted with Bardolph before he agreed to this, she would . . .

She wasn't sure what she would do, but it would be violent.

The duke glanced at her, one eyebrow raised ever so slightly, then at Bardolph, who offered a brisk little bow and walked away. Only then did she realize that she'd just won a skirmish in the war shaping up between herself and Bardolph.

But the factor was nothing if not tenacious. She left Gowan to instruct his retinue as to the afternoon's work, and made her way to the carriage. But when she climbed in, she discovered three ledgers had been placed on the seat for her husband to review. She poked her head back through the door and a footman leapt to attention.

"These will travel in another carriage," she said, dropping them into his arms.

"His Grace said . . ." the boy bleated.

So the war wasn't just between herself and Bardolph; it had a wider scope. "*Her* Grace has just informed you otherwise," she told him.

Then she settled back inside the carriage to wait.

Moments later, Gowan strode past a footman trotting away with the ledgers he had intended to review during the afternoon's journey. By rights, he should feel irritated. He deplored time lost sitting in a carriage.

But the truth was that he felt only anticipation.

Of course, he'd known from the moment he'd first seen Edie that she posed a threat to his ordered life. One cannot succumb to such a primal lust for a woman that one marries her before a month has passed, and not understand that routines would be disrupted, at least initially. Time with Edie could not be counted toward his obligations to the estate. But, on the other hand, if he indulged himself now, perhaps he would stop wanting her every minute of the day. With time, he thought, he could relegate his body's need for her to the evening. Or at least to once during the day.

He didn't believe it for a minute.

Bloody hell.

He had responsibilities. People depended on him. Whole estates. The banking system.

He dimly remembered caring about all that. But

right now he only had to think about Edie to feel a clench of desire flare in his body with mad ferocity. One look at her and he wanted to dismiss Bardolph and throw the ledgers into the fire.

He cursed again. If he didn't get control over himself, he'd discover that his days were spent in her bed, losing himself in her body. Falling for her. Worshipping her. Drinking himself to death if she played him false, the way his father . . .

That thought steadied him. Lust was nothing more than a bodily urge. It had its place in life and needed to be kept to that realm. Instead of slamming the carriage door and pulling her beneath him—servants be damned—Gowan forced himself to settle onto the opposite seat and gave Edie a measured, gentlemanly smile, reaching up and giving the roof a considered tap so the coachman would know they were ready.

Her smile, from under the brim of her bonnet, was demure and utterly adorable. Just like that, carnal desire surged in a wave that dragged him under to drown. Work could damn well wait. He opened his mouth, then snapped it shut, appalled that he had almost blurted out, *Naked. I need you to be naked.*

One didn't say that to a duchess in a carriage. He curbed the demand, but the emotion behind it slipped out: "Someday, I should like to love you in the morning."

An emotion flashed across her eyes that he

couldn't interpret. Without answering, she undid the ribbons under her chin. As he watched, she took off her bonnet and dropped it on the seat beside her. Could it be that she had read his mind, and meant to unclothe herself? The carriage was well onto the post road so no one could open the door.

A cascade of lustful images filled his head—only to evaporate when she leaned forward and tapped him on his knee with a slender gloved finger.

"Bardolph," she said, lowering her voice to an absurdly masculine growl, "I intend to tup my wife tomorrow morning from seven fifteen to seven forty-five, so be good enough to delay our departure to take account of the event." Then she gave him an impish grin.

Gowan was so surprised he burst into laughter.

"Well, thank God," Edie said, pulling off her gloves and placing them beside her hat. "I was beginning to fear that you'd lost your sense of humor entirely."

He frowned.

"I do know that you have one," she said, with a wicked little grin. "It's too late to pretend that your brain is devoted entirely to the admirable task of managing all those eel traps."

"I shall never live down the eels, shall I?" Gowan asked, stretching out his legs so that they fell on either side of her slippers. He'd made up his mind. He meant to have his saucy wife at some point during their journey. She had arranged the afternoon so that he had no work on which to concentrate.

Very well: he would concentrate on her.

"You brought it on yourself," Edie said with a delightful chuckle. "I fully expect that at the age of eighty, I'll still be pulling you away from fishy reports and teasing you into a display of humor."

"A sense of humor?" he repeated lazily. "Are you quite certain I have one?"

She nodded. "I am sure. Although the wry, funny part of you disappears during talk of wheat and eels, and instead I find myself looking at a man who's finding no pleasure in life."

He started to disagree, but she hadn't finished. "That's not quite right. You do enjoy your work, don't you?"

Work? He enjoyed the delicate curve of her cheek, the deep rose of her lips, the way her eyelashes curled. Even the way she was dissecting him.

Edie leaned forward and gave his knee a little poke. "Gowan, are you listening to me?"

"Why would I work if I didn't enjoy it?"

"Because you have responsibilities," she said promptly. "My father would much prefer to play the cello, and yet he is unable to find more than a few minutes here and there in which to practice."

"There's only one thing I'd prefer to be doing,"

he said, shaping the words with the controlled urgency of a man whose body was hard and aching.

"Gowan! That is *not* what I meant."

He dragged his mind back to the subject. "You meant that I'm a tedious bastard and unfit to be in a lady's company. I think," he said apologetically, "that might just be the way I am, Edie. I can assure you that Bardolph and I do not exchange witticisms."

"Bardolph is a *stick*," she said, turning her little nose into the air. "And you, my dear duke, must be careful yourself in that respect, because you have displayed some stickish tendencies of your own."

"I am not a stick." He gave a bite of laughter. "Though, hell, we'd be better off if I were less sturdy and more stickish."

Edie's answering smile was just a bit wobbly. She took a deep breath. "It does still hurt some, Gowan."

All amusement drained out him. He leaned forward and took her hands. "I know. I'm so sorry—but it *is* getting better, isn't it?"

She nodded.

"It means everything to me that you are finding pleasure in the act." He grinned at her. "My lack of experience was embarrassing enough, but if I'd failed you in that respect, I would have had to relinquish my claim to manhood altogether."

Edie frowned. "That's absurd."

A ridiculous wave of relief washed over him. "I never felt more happy than when you came last night." He brought her hands to his mouth and kissed their palms, first one, then the other. "I just wish that the first few minutes weren't so painful." His sweet bride was still so shy that she kept her eyes on their entwined fingers. "Look at me?" he coaxed. "We must talk about these things, Edie. A husband and wife shouldn't have any secrets between them."

"I know," she said. "That's why I . . ." But her voice trailed off.

She looked so miserable that Gowan couldn't bear it. He half rose, bending his head to avoid the padded ceiling, pushed aside her hat, and sat down beside her. "Shakespeare makes the very true point that a standing prick has no conscience."

At first she didn't understand. "A standing what?" she asked. The words had scarcely left her mouth when he watched, fascinated, as her cheeks took on a faint color, like the blush of a peach. "Gowan!" She gave a little explosive laugh. "A *standing* prick?"

"Much better than a falling one," he pointed out. "But what I'm trying to say is that I have a conscience, even if other parts of me are ravenous for you. Edie, *mo chrìdh*, if it hurts too much to make love, you merely have to tell me. You do know that, don't you?"

The color in her cheeks stained darker, as beautiful as the first plum of the season. "Of course I do," she said. "What does *mo chrìdh* mean?"

"My heart." He picked her up easily and put her on his lap, pulling her into the crook of his arm. "You're exquisite," he told her. "The most beautiful girl I've ever seen."

"I feel the same about you." Her honesty always startled him, the way she so easily said things that others hid or doled out in meager doses.

Her arms came up and around his neck and he had an odd lurching sense, as if the carriage—or the world—tilted. She gave him that secret smile, the one with the tucked-away kiss. "When I looked up and saw you coming toward me at Fensmore, I thought you were the best-looking man in the room. And now," she said, giving him a mischievous little smile, "I even like red hair. *If* it's yours."

Gowan had never given a damn how he looked—he was well aware that his title commanded admiration that had nothing to do with his physical attributes. But the look in Edie's eyes gave him a shock of pride.

She liked his looks. Edie wasn't the type of woman who cared much for titles. Nor for money, either.

She rested her head against his shoulder. "Still, I do worry about you, Gowan. My father has a tendency to be far too serious. I think life can be very difficult if a person hasn't a sense of joy."

He felt a little chill. "You think I don't?"

"Of course you do! You can even make Shakespeare's plays seem funny to someone like me, who's never managed to read one all the way through. I'm just worried that your life may be smothered under a hundred daily reports."

"I doubt it. For one thing, I lose my self-possession around you," he confessed, running a finger along her cheekbone. "I stop giving a damn about work. Bardolph suggested I bring the ledgers in the carriage because he knows I didn't truly absorb them."

She sat up straight, her brows drawing together. "Mr. Bardolph is not endearing himself to me."

"Don't bother about him. More to the point, am *I* endearing myself to you?" Gowan scarcely believed that bit of foolishness came from his own lips. Something about her was eroding his independence . . . his manhood.

"I think you may well be," Edie said.

Still, a shadow of anxiety clung to her eyes. "Don't worry," he said, dropping a kiss on her lips. "We will work out this marriage business. It's unfortunate that neither one of us has a very good example to go by. My parents would have been vastly better off had they never met."

"I can't say the same for my father and Layla. They genuinely love each other. It's just that my father has forgotten how . . ." She trailed off and started again. "He has stopped appreciating Layla for all the things he fell in love with in the first place. It's as if he wants her to become *him*. And he is quite stiff by nature, I'm afraid."

Gowan nodded.

"It makes him behave in a rather ill-tempered fashion, when in reality he isn't."

"I've seen him retain his temper in truly vexing circumstances, as when dealing with the idiots from the Bank of England."

"But he doesn't laugh at her jokes."

"I promise to always laugh at your jokes," Gowan whispered.

"If only I knew some to tell," Edie said with a sigh. "I have only a passing and distant acquaintance of the sort of puns you like, the ones about pricks and bawdy clocks." She snuggled her head back against his shoulder.

"I'm happy to provide definitions," he said, his voice growing husky.

But she wasn't listening. "I'm not used to staying up late, and then drinking wine at luncheon," she said, yawning in a ladylike way. "Could we not find some potable water, Gowan? Wine at midday makes me feel so drowsy."

"Certainly," he answered. He paused, thinking about how he'd fallen into the habit of drinking wine at every meal but breakfast. He was always testing himself, checking to make certain that he didn't turn into a sot, and follow in his parents' footsteps.

It wasn't a fear that he had ever shared with another person, but in the spirit of not keeping secrets from each other, he decided he would tell Edie . . . and then he realized that she had fallen asleep.

He stared down at her, all his plans to seduce her fading away. She was curled against him, looking utterly peaceful. His first reaction was a pulse of irritation. But that wasn't fair; it was selfish. He was responsible for her lack of sleep, after all.

If only he had his ledgers . . .

But he didn't have them. He had nothing to do.

That wasn't entirely true. He did have a small amount of paper and a pen. He could prop her against the side of the carriage and go to work.

Absolutely not. She would wake. He felt a startling sense of protectiveness. Edie was exhausted, with faint blue circles under her eyes, at least partly because he had made love to her in the middle of the night.

Holding her as carefully as a glass vase, he shifted to the corner of the carriage and then leaned back, holding his sweet, fragrant bundle of wife in his arms and examining her eyelashes and her lips all over again, just as he had at the ball where they first met.

Everything was different now, because she was his wife. He'd been the first to make love to her, and he would be the last to make love to her. He would wake every day of his life to those passionate, intelligent eyes and the stern honesty that led her to warn him that he was in danger of becoming stickish.

The smile easing the corners of his lips was neither sardonic nor rueful. He knew what Edie would call it: a joyful smile. His arms tightened around her in gratitude.

He thought about marriage as the carriage rocked on, down the road.

He never took naps.

Naps were a waste of time.

Twenty-three

As evening began to draw in and the carriage jolted from the post road to a cobblestone street, Edie woke to find herself in a sleeping Gowan's arms. The carriage rocked around a corner, heading into an inn yard. His arms tightened around her, but he didn't wake until she kissed him.

He woke up, scowling, and before she could say a word, announced that he never napped.

Edie held her tongue. Her father had similar convictions: *he* was certain that he never lost his temper.

The Queen's Arms, in Palden, was accustomed to accommodating nobility who arrived in a swirl of servants. The innkeeper led them to a private parlor, where Gowan kissed Edie absentmindedly and then sat down to listen to the groom who had arrived that morning from Scotland with the latest reports.

Reports!

Edie was starting to detest the sound of the word.

And she was tired from the long hours cooped up in the carriage, and frustrated by the fact she hadn't played her instrument in two days. To her chagrin, she discovered that she was on the edge of tears. She made an excuse, returned to her room, and ordered a hot bath. Mary bustled about the room tsk-tsking over this and that—Bardolph was not a favorite below stairs—until Edie wanted to leap out of the bath and scream.

Unfortunately, even soaking in hot water was not entirely comfortable, so it was difficult to imagine enduring another bout of lovemaking, let alone enjoying it. A flare of panic swept over her. She hadn't managed to confess everything; she had lost her courage after he told her how happy it made him that she found pleasure. Now she was facing another night in which she would fail. Another night in which she would have to lie.

"Mary," she said, her voice exploding into the room louder than she expected. "I'd like a piece of writing paper and a pen, please."

"Mr. Bardolph provided a traveling *secretaire*

for your use, Your Grace," Mary said, her tone shaded with ice as she pronounced the factor's name. When Edie was out of the bath, Mary opened up a charming leather box on the corner desk, equipped with anything a letter writer might wish.

Dearest Layla, Edie wrote, then paused. Of course, she had no idea whether Layla was still with her parents in Berwick-upon-Tweed. Perhaps her father had fetched his wife? With a sigh, she remembered his face and decided it was more likely that a groom would locate Layla at her parents' house with very little difficulty.

She wanted to invite her stepmother to visit the castle; Berwick-upon-Tweed was on the border with Scotland, so it couldn't be a terribly long trip. But how urgent should she make her plea? She couldn't detail what had happened.

In the end she kept it concise: *Please pay me a visit,* she wrote. *Please, Layla. Do you remember the secret you taught me? I need you. Love, Edie.*

Sometime later, when she and Gowan were seated in the inn's private dining room, attended by Bindle, Rillings, and four footmen, Edie produced the letter. "My stepmother is staying with her parents in Berwick-upon-Tweed, so I have written to invite her to pay us a visit in Scotland."

Gowan showed not a flicker of irritation at the notion that her stepmother would join them. Why

265

should he? He spent every waking hour with Bardolph, Jelves, and the rest of his entourage. Unless she demanded that they have privacy in the carriage, marital interaction was limited to mealtimes and visits to her bedchamber at night.

"We will send a groom ahead to Berwick-upon-Tweed," Gowan said now. "If he leaves immediately, it's possible that your stepmother may decide to join our carriage."

"We can't send someone now, Gowan; it's nighttime!"

"We must give your stepmother all possible time to consider your invitation," Gowan stated. He raised a finger and a footman ran from the room and returned with Bardolph, who managed to imply without words that it was extraordinarily thoughtless of her to dispatch a letter at this hour.

Edie eyed his whiskers and bit back her impulse to overrule Gowan. Her husband had been given his way far too often; that was clear. But she could say the same for Bardolph, and she refused to give the factor even the slightest satisfaction.

She watched as he left the room, letter in hand, with a renewed sense of hope. If she couldn't divine the secret to the *petit mort*, Layla would help. There must be a trick to it.

Gowan sent his valet off to bed and then put on his robe to cross the corridor to Edie's room. But he paused, hand on the door. He was already so aroused that he felt as if heat was rising from his very skin.

He couldn't go to her like this, like an animal. Crazed with lust, intoxicated at the mere thought of her. He retreated into the bathroom and closed his hand around himself. A few moments later he pulled his robe back on. His breath was still caught in his chest; he was still hungry, but in greater control.

When he closed the door behind him, he found Edie sleeping, face buried in her arms, rumpled hair spilling over the pillows. The room was dark except for a slender ray of moonlight that stole through the heavy drapes and played over his wife's tresses, turning them pale gold, as if all her vibrancy had been washed away. He shrugged off his robe, slipped under the covers, and wrapped an arm around her.

"Gowan?" she asked a second later, in a husky little protest.

"You slept all afternoon," he whispered, brushing a kiss against her cheek. "Wake up now and play."

She yawned and rolled onto her back, pulling her gown tight against lush breasts. A groan involuntarily broke from his lips.

"You're so beautiful, Edie." He bent his head to kiss her, but she wriggled away.

"Not through my nightdress," she said, sounding much more alert. "Last night it was quite unpleasant sleeping with damp patches over my breasts."

That was fair, if a bit cold.

Edie pulled the gown over her head. A ray of moonlight flickered over one breast, down to the curve of her waist.

Desire punched through his body, and made his breathing rough. With a struggle, he made sure his voice was even. "May I kiss you now?" he whispered, tenderly guiding her onto her back.

"On my breasts?"

She sounded altogether too rational. It was a bit demoralizing. "Yes, here," he said, curving his hand around a luscious breast.

"Yes, you may," she stated.

He felt as if he'd lost his senses, as if the world had shrunk to one creamy breast, the fire in his loins, the catch in Edie's breath when he suckled her.

"You like that," he murmured, moving from one breast to the other. He could tell she did. He was learning her body. It softened under his caresses. He couldn't stop kissing her, his hands roaming over her body. Every touch was intoxicating.

The only thing he wished . . .

"Edie," he said, and then cleared his throat. His voice sounded embarrassingly guttural.

"Yes?"

He would have preferred that her voice sounded more like his, which was stupid.

"Would you—" He stopped. He couldn't demand that a gently bred lady touch him. Perhaps when they knew each other more. Last night she had stroked his chest and back, and he longed for her hands to roam over the rest of his body. But he felt hesitant to ask . . . What if she thought he was too muscular? Too burly? Too much like a laborer?

Sweat beaded across his forehead, but he kept kissing her breasts, determined not to overwhelm her. "Does this feel good?" he whispered, closing his teeth in the gentlest of bites.

Edie shivered, and a little gasp broke from her lips. He almost couldn't hear her answer: her *yes* was a thread of sound.

His desire burned so hotly that he felt unmoored, as if every moment he wasn't inside her was a sacrifice. It didn't matter that he'd just pleasured himself. He wanted to push open her legs and lick her *there* until her body squirmed away from his and she got that enchanting hitch in her throat, and then he would bury himself in her so hard and fast that he could feel his balls against her.

He had to pause, collect himself, remind himself that he was a thinking, rational man whose young bride was still new—

Hell, *he* was still new to it.

Slowly, slowly, he kissed his way down her body until he pushed her legs apart. He may be drowning in lust . . . but all the same, the logical part of his brain was still operating, and it was offering observations. They weren't all encouraging.

When they had first kissed, in the carriage outside her parents' house following the Chuttle ball, Edie had been as feverish as he, her hands flying around his body. Now, she wasn't. One moment she would gasp and a little tremor would go through her body, but then, all of a sudden, she would go still. She didn't touch him, not really. She stroked his arms, or his chest, or twined her fingers in his hair.

For a while he lost himself kissing her, but then he knew she was ready. She was swollen and soft, and every time he licked her, she would make a little moaning sound, and her hands would tighten on his hair.

Her beautiful eyes were squeezed shut but as he came up, over her, she opened them. For a moment they looked hazy with pleasure and then something else came into them.

"Edie!" he said, startled. "What's the matter?"

"Nothing," she said with a little gasp.

He looked at her a second longer, but she arched her back and rubbed against him. "We should . . . we should make love now, Gowan. We have to be up early tomorrow."

Her touch sent his mind reeling into a smoldering place where rational thought wasn't possible.

"Tell me if it hurts too much," he told her, and she nodded.

Coming into her, his Edie, was the most exquisite feeling he could have imagined. Why didn't people do only this—make love—day and night? He went as slowly as he could, hoping that it wouldn't hurt too much. When he finally seated himself, she wound her arms around his neck and buried her face in his shoulder.

"How does it feel, Edie?" he asked. He dropped kisses on her ear, coaxing her. "Does it feel good?"

"It's fine," she whispered.

He froze.

"No, it's—it's better," she said, almost sounding surprised. "It is not so painful."

Relief swept through him. Now he just had to maintain control. It had taken thirty, forty minutes, but if he stayed the course, she would catch up to him and take her pleasure. A swell of emotion, a determination that he would give his wife the same ecstasy he felt, came from deep within him, and he braced himself above her and began moving.

Edie lay back with her eyes closed tightly, and for a time he just concentrated on keeping his hungry flesh under control. Finally, he said, "Edie, how does it feel?"

Her eyes snapped open, startling him. They weren't hazy with desire but grave and focused.

271

Gowan felt a sudden pang, a ridiculous wish that she would be playful. That wasn't fair. His Edie was serious by nature. Even having that thought was disloyal.

"It's all right," she said. She shifted under him and the small movement rippled through his loins like fire. "You feel so . . . well, you make me feel full."

Full? Full couldn't be good. Full sounded like a belly after a Sunday meal. "Is that a pleasurable sensation?" he asked.

She bent her knees, and he shuddered at the feeling that washed through his body.

"You should come," she whispered.

"Not without you," he said. "What would make this feel better for you?"

Edie met his eyes with a feeling of utter panic. Her interior parts were burning—not as badly as they had the day before, but it wasn't pleasant. And worse, she felt horribly inadequate.

Desperate.

Was she the only woman in the world who found it deeply unsettling to have a large man on top of her, with part of him inside her? Once or twice she felt a flicker of pleasure. But then Gowan would shift his position, or say something that would make her start thinking again.

She ended up lying beneath him hating herself, longing for it to be over.

Gowan watched as Edie closed her eyes tight

again, wishing he knew what she was thinking. He channeled his desire into long, slow strokes that would eventually get them both where they needed to go. Looking down at her, he was struck by a surprising wave of protectiveness so ferocious that he nearly stopped altogether.

He wanted her to be happy more than anything he'd ever wished for in his life. Fantasies were nothing like the reality of her: physical beauty was one thing, but the seriousness of her, her thoughtful kindness, her wry sense of humor, were another.

"Edie," he said, speaking his heart. "Come for me," he ordered, kissing her. "Come for me, *mo chrìdh.*"

And she came, thank God. He heard the piping sound of her voice with a thankfulness that was as deep as his pleasure. And then he was lost to it, shocked by the joy, the piercing heat, the way bone-deep delight filled his body.

To Edie's mind, the evening's end had always been inevitable.

The only difference from the other nights was that she thought Gowan might have begun to understand that she wasn't feeling the same pleasure he was. There was a concentration on his face that didn't resemble the savage joy he'd taken in her body the other times.

That thought made her heart sink.

• • •

The third day of their journey came and went. When they were installed at that night's inn, Mary told Edie with a giggle that His Grace had informed the servants that the duke and duchess would dine in his chamber.

By then, Edie was limp with exhaustion. That morning Gowan had told her, apologetically, that he couldn't sleep away another afternoon. So he and Bardolph spent the day reading about companies that Gowan might acquire, while the carriage jolted over roadways on the way to Berwick-upon-Tweed. She had practiced for barely an hour when Mary appeared to put her in nighttime attire so that she could have an intimate supper with her husband.

She went next door and found Gowan with his hair still damp from his bath. It was stupid, given all the tangled problems they had, but the moment they were alone, something eased in her. That contained wildness that was Gowan's very essence sang to her like a chord, resonating deep in her bones. He had only to wrap his arms around her and she felt safe. As if she were in the right place.

It made no sense, given that they may well have irresolvable problems. Layla hadn't mentioned any potion for a woman's difficulties in bed, only for a man's.

A half hour later they were lying side by side on

the bed. Gowan's dressing gown was pushed back from his shoulders and Edie's fingers were roaming over the planes of his chest and even, daringly, down to his muscled stomach. Though she'd heard nothing at all, Gowan suddenly lifted his head and barked, "Come."

The door opened and two footmen walked through.

Edie pulled the covers over herself, even though her nightdress still covered her legs. The head footman began to arrange ducal china on a side table, his eyes never straying to the bed. He made several trips to the hall, returning with covered silver platters. When he finished at last, he poured their wine, bowed, and backed toward the door, his eyes still lowered, as if they were royalty.

"Peters, isn't it?" she asked.

He swung his head up, startled. "Peterkin, Your Grace."

"You may leave the bottle here, Peterkin. Thank you for bringing our meal."

He ducked his chin. "I'll be pleased to wait in the corridor and refill your glasses when you have a need, Your Grace."

Edie couldn't imagine anything more appalling. "We will serve ourselves," she told him.

But later, when they'd eaten, Gowan summoned Peterkin and another footman to remove the plates, even though by then her nightdress was bunched around her upper thighs, albeit still under the covers. They had been kissing, and Gowan ran his hand up her leg. The sensation made her want to squirm away and come closer, both at the same moment.

But once the plates were gone, she knew that it wouldn't be long until they made love, and after that thought, she couldn't relax. Even so, it was definitely getting easier. When he entered, she didn't gasp aloud; she merely flinched. But she could not relax.

It made it worse that Gowan seemed capable of going on all night. "How much does it hurt?" he asked her after a while, propping himself on stiffened arms and staring down at her.

"Not at all," she said, wiping his shoulder so she could pat him. "The pain goes away after a while."

It was unnerving to feel so happy when he smiled at her. But she did, even though he was smiling because he thought . . .

Well, what he thought was happening wasn't happening, that's all.

When she swung her legs from the bed to return to her own chamber, Gowan had a tense, nearly angry look on his face, but she just kept her head down. She couldn't explain.

There was nothing *to* explain.

Twenty-four

The next morning there was blood on her nightdress, and Edie panicked. She thought for a moment that something had been ripped open inside her.

"Your courses have begun," Mary said, coming up behind her. "The duke will be sorely disappointed," she added with a laugh.

Edie laughed a little, too. Weakly, but with relief, she laughed.

At breakfast, she informed Gowan that a female complaint precluded any visits to her bedchamber for the time being. It felt good to say that. Fueled by the memory of her useless practice sessions, she launched straight into another pronouncement. "I should like a two-hour stop in the afternoon to practice."

Gowan looked at her as if she'd just announced her intention to immigrate to Philadelphia. "Our route is laid out and on a strict schedule, Edie, as you know."

"I must practice and I'm too tired to play after supper. We could remain here for another day," she offered.

"We are holding every room in the Partridge Inn tonight. And the early coaches left an hour ago."

"I kept my cello back. Gowan, I must practice. I can do it here, or we can pause at midday."

Gowan's mouth tightened, but to her surprise, he didn't argue. Instead, he decided that it would be better to lose a day on their journey, so she played until lunch and then again until suppertime. Throughout, servants kept coming and going in the parlor, attending to Lord knew what tasks, until she gathered them—all eighteen of them—and announced that anyone who interrupted her playing again would have his or her employment summarily terminated. She let her eyes linger on Bardolph for the pure pleasure of it.

She'd seen enough to know that Bardolph was integral to Gowan's retinue, but threatening him, no matter how impotently, made her feel as if she was developing the backbone Layla said she needed.

"What shall we do about your practice tomorrow?" Gowan asked at dinner.

"I would be so grateful if you could spare two daylight hours," she told him. "The cello would be quite loud in the carriage and make it difficult for you to hear your reports." That was an empty threat because, of course, she would never achieve the proper balance in a moving vehicle. But she was relying on the fact that he knew nothing of stringed instruments.

"We'll leave an hour earlier and arrive an hour later," Gowan said. That was the way he approached obstacles, she was beginning to notice. He assessed them, dealt with them, and moved on. The daily estate reports would present a problem, and Gowan would build a road around the obstacle without growing irritated.

Bardolph did not share Gowan's matter-of-factness. His back teeth were obviously clenched, so she gave him a sunny smile, the better to rankle him. "It is almost midsummer. I shan't mind if I practice in a field," she told him.

"We can do better than that," Gowan said. "We will stop in Pickleberry," he said to Bardolph. "I believe that Her Grace would enjoy playing in the Merchant Tailors' Hall. Send someone ahead to ensure it is available, and donate the appropriate amount to their charitable endeavors."

That afternoon the coach pulled over in a tiny town square. Gowan escorted her into a good-sized hall and stationed a footman outside the door to make certain she wasn't interrupted.

Edie bent over her strings with a solid sense of purpose. If she put in two hours' hard work on the Boccherini, she wouldn't feel so restless in the coach. And she had decided to bring the score with her in order to go over it a few times, just as if it were a ledger.

An hour or so later, Gowan slipped back into the hall. She raised her head and saw him, but her fingers were nimbly following a thundering cascade of notes, so she looked back at the score.

He was still there a half hour later, his arms thrown to the back of the bench, staring at the ceiling. She drew the last note to a pause. Gowan brought his chin down slowly. "Are you finished?"

Was it her imagination, or did he sound regretful?

"No," she said firmly. "I shall take every second of my allotted two hours." But she was weary of the Boccherini. Instead, she raised her bow and began the opening notes to *Dona Nobis Pacem*.

When the final note died, she began the piece again. She had crowded the third and fourth sections. She needed peace in her heart.

But her bowing knew the truth, and she began speeding up again. She had no peace inside her at the moment. Gowan was still staring at the beams far above them, and all she could see was the powerful line of his jaw.

She usually immersed herself in the music. But this time she let the music be an accompaniment as she feasted on him: the strong column of his neck, his broad shoulders, and the glint of red in his hair. The extraordinary brilliance of him. The incisiveness that was an integral part of him. The way he ruled an empire without raising his voice. The way he had bent his life around her passion for music.

She was lucky. She was so lucky, barring that one thing.

Her eyes drifted to his legs, spread wide as he sprawled on the bench. It felt wicked to ogle him when he was swept away by the music. When the piece ended, she went straight into a Telemann sonata, hoping not to stir him. His eyes were closed, so perhaps he was dozing.

For the first time, she found herself wondering what it would be like to lick *him*. She could imagine her tongue tracing patterns over his flat stomach, even lower perhaps.

When she was on the final measures, he opened his eyes and then stood, stretching. She felt as if spangles of fire were racing through her in time to the music. If only they could be like this all the time: alone, with no Bardolph and no reports.

She slowly lifted her bow from the strings.

Twenty-five

By a week later, Gowan was fairly certain that he was losing his mind.

Edie spent the days tucked in the corner of the carriage with a score. At one point, she actually declared in a surprised tone that she now understood his method of traveling.

"Normally I would sit in a coach laughing with Layla while my father rode outside. But even without an instrument I have made astonishing strides on this score." Then she bent her head over the score again, and he had to fight not to throw her pages out the window.

She may be concentrating, but he wasn't. He couldn't stop looking at her. Over the hours and days and miles, he had studied everything from her delicate little nose to the tiny dent in very middle of her lower lip. When she reached a difficult part in the score, she would worry her lower lip with even white teeth.

He wanted to bite that lip. He wanted to throw himself on his knees in front of her and push up her skirts. Push her onto the seat and . . .

If things were different, Gowan would lay Edie on the carriage seat and kiss every inch of her.

He would throw himself down on his back and lift her on top of him. He would . . . It wasn't pleasant to spend the day ravaged by desire, knowing full well that his wife did not share the feeling.

Poor Edie had had a terrible time accommodating him. He knew it, and yet it didn't stop him from succumbing to lust. Every time he closed his eyes, he saw her long, pale legs and the luxurious fullness of her breasts. She sat there in the corner of the carriage, chewing on a pencil, then making sudden marks on the score, oblivious to him, and he could scarcely breathe because of the intensity of his hunger.

Knowing that making love hurt her made him feel like a brute. The second, third, the fourth times, her body had gone rigid when he entered, and a whimper had broken from her lips that made his blood run cold.

But even so, he longed to thrust into her warmth.

A mere glance at her bent neck, and lust seared his groin. Yet her orgasms were paltry, thin affairs compared to the way his body caught fire, shuddering as he gave her everything he had.

She . . .

Edie was a mystery to him, and it didn't help that he knew damned well that most men thought all women were mysteries. Even before her monthly courses arrived, he was already putting away the fantasies he'd had that someday she might pull up her skirts and seduce *him,* riding him to the jostle of the carriage wheels.

Edie wouldn't care for that. She remained primly in place under him when they made love. She froze at the sound of footsteps in the corridor outside; he couldn't imagine that she would welcome caresses in the daylight, in a carriage.

Except that reminded him of the way she had trembled when he touched her after the Chuttle ball. She seemed to think that he had lost his sense of humor, but he would say she had lost something as well.

Perhaps that was the nature of marriage. You started out enchanted with each other's sense of humor and responsiveness . . . and then real life intervened. But everything in him revolted against accepting that notion. The sensual Edie he had first met could not have disappeared, leaving a woman uninterested in making love.

It wouldn't bother him in the least to make love

during her courses, but she was fastidious. He hated the way she dried him with a sheet, as if she were rubbing down a horse.

It emphasized how much their intimacy was a failure.

Failure.

It felt better to acknowledge that, if only to himself. Something didn't feel right. It wasn't all he'd hoped . . . not what the poets described. Even in the depths of pleasure, he felt as if she were doing him a favor. He even suspected that she was thinking about music while he was shuddering over her.

The worst of it was that he felt as if Edie wasn't really his. She laughed and talked, and she wore his ring, but he had failed to imprint himself on her. When her courses were over, things would have to change.

Still, it would only make things worse if he tried to persuade her into intimacies that she wasn't ready for. He had no idea how long these female complaints lasted. Would it be another week? A few days?

When they reached Berwick-upon-Tweed three days later, Lady Gilchrist joined their carriage, and he even felt jealous of her, of his own mother-in-law, because Edie was so blindingly happy to see her. She and her stepmother sat together, holding hands, throughout the afternoon, until they stopped for the night at the Bumble and

Berry, a mere two-hour drive from Craigievar. He didn't want to introduce Edie to the castle and its residents in the dark, so he sent Bardolph and most of his retinue ahead, but the three of them and their private servants stopped to rest.

After supper, they bade each other a genial good night in the corridor of the inn and retired to separate chambers. But Gowan lay awake, thinking about his marriage.

The next morning he entered his wife's chamber and sat down on the bed. Edie was just waking up, her hair tousled and her eyes heavy-lidded and languorous. He choked back the lust that flooded his body, leaving him with an ever-present erection, and asked, "Are your courses over, Edie?"

She stretched in a way that outlined her magnificent breasts and nodded. The words burst from him. "When were they finished?"

Edie didn't lie to him. She looked him straight in the eye and told him that they'd ended four days ago. Yet she hadn't mentioned it to him. She hadn't once touched him, or let him know in any way.

He felt a wave of nausea that must have shown on his face, because Edie said, "Should I have informed you, Gowan? I thought if you wanted to come to my bed, you would have asked. Or just come."

She looked genuinely confused.

He managed a smile and left for breakfast.

Sometime later, Lady Gilchrist appeared downstairs, looking like a lush Frenchwoman, dropped by accident in the Scottish Lowlands. Her fetching bonnet dipped over one ear with just the right élan; her skirts were a tad short, exposing slippers whose ribbons crisscrossed up her ankles.

When they were all in the inn's courtyard, ready to leave, he announced that he would ride alongside the carriage. Relief flashed through Edie's eyes, giving him another wave of nausea. He handed his wife and her stepmother into the carriage and leapt onto his horse as if the Furies were behind him. He needed the wind screaming in his ears so he couldn't listen to the bitter, cynical voice in his head.

He'd always condemned both his parents for their despicable morals, but now he fancied he understood them better: they'd probably found themselves alone in the middle of a marriage.

There was nowhere colder, nor lonelier.

Even angry as he was, he still yearned to touch Edie, to kiss her, to make love to her. Given the chance, he would follow her as a falcon does the falconer, as if there were a string about his leg. And yet she didn't want him. That was manifestly clear.

If she were a falconer, she'd toss him into the sky and tell him not to come back. The realization made Gowan's heart thud heavily in his chest. He didn't even notice that his horse's flanks were white with foam. Finally, he slowed to a walk, but he couldn't stop his mind reeling from point to point.

Edie did care for him. During the last ten days, they had had conversations about everything from the castle sewers, to his aunts' piglets, to the state of the empire, to the future of the pound note. Even when she was studying her musical scores, he found himself interrupting to ask her opinion, drawing her into the conversation, making Bardolph wait to see whether she had thoughts about the future of coal or the economical implications of the new blast furnaces.

When they sat at meals, time flew, even when she talked about music, which he hardly understood. But he loved to see her excitement and the way her slender hands gestured in the air as she told him about the "blasted" Boccherini score, and then looked so guilty for cursing that he couldn't stop laughing.

Yet caring for him and wanting to make love to him appeared to be two distinct things. After his horse had cooled down, Gowan spurred him again, widening the distance between the carriage and him, creating a space between his mindless, sensual need and his wife. He felt like a wild animal, howling into some dark night.

It wasn't as if Edie had ever refused him her body. She hadn't. She even enjoyed it . . . he thought—no, he knew—she enjoyed it. At least, parts of it. But he ended up feeling like a heartless bastard. No matter how many times he told himself that she found pleasure bedding him, he didn't believe it. Some part of him felt like a rapist while taking his own wife. That was the raw truth of it.

He was pushing his horse harder than he ought, but he couldn't run from the truth. Every time he made love to Edie, he felt a kind of raw openness, as if her slightest touch turned him vulnerable. There was a touch of magic about it.

Yet she did not feel the same.

In fact, he had the shrewd feeling that Edie felt that kind of joy only when playing the cello. Whenever he could, he fobbed off Bardolph in order to listen to her. He'd even learned to recognize a few of the tunes she was working on. Though she wouldn't approve of the word *tunes*. They weren't "tunes" to her; they were arpeggios and barcarolle and the like. The words were like arcane formulas that only she knew.

That was when he saw the passionate, brilliant woman he wanted in his bed and his arms. When Edie played, her eyes went soft and unfocused, her lips parted, and her body swayed. The sight ripped him open with longing. Seeing her drop into that ecstatic state woke a dark monster that drove him to try harder and harder in bed.

He had kissed her in her most private places

until she writhed in his arms. He had caressed her every curve; he had whispered endearments in her ears. He had kissed her like a man possessed, which he was. None of it seemed to matter.

There was a wall between them, a separation. He only had to look into her eyes to know that whatever erotic excitement she felt in their bed was nothing to what she felt with that damned bow in her hand.

Music was her true love.

He had his horse back at a walk by the time he neared his estate. He heard a whistle in the woods, and whistled back; one of his sentries had spotted him.

A moment later the man trotted out from under the shadow of an oak tree, doffing his hat.

"Maclellan," Gowan said. He wanted to smile, but couldn't quite manage it.

The man fell alongside, giving a succinct report of events during Gowan's absence. A wild boar had attacked near the granaries; a hunting party had shot it the next day. The carcass had been butchered and the meat was drying, ready to be made into boar stew next winter. One sentry had fallen from the battlements and broken his shoulder, but he was healing well.

This was nothing that Gowan hadn't already learned from his daily reports, but he had found that one often learned more from hearing a report again in person. He asked about the clumsy sentry.

"The lad's not handy with a gun," Maclellan reported. "I've my worries about that. His father had perfect aim, but the lad doesn't. I think he's a sentry to please his da, but his heart isn't in it. I'm worried he'll point that gun in the wrong direction one day and shoot his own foot off, or worse. I've in mind to let him go, but his father will be right grieved to see him leave."

"Let's try him in the stables," Gowan said. "Perhaps he has a hand with animals. We can use him somewhere."

They rounded a bend and there before them lay Castle Craigievar, the centuries-old stronghold of the Clan MacAulay. The noon sun shone down gold over its ancient walls, battlements, and drum towers. Sentries caught sight of them. He heard the blare of a trumpet. As they made their way down the drive, the MacAulay banner—argent, a crimson dragon grasping a sword—was slowly raised above the keep.

The Duke of Kinross was back in residence.

Gowan pulled up his horse. His heart lifted as he watched the flag unfurl, the dragon's lip curling with fury. This was *his* place, where he was master. All would be well here.

He could woo his wife into loving his bed.

Of course he could.

He just had to try harder.

Twenty-six

The minute the groom closed the carriage door, Layla pounced. "What on earth is happening with that delicious husband of yours?" she cried. "Here I am, springing to the rescue like Sir Galahad himself. Tell me *all*."

Edie burst into tears.

Layla hugged her, but Edie had held her tears for too long. After a while, Layla said, "Darling, that's my last handkerchief, so unless you want me to rip something off my petticoat, you must stop blubbering. I'll be brutally honest and admit that my petticoat is trimmed with Alençon lace, so I would rather not turn it to handkerchiefs."

"I will," Edie gasped, struggling to take a deep breath.

"Tell me the worst," Layla said, giving her another squeeze. Her voice dropped. "Did he turn out to have some sort of perversion? Does he tie you to the bed or something of that nature . . . even *worse?* I will take you away directly and you will never see him again. Your father will have the marriage annulled before the duke realizes you're out the door."

"It's consum-consummated," Edie said, getting herself under control. "And I don't want to annul my marriage."

"Of course, there are some perversions that I'd

quite like to try myself," Layla said encouragingly. "Why should we be so rigid, after all? If two people wish to indulge themselves, and are in perfect agreement, why not? I've never tried to talk your father—"

"Gowan isn't perverted!"

"Oh, so it's a more mundane problem?" Layla looked quite relieved. "Let me guess. He's a five-second-miracle. I should have brought a potion or two with me. Those big, burly men, they're the—"

"It's the opposite," Edie interrupted, hiccupping.

"The opposite?" Layla frowned. "Please tell me you're not complaining about a situation that most women merely dream about."

"There's something wrong with me," Edie cried, her darkest fears tumbling out. "It hurts so much."

"That probably just means that your husband is well-endowed. Let's see . . . would you compare him to a carrot, a marrow, or a courgette? I do hope we're not talking about a string bean."

"But—but you told me pain was an old wives' tale." A last hiccup escaped. "I hate it. I just hate it. I feel so stupid and—and I'm such a *failure* at the whole business."

Layla gave her knee a pat. "Darling, I couldn't possibly have revealed that there was the risk you might feel as if you'd been skewered like an unlucky matador."

"It would have helped!" Edie cried. "All this

time I was afraid that something was wrong with me."

"There *is* something wrong with you. You're a chucklehead. What's all this about failure? There's no failure about it. After her wedding night, my cousin Marge locked the door to her bedchamber and wouldn't let her husband back in for a solid month. And even then, she didn't enjoy it."

"I've met your cousin and her husband," Edie observed. "There might be more than one reason for her lack of pleasure."

"So true. The man has lips like a sturgeon. It's most repellent. Do you think the windows open in this carriage?"

"No, and you mustn't smoke in here. The smell would never come out of the velvet."

"A bit overdone, don't you agree?" Layla said, poking at the seat. "Not that I have anything against copper-colored velvet. I think this would make a wonderful pelisse. But just think if you spilled some wine!"

"Gowan doesn't drink wine in the carriage," Edie said, feeling even more despondent. "He works all the time."

"Works? Works at what?" Layla had taken a small implement from her reticule and was prying at the window.

"What are you doing?"

"Fresh air is good for your skin," Layla said

over her shoulder. "The perfume of Scottish wildflowers and the deep forest. You don't want to have spots, do you? You're already all blotchy from that virginal wailing."

"I'm not a virgin anymore," Edie protested, feeling better just for having told someone. "Do you think the pain will go away?"

"No question. If it didn't, the human race would have dwindled out long ago. I've never heard of anyone having a problem that lasted more than a few weeks. And believe me, married women discuss this sort of thing for hours on end."

The window popped free and sailed away behind the coach. "I didn't even hear a crash, did you?" Layla asked.

A pungent smell of manure blew in the window. "The odor of these Scottish wildflowers is astonishing," Edie said, wrapping her pelisse around her and watching as Layla opened a tinderbox to light her cheroot.

"Ah, that's better," Layla said, a second later. "A nice glass of champagne would be marvelous, but it is before noon. One must maintain one's standards. So, darling, how terrible is it?"

Edie shuddered.

"Dear me, that *is* bad. Throw me one of those extra cushions; we might as well make ourselves comfortable."

The carriage's seats were so padded that the seat felt as soft as a bed. Edie propped herself in one corner, stretched her legs out on the seat, and crossed her ankles. It felt rather naughty to put her slippers on all that plush velvet.

Her stepmother did the same on the seat opposite. "So you're in positive agony, but it's getting better. Here's the most important question: Are you berating Gowan nightly, thereby making him understand just how lucky he is that you even allow him near your delicate lady parts?"

"No." The word dropped into the carriage with all the desolation Edie felt.

"Darling, you really must cheer up. It's hardly the end of the world, and you are not the first young couple to find yourself initially incompatible." Layla pushed herself up a bit and blew some smoke in the general direction of the broken window. "Why on earth aren't you scolding your husband for his—ahem—magnificent proportions? You might as well get a diamond or two out of all that misery."

"It was all so horribly embarrassing. I thought it would go away."

"Don't tell me he doesn't have any idea." Layla sat even further up. "Is that what you meant in your note, about my 'secret'? *That's* not what the secret is for!"

Edie sighed. She hadn't even used the secret correctly.

"It's meant to give *you* some relief, not him. If

295

he's hammering away at you and it hurts, you should be yowling like a cat on All Hallows' Eve, not befuddling him by making him think that you're enjoying it. You're doing it all wrong, Edie."

"I think he may have guessed, but is just too polite to say so."

"Men are never polite in the bedroom." Layla made a sweeping gesture that sprinkled ashes all over the upholstery. "It is you who are being too polite. So let's tot it all up. It doesn't hurt as much as it did. Are the two of you making a regular go of it?"

Edie shook her head. "Not since my courses began ten days ago."

"So what? Oh, don't answer that. You look as horrified as when you were young and I told you about how babies are made."

"You told me they came from eating suet pudding with treacle!"

"Well, I couldn't tell you the truth, could I? Even in the earliest days of my marriage, I had already grasped that your father was on the sober side. You wanted to know and I had to tell you something he wouldn't mind. Suet pudding is very fattening. I was giving you a helpful tip about adult life."

"It doesn't matter," Edie said, staring at the toes of her slippers. "I've made a mess of my marriage. I don't want to spend the rest of my life gasping out faux moans. I simply can't. I'm not even any good at it. *I* wouldn't believe myself."

"Let's go back to what you told me in the beginning." Layla tossed her cheroot out the window.

"Layla! What if you start a fire?"

"I extinguished it." Layla pointed to a dark mark on the floor. Then she peered closer. "Don't tell me His Almighty Grace has put carpets in here."

"He has."

Layla collapsed back into her corner. "So the duke goes at it so long that you're wincing."

"He's simply too big."

A short silence ensued.

"I could say something, but I won't," Layla said with a sigh. "It would be indelicate."

"When has that prevented you?"

"I'm getting older. Listen, darling, the important thing is that it's hurting less than it did at first."

"It does seem to stop hurting as he keeps going. But that's not the only problem, Layla." Edie made herself say it. "That *petit mort*? It's not happening to me, obviously. I don't think it ever will."

"Do you feel good down there?"

"Sometimes, but then it drains away as soon as I think about it."

"Believe me, I know what you're talking about," Layla said, sighing. "I remember the mindless days—or, I should say, nights—before I started thinking too much about babies. Those brains of yours are the enemy of a happy bedchamber."

"What am I going to do? I can't tell Gowan; I just can't."

"Why not?"

"He never fails at anything. *I* have to solve this problem, because the failure is mine."

"There's no failure," Layla said decisively. "Don't you dare blame yourself; it's a bad precedent in a marriage. What's missing is romance. The air of a boudoir. A bottle of champagne."

"He tried that," Edie said, tears welling up again. "He ordered supper in his bedchamber and served champagne. But there was a footman to bring the meal in. And then, just when I was starting to relax, he had the footman come back in, with another fellow as well, to remove the plates. I feel as if Bardolph is hovering in the corridor all the time. And when Gowan spent the night in my chamber, his valet marched straight into the room in the morning. *I hate it!*"

"It sounds as if you're trying to be intimate in the middle of Hyde Park," Layla offered. "Do you know, darling, I've never heard you be so passionate about anything other than music in all the years I've known you?"

"Gowan is never alone," Edie continued. "I'm never alone anymore, either. I had to threaten to dismiss everyone in his retinue if they didn't keep interrupting me while I was practicing. *While I was practicing,* Layla!"

"You simply need to get your husband alone."

"It's impossible. I was thinking the other day that his life reminds me of throwing a piece of bread into a stream and watching a whole flock of little minnows come up and start nibbling at it. People come and go around him at all hours."

"I don't think minnows flock," Layla commented.

"Who cares?" Edie demanded. "You see what I mean, don't you?"

"So you need to make changes in his household. That's not as easy as keeping footmen out of your bedchamber, but it can certainly be done. You're simply going to have to intervene."

"He takes care of every problem that arises, the moment it's presented to him," Edie said disconsolately. "He doesn't need anyone. He's perfect in every way, Layla. I could hate him."

"Except you love him instead," Layla said calmly. "Do you mind if I smoke another?"

"Yes, I *do* mind!" Edie said.

Layla reached for her cheroots.

Edie sat up. "I mean it! I hate those things. I hate the way they make my clothes smell after I've been around you. I hate the way they make *you* smell. I hate the way they make your breath smell."

Layla's mouth fell open.

Edie had the impulse to say something to smooth it over, but she did not give in. "I shan't apologize."

"Very well," her stepmother said cautiously. "Is there anything else you'd like to tell me?"

"No." Then she added, "Not that I can think of right now."

"My *breath?*" Layla frowned at the box of cheroots she was holding. "I don't like that."

"You shouldn't," Edie snapped.

"Right." The box flew through the window. They heard a faint thump as it hit the road.

"Thank goodness the second coach is a distance behind us," Edie said. "You could have brained one of the horses."

"If I were going to brain anyone, I'd brain that Bardolph," Layla said, reclining again. "I don't like the way he looked at me, as if I were some sort of aging hag come to steal the virtue of the young prince."

"Wait until you see what he thinks of me. Are you really going to quit, Layla? Just like that?"

"I began smoking in order to irritate your father. Why keep it up, now we're no longer living under the same roof? But I don't want to talk about my miserable marriage. You need to teach your husband to be romantic."

"I suppose I could ask him to give me flowers," Edie said dubiously. "Is that what you mean?"

"Picture His Dukeness on one knee, handing you a bundle of violets tied with ribbons. How do you feel?"

"A little sick. Violets are so funereal."

"Very fussy," Layla said reprovingly. "If your father handed me a bunch of daisies he'd plucked off a coffin, I'd be thrilled."

"Have you written to him?"

"I wrote and said I would be paying you a visit. He didn't reply, which is unsurprising, because he didn't reply to my first two letters, either."

Edie sighed.

"So we've decided that you need to reform the duke's household," Layla continued, "and teach him how to protect your privacy. What else? Is he a bungler in bed?"

Edie thought about it. "I don't think so."

"Have you told him what you have particularly liked?"

She shook her head.

"You have to take some responsibility in that respect," Layla advised. "Men like a road map. No: men *need* a road map. My mother told me that years ago, and she was absolutely right."

Edie was trying to imagine herself giving Gowan directions, when Layla sat up jerkily. "Are we going to be sitting in this carriage all day long? We've been here two hours at least." She reached up and thumped on the ceiling.

A slat slid open. "Yes, Your Grace?"

301

"It's Lady Gilchrist!" Layla shrieked. "Stop this carriage. I need to stretch my legs."

"We're very close to His Grace's borders," the coachman hollered back. The horses didn't slow.

"'His Grace's borders'?" Layla repeated, throwing herself down on the seat again. "Have you noticed that they act as if your husband is a monarch?"

"Because he *is* a monarch to them, Layla. They practically kiss his toes every time he leaves a room."

"I wouldn't mind if people kissed my toes. You know, I might be a wee bit irritable in the next day or so," Layla said, drumming her fingers against her seat. "Cheroots give me a sense of calm that seems to have gone missing at the moment."

"You can howl all you wish, as long as you give them up," Edie told her.

Layla sighed. "Right. Well, darling, what we're going to do is set the scene for an evening of romantic bliss. Champagne, flowers, poetry."

"Poetry?"

"I'll instruct your husband myself. You know I've seen every romantic play performed in the West End in the last three years. I'm an expert."

"You *cannot* tell Gowan what we've discussed!" Edie ordered.

"I would never do that," Layla said, looking injured. "Trust me. I'm as wily as a fox."

At that moment the carriage rocked around a turn. Edie looked out the window and gasped.

Before them lay a fairy-tale castle. It was pale yellow stone, the exact color of October beer, its battlements sharp-edged against a sky so pale that it looked like skim milk.

"God, I hope your husband had bathrooms put in," Layla said, sliding across the seat so that she could look out her window. "Castles have garderobes; did you know that? I gather they're nothing more than holes that empty straight into the moat."

"No moat," Edie said. "I'm looking at the flag."

"Good Lord," Layla said, in a shocked voice. "Just look at the size of that dragon's sword. Either it's a mighty boastful flag or you really do have something to complain about."

Edie squinted at the sword the dragon held. "It's a trifle out of proportion."

"No wonder the man is so autocratic. Every time he comes home he likely forgets he's a mere mortal. Do you suppose trumpets will sound when you step from the carriage?"

"I hope not."

"That's what happens in threepenny plays when the princess marries a swineherd who turns out to be a king," Layla said. "Trumpets, and lots of them. Who would have known you'd marry someone like this? I can't wait to see you drinking pearls dissolved in wine and generally carrying on like Cleopatra. Given the size of that castle, Gowan should be giving you a diamond for every squeak of pain you suffer."

"Layla!"

Twenty-seven

Edie climbed down from the carriage, clutching the doll she'd bought for Susannah, to find Gowan and company waiting in front of the castle.

"I feel as if we've traveled through time to a medieval fiefdom," Layla said, stepping onto the ground next to her. "Weren't those the days when a returning duke was met by servants running in from the fields and the like?"

Edie was watching people stream out from the portcullis. "I suppose."

Gowan moved to her other side, his expression as grave as ever. He had helped Edie from the carriage, but he hadn't said much. Now he stood silently with his hands clasped behind his back. She had the feeling he was angry at her, but she wasn't sure why. When he asked about her monthly courses, she'd told him the truth. If he had asked, she would have allowed him into her bed.

But he hadn't asked.

At that moment, all the assembled servants bobbed up and down at the same time. Gowan lifted his hand.

They were so silent that Edie could hear a bird singing over the wall.

"I present to you the Duchess of Kinross," Gowan said. His voice was quiet, but utterly commanding. "She is your mistress. Respect her as you respect me, obey her as you obey me, and love her as I bid you."

They all bobbed more curtsies and bows.

"Thank you," Edie called, looking from person to person with a hopeless sense that she would never come to know all the people who lived in her own house. What's more, if she couldn't talk Gowan out of his habit of allowing his retainers carte blanche in his bedchamber, in the breakfast room, and in the dining room, she'd have all these strangers wheeling through her life on a daily basis.

Bardolph stepped forward. "On behalf of your clansmen, Your Grace, we welcome you to Castle Craigievar."

"Ah," Edie said, fascinated to see Bardolph's lumpy knees poking out from beneath a kilt. "I am grateful for your kindness."

"I shall now introduce you to those who work here. The housekeeper, Mrs. Grisle." Mrs. Grisle was a very tall woman, with teeth so large they seemed to rattle in her mouth when she spoke. She didn't look like the sort of person who needed constant supervision, but Edie reserved judgment.

"You have already met Mr. Rillings, Mr. Bindle,

and the chef, Monsieur Morney," Bardolph continued.

"Good afternoon," Edie said.

"The kitchen workers," Bardolph announced. A group of some twenty stepped forward.

There was a short lull as the housekeeper marshaled a group of maids in preparation for presenting them en masse. Edie glanced at Gowan and had to restrain herself from shivering. There was an odd distance between them, but at the same time . . .

No woman could look at Gowan and not think about kissing him. He had such animal magnetism that his very walk promised a woman that he could pleasure her for hours.

"Edie, where's your new daughter?" Layla asked. "Your father is not going to be happy if she turns out to have been a figment of the duke's imagination. And neither will I, though I suppose I could eat the gingerbread I bought her myself."

"Where is Susannah?" Edie asked, turning to Gowan.

Gowan lifted a finger. Bardolph snapped to attention.

"My sister."

There was a bustle of activity toward the rear of the crowd, and another group was ushered forward. "Miss Pettigrew, the nanny," Bardolph announced. "Alice, Joan, and Maisie, the nursery maids. Miss Susannah."

Miss Pettigrew was quite large and swathed from neck to slippers in immaculate starched linen. She was flanked by three nursery maids, similarly attired. And to the side, arms folded over her narrow chest, was a child, dressed entirely in black, who looked like a very small crow next to four looming white storks.

Bardolph beckoned. "Miss Susannah, you may greet the duke and duchess." There was a hint of asperity in his voice.

Lady Susannah bobbed in a knee flex that only remotely resembled a curtsy. She favored Gowan with a scowl that he seemed to find unsurprising.

"Susannah, this is my new wife, the Duchess of Kinross," he said.

The child shifted her scowl to Edie. Her red hair stood out around her head like a flame in contrast to her attire. It suddenly came to Edie that although Susannah wore black from her slippers to her hair ribbon, Gowan was not wearing mourning for his mother. Indeed, she had never seen him in black.

"How do you do," Edie offered.

Gowan folded his arms over his chest. "Curtsy to the new duchess, if you please."

Susannah bobbed her knees again.

"She looks just like you!" Edie exclaimed.

"No, I don't!" Susannah retorted, speaking for the first time. It was astonishing how such a very small person could look down her nose. A family trait, one had to suppose.

Edie threw a slightly panicked look at Layla, who whispered, "Stoop down so she doesn't have to look up at you."

Edie crouched down, balancing on her toes, and held out the doll she'd brought all the way from London. "I brought you a present."

For a moment they both looked at the doll. She was very stylish lady, with painted yellow hair and a frock trimmed with real lace. Susannah did not reach out for the doll. Instead she looked away, to Gowan. "Is she my sister?" she demanded, pointing to Edie.

"She's your new *mother*," Gowan stated. "And ladies never point."

Susannah's chin firmed. "I wanted a sister. I told you. I said I wanted a sister. I don't need a mother." Her voice rose higher with each declaration. "I told you to bring me a sister smaller than I am."

"And I informed you that I could not bring you a sister." Gowan was clearly in danger of losing his usual imperturbability.

"I don't need a mother because I've already had one of those," the girl said, turning back to Edie, who was frozen in place. She came a step closer, so close that Edie could see a faint pattern of freckles on her nose.

"I'm sorry," Edie said awkwardly. "I certainly don't wish to replace your mother."

Susannah's eyes darkened. "No one can replace my mother because she's *dead*. She's gone. I don't like you very much. And that doll is ugly." She reached out and gave it a push.

Edie was still balanced precariously on her toes, and Susanna's shove sent her tumbling backward, landing on her bottom in the gravel. Edie was so startled that she didn't move, even though her legs were inelegantly splayed before her.

A murmur arose from the surrounding servants. They likely hadn't witnessed such an interesting family drama since the death of the former duke. Not to mention a lady's ankles, albeit ankles clad in lacy white stockings.

"Blast," Layla muttered.

"Susannah!" Gowan bellowed. He bent down and helped Edie to her feet.

At the same moment, Miss Pettigrew stepped forward and grabbed the little girl by the elbow with one hand, giving her a hard whack on the bottom with the other. "You will apologize this moment," she hissed. The nanny had red patches in her cheeks, and she was so furious that her eyes looked like black currants.

"It was just an accident," Edie put in, not liking the way that Susannah's body had jolted forward when she was spanked.

"No, it wasn't!" Susannah retorted, her voice as strong as ever. "I don't need a mother, and I told him. I don't like you. So you can just go back

309

where you came from. And take that ugly doll with you." She tried to pull free of her nanny but couldn't manage it.

Gowan stepped forward, his eyes kindling.

Edie quickly stooped down before the small girl. "I expect you are very sorry for hurting my feelings, aren't you?"

"No."

But something about Edie's gaze must have sunk in. "I'm sorry," Susannah said sullenly.

"If you don't wish for this doll, I'm sure that someone here has a little girl at home who would love her." Edie held out the doll again.

Susannah's eyes went from the doll's golden head to Edie's. "I don't want it," she said, her tone hard. "You can throw it away."

Edie straightened and handed the doll, rather blindly, to Bardolph. She felt as if she'd been kicked in the stomach.

"Edie, would you introduce me to Miss Susannah, please?" Layla asked gently.

"Susannah, this is my very dear stepmother, Lady Gilchrist." Edie put a steel undertone in her voice. "Please make your curtsy."

Susannah bobbed a curtsy.

Layla knelt down with no regard for her skirts. "Hello, Susannah."

Edie was battling a sharp sense of utter failure. She looked down, trying to see Layla's tip-tilted, smiling eyes and sweet mouth through a little girl's eyes. Sure enough, Susannah's shoulders softened a bit. "Hello."

"I've brought you a present as well, though it's not as nice as that beautiful doll."

A cautious light shone in Susannah's eye. "Really?"

Layla nodded. "It's something I loved when I was your age."

Susannah stepped closer, enough so that Layla could take her hand. "What is it?"

"A gingerbread princess. Have you ever eaten gingerbread?"

"No. Where is it?"

"She's in the carriage," Layla said, standing up. "Shall we find her?"

Miss Pettigrew moved forward. "I regret to say that it is time for Miss Susannah's French lesson. Because she was extremely misbehaved this morning—which I am sorry to tell you is not uncharacteristic of her—she will have a double lesson, followed by an hour practicing deportment, after which she will lie on a board for an hour. Her posture is deplorable."

Susannah slanted her nanny a look that was far too worldly for her age.

"Susannah!" Gowan thundered.

That scowl must also be a family trait, like the ability to look down one's nose. And yet Edie thought she could see a heartbreaking vulnerability behind Susannah's frown.

Layla said, very quietly, "Edie."

Edie knew exactly what Layla wished to convey with that one word: to wit, that Miss Pettigrew wasn't a suitable person for the nursery. If Edie didn't dismiss her, Layla probably would, despite having no authority. Edie squared her shoulders. She had to take responsibility; this was her household now.

"You must be polite to your nanny," Gowan was saying. "And to the duchess."

Susannah bobbed up and down in her version of a curtsy, looking like a cork thrown into the water. "I apologize, Miss Pettigrew." At the age of five, she had mastered a perfectly expressionless tone.

Miss Pettigrew lowered her chin in a gesture that bore no resemblance to a nod, and turned back to Edie. "As you can see, Your Grace, the child has been sorely spoiled. She has no languages, no music, and no understanding of polite comportment of any kind whatsoever."

Edie didn't think that Susannah looked spoiled. She looked like a person who had learned very young that it was better to be scornful than to cry. Frankly, Edie agreed with her.

"I myself speak no French," she told Miss Pettigrew.

The nanny's thin lips tightened. "As the daughter of a duchess, Miss Susannah ought to be fluent in at least three languages. Given her questionable paternity, her behavior must be exemplary. As you can see, much work remains to be done."

After that speech, Edie needed no further prompting from Layla. She looked the woman squarely in the eye and said, "Miss Pettigrew, I thank you for your service to the family, but I am terminating your employment, effective immediately. Bardolph, make all due arrangements. Miss Pettigrew shall have a generous severance and transportation to wherever she wishes."

Shockingly, the nanny opened her mouth as if she might argue, so Edie fixed her with a look. "As I said," she repeated, "a generous severance. But there will be no letter of recommendation."

Bardolph seemed rather stunned, but snapped to attention and drew Miss Pettigrew to the side.

Susannah's eyes widened, though she didn't move or say a word.

"Now then, shall we find that gingerbread?" Layla dropped her reticule on the ground, bent down, and scooped up the little girl. Susannah's legs looked birdlike against Layla's curves.

There was one long moment when Layla and Susannah stared at each other, and then the little girl smiled. Some of her teeth appeared to be missing, which was oddly adorable. Layla turned to Edie and said, "Susannah and I will find the gingerbread in the carriage and return shortly." She walked away, holding Susannah as if she were very precious.

Edie took a deep breath and picked up Layla's reticule.

"I see why you were concerned," Gowan said, his voice offering no judgment. "Clearly, you are not accustomed to children, but Lady Gilchrist is. Perhaps she will offer a solution to the question of Susannah."

Edie stared at him. Had he just offered to give away his sister?

"Are Lord and Lady Gilchrist permanently estranged?" he asked.

"I certainly hope not."

"Perhaps we can persuade Lady Gilchrist to live here in the interim." That was Gowan. When a solution to a problem presented itself, he moved swiftly to carry it out.

Edie gave herself a mental shake and turned to the nursemaids. "Do we truly need all three of you for one child?"

"The best nurseries have at least three nurse-maids and a nanny, if not a governess as well," Bardolph put in.

Edie looked at him, and he fell back a step. "Which of you does Susannah like best?" she asked the maids.

After some hesitance, a chubby-cheeked girl with a sweet mouth stepped forward and said, anxiously, "My name is Alice. But I don't speak a word of French, Your Grace. Nor any other language except the King's English."

"You shall be the head nursery maid for the time being," Edie said. "Susannah is still in blacks, so languages can wait. The more important thing is to find a music instructor. The younger she is when she begins, the more proficient she will become." It was the one thing she felt confident about. She herself had picked up a cello around Susannah's age.

Gowan seemed faintly amused. "Find a musician who can tutor the child," he said to Bardolph.

The nursemaids curtsied and departed. Bardolph ushered forward a group of women who wore dark crimson gowns and snowy white aprons. "The downstairs maids."

"Good morning," Edie said.

Bardolph waved forward another group. "The dairy maids."

"Good morning."

The second-floor maids were followed by the scullery maids, who were followed by some other groups, and then by the bootblacks. The very last cluster were the swineherds, of whom there were a surprising number.

"I'm very happy to meet all of you," Edie said when the final group had been introduced. "I hope that in time I shall learn all your names." There was a round of smiles at that.

"Good morning," Gowan called, followed by a tidal wave of curtsies and bows, and then it was

315

over. "There are others," he told her. "The bailiffs and the stewards, the keeper of the tower, and so on. But they can wait."

They walked across the courtyard toward a huge open pair of richly carved wooden doors, as Edie absorbed the idea that there were still more people to meet. "The 'keeper of the tower'? Which tower? I saw several as we approached in the carriage."

"I shall give you a tour of the grounds, when I have the time. The towers in the castle fall under the purview of the groundskeeper, who is under Bardolph, of course. The tower to which I refer is an unattached structure built in the thirteenth century, down in the meadow by the Glaschorrie River."

"It sounds very romantic."

"No," he said uncompromisingly, "it is not. It presents constant trouble, as fools cannot resist climbing it. One boy fell two years ago and cracked his head so badly he nearly died. After that, I appointed the keeper to make certain no one approaches it."

The entry hall was large enough to roast four or five suckling pigs and still have room for a maypole. The acoustics, Edie noted automatically, would be terrible, given the fact that the ceiling disappeared into the gloom far above their heads.

Bardolph immediately caught Gowan's attention and bore him off to the side of the hall. Layla had emerged from the carriage and followed them into the entry hall with Susannah trotting along beside her, so Edie took the opportunity to ask the little girl, "Do you know where your brother's bedchamber is?"

"No," Susannah answered, unsurprisingly. "You'd have to ask her." She nodded toward the housekeeper, Mrs. Grisle, who had been drawn into the conversation with Bardolph and Gowan.

"Let's try to find it ourselves." Edie started up the great stone staircase, followed by Susannah and Layla. At the top, she began pushing open doors. "Do you like living here?" she asked Susannah.

"It's lonely. My mother is dead." She put a bit of vibrato into her voice.

"So is mine," Edie said.

"But you are old."

"My mother died when I was only two. Younger than you are."

"Oh." Susannah digested that for a while. "Did your mother fall into a loch and drown?"

"No, she did not. She took a chill and caught pneumonia."

"Were you sad?"

"I don't remember, but I've been sad about it since. I would have liked to have a mother."

"They're not so important," Susannah told her.

Edie tried not to take that personally.

"I think mothers are very important," Layla put in.

The next door led to a large bedchamber, but it had no connecting doors leading to a bathroom or dressing room.

"This appears to be a guest room," Layla said. "Shall I stay here, Edie?" It was a bilious room, completely done up in mustard yellow, from the drapes to the rugs to the bed hangings.

Before Edie could answer, Susannah said, "You can sleep in the nursery, if you want. Miss Pettigrew had a bed there but now she's gone. The room is small, though."

Edie instinctively recoiled at the idea, but she caught herself. Layla never saw a baby on the street without stopping to coo. She paid calls merely to catch sight of children who might be paraded through the morning room. Of course, she already adored Susannah, and it seemed Susannah adored her.

"I like small rooms," Layla said. "I think they're cozy, don't you?"

Layla wasn't one to travel light and had brought three trunks full of clothing with her. *Cozy* would not accurately describe Edie's understanding of her preferences.

The duke's bedchamber turned out to be just down the hallway. Here the rugs, drapes, and bed hangings were brown.

"I like the nursery better." Gowan's little sister planted herself in the middle of the room with her arms crossed over her narrow chest. "This is not a good room," she stated. "This is a bad room, and maybe someone died in here."

"There are no ghosts in my castle," Edie said, walking over to an interior door, which led to a large chamber, with a built-in bath and an adjoining water closet.

"There are three ghosts in the tower," Susannah said. And then: "The bath is large enough to swim in." She sounded impressed for the first time.

"How is the bath in the nursery?" Layla asked.

"There isn't one. I have a tin tub."

"Then you shall bathe here tonight," Layla promised.

The far door, on the other side of the bathing chamber, led to the duchess's room. It was blue. All of it: rugs, hangings, curtains. Just as she noticed that the ceiling was also blue, Gowan strode in from the corridor.

"This room looks as if someone vomited the sky," Layla said.

Susannah burst into hoots of laughter until Gowan gave her a quelling look.

"It's more efficient for the staff to carry out their duties if each room is known by its given color."

Edie was fascinated by the uniformity of the furnishings. Even the fire screen was blue. "I gather blue was a particular favorite of your mother?"

"I have no idea what colors my mother preferred," Gowan said, his face unreadable. "The room was refurbished a year ago."

"And you directed the work? I finally found something you're not good at," Edie exclaimed, feeling rather relieved.

He aimed the family scowl in her direction.

"Could I see the gingerbread princess now?" Susannah said. She was jumping from foot to foot.

Layla drew a cookie larger than her hand from a gaily colored cambric bag. "We'll save the princess for after supper. This is a gingerbread man, though it would be more accurate to call him a gingerbread *gentle*man, because he has gold buttons and a particularly elegant hat."

Susannah took the treat carefully. "He smells good. What do I do with him?"

"Is he your very first gingerbread man?"

She nodded.

"You eat him."

"Eat his *head?*"

"I always start with the feet," Edie suggested.

Susannah kept her eyes fixed on Layla. "But if I eat him, he'll be dead."

"No, he'll be in your tummy," Layla said. "There's a difference."

"I think I'd better eat his head first," Susannah said, just when the silence grew a second too long. "That way he won't know what's happening to him."

"That's a very kind thought," Layla approved.

Susannah turned and climbed up on the bed. "This room is not pretty," she said, nibbling on her gingerbread. "But the bed is nice. Mine smells like straw, but yours is soft."

"It's probably a feather bed," Edie said. Gowan cleared his throat and Edie was suddenly, vividly aware of him—not to mention the proximity of the feather bed.

Layla glanced at them, strolled over, and said, "You promised to show me the nursery, Susannah love," and held out her hand.

Susannah climbed down and they walked out without a backward glance.

Twenty-eight

Gowan had experienced emotions like this before. They were as profound as an atmospheric effect, as if sea pressure were bubbling up his legs. He had felt it when he was a boy, when his father was drunk . . . but rarely as a man.

But he felt it now.

The moment Susannah pranced out of the room with her gingerbread, holding Layla's hand, Edie threw him a nervous glance, muttered something about the housekeeper, and fled. Clearly, she didn't want to be alone in a bedchamber with him.

This emotion was a blinding, inarticulate *thing* that reminded him of days when his father would topple from his stool by the fire and sprawl across the floor, so filled with whisky that he sloshed as he rolled.

Every time Gowan looked at Edie, he felt a rush of possessiveness that felt as fundamental to his nature as being a Scot. But that emotion didn't belong in the civilized world.

He had married Edie. He had put his ring on her finger. He had bedded her. And yet there was some part of her that eluded him. He felt it, more and more clearly, and it was driving him mad. He had wanted her the moment he saw her, so he'd arranged to marry her. And yet he didn't have her. The truth of it made an animal howl threaten to break loose in his chest.

Perhaps it was the music. He loved the fact that his wife's body was shaped like her instrument. But she played the cello, not his body. She hardly touched him in bed. Of course . . . what did he expect? He knew aristocratic women weren't as lusty as barmaids.

Gowan had been eight years old when his father had told him the facts about what happened between men and women, grabbing him by the wrist and pulling him close. His reeking breath had struck Gowan's nose like a blow.

"Ladies aren't worth the straw they lie on," he had said, his eyes lit with strange glee. "They lie as flat as a Shrove Tuesday pancake. Go get a lusty barmaid, my boy. Go down to the Horse and Poplar. Annie is the one to teach you what's what. She taught me. And she'll take you on as well."

He must have shown revulsion, because his

father had given him a hard shove, sending him across the floor and into the wall.

"Think you're too good for Annie, do you? You'd be lucky to have a sprightly lass like her. She'll do anything, she will. Can twist like a cat and eat you like—"

So that's why this particular vile memory had come back. The barmaid would eat him—or so his father promised—like a gingerbread man.

The lurch of nausea in his stomach was like an old and unwelcome familiar. He hated whisky. He hated gingerbread.

Damn it.

Bardolph opened the door and walked in. "Your Grace, I bring—"

"Do not enter without first knocking," he said harshly. "This is Her Grace's bedchamber."

Bardolph's face was the pale yellow of a raw potato, his eyes a darker brown. Like the bruise on an old potato. "Her Grace is speaking to Mrs. Grisle," his factor replied, with the injured air of a man used to knowing precisely what was happening in every room of the castle at any given moment. "I wanted to consult with you about arrangements for Lady Gilchrist's lodging."

In a house with this many servants, there were no secrets. Gowan had known when his father got the second housemaid with child, and he'd known when the poor lass lost the child, the same as he'd known when his own mother had insisted on riding after the hounds while carrying a child, and had lost it.

She had started drinking to excess after that, and that was no secret, either.

"Not the yellow chamber," Gowan stated. He'd be damned if he'd have his stepmother-in-law next door, hearing . . . whatever there was to hear. He walked out the door and started toward his study, Bardolph on his heels. "Put her in the room closest to the nursery."

"The nursery? The nursery is on the third floor. Your Grace offers the lady an insult."

"You should be asking my wife these questions, not me," Gowan snapped. At that very moment he knew that it would be madness to go to Edie's bed after the meal. If he snarled at her, she would recede even further.

"As you wish, Your Grace. I have located a musician."

"What?"

"Your Grace asked me to find someone who could teach music to the child. Miss Susannah's French tutor, François Védrines, is a relative of the late Comte de Genlis, and professes to be a violinist. When we hired him, he was traveling through Scotland collecting tinker's ballads."

"Why are you telling me this?" Gowan asked, walking into his study and turning about.

"You wish to hear details of all significant appointments in the household," Bardolph said, his mouth tightening into a pucker that looked like a potato's eye.

"Inform Her Grace of his credentials," Gowan said. Then he remembered that Edie would wish to practice rather than listen to Bardolph. "Never mind, just get the man here as soon as possible."

"He's already here," Bardolph said, "in the capacity of Miss Susannah's tutor."

After luncheon Gowan retreated back to his study and was working well, having managed to push Edie from his mind, when she poked her face around the door. Her hair was curling around her face and the sun coming in the windows lit a strand as brilliantly as gleaming gold. "There you are!" she cried. "I've been touring the castle with Mrs. Grisle. Layla, Susannah, and I are about to walk down and see the river. Will you join us?"

The moment he saw her, his body sprang to attention. "Of course," he said, standing and pulling his coat down in front.

"Would you mind if Susannah left off her blacks after today?" Edie asked as they made their way through the castle's maze of rooms, all connected to each other rather than to a corridor.

"Not at all."

"I see that you yourself are not observing that custom."

Gowan glanced at Edie and then looked away, shocked by his reaction to a mere glimpse of her rosy lips. "I made a decision not to wear mourning for my mother," he said, pulling himself together.

"I suggest that we view Susannah's three months of mourning garments as sufficient."

He nodded, not trusting himself to speak. Even thinking about his mother made the inarticulate feelings of anger and possession in him gather force. The last thing he needed was to crack apart. Somehow he had to make Edie understand that the mere mention of the late duchess felt as if a torch had fallen on kindling.

They made their way to the entry hall to find Layla standing in the middle of the cavernous space, holding Susannah's wrists tightly and spinning as she swung his sister around and around. Susannah's legs were parallel to the ground, her skirts billowing. And her red hair was flying around her shoulders in a tangled cloud.

Needless to say, she was shrieking with pure joy. Layla was laughing, too, and so were the six footmen ranged along the walls, though their mouths snapped shut when they saw Gowan.

It appeared that Layla had managed a miracle, and in no time at all: she'd won over his half sister. As Layla brought her gently back to the floor, he saw that Susannah's peaked little face, ordinarily pallid, was flushed with color and her eyes were radiant. It made him feel guilty.

Susannah had not noticed their arrival; she was hanging on Layla's hand and demanding to be swung again. Gowan strode forward. "I must be back at work shortly; we shouldn't delay." Two footmen sprang to attention, pulling open the great doors.

"What do you know about the tower?" Edie asked as they walked through the courtyard toward the open portcullis in the wall. Her voice was utterly calm; she hadn't responded to his irritability at all. He didn't know what to make of that.

"It's a freestanding tower, much older than the castle we live in," he said.

Susannah ran past them, her thin legs scissoring like a black-legged sandpiper, if such a creature existed. I should have visited the nursery more often, Gowan told himself. I should have put it on my list, made it a priority.

They took the long, gently sloping path that led down and around the side of the hill on which the castle stood. "The tower is likely all that remains of a castle that stood there in the thirteenth century. If so, it would have been the castle keep." They rounded the hill. "Over the years it's gained a reputation for being unclimbable among some of the more foolish local people."

"And Susannah says there are ghosts?" Layla prompted.

Gowan snorted. "Bollocks. Three fools climbed the tower in order to impress their ladies, only to fall to their deaths. I fail to see why their failures should cause them to recur as apparitions. Needless to say, I've never seen any ghosts."

Below them flowed the Glaschorrie, placidly making its way through the fertile land of the Kinross estate and then out to the Atlantic, far in the distance.

"It's rare to have a plain of this sort in Scotland, isn't it?" Edie asked, looking over the fields of wheat.

"It is. That's probably exactly why an ancestor built a castle, or at least a tower, here on the river. He wanted to protect what was his."

"It must have a lovely view."

"He was a fool," Gowan said with a shrug, "because the plain floods every spring and often in between. The Glaschorrie becomes a raging torrent heading downhill all way from here to the sea."

"Yet the tower has survived."

He nodded. "Flood and fire both."

They had walked far enough that they entered the orchards that lay around the base of the tower. Layla and Susannah now trailed them, walking hand in hand and pausing now and then to look at a butterfly or an interesting stone in the path.

"Aren't these trees injured when the river overflows?"

Gowan reached out and pinched a leaf from an apple tree. "They seem to manage. Once, when I was young, I remember looking down from the castle and seeing only the smallest branches above the water. A day later all that water was gone, drained off to the ocean."

"It sounds ferocious."

"We've lost men to this river, though I've put in place evacuation orders. Last year we lost only three goats, and that was due to a fool of a tenant who thought it would be enough to put the animals on the second floor of his house."

"It wasn't?"

Gowan shook his head. "The flood took the house, and the goats with it. The land here is so flat that when the Glaschorrie rages, she often cuts a new route for herself. What is safe one year is no longer safe the next."

Edie walked beside him silently; he couldn't tell what she was thinking. They reached the broad base of the tower, into which was set a small but very stout oaken door, and Gowan pulled the great iron key from his coat pocket. After he'd set workers swarming over it for months, the stonework and mortar looked as good as new.

When he opened the door, they were met by the sultry sweet odor of ripe apples. Up above were the attics, where the apple harvest was stored every autumn, allowing his household to enjoy apples all year round.

Gowan pushed the door all the way open, stooped a bit in order to pass under the lintel, and entered the small dark room at the tower's base. He took a quick look around, making certain all was well before stepping back so Edie could enter. Susannah slipped past and began trotting up the narrow uneven stairs, her black skirts disappearing around the corner.

"I am not fond of small spaces," Layla said, hovering on the threshold.

"The upper floors are far more commodious," he told her.

Layla started to climb the stone steps but Gowan caught Edie's arm, holding her until her stepmother turned the corner.

He looked down into her face, and the yawning chasm in his chest cracked open a little wider. Edie was so beautiful. She was everything he'd thought on the very first night he met her—an ethereal, glowing creature who danced to music only she could hear—but she was also a musician, a prodigy, a woman whose musical ability would have had the world at her feet, had she been born a man.

Being Edie, she didn't seem to care. She lived for her music . . . and he wanted her to live for him.

"You're mine," he growled, the words coming out with all the force of jealousy and possession that he felt.

Her eyes widened and then she did an unexpected thing. She put her arms around his neck. She hadn't touched him voluntarily since the first days of their marriage.

And now . . .

She rose up on her toes and brushed her mouth across his. "Then you are mine, as well," she breathed, a smile dancing on her lips.

He was at her feet and had been since the moment he saw her. She knew it; hell, the whole world knew it, at least those people who had attended Chatteris's wedding. Still, there was a trace of uncertainty in her eyes. So Gowan kissed his wife, pouring everything into that kiss: his love, his obsession, his dominance, his uncertainty, his ruthlessness, his . . .

Everything.

Edie murmured something unintelligible and tightened her arms around his neck. Her tongue met his and set his heart pounding at a hectic pace in his chest. Her hair fell from its bun and slid through his fingers as if it was water from the river outside. For a moment he was perfectly happy, as if merely by holding stands of her hair he could keep her close.

Then Edie pulled away. "Oh no!" Her hands flew up a second too late; loops of hair began tumbling down below her shoulders.

"I love your hair," he said, satisfied with life for the first time all day. "Even in this dark room, it shines like moonlight."

"You've pulled it down again," she said,

wrinkling her nose at him. "I had to sit still for nearly forty-five minutes this morning, and I am not patient when it comes to my toilette."

"I'm sorry," Gowan murmured. He captured her mouth again . . . but then he realized dimly that he was trying to impress his seal upon her by kissing her, as if that would make the difference.

It wouldn't, and he pulled back, his soul filled with disappointment. She made a little sound of protest. He'd kissed her lips until they were cherry red and swollen. Just two weeks ago, he would have caught fire at that sight, imagining her lips caressing his body. But now he couldn't quite imagine her on her knees before him.

It wouldn't happen. She wasn't present enough for that sort of love play. She wasn't . . .

He was missing her, even though she stood right in front of him, though he wouldn't be caught dead voicing such a half-assed idea. That ache in his chest? It was idiocy.

"I must talk with you," he said abruptly.

Edie swallowed, and his heart sank. Some small part of him had hoped that it was all in his head, and that in reality she was perfectly happy with him.

But that tiny convulsive movement in her throat told its own story.

"We'll have a private dinner in my bed-chamber," he said, rapidly turning over the possibilities. "I'll banish all the footmen."

Her eyes clouded. "We can't, not on Layla's first night here. Bardolph mentioned that he believes Susannah's French tutor would be able to teach her music, and he eats with us as well."

"Tomorrow evening, then." He couldn't stay with her now, or he'd make a worse fool of himself by falling on his knees and begging her to love him. "I must return to work. I am late for an appointment."

Far above them they could hear little squeals of laughter as Edie and Layla explored.

Edie nodded. Her eyes were the green of the wild heart of a Scottish forest. He gave her the key, turned, and walked away.

In that moment, he hated the fact that men waited in his study. He wanted to scoop up his wife and carry her somewhere, to a place where there wasn't a little sister to make him feel guilty.

He wished he could swing his wife into his arms, set out on the path to the river, and find some curve in the riverbank where they couldn't be seen. He was rock hard and so lustful that he felt as if desire leaked out of him like mist.

But his instincts had never led him astray. It was best to wait for the morrow. If there was anything Gowan hated, it was going into battle half-cocked.

That was such a bad joke that he didn't even bother to grin.

Twenty-nine

Edie plodded up the tower steps. Being with Gowan—being married to Gowan—was like finding herself mated to a tornado. A centrifugal force spun her about until she couldn't think, and she just wanted to cling to him and gaze into his midnight eyes.

And then she would wake up and realize that she was merely another appointment in his life. Not important enough to justify any of his time, it seemed, other than at dinner. She felt a surge of anger, followed hard on by a moment of clarity: neither one of them was willing to give up their time. She guarded her practice hours with as much intentness as he did his working hours.

She continued up the stairs, thinking about that. The first level was completely empty, but just as Gowan had promised, much less dim. The tower had charming mullioned windows, with little diamond panes. She paused for a moment to look out over the river below.

It was hard to imagine the Glaschorrie in full flood; at the moment its lazy current was barely perceptible. Small bubbles rose to the surface, but otherwise it was as flat as a dinner plate.

She heard another burst of laughter and went back to the narrow, uneven steps and kept climbing. She reached another room, large enough for four people at the most, that might have once served as a dining room. Its table was blackened oak but there were no chairs. She looked at its battered surface for a moment and then checked the legs: sure enough, there were water stains.

She climbed higher still and emerged in a bedchamber, identifiable by a wooden bed frame off to the side. Layla was sitting in a rocking chair before the unlit fireplace, pushing off with one toe to keep the chair in constant motion.

Susannah was in her lap. She was curled up, facing away, so that she couldn't see Edie. Layla put the index finger of her free hand to her lips, and Edie sank onto a stool at the side of the room. Her legs were tired after that climb.

"Probably lots of people have died in the castle," Susannah was saying sleepily. "Cats, too. Lots of cats. The whole courtyard is probably full of graves, and we walk over them all the time."

"I think," Layla said, quite seriously, "that people and cats turn back to the earth after a while. So what you walk over is just earth, Susannah."

Susannah had her thumb in her mouth so Edie couldn't understand what she said next.

But Layla said, "I don't think so. Their souls went up to heaven."

Then there was silence, but for the creaking of old wood rockers against the stone floor.

After a while, Layla raised her head and said, quite calmly, "She's mine, Edie."

"I can see that," Edie said, feeling a little tug at the heart. "She's had a hard time of it, hasn't she?"

"Not particularly. She was warm and fed, and I think the maids were quite nice to her. She's dramatic because that's her personality." Layla smiled faintly. "I know all about that."

With her penchant for drama, Layla was exactly the right person to bring up Susannah. Of course she was.

"I wish your father were here," she added. "He will love Susannah."

Edie wasn't so sure. Her father turned from merely stiff to downright rigid when it came to improprieties. How would he feel about a child who may or may not be illegitimate, who didn't seem to have a baptism record?

Layla guessed her thought. "You're wrong, Edie. He would love her—will love her—because she's bold and fearless, quite like you."

"I am not fearless."

"Most English ladies would have been terrified to marry a stranger and head off to the wilds of Scotland. And your duke is no milksop. Yet you are not in the least afraid of the marriage, or of Gowan, are you?"

"I probably should have been. I was thinking earlier that I feel as if I've married a tornado."

"But you're not afraid of him, are you?" Layla looked at her quite sharply.

"How could I be afraid of him after growing up with Father? Father pretends that everything he sees is logical, but underneath he's all emotion."

Layla sat with her arms wound around Susannah's little body, her toe still pushing the chair back and forth. Then she said, "Yes, he is, isn't he?" And she put her cheek down on Susannah's tangled hair.

So Edie sneaked away, back down all those stone steps, and wandered through the orchard before climbing back up the hill, following the path all the way around until she could see the opening in the castle gates. Then she stopped and looked back at the tower. It looked very squat, if tall, from this height.

Gowan was right to preserve it. And he was right to say that they needed to talk.

If she and Gowan talked seriously, she would have to confess that she had only pretended to achieve pleasure, rather than truly feeling it. But if she tried Layla's ideas for a romantic evening, perhaps she wouldn't have to confess. Ten days had passed since they last tried, and she was hopeful that it wouldn't hurt any longer.

Either way, there would be no more pretending.

Cow parsley grew in the shelter of the wall. The stems were very long, and had grown sideways and tangled with one another before erupting into spangled white flowers.

She knelt down and began gathering flowers until she had a great armful of twisty, spare blossoms. They didn't have the beauty of flowers bought at Covent Garden, in London, those with straight stems and regular petals. These were wild and unruly. Her first Scottish flowers.

At first she thought they were odorless, but very close up, they had a faint sweetness, a windy scent. With one final look at the tower, she came back to her feet.

She walked under the portcullis, thinking hard. In truth, she wasn't brave, as Layla believed. A brave person wouldn't have left it to Gowan to acknowledge that something was wrong, when the problem stemmed from her failures.

Bardolph was passing through the entry— heading, no doubt, for Gowan's study. He stopped and said, "Those are not flowers, but weeds, Your Grace."

Edie let a silence build precisely long enough to suggest that he had overstepped. "I would be grateful if you would send a maid to me with several vases. I shall be in my bedchamber. Oh, and Bardolph, my room needs to be completely redecorated."

He bowed, so rigid that his back looked like a tabletop. "I will summon Mr. Marcy, who directs renovation in the castle."

"Was Mr. Marcy responsible for the blue room, and the yellow room, et cetera?"

"Yes, he was."

"In that case he will not do. I'm sure you can find someone else. Thank you, Bardolph." She began climbing the stairs, aware that small white flowers were brushing off on her clothes and falling to the ground.

Once in her room, she managed to get the flowers wrestled into vases. The stems curled madly in different directions before blossoming into tight little white flowers. They brought a touch of welcome wildness to her sterile, blue room.

Mary had removed all her clothing from the trunks. And it seemed that she had encountered Susannah's French tutor, who was now being recruited to teach music as well.

"He's pretty as a picture," Mary said. "He wears his hair quite long and tied back. He is the son of a marquis, or so they said." The maid folded a frilly petticoat into a neat square with brisk flicks of her wrist. "He should not work. He should not be living here at the command of a Scottish duke, ready to teach music to a child of five."

She glanced at Edie. "And no one thinks that Miss Susannah will be able to learn to sing, let alone to play an instrument, Your Grace. She's an ill-tempered little thing, by all accounts. She spilled her milk on purpose, more than once, or so they say. What will you wear to supper?"

"The sea-blue one," Edie said. She had left all her white gowns behind.

"The pongee silk," Mary said, lifting the evening gown reverently from the wardrobe. "Your hair is a disaster. I shall put it up again and weave pearls through it."

Edie sighed and sat down. The whole day was lost.

"Tomorrow I shall practice all morning," she told Mary. "No interruptions after breakfast."

Mary nodded. "His Grace said that you were to have a footman outside your door to ensure you are undisturbed."

"No need for a footman," Edie said. "I shall practice in the tower."

Mary wrinkled her nose. "Bardolph said that no one is allowed near that tower." Then she started unbuttoning, and all the while, Edie looked at her flowers, thinking about how their curling stems resembled an intricate stave of music.

It was as if Scotland had wild music growing just outside the castle walls.

Thirty

Supper was hellish.

Edie and the Frenchman kept laughing at Layla's gossip—which Gowan thought was rather coarse, though her stories never edged over into pure vulgarity.

"From what I heard," Layla was telling them, "being married to Lord Sidyham was like finding oneself a Christian in the Colosseum, whisker to whisker with a large tiger. I mean to say that he was absurdly primeval. Rabid. I was at a dinner party once when he accused his wife, in front of all of us, of being infatuated with anyone wearing a clerical collar. She was merely enjoying a conversation with the Archbishop of Canterbury, and anyone who has met *him* knows that one would have to be truly devoted to the cloth to find him attractive."

"His was a quite unkind attack," Edie said, adding, "though oddly specific."

"My thought precisely. As it turned out, Lady Sidyham had indeed allowed her respect for the priesthood to prevail over principle, because a few months later she and the local vicar disappeared and were last heard of in the Americas, where I believe they are quite happy."

Gowan couldn't bring himself to look even slightly interested, not with coals heating the base of his stomach and bitter acid coating the back of his throat. He had taken one look at Edie as she walked into the drawing room, wearing a gown whose design emphasized the line of her legs, and then celebrated her breasts with a burst of ribbons and frills . . .

And she had turned to him with a smile in her eyes. It was like being tossed on a rough sea, being married to Edie. One moment she was incalculably elusive, and the next she was within reach. One moment there was complete awareness in her dark emerald eyes, and then she turned to greet Layla, and all he could see of her face was the delicate curve of her cheek.

For the first time he considered that perhaps madness was hereditary. Perhaps his father felt the same for his mother, and when she strayed, he had no recourse but to drink himself into a stupor and sleep with barmaids.

Though, of course, Edie would never stray. Still, he had a terrible feeling that he couldn't pin her down, couldn't keep her by his side. She would lock herself in a room with her cello and be gone.

Not that he would ever think—or want—to take her music away.

But he couldn't help the gnawing sense of jealousy. He wished she weren't a musician. If she were an ordinary woman like Lady Edith, the young lady whom he thought he met at the Gilchrist ball: that chaste, wistful girl who scarcely said a word . . .

She wouldn't be Edie, he realized with a sigh.

He was sitting at the head of the table, where his father had sat a million times, watching silently as Edie and Layla jested with Védrines, the violinist whom Bardolph had produced like a rabbit from a magician's hat.

This particular fellow was supposedly related to the Comte de Genlis, who was rumored to have met his fate at the guillotine, though one wouldn't want to ask. Presumably, Genlis was his grandfather, and since Védrines had dressed in black velvet for the evening meal, there must have been a jewel or two smuggled out of France.

Layla caught Gowan's attention with an emphatic wave of her hand. "That liverish fellow with the mustaches, Bardolph, doesn't approve of me."

"I find that impossible to believe," Védrines said gallantly.

He was a handsome man, the Frenchman, lean and tall. "You play the cello?" Védrines was saying to Edie. He leaned toward her, and Gowan had to suppress an instinctive urge to shove him back into his chair.

"I do." Edie smiled at him, her lips so plump and inviting that Gowan's head swam for a moment. Why the hell didn't he sleep with a hundred women before getting married? At least then he might have some control.

Then he realized that Védrines was giving Edie a condescending smile and was crooning about how he felt certain he could help her improve her craft, although the cello wasn't his own instrument. "The viola de gamba has a better tone," the Frenchman said.

Edie briskly disabused the man of his prejudices,

which was amusing. But then the two of them began talking of things that he didn't understand.

"This will happen to you as often as you allow musicians at your table," Layla said, from his left side.

He turned to find her smiling at him, with a twinkle in her eye that he found far more appealing than her seductive ways.

"Edie and her father are capable of talking like this for hours at a stretch."

"Have you ever tried to learn the language?"

"It's too late. They've both been studying for years." She paused, just long enough so that Gowan heard Védrines say, "Monsieur de Sainte-Colombe," and Edie reply, nodding, "added the seventh string to the bass viol . . ."

"You see?" Layla continued. "They'll come back to the realm of us mortals at some point. It's like a secret society."

Gowan didn't like it. He didn't want Edie in a secret society, especially not with a handsome young Frenchman with an enticing air of tragedy hanging about him like a tattered cloak.

"I prefer to play out of doors," Védrines was saying now. "It is my deepest pleasure to take my violin into the gardens."

"I have never thought of such a thing." Edie turned to Gowan and touched his hand. "Shall the two of us give you, Layla, and Susannah a recital tomorrow? We could perform in the orchards at the base of the tower in the afternoon."

"I shall be busy," Gowan said, the words coming automatically to his lips. Why would Edie think that he would be free for an afternoon recital? Every hour of his day was scheduled. "Perhaps after dinner?"

"I doubt we could see well enough to play outdoors after supper. Though we may be able to manage it with time. We'd have to learn each other's rhythms enough to play without a score or very good vision."

He'd be damned if Edie would learn another man's rhythms. And no other man was going to see her with that instrument between her legs. That was unacceptable. He could tell her later, when they were alone.

"Layla, you can be our audience," Edie continued, giving her stepmother a smile. "I promise we'll play *Dona Nobis Pacem*."

That made the rage rise higher in Gowan's throat. What had Edie said in that letter that made her stepmother follow them into a different country?

Edie's hair turned to dark honey in the candlelight, gold with glints of sunlight trapped inside. Pearls in her hair gleamed pale silver among the gold, turning Edie into a jewel.

His jewel.

He hungered to take her to bed, to thread his

fingers through her lavish strands. But then some part of him shied away. It didn't seem right that his orgasms were so overwhelming, sliding over him like a tidal wave, not when he would open his eyes to see that she was watching him, a faint haze of relief in her eyes.

They had to talk first, in private. Tomorrow.

He felt lonely.

Feeling lonely was hell.

After supper, Edie played for a couple of hours and then lay awake, waiting for Gowan to come to her chamber, but he didn't. She heard, very remotely, the bustle of his valet . . . then silence. She lay awake a long time.

The next morning she dressed and then went up to the nursery to see if Layla had truly slept in the governess's narrow bed. She found her sitting on the floor, her hair a tousled mess around her shoulders, apparently marshaling a battalion of soldiers.

"Hello," Susannah said, getting up and going to stand at Layla's shoulder, as if Edie meant to steal her away. Obviously, Layla and Susannah had fallen in love with each other. It had nothing to do with her mothering of Susannah, or lack thereof.

"Hello yourself," she said to Susannah. "You may call me Edie, if you wish." Since *Mama* wasn't an option.

Then she crouched down and examined the way

the soldiers were arranged. There were a great many of them; it seemed that Layla was in charge of the redcoats and Susannah of the blue. "Who is winning?" she asked.

"It's the third battle of the English against the Scots," Layla said, stifling a yawn. "By some miracle, the Scots always win." She had wound an arm around Susannah's waist as naturally as if she'd known her from the moment she was born.

"Three battles," Edie exclaimed. "And you lost every time. Dear me, Layla. We Englishwomen have to do better than that."

"This Englishwoman has been up since the crack of dawn," Layla said, with some dignity. "Naturally, His Majesty's forces would win any battle conducted at night."

Layla never rose early. "How are you doing without the cheroots?"

"I seem to be hungry all the time," she answered, a frown pleating her brow. "At this rate, I shall become as round as a turnip."

Susannah hooted with laughter. "A turnip, a turnip!" she shrieked. She apparently decided that Edie didn't pose an imminent risk, because she twirled across the room to where Alice sat sewing by the fireplace.

"Were you really up at dawn?" Edie asked. She'd never seen Layla like this. Tired, but with a glow of deep contentment.

"I gather children are early risers, at least Susannah is. She woke me up by climbing onto my stomach. My turnip-sized stomach."

Susannah hurtled back across the floor and wound her arms around Layla's neck from behind. "Susannah does not care about the size of your stomach," Edie pointed out.

"Who's this?" Layla cried, capturing a squirming body that she promptly started tickling. "Not this absurd creature who woke me up before it was even light outside!"

Edie would have guessed that Susannah's shrieks indicated pain, but Layla obviously knew the difference. "I thought I would ask Gowan to a private supper tonight," she said.

Layla's fingers stilled. "Brilliant!" She set Susannah free, and the little girl sat back down next to her soldiers. "I suggest champagne. In fact, Edie, you should get properly tipsy."

"What's 'tipsy'?" Susannah asked, raising her head.

"Tipsy is what you are when you spin around," Layla said, pulling her onto her lap as if she couldn't stop touching her. "Come here, you horrid child; you've worn me out. I refuse to stage another battle with those soldiers."

"You think so?" Edie asked, a bit dubiously.

"Do you remember the evening when we went to Lady Chuttle's ball?"

"Of course."

"I had drunk rather more champagne than was strictly good for me."

"You were pickled!" Edie said with a gurgle of laughter.

"That evening, I forgot all about babies and just enjoyed myself. If you stop worrying, all will be well."

"I hope so," Edie said. "At any rate, I must go. I have to work."

"Play for him," Layla whispered. "There is nothing more erotic. When your father plays something just for me, it makes me melt all over."

Edie walked back to the small sitting room thinking about what she might play for Gowan, but Bardolph was there to inform her that His Grace had asked to see her. She went downstairs to her husband's study, where a pudding-faced footman informed her that he would have to ascertain whether His Grace was free, as he had left strict orders with regard to interruptions.

A moment later, it appeared that Gowan was able to see her, so, trailed by Bardolph, she followed the footman into the room. There was a new bailiff to meet, and the mayors of two neighboring villages.

Then her husband made an apology and drew her slightly to the side. The three visitors had the good manners to withdraw to the other side of the room, but Bardolph walked over to the desk that stood to the side of Gowan's own desk and sat down. He could hear their conversation perfectly well from there.

Edie took a deep breath. Bardolph was not a problem she could address at the moment.

"I summoned—" Gowan broke off and gave her an entirely charming smile. "Excuse me. I requested to speak to you because we must discuss the recital this afternoon."

Edie blinked with surprise. "You can come, after all? That is wonderful."

"I'm afraid that my press of work is such that I cannot lose an afternoon. But more to the point, Edie, I cannot allow you to play your cello before an audience, particularly one which includes a man."

Edie was dismayed, but unsurprised by this. "I have a special drape that my father had made for just that circumstance. It's made of pleated silk so it billows around the cello. But the truth is that a true musician is only interested in how I play, not what I look like doing it. I have hopes that Védrines is just such a musician, but of course I cannot know for certain until I hear him play."

"I'm sorry to disappoint you, Edie."

"You do not disappoint me," she assured him.

"I'm glad to hear it." He gave her one of those caressing smiles that apparently indicated he had remembered how much fun their bed sport was. For him.

"You will not disappoint me," Edie stated,

"because I shall play when and where I please." Her entire body had lit with an anger so incandescent that she felt as if she'd caught on fire.

His eyes narrowed. She held up her hand before he could speak. "Perhaps you have misapprehended, and believe that my father dictated the circumstances under which I played. He did not. I did him the honor of acquiescing to his wishes by not performing in public. I have been asked to practice with the Smythe-Smith girls and I declined. Although," she added punctiliously, "that was not the sole reason for my refusal."

"If you would like to come to such an agreement with me, that would be more than satisfactory."

"An agreement," Edie said, "involves *agreement,* Gowan. I do not agree to your directive. In fact, given your presumptuousness, I shall agree to no rule whatsoever. You shall have to be guided by my sense of priority, and if I choose to invite the entire Smythe-Smith clan up here and hold a public recital in the nearest town hall, I will do so!"

Gowan had gone utterly still, which struck Edie as ominous. She abhorred altercations. In fact, she never argued—but this was different. She had to make a stand. He was trying to infringe on her music. It was the most important thing to her. Her soul.

"What if I were to attend the recital this afternoon?" His lips hardly moved.

Edie could practically feel Bardolph's interested stare boring into her shoulder blades.

"I would be happy to see you."

"But you will not agree to my request that you not play in front of men."

"I did not hear a request, but a command," she observed.

"Please, will you refrain from playing in the presence of men?"

"I will not play public recitals, if you wish."

"Thank you," Gowan said. His face was expressionless, but the image of an icy lake came into her mind as she looked at his eyes.

"You are welcome to join me during the recital, as I gather you are worried that I . . ." What? Did he imagine that she would start flirting with that young Frenchman? Throw aside her cello and embark on an act that she found not only painful, but distasteful?

His eyes hardened. "I trust *you* implicitly. What I do not like is the fact that your partner will be able to savor his lust during every moment in which you play together."

She shook her head and, against all odds, felt a pang of sympathy for him. "You do not understand what duets are like. I would play only with a true musician. If I hadn't talked to Védrines for two hours last night, I would never have considered it. I assure you that he will be thinking about the music, not my posture.

"We shall practice this afternoon in the orchard, if you would like to join us." Then she turned, curtsied rather blindly to the room at large, and fled.

She didn't get far. Mrs. Grisle caught her, dragged her into the housekeeper's sitting room, and plied her with question after question. Two hours passed. Bardolph joined them, and droned on for fifteen minutes about the linen closet at the Highlands estate near Comrie. They had mice.

Mice?

Mice were everywhere. She managed to impress upon Bardolph the concept that said mice— indeed, *all* mice—were his concern.

It took another hour before Edie realized that if she didn't organize the household better, she would never have time to put bow to strings.

There were bound to be a few problems in running a household of this size. Every once in a while, she thought about how Gowan had stated that she should not play in front of men. It lent her a spark of rage that she had never experienced before.

By the time Bardolph summoned her to the midday meal, she was reasonably certain that the household understood the way things were going to go from now on.

Meanwhile, Gowan deserted all the men in his study and engaged in a brief conversation with Védrines. It took only a couple of minutes to establish that Gowan would slaughter him if his eyes fell below the duchess's neck.

"I would not," the Frenchman stated. And then he added, rather defensively, "When one plays, one thinks only of the music, Your Grace. Though, of course, one's concentration depends upon the musical abilities of one's partner."

A faint undertone implied that he was as uncertain of Edie's musical prowess as she was of his. They both held their own playing in damned high esteem. Gowan took a good look at the Frenchman's indignant eyes and realized that Védrines was no threat to his marriage. He didn't think of Edie as a woman at all. There was some other currency in play here.

"Right," he said, holding out his hand. "I offer you my sincerest apology for the insult."

The man looked at his hand for a moment, but he took it. For some reason, Gowan liked that the most of all. Védrines was on the verge of walking out of the castle, even though he desperately needed the income. "What are we paying you?" he asked.

Védrines flushed, and named a sum. It must rub at the man to have to accept employment.

Gowan nodded. "From now on, we'll pay you twice that."

Védrines's brows drew together. "Why, Your Grace?"

"Every castle should have a musician," he said.

The young Frenchman pulled himself upright, although that put his eyes only at Gowan's shoulder. "I should be remiss in my duty as a gentleman not to point out that you do your duchess a dishonor."

"How so?"

"You imply base things. Her Grace is all that is gracious and virtuous."

Gowan felt even more cheerful now. He had acquired an employee with just the right kind of reverence for his wife. "Just wait until you marry."

"I shall both maintain and display faith in my bride," the Frenchman said coldly.

"As do I," Gowan assured him.

He wasn't sure what to expect when he left his study for luncheon sometime later. Apparently, there had been quite a fracas. Bardolph had actually interrupted him to deliver a complaint, but Gowan had cut him off: the household was now the duchess's domain.

The first person he encountered was Layla. "Did you really sleep in the nursery?" he asked.

"I did, and your servants sleep on deucedly hard mattresses, Gowan. I had to tell Barlumps to bring me a new mattress or I won't be able to straighten my back tomorrow."

"Bardolph," Gowan corrected.

Edie entered the morning room, greeting him with a face that betrayed no irritation stemming from their earlier conversation. In fact, it betrayed nothing at all, which he found annoying. He had the trick of concealing his own feelings, but he didn't appreciate it in his wife.

"How was your meeting with Mrs. Grisle?" he asked, as they sat down.

Edie smiled at the footman offering her a helping of cheese pudding. "I dismissed her."

"What?" Whatever he expected, it wasn't that his wife would toss out a housekeeper who had held the post for a decade. Not that Mrs. Grisle was particularly pleasant, or particularly efficient, but she didn't steal the silver.

To his left, Layla drew Védrines into a conversation.

"Why did you dismiss her?" Gowan asked, reminding himself that marriage entailed sharing power, at least in the household.

"She was unable to trust herself to make decisions," Edie replied, looking quite unperturbed. "She felt she had to constantly check with me and actually requested that I spend two hours with her every morning. I told her that I would be happy to give her a few minutes in the evening, but I did not wish to be interrupted during the day, and she was quite discomfited by that. Were you really giving her an hour or more daily?"

Gowan nodded.

"The housekeeper should report to the factor, if she must recapitulate her daily accomplishments,"

Edie said, cutting up her roast beef. "Your time is far too valuable to waste learning whether the laundry is drying properly. And, frankly, so is mine."

Something like a smile twitched at the corners of Gowan's lips. He would have loved to witness that conversation.

"In the end, we agreed that it would be more comfortable if I found someone able to work in the manner to which I am accustomed. Mrs. Grisle was agitated by our conversation, which merely confirmed my decision. I cannot abide people who raise their voices when angry."

That was reasonable. "Have you dismissed anyone else?" he inquired.

"Two upper housemaids, a kitchen maid, and a footman."

"Have you tasked Bardolph with finding replacements?"

"No," Edie said. "I am quite certain he can take that initiative without my having to prompt him. I did instruct him to give each a substantial severance payment. The morning was disruptive, but from now on, I expect the servants will be far more self-directed."

Gowan wondered what the footman had done to offend, but decided there was nothing to be gained by asking.

"Hopefully, there will be no further need for encouragement on my part." She smiled at him without a bit of irritation in her eyes. It was as if their battle of the morning had never happened. "You are probably thinking I am headstrong, but my excuse is that I took housekeeping lessons at Layla's knee."

She touched the back of Gowan's hand and an embarrassing streak of heat shot from her touch. "The household will settle down once they know my ways."

Gowan thought they might well be dealing with an entirely new group of servants by then, but, as Edie said, that was Bardolph's problem.

Edie went upstairs to practice after the meal, and Gowan invited Layla to come to his study. She was wandering about looking rather critically at the towering stacks of ledgers on Bardolph's desk, when he simply said what he'd been thinking.

"It seems to me that you and Susannah are enjoying each other's company."

Layla whipped around, her face more serious than he had ever seen it. "I love Susannah." She came over to him, her face alight with determination. "I—"

He held up his hand. "I agree that you would be an entirely appropriate person to care for Susannah."

"I don't want to merely be her nanny," Layla said firmly. "I am her *mother*."

"Do you mean that you wish to adopt her?"

"Of course."

He thought about it for a moment. His mother had never bothered to tell him of the child, but even so . . . "I would be quite uncomfortable if I were not responsible for her education, wardrobe, and other expenses." He hesitated. "And I don't want to lose her entirely."

Layla smiled, a wide, generous smile without a trace of the coquette in it. "How could that be? Edie is one of my favorite people in the world, and the person my husband loves best. You will see far too much of us, I'm sure."

"Very well. We can work out the formal side of it when Lord Gilchrist arrives."

Her mouth tightened.

"And if he doesn't pay a visit in the near future, I will send the papers to him," Gowan added.

Something eased in Layla's eyes and she embraced him. "We are family now. This simply binds us closer together."

"Of course," Gowan said. "I am certain that Edie will feel the same."

The smile fell from Layla's face. "You did speak to her before you asked me to care for Susannah, didn't you?"

He didn't like the tone of her question. "I assure you that Edie will not disagree with my choice for Susannah's guardian. Your affection for my sister is obvious."

"Edie should have been consulted. Just yesterday,

she was to be Susannah's mother, and now you are giving the child away?"

"I think we can both acknowledge that Edie showed no great aptitude when it came to mothering Susannah. She had already informed me by letter that she didn't welcome the role, so I did not find it surprising."

"Edie will be a wonderful mother!" Layla snapped.

"But a person would have to be blind not to see that you and Susannah belong together," he offered.

Her face eased into a smile. "She is the child of my heart. Not being able to conceive a child has been heartbreaking. But now I can only think how glad I am that it never happened." A haunted look crossed her eyes. "If I had my own children, I wouldn't have come to Scotland. I would never have met Susannah."

Gowan was not a demonstrative man, but even he could tell when something other than a bow was required. So he allowed himself to be enfolded in Layla's perfumed embrace once again. It wasn't as unpleasant as he would have thought.

She drew back. "I have a present for you." She put a book into his hand. "Love poems. These collections are quite the rage at the moment; everyone is reading them. I thought that, because you quoted *Romeo and Juliet* in that entirely outrageous letter you sent Edie, you would appreciate them."

Poems . . .

His head snapped up. "Are you suggesting that I need to write poetry to my wife?"

Layla frowned. "Why on earth would I suggest that you write poetry? With all due respect, Duke, you don't strike me as having a poetic soul."

"I apologize," Gowan said, turning the book over. "Of course you weren't saying that."

"In any case, Edie has a tin ear when it comes to poetry."

"She has?"

Layla nodded. "Her governess tried to drum some into her head, but she is a proper dunce about the written word."

"She *is?*"

"I think it must be concomitant with her aptitude for music. Edie does not read with pleasure. But she does love to listen to poetry read aloud."

"Of course. She prefers sound." The book was leather-bound and embossed in gold. On the cover it said *Poetry for a Lonely Evening.*

"You could read some to her."

"All right," Gowan said, thinking that he scarcely had time to kiss his wife, let alone read poetry to her. He put the book to the side and went back to work. But when the bailiff from the Highlands estate missed his appointed hour, rather than attend to the hundred items awaiting his attention, Gowan picked up the book again.

He skipped Shakespeare's sonnets; he'd memorized all those in his youth. There was a great deal of verse written by a man named John Donne, who seemed to have a sense of humor, at least. *I am two fools,* he read, *for loving, and for saying so in whining poetry.* Gowan gave a bark of laughter, and turned the page.

He read the next poem four times . . . five. It begged the sun not to rise and call lovers from their bed. *Shine here to us, and thou art everywhere; This bed thy center is, these walls thy sphere.*

The element that was missing from his marriage was printed here in black and white. The bed gave no center to their lives. *She's all states,* Donne wrote, *and all princes, I. Nothing else is.*

Gowan looked around himself with a bleak sense of futility. If he was a prince, Edie was not his state, nor his dominion. He was a prince of land and soil, of small villages and wheat fields.

Not of a woman as elusive as the wind. He had failed. He had failed in their bed, and his heart squeezed with the pain of it.

Later that afternoon, he looked out the window and saw the recital. Layla and Susannah were sitting on a blue blanket, looking like bright flowers. Edie sat in a straight-backed chair, her back to the castle, and Védrines stood to her right, a violin tucked under his chin.

Even from this distance, he could see Edie's body sway as they began playing. And he could see that Védrines was standing at an angle, facing away from her, his eyes presumably on the music stand before him. He had probably concluded that his employer was stark raving mad, but he was keeping to his word.

Gowan's heart began hammering in his rib cage. One of his bailiffs was talking, but the words made no sense. He snatched up the legal papers Jelves had prepared with regard to Susannah's upbringing.

"Gentlemen," he said, pivoting on his heel. "If you will please excuse me for a few moments, I will deliver these papers to Lady Gilchrist myself."

He was down the hill a moment later, but he skirted the trees so no one saw him. Védrines's face had the same transcendent joy on it as Edie's had while playing, damn his eyes. Just then the Frenchman lifted his bow and said, "A C-sharp is quite different in the open air."

Whatever that meant.

But, of course, Edie knew. She plucked a string, and one note quavered before dying away. "I hear just what you mean."

Védrines turned a page on the stand before him—which Gowan recognized as the one that usually stood in the library, supporting the Kinross Bible—and nodded. Then they were off.

Edie's slow, sweet notes played beneath the violin's, sounding like the wave of the sea. Her sound would die just as the violin picked up and yet it was never subdued: a moment later it would rise up again. In contrast to her lines, the violin bounced like a nursery rhyme, childish and thin.

The look on her face . . .

He turned and walked back up the path before the piece was finished. For the first time, he understood that a man could just give up his life and walk away from his wife. He could put his back to his castle and cease to be a duke. He could walk until the jealousy in his heart was silenced, and a woman's face didn't wring his heart's core.

Back at the castle, he handed the papers for Lady Gilchrist to Bardolph, telling him to get them signed. It didn't sit well with him to know that Susannah would grow up an Englishwoman. But their mother had not shown the slightest interest in mothering either him or his sister; nationality surely mattered less than Layla's clear love for Susannah.

Later that afternoon the butler informed him that Her Grace had requested they dine privately in her bedchamber. And shortly thereafter, the bailiff from the Highlands estate finally arrived; he had been delayed by a broken axle. At some point Gowan asked Bardolph to inform the duchess that he would be late.

But even he was astonished when he raised his head and discovered it was ten o'clock.

Bardolph had an uneasy flicker in his eyes when Gowan emerged from the study, the book of poetry tucked into his pocket. His factor had apparently been hovering outside the door for some time. "I fear the meal is cold, but I believe Her Grace would not have wished me to intrude with warmer food, as she is playing her instrument."

Bardolph was learning, Gowan realized. Edie had somehow put the fear of God in his grumpy factor.

Thirty-one

Edie was playing something low and languorous; as he climbed the stairs, he heard notes spilling out into the corridor.

Gowan climbed faster, prodded by guilt. She had been waiting for at least two hours. Perhaps three. He couldn't remember when Bardolph had first asked him if he was ready to break off for the day.

That was the life of a nobleman. She would simply have to endure it, just as he did. The alternative—to be the sort of desultory duke his father had been—was unthinkable.

Still, she would likely be angry. Ladies were not happy when their arrangements were disrupted.

He walked into the bedchamber and stopped short. The room had been transformed. The blue walls had been hung with saffron-colored silk that seemed to ripple in the light of the candles. And candles crowded every surface—on the tables, on the mantelpiece, on the table. The illumination was superfluous, because Edie wasn't using a score.

Instead, her eyes were closed, and she was playing something so low and soft that it felt as if she were humming it. He listened without moving, his back to the door, as notes built and subsided, as if a giant were softly breathing them, as if each note was a drop of water going down a stream filled with rocks.

Then he entered into the room. He took the book of poetry out of his pocket, put it to the side, and dropped into a chair. Edie didn't open her eyes, but surely she knew he was there.

The stress of the day seemed to slip away with the music. It took him to another world, away from numbers and reports and stocks, giving him a feeling that he had only occasionally, when standing deep in the loch in the Highlands, fly-fishing. Those were his happiest moments . . .

This made him pretty damn happy, too.

Even with all their problems in bed, he and Edie had a deep, thrumming awareness between them, a tension so taut that it overtook the music. Her bow quickened and he thought she went straight into playing something different, a piece less melancholy.

When she lifted her bow, he said, "Was that played allegro?"

"Yes, it was."

"And the first was largo. Was that last written by Vivaldi?" he asked, trying out the new names that he was just beginning to store in his memory.

She beamed. "Exactly! The Vivaldi piece is one of the first I learned as a child."

"It sounds as if they were written by the same person," he said. "As if he was trying to capture birdsong."

"What a lovely thought." She put the bow aside and hoisted up her instrument.

Instantly Gowan was on his feet, reaching out for the cello.

"Careful!" she cried. Then she fell back with a shamefaced smile as he placed the instrument face up in its padded case. "I love my cello. I don't know what I'd do if it was injured."

She said *injured,* Gowan noted. As if it were a living being.

"Are there differences between one cello and another?"

"Absolutely. Mine was made by Ruggieri. My father and I think he is the finest cello maker in the world."

"Was it costly?"

She named a sum that made his jaw drop. "You could buy a house in an excellent area of London for that."

"That's why I'm so fussy, and why it travels in a padded case."

"I should have suspected when Bardolph informed me that the cello required a carriage of its own."

"And a footman to keep it steady during the journey," she said, nodding. "It's an expensive business, being a musician. But I imagine we won't travel for some time." She looked up at him, a smile glimmering in her eyes. "I have to warn you, Gowan, that I may spend the rest of my life playing outdoors, in the orchard. It's so quiet except for the river, and the acoustics are wonderful. It's everything I ever wanted."

Everything she wanted?

She picked up a glass of champagne and took a sip. "May I give you a glass? I thought we might celebrate our . . . well, arriving home."

She poured a glass for him. He accepted it, but set it down on the table without tasting it, and curled a hand around her neck. He kissed her openmouthed, and the taste of her struck deep into his body. He already had an erection; these days he lived in a constant state of readiness. By the time he pulled back, in need of air, she was trembling in his arms and making little stifled noises in the back of her throat.

"You should eat," he whispered, running his teeth down the slender column of her throat.

She pulled back. "No."

"No?" Was she rejecting the cold food, or dinner altogether?

Edie had an endearing gleam of uncertainty in her eyes, and he swooped to kiss it away.

"I don't want to follow a plan," she said.

"Ah," he said, remembering their wedding night. He wrapped her even more tightly in his arms, sliding one hand down onto her beautifully rounded rump. "In that case, my lady, would you mind if we took an indirect route to dinner via our bed?"

"I think you should drink your champagne," she said, a little wildly. She turned to the side and groped for hers, found it, and then tossed down the glass.

Gowan didn't like champagne. It was the kind of wine that tried to claw you in the throat. He couldn't imagine why anyone liked it, but then he felt that way about most spirits. He took a sip.

Edie picked up the bottle and refilled her glass. He watched her and wondered. It seemed he wasn't the only one who had a plan for the intimate side of their marriage. Then he gave a mental shrug. With luck, her plan would work better than his had.

When she turned back, her eyes shone from the wine. "I thought I might play for you. I mean, just for you, since you were unable to join us this afternoon."

"I would enjoy that."

"But I forgot, and now my cello is put away."

"I would be happy to retrieve it for you."

"Thank you," she said, beaming as she finished her second glass. Or perhaps it was her third? He glanced at the bottle, but the glass was too thick to tell if it was half empty. The butler had probably opened the bottle for her some three hours ago.

Edie fussed with a chair as he brought out the cello, putting it directly in front of the couch. "You sit there," she ordered, pointing. He sat.

"You forgot your champagne!" she exclaimed. She handed it to him and then apparently realized that her own glass was empty.

He was out of his seat before he knew what he was doing, stopping her hand as she reached for the wine. "Don't. Please don't." He uttered a silent curse, hearing the note of pleading in his voice. This marriage was turning him into a bloody infant, begging for what he could not have.

"Oh," Edie said. And then: "Do you think I'm tipsy yet?"

"Absolutely."

She sat down on the chair and reached for her cello. "Good. Oops." She popped up again, holding her instrument around the neck. "Will you hold this for a moment?"

He was already standing, the command to rise

with a lady so ingrained that he felt like a jack-in-the-box. The cello's wood was satin-smooth under his fingers, as smooth as Edie's own skin.

As he watched, she untied what seemed to be some sort of robe and tossed it away. Underneath, she was wearing a nightdress of thin lawn, trimmed with lace at the bodice, and the elbows, and the hem, and . . . She sat down, a slit fell open, and there was Edie's utterly delectable leg. The lace fell on either side of her thigh, like a ribbon on the best cake he ever saw. Her thigh was plump and luscious and—

"May I have my cello again?" Her voice broke his trance.

He handed it back.

She spread her legs wider and he almost lunged forward and called for the recital to be postponed, but instead he lowered himself slowly into the couch as she fussed with her instrument, positioning it correctly.

Then she looked at him rather shyly. "I've never played for anyone like this before."

"I should damn well hope not!"

Her smile broadened. "What would you like me to play?"

"Something brief." He couldn't stop looking at the way that big instrument balanced between her open legs. It was the most erotic thing he'd ever seen.

Edie always seemed transformed when she

played. But this was a different sort of trans-formation: while it was about the music, it was also about *him*. She kept peeking from under her lashes, even as she played some sort of rippling thing that made her fingers dart among the strings.

Listening, Gowan had an idea. He had discarded his coat and neck cloth while in his study; now he stood up and began unbuttoning his waistcoat.

Her eyes grew a bit wider, but she continued to play, even when he pulled his shirt over his head. She made an error when he bent over to pull off one boot. He had catalogued the way a cascade of notes fell down a scale, and one of Edie's struck a sour note.

He had a distinct impression that his wife liked his muscles. So he bent over again, slower this time, twisting like some sort of Roman statue to pull off his other boot and roll down his stocking. She was watching . . . the tempo of her piece was not allegro any longer.

The room was half in shadow now, as some of the candles were burning low and the last midsummer daylight was gone for another night. He put his hands on his waistband.

Her bow lifted, and the last note was cut short. In the silence, he became aware of the patter of raindrops against the windows.

"Dear me," he said, unbuttoning the top button of his breeches, and meeting Edie's eyes. "That note should have lasted longer, shouldn't it?"

"How did you know that?" She looked surprised, but her eyes drifted back to his hands. He undid another button and shoved his breeches down a little, showing off his rippled abdomen.

"It's the piece you played with your father." The notes were stored in his mind, like everything else.

"You remember the music that closely after having heard it only once?"

He had to work his breeches around that part of him that was barely fitting in his smalls as it was. So he dropped his smalls along with his breeches. It was oddly liberating to stand naked in front of his wife. No servants. Just the two of them.

Edie rose and pushed the cello in his direction. He laid it in its case. She turned to the mirror and began pulling pins from her hair. He came up from behind and ran his hands around her, cupping her breasts.

That luscious hair of hers came tumbling down, down over his arms. "God, you have lovely hair," he whispered.

She dropped the pins. There was a faint tinkle as they scattered over the ancient wood floor. But then her hands came warm over his and she leaned back and looked up at him. "I've thought of cutting it a few times."

"*Never* cut it," he said. "Promise me, Edie."

She hesitated, and her brows drew together. "What if I want to cut it?"

He pulled her tighter against him. He couldn't own her. She owned herself. He couldn't . . . "Forget I said that." He bent his head and licked her cheek, a blatant, sexual caress. His fingers spread across her breasts. "May I take you to bed, Madam Wife?"

She smiled, meeting his eyes in the mirror. "Yes, please."

As long as she said *yes* at the right moments . . .

In the length of their short marriage, they had made love four times. Gowan lay Edie on her back, thinking about this, the fifth time. It had to be different.

Better.

She began wiggling right away, though, batting his hands away. "I want my champagne," she announced. And then, when she was upright again and holding another glass, she looked at him through those thick lashes of hers and said, "I'd like *you* to lie down."

"What?"

She pointed. "On the bed. On your back. You're my husband, so . . ."

Edie would have laughed at the expression on his face, except this was too serious. She sipped her champagne again, hoping that Layla was right. It made her head swirl, which had to be good. Just let go, she told herself again. Let go.

But first . . . For a moment she thought Gowan wouldn't do it. He was the most dominant man she'd ever met in her life, after all. But then he lay on his back, except that his face turned blank.

She crawled up beside him and pressed a kiss on his lips. "I don't like your expression," she informed him. Yes, the champagne was definitely helpful.

"What do you mean?"

"Sometimes you have nothing in your eyes. Are you certain that you don't want champagne? It's quite good."

His eyes narrowed. "No." The word came out with a wolfish snap, and made her remember that his drunken parents complicated the whole question for him.

"All right," she said, putting her own glass away. "Now I'm going to learn what pleasures you."

"What pleasures me?" He rose up on his elbows, staring at her incredulously. "It all pleasures me. If you let me touch you, I'm pretty damned near in heaven."

Edie could almost wish she hadn't drunk that fifth glass, because her brain wasn't working properly. "Well," she said, "all right then."

He gave her a gentle tug. "What if we did it the other way around?"

"What way?" His chest was in front of her, and she ran her fingers across his muscles.

"What pleasures you?" Suddenly she found

herself flat on her back, both of her wrists loosely pinned above her head.

She frowned at him. "Not being held down."

"Damn." He let her go.

"Unless you want to," she said, feeling a sudden streak of excitement.

He cocked his head. "This isn't about what *I* want to do. This time is about what *you* want to do."

"That's right," Edie said, nodding. "I need to give you a road map."

Gowan came back on his heels, looking down at the luscious, delicate body of his wife. He required every ounce of his self-control not to fall on her and bite her all over. "Tell me what to do, sweeting."

To his horror, her eyes filled with tears. "I don't know. I forgot to ask." Then her brows drew together. "You were the first one, you know."

He cupped her face in his hands and gave her a kiss, because he simply couldn't *not* do that. "I know," he whispered. "I know." Consummating their marriage was one of the most profound moments of his life. Though it would have been better if it hadn't hurt her so much.

She popped her bottom lip out in such an enchantingly sensual fashion that he had to kiss her again. They lost track of the road map for a while, but then he got back to the point.

"I don't know," she confessed.

A slow grin shaped on his lips. "Experimentation," he murmured, "is one of my favorite pastimes. And I already know some things about you."

"You do?"

He nodded. "You like this." He rubbed both thumbs across her nipples. She gasped. "Don't you?"

She didn't seem to want to answer as long as he kept doing that, so he stilled his hands and said, "Edie."

"Yes," she said, her voice coming in a little pant. "I like that." He bent down and . . . aye, she liked that, too. She pretty much liked everything, it turned out, except when he licked her under her chin. And she actually started scolding him when he licked her armpit.

"I love it," he said thickly. "You smell so good, like essence of Edie, my favorite scent in the world."

"Ugh!" she cried, pulling away. "Stop that!"

But an experiment needs to be thorough, so he just kept licking and kissing and nibbling his way down her stomach. Then he pushed her legs apart, giving one throbbing second to the memory of her legs straddling her cello before lowering his mouth onto her plump, tender flesh.

He'd kissed her here before. But he'd done it to make sure she was ready for him. The road map wasn't about him.

It was about *her.*

Every time Edie felt that little pulse of embarrassment that threatened to make her think too much, she let the champagne drag her back into a floating place. What Gowan was doing felt so good that her breath came sobbing from her chest. And then he pushed her knees back, which made her so vulnerable and oh God, he could see *everything,* but he didn't seem . . .

He was growling, deep in his throat, and when she took a quick glance, she could see that his private part was still standing up. So he desired her, even though he was doing that. For the first time, it made her feel empty, as if she needed him to fill her up. So she pulled at his shoulders, but he wouldn't pay any attention to her.

And all the time a feeling was building in her legs until she was moving them restlessly as if a fever was coming over her. Gowan ran a hand over her stomach, farther down . . . put one broad finger into her.

She shrieked and arched her back. It wasn't enough, so she sobbed and begged him, but then he slipped in another finger and did something with his tongue and her hands fell away from his shoulders altogether.

A moment later a flash of heat rolled her down and under, as if she'd been caught in a tidal wave: utterly engulfing, magical, terrifying, all at the same time. She heard herself crying out, her voice guttural and hoarse, and even that frightened her, a little.

But there was no avoiding it, no stopping it. The feeling swept up from her toes and dragged her in a storm of sweet pain that her body welcomed. When she broke free, she was panting, her face was wet with tears.

Gowan's fingers slipped from her, and she began shaking again. She wanted more than that. Without thinking, she sat up and reached for him. There was a song in her veins and she wanted to give him the same.

She caught sight of his face.

Thirty-two

"What?" she whispered, realizing that her fingers were trembling as if lightning had forked through her. She withdrew her hand. "Did I do something wrong?"

His face was dark. The silvery feeling drained from her body as quickly as it had come.

"You came," he said, his voice clipped.

Edie drew her knees to the side and managed to sit up. "Ah . . . yes?" It seemed such a paltry word for what had just happened. She could feel pulses in parts of her body where she had never felt them before.

His jaw tightened. "Was it your first time?"

Edie froze, realizing her mistake. The champagne . . . the pleasure . . . it had made her recklessly abandoned. She nodded.

First disbelief, then fury, ripped across this face. His words came as hard as hammer blows. "Then what happened when you supposedly came the other"—he paused—"three times?"

Her mind was spinning from the champagne, and the only solution she could come up with was to pull the sheet over her head. Instead she drew it up so her breasts were covered. "I just thought—I can explain."

"Do that." He folded his arms. "Explain to me why you've been pretending that I pleased you."

The problem was that she couldn't quite remember what her reasoning had been, but she hadn't known him then. Not the way she did now, after spending hours and days confined in a cramped carriage, listening to him patiently dealing with problem after problem. "I didn't mean it that way," she said, finally.

"*You didn't mean it that way?* How else could you explain what you did, other than to say that you lied to me in the moment when I thought we were closest? When I thought—" He broke off.

"It hurt," she said, stumbling into an explanation. But she couldn't put the words together. She tucked the sheet tighter around her breasts, feeling tears press at the back of her throat. "This time was different."

"This time you were drunk." His voice was utterly even. "God, Edie, of all things I wouldn't have thought you were a liar."

"I'm not!"

"I knew something was wrong. No wonder I damn well felt as if I didn't own you."

Her breath caught at this, and she recovered some presence of mind. "You do *not* own me," she said, feeling her own temper spark. "What we do in bed has no bearing on the fact that I am my own person."

"So I'm facing a lifetime of asking my wife whether she really liked it or whether she was just acting—being as she's her own person."

"That's cruel." It went against Edie's nature to argue. She wasn't good at fighting back. Instead, she resorted to the method by which she'd learned to negotiate her father's and Layla's fraught union. "If you would just be reasonable—"

Gowan actually growled at her, lunging from the bed and walking away to the darkest part of the room to stand with his back to her, clearly fighting to control his rage. "I hate it when you use that tone of voice with me."

"What voice?"

"That sugary, peacemaking tone. You're condescending, and if there's anyone in this room who should be condescended to, it's you." He swung about. "You lied to me, and I hate liars."

"I was just—I was a virgin!"

"So?"

"I panicked!" she cried. "It hurt, and you just kept going on, and I didn't know how to make you stop."

His head snapped back, and he made a sound as if he'd been slugged in the gut. "Now you're telling me that I forced myself on you?"

"No!" But she was so rattled by his snarl that the right words didn't come. Her eyes fell under his glare. "I just couldn't . . . I kept thinking about what you expected, and that I couldn't be what you wanted in a wife. I was failing," she said, saying it because it had to be said. "You were trying so hard, and I tried, too, I swear I did. I didn't want you to think—"

"I was *trying so hard,* like some rutting animal?" His eyes blazed at her. "You thought I'd prefer to be deceived than told the truth, no matter how difficult it was? What you're saying is that when I failed you in bed, you didn't think I could shoulder the truth." His jaw flexed again. "Bloody hell, Edie. How could you think that of me?"

"It wasn't like that," she cried.

He bent over and pulled on his breeches, not bothering with his smalls.

"Where are you going?" she asked, hating that her voice was shaky. She couldn't let him go like this. She slid from the bed.

"For a walk."

She stepped forward, but tripped on the sheet, stumbled, and nearly fell.

"Careful," Gowan said, his tone cutting. "My father took to sitting on a three-legged stool because it was a shorter distance to the floor once the whisky went to his head."

Edie took a breath and tucked the sheet securely around her breasts. Any pleasurable effect of the champagne had evaporated. "Couldn't we talk about this? I'm truly sorry."

"What would we talk about?" Gowan buttoned his placket, not meeting her gaze. "I was under the impression that I was making love to you. That you were *with* me, in a moment I thought was . . . But, obviously, I had my head up my arse. You were shamming, and I was fool enough to believe you. Fool enough to think that there was something special about the moment."

He gave a short laugh. "That's the real travesty. Every time you moaned through your supposed pleasure, I prided myself that we were perfect together. I kept thinking that even though you yourself told me in a letter that you had very little interest in the 'pursuits of the flesh,' I was proving you wrong."

"I shouldn't have pretended," Edie said, her hands wringing together. She feared the bleak look in his eyes even more than she had feared his rage. "But I didn't know you very well yet, and I found what happened in bed embarrassing."

"Well, now we know each other. And how in the hell am I ever supposed to trust you now?" He grabbed one of his boots. "You're at your most honest when you're drunk!" The words burst with rage.

Edie tried to form an answer, but nothing came. Her stomach was churning, and she had a sudden panicked thought that she would throw up at his feet.

"I had hoped to marry a woman who would love and care for Susannah," he went on. "I didn't question my decision, even after you told me in the same letter that you had no maternal inclinations."

He slammed one foot down into his boot with a thump that rang through the room like a gunshot. "You warned me, and I ignored it. I have no one to blame but myself for the fact my sister will grow up in bloody England."

That hurt so badly that Edie couldn't even speak. A hoarse sound burst from her chest. "I wanted to be her mother; I did, I did."

The flash of disbelief in his eyes was almost more painful than his rage. Then he turned aside, looking for his second boot.

"I would have loved her," Edie said, her voice wavering. "But Layla was there, and . . ." Tears spilled down her cheeks.

He shrugged. "I took one look at you and lost all capacity for rational thought. I marched in to your father and bought you with no more thought than if I was purchasing a horse."

Gowan slammed into his other boot. "Then I failed in bed—not to mention the fact that I was such an ass that I didn't even know all those oohs and aahs were mere lines, performed by my wife, the actress." She saw him shudder. "Did I tell you *why* I didn't sleep with a woman until marriage?"

The question was so savagely asked that tears spilled down Edie's cheeks.

"I had this quixotic idea that honor demanded honesty between myself and my wife. *Honesty.* And the moment I met you, I decided that you were that person. Hell, I even fell in love with you—"

She made a sound, and he looked up. "Go ahead and call me a damned fool, because I am. I fell in love with you and decided you were a perfect woman, evidence to the contrary."

"And now you don't think I'm perfect for you?" Edie's voice cracked.

"What you are perfect for is playing the cello. In truth, the only thing you really give a damn about is that instrument. Your father as good as told me that, but I ignored him as well. You're married to the cello, not me, and I'm married to a woman who had to get drunk in order to enjoy intimacy."

"It's not true," she whispered. "I—I did like it at first. You know I did. And I married *you*." She searched his face, looking for that spark of warmth that was always there when he looked at her. The way he watched her, the way he reached out to touch her. She had always felt he wanted her . . . yes, that he loved her.

It was gone.

"You said you love me," she cried, hating the sound of her own voice, the way she was pleading with him. "That can't just disappear."

"I love the woman I created in my own mind," he snapped. "The woman who had a fever so high she couldn't even hear me, but I didn't notice it. You told me yourself that you didn't want to be a mother, but I blithely thought you'd change your nature for me. I was as drunk as my father on a bottle of whisky, but it was on a product of my own imagination."

"Don't," Edie cried, sobs rising in her throat. "Please don't say these things."

"I'm simply acknowledging the truth." He looked suddenly exhausted, the skin drawn tight over his cheekbones. "It's as much my fault as yours; I forced our wedding before we had time to truly know each other, and now we both have to live with the consequences. Most importantly, I fell short in the most profound way a man can."

He pulled on his shirt. "I need to rearrange my view of the world. A matter of priorities. I can—it will all be fine." He enunciated the words with savage precision.

"Gowan!" She put raw emotion into her cry.

He walked to the door, leaving her standing in the middle of the room. "Drama doesn't suit you." His voice hardened. "My father warned me, you know. He said that there are two kinds of women: the ones who give and take pleasure, and the wives, who lie in bed like pancakes."

Tears were streaming down Edie's face, blurring her vision.

Gowan had opened the bedroom door, but then, at the last moment, he suddenly wheeled and lunged back into the room. She jerked aside as he snatched up a book that lay on a side table. The earlier rage had reappeared on his face . . . and not just rage. He looked like a warrior king betrayed by his own men. Like Caesar, when his friend Brutus raised the dagger to his chest.

"What's the matter?" she asked, fear washing her body.

He turned to her slowly. "I'm not the only one who knows that I failed you in bed, am I?"

Edie felt the blood drain from her face, as a wave of guilt flooded over her.

"You told Lady Gilchrist. In fact, you wrote her a letter describing my shortcomings, didn't you?"

"I didn't reveal any details," Edie said in a choked whisper.

The next word out of his mouth was flatly blasphemous. Then: "How could you do that? You told someone about what was happening in our bed?" He wasn't even bellowing, but this was worse than shouting. There was a desolate acceptance of betrayal in his voice that cut her to the heart.

A sob rose up in her. "I didn't mean it that way!" She ran forward and threw her arms around his neck. "Layla is like my mother. Please . . ."

Gowan removed her hands and stepped back. "You told the woman who will raise my own sister that I hurt you in bed. You told the wife of one of the governors of the Bank of England that you had to feign pleasure . . . because I couldn't take the truth." He bared his teeth, and his final sentence came out in a growl. "Damn you—you took my manhood and made me a laughingstock!"

Edie was shaking with uncontrollable, violent sobs. "Gowan, no," she implored. "Layla will never mention it."

"Layla already has." His face was savage, but his voice had gone icily calm. "Your stepmother did me the kindness of lending me a book of poems about copulation. I thought it was odd. Now I see that she was giving me lessons on how to bed my wife."

Edie's legs gave way, and she went down on her knees before him, her shoulders shaking, hair falling over her face. "Please don't do this to us," she choked out. "I love you. And I'm sorry."

"As am I," Gowan stated.

Then he walked out the door.

Thirty-three

It was a long time before Edie stopped weeping. She wept for her marriage, and she wept because she had hurt someone who loved her. He had loved her. Gowan had fallen in love with her, and she hadn't even known it.

When the tears finally stopped coming, she felt so sick that she got to her feet and staggered into the water closet, where all the champagne that had gone into her came back up.

She returned, still shaky but with a clearer head, and sat down on the bed to think. She wasn't crying merely because she had hurt Gowan; she was crying because she was in love with him. She'd fallen in love with him—probably between one mile post and the next, while watching him solve problems, while watching him endure an endless description of roast chicken because it made Bindle happy, while watching him listen to music, the music he'd been taught was a waste of time. Even so, he respected her love for the cello, and had changed the itinerary of their journey, and . . .

And loved her.

The next morning, she woke feeling empty, like a shell whose inhabitant had died long ago. Gowan was right: she was useless as a woman and as a wife. She had to drink to have an orgasm.

That could lead to a life as an inebriate. Like taking laudanum to get that lovely floating feeling Layla described.

She refused to be that woman.

And he was right about Susannah, too. The child had taken one look at her and turned away. Stupidly, it wasn't until Layla had stepped in that Edie knew she wanted to be Susannah's mother. But, of course, the little girl would be happier with Layla. Her stepmother had known exactly what to do. Susannah didn't push *her* away; instead, Layla picked her up into her arms. It was petty to weep over the fact that the two of them loved each other.

The truth was that she wasn't any good at the things that made a woman a woman. Not only did she lack maternal instincts, but she didn't seem to have the right instincts when it came to intimacy, either. She didn't really know what she did wrong in bed. He had a disgusted look on his face when she opened her eyes. It made her wince even to think of it.

She *had* needed half a bottle of champagne to relax enough to enjoy his touch. And she'd rather kill herself then spend hours organizing Gowan's household the way everyone expected her to do.

She stood up slowly from the bed; her stomach muscles still ached from all that sobbing. Deep down, she'd always known the truth. Music was all there was for her. She just hadn't realized how much it would hurt to acknowledge it.

Her father would have the marriage annulled. He was rich and powerful; he'd make all this go away. She just had to get word to him, and he would come and take her away. She was fighting tears again when she heard footsteps outside her door. She took a deep breath, expecting Mary—but it was Layla.

"What in the hell happened?" Layla cried, rushing in and closing the door behind her. "Your husband has apparently left, in a fury, for the Highlands. The whole house is in a twitter about it because the man never makes a move without Bardolph, and he left him behind. He took two footmen, six grooms, a solicitor, and a valet, but they all seem to think that he's traveling light."

Edie swallowed hard. "I'm leaving, Layla. I'm returning to England."

"Leave? You can't leave! You're *married,* Edie. You can't desert your husband. Unless . . ." Her eyes narrowed. "He turned out to have some disgusting perversion, didn't he?"

"No! It's me!" Edie shouted. "Me, don't you understand?"

"*You* have a perversion?" Layla said, looking bewildered. "Well, couldn't you—we—"

"No," Edie said, her voice catching. She turned away, curling her fingers hard around the side table until she regained control. "I'm no good at marriage, Layla. Could we just leave it there? Gowan deserves better: someone who is good at bedding, and doesn't lie to him, and wants to have children."

"What are you talking about? You lied to him? About what? And where do children come into it?"

"I wouldn't be any good at raising them, as he pointed out," Edie said steadily. "And I don't want to run a castle, either, Layla. I should never have married. I'm good at only one thing, and we both know what that is."

"You're wrong," Layla said, sitting down on the couch. "Come and sit beside me, darling. I've always thought your father laid too much emphasis on your playing. You are so much more than a musician."

"Gowan wouldn't agree with you." Edie had a little struggle with herself again, but she bit her lip hard, refusing to succumb to self-pity. "I'll go to Italy. Father will support me; I know he will. I shall take another name and begin playing seriously, for audiences."

"But Edie—"

"I've made up my mind," she said, breathing more calmly now that she had forced the tears back down again. "My marriage is over, Layla. Gowan was so furious because I had pretended those times. You know how much I hate it when people rage. Even though I deserved it."

"Oh, sweetheart." Layla was at her side in a moment, pulling her into a protective hug. "He shouldn't have. He's a beast. He should apologize."

"What would be the point? A man who bellows will just keep doing it. He guessed that I told you, by the way."

"Oh Lord. No wonder he's furious."

"I betrayed him with the one person he cannot avoid, because you'll be bringing up Susannah. I can't live like this, Layla. I just—I just can't bear to be shouted at like that."

Layla held her so tightly that it almost hurt. "I can't understand it. The man *loves* you."

"According to him, he loved the woman he imagined me to be." Edie freed herself and sniffed ungracefully. "Do you have a handkerchief? I used all mine and almost took to tearing up the sheets during the night."

"Time for my French petticoat," Layla said, but the joke fell flat. "I don't think Gowan will let you go," she said a second later, having given Edie a handkerchief, and pulled her down on the couch beside her.

"He doesn't want me any longer. He told me that he made a mistake in purchasing me, because I'll be a dreadful mother." The pain felt like some sort of black thing pulsing inside her. "He says I lie there like a pancake in bed."

"He said that?" Layla surged back up to her feet, her fists clenched, the very picture of a vengeful Greek goddess. "How dare he say such a condescending, horrible thing? He's not even

English! He should be slaveringly grateful that someone as beautiful and talented as you accepted his hand! Let's not even address your dowry or your title. Your father will *kill* him."

"There's no need for that. But I—I cannot spend my life feeling like a piece of chipped threepenny china, Layla. Let alone a pancake. I just can't."

"Your father will take care of it. Bardolph is a pain in the arse, but he's a master organizer. He'll have us in carriages in no time."

"What are you saying? You needn't come with me! You have Susannah to consider now."

"We were leaving for England in a few weeks anyway. We'll simply go a bit earlier."

"What if Gowan comes after us?"

"Given that he left for the Highlands, he won't be back for at least a week. I suppose there's a faint chance that the man will come to his senses twenty miles from here and realize that he's a craven, hell-born pig."

"That's too harsh."

"No, it's accurate. Your father has lost his temper with me many a time, but he's never tried to strip me of all self-esteem." Layla rang the bell. "We'll be out of this godforsaken country in no time."

Edie looked at her wildflowers, still holding up in their weedy, tangled way. "I like Scotland."

"Wait until you see the South of France. My mother took me there when I was a young girl, and I've never forgotten it. I can't wait to see it again."

But Edie shook her head. "No, I refuse to steal away behind my husband's back, like a housemaid stealing the silver. I have to speak to Gowan face to face. I'll send word to Father, and then wait until he comes for me. I'm sure Gowan will return before then."

"Your father may ignore you, because I've already written to tell him I am here," Layla said dolefully.

"Darling," Edie said, using her newfound determination to say just what she was thinking, "you need to stop flirting with other men, because you are breaking your husband's heart."

"But I never—"

"That is not the right way to behave, even though we both know that you would never be unfaithful to Father."

There was a moment of silence. "I'm not sure I like this new Edie," Layla observed. "First you make me throw my cheroots out the window, and now you're doling out marital advice."

"Ironic, isn't it?" Edie said flatly. "The blind leading the blind."

"Someday," Layla said, her voice musical in its sincerity, "you'll meet a man who will love you so deeply that he would forgive you instantly for a silly fib. That man will change your mind about bedding. When it's good . . .

it's as if the two of you become one person. There's no way, and no need, to call someone a pancake, because you're speaking to each other without saying a word."

Edie bit her lip. "If it's like that for you and Father . . ."

"We forgot," Layla said. "And I mean to do everything I can to bring us back together. You're right, Edie. I damaged what we had between us."

"He's responsible, too. He needs to learn to be less judgmental."

"But we will talk, really talk, I promise you. We have Susannah now. We're parents."

Suddenly, Edie didn't care anymore that Susannah hadn't liked her. "She's so lucky to have you as her mama," she said, smiling.

"And she has you as her aunt," Layla said. "A famous, exotic aunt, who will marry a gorgeous, tender Italian man—a *prince*—and live in a tower on a hill."

Thirty-four

On the way to the Highlands, Gowan rode alongside the carriage carrying the bailiff and solicitor with whom he was supposed to be consulting. Fury drove him for hours, partnered with a pounding, leaden sense of betrayal.

But somewhere between one league and the next, his anger slipped away and was replaced by a much crueler truth: he had failed. He was shite in bed, as his father would have put it.

He'd never really failed at anything before. Oh, there'd been the occasional problem with leaf rust on the wheat or sheep infected with murrain. He'd made mistakes. But failure was another thing. Failure . . .

It took him two days, all the way to the Highlands estate, to grasp something important. Edie had never before failed at anything, either. That's why she couldn't bear to tell him the truth—because she believed what had happened to be *her* failure.

But it was manifestly his. Bloody hell. All that posturing about his honor, when what he should have been doing was tupping the barmaid, just as his father had told him to do. If he had, he would know what in the bloody hell he had done wrong.

He walked through the door of the ancient lodge and went straight to his bedchamber, ignoring the butler, the assembled staff, and the men who had accompanied him from Craigievar, and now trailed behind him. His valet followed him up the stairs, only to be met by a slammed door.

Two hours later he was still sitting, head in his hands. But something like sanity was beginning to filter into his mind. He could solve this. He *had* to solve this. What the hell had he been thinking all those years? He should have—could have!—spent every minute since he turned sixteen learning about women, the way other men did. Instead he acted like a hidebound stuck-up prick, looking upon others with condescending coolness. He'd never felt such bitter contempt for anyone in the world—except for one person.

His father.

Right.

At length he straightened painfully and returned downstairs, where he gathered his angle-rod and tackle, waved away the offer of a groom, and waded into the loch a short distance from the house.

There is something about a Scottish loch and a fishing line that doesn't allow a man to live with self-hatred. Peace crept into his heart a couple of hours later with the splash of a fish jumping from the surface of the water.

When he came back to the castle, he was cold and wet and his clothes were covered with fish scales. It took another's day casting his line to think out the rest of it.

In the end, he concluded that he was a creation of his depraved father. Avoiding whisky, avoiding women, avoiding three-legged stools . . . all the posturing of a child telling the world that he would never be like the only exemplar he'd known. In other words, it was never about virtue —it was all about a dead man.

The third day, he found himself noticing that the water was shining dark green, but the edges were dark silver. Trout slipped below the surface avoiding his line with the ease of wise men. Pink-legged buntings greeted him at the heathered edge.

That afternoon, he realized that he never wanted to hear another lecture about a bottle of wine ever again. And he was sick of eels as well. And wheat.

An osprey plunged straight down into the water not so far from him, rising with a trout in its claws; Gowan swore at it in Gaelic for taking his fish. A thread of happiness snuck up on him. But he wasn't completely happy by any means. The thought of Edie was like a hole in his heart.

Every day his longing for her grew worse. He craved her like a drug, like opium, and it wasn't all about the bed. He wanted her to hear the haunting calls of the rain geese in their endless mating conversations. He wanted to bring her an armful of dripping water lilies and hold the creamy petals up to her skin.

One morning, he didn't head for the loch until he set up a chain of command whereby he would hear only the most significant reports. By the next day it was clear that one secretary and two bailiffs would be unable to carry their own weight without his constant guidance. He dismissed them.

Since he'd inherited his title, at age fourteen, he had never allowed himself more than an hour of angling; there were too many important things to do. Now he understood that almost nothing was important except perhaps regaining control of his emotions. But every day it seemed a bit more possible that restraint wasn't an option, not when it came to Edie.

Perhaps love was the only choice.

He had to go back and make it work—not the bedding, though that was important. The rest of it. They needed to talk, really talk. It wasn't something that came easily to him. He'd never had anyone to talk to, for one thing.

He was standing on a promontory, watching his line drift on the surface of the loch, when a ray of sunshine struck something gold, the gold of Edie's hair. His body went taut, his mind dark with lust. A moment later a bird sang, not half as beautifully as the music Edie coaxed from her cello as her left hand rocked on the strings, making notes float from her instrument.

His heart clenched, and her name choked in his throat. She was the only thing that mattered in the world. Not this loch, not Craigievar, not the servants . . .

They were nothing.

Edie was—

He had to go home. He strode out of the loch and back to the house, shouting for a bath. Before he returned to the castle, he had to deal with a backlog of complaints relating to his position as justice of the peace. That afternoon he strode into Great Hall, cursing the fact that he'd stood around in the loch when he should have dealt with these cases and returned to his wife.

He doled out justice—more or less—for the first four to five cases. Then a brewer and his wife, who found themselves unable to live in harmony and had decamped to separate houses, appeared in front of him. Her dowry had been a number of pigs, and now she wanted them back.

The brewer's wife had no chin. Her husband had a chin that came to a point. They glared at each other as if the pigs were there in the room, rootling about in front of them all.

What right had he to sit in judgment over these two? He wanted nothing more than to leave, but he couldn't leave the pigs—who were blameless—in metaphorical limbo.

"Half and half," he barked. "Five pigs to you, and the others to you."

The brewer turned plum-colored. "She's me damned wife and what's hers is mine," he shouted. "Them's me pigs and I'll pickle them before I let her have a single trotter."

Gowan walked over to him, knowing that he looked like a man emerging from the gates of hell. He couldn't sleep; he couldn't eat; he couldn't take a damned piss without thinking of Edie.

"You do not own your wife." His voice boiled with barely suppressed rage.

The brewer fell back a step.

"No man owns a woman. You're lucky she tolerated you for five minutes, you shriveled excuse for a fool-born ruffian!"

"Here!" came an indignant voice behind him. "You hasn't the rights to say that!"

Gowan turned his head.

The brewer's wife was on her feet, hands on her hips, scowling at him. "He's no ruffian. He may be a clotpole—and I say that he *is*—but you've no right to call him names just because yer a duke."

Gowan glared at her until she paled, but she didn't back down. The brewer's mouth was half-cocked. Gowan took him by the collar and gave him a shake. "There's a chance she might take you back, you useless, witless clotpole."

The man gulped.

Gowan shoved him away. "The pigs are confiscated until these two idiots work out their marital problems."

A babble of protest rose instantly. Gowan looked at the brewer. "Do you love her?"

He gulped, and then nodded.

Gowan turned to his wife. "He don't act so," she said shrilly. "He stays at the pub till all hours."

"No pigs," Gowan told the man. "Not a single pig until you learn to keep your arse in your own kitchen."

Then he left.

Thirty-five

By the third day of Gowan's absence, it was clear to Edie that he wasn't coming back. The first night and the second, she woke at every sound in the castle, certain that he would be home any moment. On the morning of the third day, she took a walk outside the castle walls for the first time since Gowan had left. Standing amidst the cow parsley that she thought of as her own, staring down at the tower, the idea came to her.

The tower was essentially abandoned. And yet it had everything she so desperately needed: time and space, silence, a place to practice.

If she moved there, Gowan could not surprise her by walking into the room and savaging her heart. She went back into the castle and found her maid. "Mary, will you ask Bardolph to attend me? I have decided to move to the tower, and I need him to make arrangements."

"The tower!" Mary's eyes rounded. "I thought it was dangerous or the like. The kitchen maids say it's haunted. There's a black knight who walks the top with his helmet under his arm, and his head is *in* that helmet, if you take my meaning!"

"I will risk the black knight," Edie stated.

"His Grace put the tower right off limits," Mary said earnestly. "The place is probably cursed, my lady. All sorts have died trying to climb it. Please don't do anything so dangerous."

"You wouldn't mind coming down there a couple of times a day, would you?"

"As if I'd let you go somewhere alone!" Mary said indignantly. "I shall move to the tower as well." Her face took on the harrowed but brave look of a martyr facing an angry mob.

"There's no room for you," Edie pointed out.

Mary gasped and dropped the pillow she was holding. "You're leaving the duke, aren't you, my lady? You're moving to the tower because of him."

"I've already sent a letter to my father; I plan to return to London once he comes to fetch us," Edie said. "I expect it will be something of a shock for the household."

"A *shock?* They won't believe it. They act as if that man is God himself, come down to walk among mortal men."

Edie managed a laugh, as if it wasn't something she'd thought of herself.

Whether or not he was shocked (Edie couldn't tell), Bardolph pressed into service a large number of men, who began carrying furnishings back and forth down the hill, while an army of maids with mops and buckets attacked the dust and cobwebs.

That afternoon, after the plates were cleared from luncheon, Layla announced that she simply had to lie down for a bit; Susannah had woken her the moment the sun peeped over the horizon, and she was desperate for a nap. Asked if she wanted to return to the nursery or stay with Edie, Susannah pointed at Edie.

So Edie took Susannah back upstairs, to her bedchamber. She sat down and pulled her cello forward. After a while, Susannah sidled over. "What are you doing?"

"I'm cleaning the strings of my cello."

"Why?"

"I need to remove the resin that collected on them."

Susannah sniffed. "It smells nasty."

"I'm using distilled spirits." Edie didn't elaborate; she was determined not to make embarrassing overtures to the little girl. The doll hadn't worked. She had tried smiling at her, and complimenting her hair. She'd gone to her knees and tried to play with toys. Nothing had worked. She was done.

Susannah watched her for a while, as Edie swept a soft cloth up and down the strings. Then the child started to ask more questions, and before she knew it, Edie was plucking a string and telling Susannah the pitch, and then letting her pluck it. She could still remember her father patiently doing the same with her.

A few minutes later, she looked down and discovered that Susannah was leaning against her knee. "Can you play me something?" the little girl asked.

"What would you like?"

"Three Blind Mice."

They worked out how to pluck the strings correctly for the nursery rhyme. "That's my favorite," Susannah announced.

"Why?"

"Because the farmer chops off their heads," she said. "And then they're dead, see? All dead."

Edie thought for a moment about whether she should express concern to Layla, but decided it was probably just the way things were. Your mother dies; you think about death. Your marriage dies; you think about . . . She quickly made herself think about something else.

After an early supper, Bardolph escorted her down the hill, Layla and Susannah trailing behind.

"You've done a wonderful job, Bardolph!" Edie exclaimed, as she emerged from the stairwell into the tower's first habitable room. The previously empty chamber had been transformed into a cozy dining room, including a small sideboard with a stack of ducal china. On the next level was a sitting room, with a pretty Aubusson rug on the floor, and chairs upholstered in brocaded silk. "This is so much nicer than my bedchamber in the castle!"

"These are the late duchess's things," Bardolph said, thawing a bit at the unaccustomed praise. "They have been in the attic since her untimely departure."

Edie cast him a sideways glance. Could it be that Bardolph did not approve of the bedroom furnishings in the castle?

Her new bedroom, another flight up, was as charming as her sitting room. A large bed took up most of the room, but there was enough space on the side for a comfortable armchair, as well as a straight-backed chair, and her cello—which was there, in its stand, waiting for her. "Oh, Bardolph," she said, with sincere gratitude. "Thank you so much."

"I know better than to ask whether you'd like company for luncheon tomorrow," Layla said. "Her Grace will undoubtedly practice all day, Bardolph; you can send a footman out with a light luncheon. I shall join her for supper at night after Susannah is in bed."

A little pang hit Edie's heart, but it was better not to spend any time with Susannah. What was the point?

"Although we shall pay you a visit every morning," Layla continued. "And you will simply have to put your cello aside to greet us."

Edie's heart lightened. She would get used to living alone, but for the moment, it was reassuring to think that Layla would visit.

"Will you be afraid, alone here at night?" Layla was standing at the door, holding Susannah's hand, about to descend the steps.

"I will not be afraid. I shall be perfectly happy

here." That was a lie, but what was another lie, given all the lies she'd already told?

"There may be vagrants about," Bardolph said. "I would feel much better if you would allow me to station a footman near the entry door, Your Grace."

"Absolutely not," Edie said firmly. "Now, shoo, all of you. Bardolph, if you could ask Mary to attend me, I am longing for my bed."

"We could stay with you," came a little voice. It was Susannah. "We could all fit in that big bed." She nodded toward it.

Edie felt the first real smile she'd had all day cross her face. She went over to the door and knelt down in front of Susannah, and it was an utterly natural gesture. "I so much appreciate that you offered."

Susannah backed up, just a single step. Clearly, she was still afraid that Edie would try to keep her from Layla, so Edie stood up and put a finger on her nose. "If you visit me tomorrow, we'll work out another nursery rhyme." She smiled at Layla. "I hate to say this, knowing your poor opinion of musicians. But the moppet has a lovely soprano voice."

Susannah, who had no idea what that meant, beamed up at Layla. "I got it," she said.

Layla scooped her up and put her on her hip. "You need to go to sleep." She blew a kiss to Edie. "Good night, darling. Oh, listen to that! It's started to rain again."

"Footmen are waiting below with umbrellas," Bardolph said. "It could be that the ground will become soggy," he said to Edie, "but you have no reason to worry. This tower has stood since 1248, and although the river floods, it has never in its long history threatened the tower. No matter what, the tower will stand; His Grace had the foundations reinforced and the stonework newly pointed."

Gowan was nothing if not thorough. Edie insisted on accompanying them all the way down to the ground floor, where she gave Layla and Susannah quick hugs before climbing back up to her new bedchamber. There were lamps everywhere, and a fire burning in the fireplace. But for the occasional crackling log, the tower was utterly silent.

"This is just right," Edie said aloud, reassuring herself. Beginning tomorrow morning, she would pick up her cello and return to the practice regimen that had once, in less complicated times, made her so happy.

For the moment, though, she threw open the window that faced the castle. There it sat, up on the hill, looking even more fairy-tale-like now that twilight was settling over it like a gentle blanket. Lights shone from many windows, a sign of the hundred souls within. She could see Mary trotting down the path, coming to prepare for bed.

It wasn't that she didn't like the servants, or appreciate what they did for her. But this tiny room was peaceful, and so quiet she could hear every note of birdsong coming from the orchard below.

Yet all she could think about was Gowan. She had no doubt that he would be livid when he found that she had countermanded his order as regards the tower.

She would be clear, direct, and mature.

She would be calm, sympathetic, and yet resolute.

Hours later, lying in bed, she was still thinking about it. By now, Gowan would have bent his problem-solving abilities to the task. His wife was a problem. That problem was exacerbated by his failure in bed—not that she saw it that way, but he did, and she had a shrewd notion that failure was not acceptable to Gowan. He would tie her to the bed if he had to. He would *solve the problem.*

The outcome wasn't hard to imagine. She would lie there tense, while he went on and on. She would have no way to stop him, unless she got drunk and then she would just embarrass herself by doing . . . whatever it was that put revulsion in his eyes. After he kissed her, the first thing she saw when she opened her eyes was his face, utterly transformed by disgust.

Never. She shuddered at the thought. In fact,

there was a great deal about bedding that made her shudder. All that sweat, for one thing. The way fluids leaked out of her for hours. The whole event.

She would have to make it clear that he had no right to try to mend her chips and cracks. Her problems were her own. She wasn't naïve enough to think they could be solved: there were some things that couldn't be solved. Their marriage was a case in point.

After she told him she was leaving, Gowan would undoubtedly shout at her for a time, but the bailiffs and the solicitors and all those servants would be waiting for him. Eventually, he would turn back to the castle, and someday he would marry a sturdy Scotswoman who would bear him ten red-haired children.

The thought made her feel sick, but that was to be expected. One couldn't get over a marriage, even such a short one, in a matter of a day or so. Gowan was so . . . *full*. So intense, so intelligent, so driven.

There was a magnetism about her husband that came from the way he faced everything head-on, sorting through a problem in a minute, searching for the answer, solving it. Gowan would apply all that energy to her, when he returned. In fact, she shouldn't permit him in the tower or he would put in motion a plan to ensure his wife's happiness in the marital bed. She shivered at the thought.

They could discuss whatever he wished through the window.

He was the most masculine man she had ever met, and she had inadvertently injured his masculinity. He would stop at nothing to succeed, to make sure his *possession* stayed where she belonged, thus proving himself a success between the sheets.

He could prove himself with some other woman. She went downstairs, took the key that Bardolph had given her, and stuck it into the keyhole from the inside. It took the strength of both of her hands to turn the key, but she managed it.

And then she went back upstairs, proud of her resolution. She wasn't proud of dissolving into tears . . . but that was only to be expected when one's heart felt torn in two. Finally she slept until morning, worn ragged by crying. Woken very early by the sound of birds in the trees, she hopped out of bed, went to the window, and pushed it wide open to greet the day.

Layla and Susannah were coming down from the castle, hand in hand, and Layla was already dressed, even though it couldn't be long past six in the morning. She was wearing a gown that Edie had seen before: sprigged cotton, with a seductive, low bodice. But now there was a fichu tucked in that bodice, concealing Layla's considerable assets.

She propped her chin on her hand and waited for them.

"You look better!" Layla called up to her. Her voice carried easily across the still morning air.

"I am fine." It wasn't true. Some part of her was still so raw and hurting that she could hardly bear it. But she was learning how to shut that voice into a dark box and lock it away.

Susannah was hopping from foot to foot. "What are you doing?" she shouted.

"Nothing much."

"You look like the princess in a fairy tale," Layla said.

Edie couldn't quite manage a smile.

"Like Punzel," Susannah put in.

"Who?"

"Punzel!"

"Oh, she means *Rapunzel*," Layla exclaimed. "It's your hair."

Mary had braided her hair for bed, as she always had before Edie married and discovered that having a husband meant you had to let your hair tangle all night long. Another thing to be pleased about with regard to the demise of her marriage, she thought, adding it to a short list.

Edie picked up her fat braid and dropped it over the sill. It reached only a short way below.

"A prince can't climb that," Susannah said scornfully. "The lady in my book has hair so long that it trails right onto the ground."

"Would you like to come in the door instead of climbing my inadequate braid?"

"Mary will be coming with a footman or two to bring us breakfast," Layla said. Edie padded down the stairs, turned the key in the lock, and opened the door to them.

Gowan never came that day, which was a relief, of course. Nor the following day, nor the day after.

If Edie had learned how to lock away her grief during the day, she wasn't so successful at night. The chasm in her heart seemed to open the moment she put her cello down. But the steely discipline of her childhood had snapped into place. If her father were to drop everything and head to Scotland—as she was quite certain he would do when he received her letter—he should be with them in another week or ten days.

She merely had to survive until then.

Thirty-six

It took two days for Gowan to find a decent man to appoint as justice of the peace. Everything in him longed to return to Edie. But he had come to the conclusion that he couldn't, not quite yet.

He had come to her frozen, like snow, but he was learning to be the man she deserved. He was making time for her, for their marriage. In addition to the justice, he'd appointed a new bailiff to replace the one he'd dismissed. This one was young—just his own age, in fact. He would make mistakes, but he would learn from them.

There was only one more thing that Gowan had to master.

That night he bathed grimly, handling his body with the same exacting distaste that he had felt since leaving the castle. He called for a carriage, and a short time later he was ensconced in the warm darkness of the Devil's Punchbowl.

No one in the pub had any idea who he was. He'd left his fine clothes at the castle; he was wearing sturdy Scottish woolens that beat back the rain and sleet, but rarely graced the shoulders of a London gentleman. And he'd come without servants, sending his driver to the stables to keep himself and his horses warm.

"What'll you have, then?" the bartender asked, giving him an indifferent look.

"Whisky," Gowan said, remembering the way Edie's hair took on the burnished color of liquor in the candlelight. He pushed the memory away. This smoky place had nothing to do with Edie. He felt as if he were on one side of an enormous loch, and she was tucked away on the other.

After a second glass of whisky, he had started to feel warmer. It's easier to bear loneliness when your vision is blurred.

"I know who you are," the cottager next to him said suddenly. "Yer the duke!"

He grunted.

"The image of yer father."

Gowan turned away. There were barmaids, of course. Pretty ones, too. Bonny girls with red cheeks and sweet giggles. Their bosoms glistened like butter in the lamplight.

He smiled, sharklike, at the prettiest one of all. She was perhaps twenty, with no wedding ring. Not that he cared if she was married. It occurred to him that he was punishing himself, and he pushed it aside.

He was done with blundering. He wouldn't return to his wife until he knew his way around a woman's body as surely as he did the loch.

The barmaid came to him as easily as a caught fish, threading her way through the crowd until she was standing between his sprawled legs, smelling like spilled beer and warm woman. Her smile had a cheerful lust to it.

She ran her hand up his thigh. He'd always told himself that no woman would be able to resist his rank, and therefore he couldn't take advantage of an offer. He realized now that his thinking had been flawed. This woman knew nothing of his rank. What she wanted was the thick muscles she was caressing. She smiled more deeply. "My name's Elsa," she said, her fingers slipping inward.

"Gowan." He leaned back against the bar, and let her do as she wished.

"You're the brooding type, aren't you," she breathed. "I like that. Big and brooding."

Her fingers slid toward his groin and his hand shot out instinctively, stopping her caress.

"It *is* a bit public here," she said, her smile widening. The smile had nothing to do with his rank, he noted dispassionately.

"Would you like to come upstairs for a bit of sport?" she said, leaning in and nipping his ear. Her large breasts brushed his chest. "I can take a wee bit of time to meself." She turned her head to kiss him and he jerked back.

"No kisses."

"Perhaps I can change your mind," Elsa said with a giggle.

He stood up and took her hand.

"Like father, like son," the man next to him muttered, just as the barmaid pulled Gowan away from the stool. Gowan gave him a look. The man snorted. "Aye, and he had a cracked look about his eyes, just like you."

He hunched back over his glass, and Gowan followed the barmaid's round arse through the crowd.

Thirty-seven

Edie was slowly coming to accept that Gowan might not come home for weeks. He didn't want to see her. She represented a failure so absolute that he couldn't bear to return. He understood that she would never be what he wanted in the bed. Or

417

he had decided that he could never trust her to tell the truth.

Tears made her throat scratchy, she discovered. They took away her appetite. It was easier to just push it all out of her mind and play the cello for hours. She kept playing even when her bow arm was tired, not wanting silence because her thoughts were loud enough.

Her father would come in a week or so. Meanwhile, the servants moved back and forth from the castle and the tower like toiling ants. She grew unexpectedly fond of Bardolph. He never showed by the slightest gesture that he disapproved of her move, though—as Layla said —perhaps that was because he disapproved of everything.

He stationed a footman at the base of the tower during the day so that she could easily send a note to Layla or summon Mary. And he visited twice a day. One morning he told her that there had been a quarrel over the footmen's two-hour rotations at the tower.

"Why on earth?" she asked.

Bardolph's mouth pursed. "The Scottish are not philistines, Your Grace. They wish to hear you play."

Later, Layla told her that there was often a group under the tower window, a group that grew every day.

So Edie had her first audience. They never

made a sound, so she ignored them, working over and over on a few measures until she was satisfied with it before she allowed herself to play an entire piece.

One day she heard Layla calling breathlessly, and threw open the window. Her stepmother was running down the hill, hand on her side, waving a letter.

"What is it?" Edie called down.

"Your father," Layla panted. "He's coming!"

"Yes, I asked him to come." Even as she said it, Edie's heart plunged to the bottom of her feet. He would take her away, of course. That's what she wanted.

"No—no, he doesn't seem to know of your letter!" Layla cried, flattening the page out. "He must have already left by the time yours arrived. He says he's coming because he wants—he misses me!" Her face was shining. "He's only three or four days away."

"How wonderful! He'll be so happy to meet Susannah."

"Yes," Layla breathed. Then she glanced down at herself with horror. "I've grown even plumper!"

Edie laughed. "You look wonderful." Layla looked like a rosy, curvy young matron who loved her daughter and her husband, and had no worries about mistresses named Winifred.

Layla was reading the letter again. "He's coming to take me home," she said, brushing away a tear. "He says he didn't realize until I was gone how much he loved me." Edie pulled her head inside the window and ran down the stairs.

"Oh, Lord," Layla cried as Edie opened the tower door, "what if he changes his mind?"

"He won't," Edie said. "Father adores you, Layla. It may have taken him a while to realize it, but he does."

"We can all go home together," Layla said. "It's like a dream." She crushed the letter to her bosom. "I read the letter ten times before I came to find you, because I couldn't believe it. But I know his writing. He meant it."

"He did," Edie said, nodding.

"He says there is no Winifred and there never has been one. It felt so terrible to be the only one who cared," Layla said, sniffing. "There's nothing worse than being in a marriage when the other person despises you, rather than loves you."

Edie's heart gave a terrific thump—and then started again.

"Oh, darling, I didn't mean you," Layla cried. "You're so brave about everything!" They had spent many hours in the last days dissecting Gowan. Layla hated him. Edie felt more desperately in love with him than she had imagined possible. She spent her nights alternately crying and waking up in a sensual daze, reliving the night when she had played the cello for him and he . . .

He had kissed her in that intimate fashion. She

420

could have kissed him in the same way. In her dreams, her fingers skimmed every inch of his body.

Her eyes had been closed a great deal of the time when they were bed together, but she'd seen enough. The memory of the way he looked in Nerot's Hotel when he climbed from the bed and turned away from her kept coming back to her. The twist of his body, with its pure strength and beauty . . .

Inevitably, she would remember the way his dark eyes looked at her, as if she was everything he wanted in the world. And then she would dissolve into tears.

Just then Bardolph rounded the path and came to join them. "As I'm sure Lady Gilchrist has told you," Edie informed the butler, "my father will be here in a few days. I expect he's traveling with his valet."

Bardolph bowed. "I shall prepare a room for Lord Gilchrist."

"We will remain only a couple of days. When he is rested, we will all leave. We shall require two other carriages, one for my cello and another for our maids and Susannah's nursemaid."

It was the first time she'd seen a true reaction on the factor's face. His eyes went blank and his entire face slackened. "What?"

She raised an eyebrow. "Are you quite all right, Bardolph?"

He bowed, recovering himself.

"I think we'll need three more carriages, not two more," Layla put in. "I have a good deal of luggage, and Susannah has a great many toys that she will not want to leave behind."

Edie smiled at that.

"The village," her stepmother said guiltily. "It is such a nice place to visit of an afternoon. And once I determined that Susannah needed new dresses, it began to be as easy to pay a visit there as to summon the seamstress to us."

"Three carriages, if you can spare them," Edie said, turning to Bardolph. "We will, of course, send them back directly once we reach London."

Bardolph had turned an odd color, like a weathered piece of parchment. "Are you quite certain you're all right?" she repeated.

"Yes, Your Grace," he said, with that withering tone she hadn't heard recently.

She nodded and he left, walking quickly back up the path.

"Just when I think that man is turning human, he shows a reptilian side," Layla commented. "I have to say, though, I've never seen anyone work so hard. He's up at dawn and never sleeps."

It started raining again, only pattering down. Edie drew Layla inside and they began to climb the stairs. "Who would have thought that Scotland was so damp? I thought that England was famous for rain, but I've never seen so much water in my life."

"It's very snug in your tower," Layla said. "You should see how chilly the nursery becomes on occasion. I have moved the majority of Susannah's toys into another room while . . ." And she talked on while Edie tried to imagine herself climbing into a carriage. Leaving the tower, Bardolph, the servants who populated the castle. And Gowan.

The fact that he hadn't cared to return or even to send a message made it easier. If her problem-solving husband had wanted to solve their marriage . . .

He would have returned. Layla had turned completely against Gowan; she kept saying that a different man would come along. But every time Edie tried to imagine such a thing, she saw Gowan's eyes and the way he used to look at her.

The truth was heavy in her soul: she would not love any man other than Gowan. So, for her, it would have to be music.

Thirty-eight

It was time to go home. The loch was whipped by rain, its edges beaten into froth by a brutal wind. All this water would be flowing to the Lowlands, Gowan thought absently. It didn't matter. His evacuation plans for the villages bordering the Glaschorrie were in place, and Bardolph would see to it they were carried out, if need be. He would leave the next morning.

The door opened, and Gowan's head jerked up. The daily report had arrived. This week Bardolph hadn't written a word about Edie or Susannah, or even Lady Gilchrist, although he reluctantly found himself thinking of her as Layla again. It was hard to loathe Layla, even knowing that she thought him less than a man. He kept hearing Edie's sob, "She's like a mother to me." Would he condemn her for telling her mother?

At the time, that word had whipped his rage higher. But it was unreasonable to loathe mothers, and he knew it. Stupid, really.

After reading Bardolph's report, Gowan summoned the groom who brought it from Craigievar. The man reported that everyone in the castle talked about nothing but the duchess's music.

Gowan frowned, confused. "Do they hear it from the corridor?"

The groom had spent only an hour or so in the castle before turning back. But his understanding was that Her Grace put on a recital every afternoon, somewhere other than the castle. Down by the river, he thought. Anyone who was free went along to listen.

Edie was holding recitals for his servants. The idea that his own footmen were seeing her with her legs spread on either side of her cello, ogling her as she closed her eyes and swayed with the music . . . It opened up a gaping pain in his chest.

The feeling wasn't a new one. One night, when he'd been a boy of around six or seven, his father had caught his arm, gripping it so tightly that Gowan began to cry, even though he knew better than to show even the slightest weakness in front of his father. Sure enough, the sight had infuriated the duke. He had gripped him harder, twisting the skin so that Gowan cried out . . . and then his dog, his brave, loyal Molly, had barked and leapt in the air and bitten the duke's cheek. It was just a scratch, but it didn't heal properly, and His Grace carried the scar to the day he died.

Gowan never forgot the moment when his father took Molly by her hind legs and threw her far into the raging river. He saw her head for a moment, and then she was gone.

He had walked the river for hours the next day. Bardolph was a young footman at that time, assigned to keep an eye on the heir. They walked and walked; Bardolph never suggested they turn back, and he never said a word about the fact that Gowan stumbled along crying.

They never found her. She could have been swept out to sea, all the way. She could have washed up somewhere . . .

He didn't believe that, though. He was no good at believing in fairy tales, even at that age. He'd seen her head go down, and he hadn't seen it come back up.

The memory brought the pain back as if it had happened yesterday, though surely it was sacrilege to compare one's wife to a dog. Molly had been a gallant, foolish creature. She'd loved him and been loyal to him. She had no resemblance to his will-o'-the-wisp wife, who wasn't *his* and would never be *his*.

And yet he was like a man possessed. It didn't matter what Edie had done or not done. He loved her. It was as if part of him, some vital part, was cut off merely because he couldn't walk into a room and see her.

The butler opened the door again just as he turned away from the rain-streaked window. "Your Grace, there is an urgent missive from Mr. Bardolph."

An electric shock went from the roots of Gowan's hair to his ankles. Nothing was ever urgent except death.

Death was always urgent.

He ripped the letter open so fast that a corner of paper tore off and spun to the ground. He read it. Read it again, read it a third time. Bardolph must be mistaken. Edie couldn't *leave* him. What was she thinking? She couldn't leave him. They were married.

He had considered leaving *her,* to be sure. But the idea had evaporated twenty minutes from the castle. Even the very first night, lying in an inn on his way to the Highlands, it had taken all his considerable willpower not to return to the castle and beg her to let him back into her bed.

His attention spun back to the paper in his hand. Layla, Susannah, and Edie were all leaving. His family. *No.* He threw the letter down and strode from the room.

"Of course, Your Grace," his butler said a moment later, bowing. "The coaches will be ready early in the morning."

Gowan looked out the window. It was still early afternoon, but the sky was an ugly gray. "I'm leaving now."

The butler blinked. "I could have a carriage ready in two hours . . . an hour . . . without your valet?" The last part squeaked out, but Gowan was already striding down the corridor.

He had horses stabled all along the road. If he rode steadily, trading horses, he could be at Craigievar in thirty hours, give or take.

Fifteen minutes later, he was warmly dressed and watching with irritation as his stable master checked the saddle. "He don't like rain," the man advised. "He might spook, so watch your seat, if you don't mind my saying so, Your Grace."

He did mind. He never fell from a horse. Ever.

There's always a first time for everything.

After three days, Edie finally gave in and asked Bardolph if he had informed the duke of their departure. Bardolph managed to convey with a bow that he disapproved of Gowan's continued absence, which was consoling, in an odd way.

By the following morning, the ground had become spongy all the way down the hill to the tower, and the river had broadened and quickened. It was no longer a fat, lazy snake: now it rushed—with purpose. Its murmur had turned to a loud conversation, and her cello wound through the music of it as if the river played counterpoint.

Lord Gilchrist's carriage drew up at the castle around noon. Edie saw it from the tower, but she decided that Layla and her father needed privacy. They would come to her when they were ready. She added a little prayer that her father would love Susannah as much as she and Layla did.

A couple of hours later she heard laughter and looked out her window. They were walking down the path, all three of them. And Susannah was holding the earl's hand, bobbing beside him like a very small cork.

In the end, she had no need to inquire about happiness. Layla's face was shining—and so was Lord Gilchrist's.

"He is sorry," Layla whispered, while Edie's father was showing Susannah the strings to pluck out a children's song, *Frère Jacques*, and teaching the little girl to sing it. "I said I was sorry, and that I hadn't meant to flirt with other men. And that he was the only man I'd ever loved, and ever would love. And he . . ."

Edie stopped her with a kiss. "That's between the two of you, darling."

Layla pulled her into her arms. "You are my best and wisest friend."

They went back to the castle after a bit, all four of them. On the way up the path, Susannah pulled Layla ahead, and Edie's father said, very quietly, "I'm so sorry, my dear. I made a terrible choice when I accepted Kinross's offer."

Edie's eyes filled with tears. "No, you didn't. I love him."

He shook his head. "You are coming home, and I shall have this marriage dissolved if I have to speak to the king himself. I *shall* speak to the king himself. And I fancy that he will respect my wishes."

"You must rest after the journey," Edie said, not managing to squash the errant hope that Gowan might still come, that she might see him once more.

"I can rest in the carriage," her father replied. "It's time to go home, Edie."

And though it made her heartsick, she nodded. It was foolish to be shut up in a tower, barricaded against the husband who didn't bother to knock on the door.

After an early supper, she returned to the tower and locked the door against a man who never came, pulling herself up the stairs with a sense of leaden exhaustion. Layla and her father were blindingly happy. Clearly, they had talked—*really* talked. What's more, Edie had the distinct feeling that Susannah would bind them together like glue. Layla's restlessness was gone, and her eyes were luminescent with happiness.

The rain beat against her windows like an unanswered voice, so finally she opened them to the cool air and crawled into her bed. It was only eight o'clock, but she fell asleep listening to the call of the river as it rushed to the sea.

Thirty-nine

Gowan rode into the stables around nine in the evening and dismounted, throwing the reins to a sleepy stable boy. He entered the castle through the kitchens so he wouldn't be seen by any footmen, who would certainly inform Bardolph.

The great oven fires were banked for the night, and no one stirred except the kitchen cat, whose slitted eyes gleamed yellow from the hearth. Gowan grabbed a lamp and lit it, then went up the servants' stairs and along the corridor. Not to his bedchamber: to hers.

He pushed open the door to find the room perfectly dark. The curtains were drawn, and the fireplace cold. The entire room was cold, far too cold. And it was empty. It even smelled empty, as if no one had inhabited it for a long time. He put the lamp on the mantel, noting indifferently that his hand was shaking. A sickening fear bloomed in his gut. He stood for one terrible moment as he realized what he was seeing.

She was gone. The bed was stripped and the room was empty.

There was only one object left in the chamber: the book of poetry. His soul roared with pain and his stomach churned as if he might vomit. He walked over, picked up that damned volume, and slipped it into his pocket.

Still, he had calculated the days since Bardolph's dispatch arrived in the Highlands. He should have been able to catch her before she left for England. But she hadn't left this room mere hours ago. There was dust on the hearth. She'd been gone for days.

He strode from the room, his face rigidly set. When he reached the ground floor, two footmen sprang from their chairs, alarm written on their faces.

"When did the duchess leave?" he demanded, his voice growling out of him in its new, angry cadence.

One gaped; the other said, "Leave, Your Grace, leave?"

They were idiots.

"When did she leave for England?" His voice rose to a bellow. "When did my wife leave me?"

Edie dreamed that the tumbling roar of the Glaschorrie River summoned her. The impossibility of it woke her: the river couldn't be calling her by name. But even awake, she heard her name again. She went to the window and leaned out. Night had fallen, and although it was spitting a bit, the rain had let up considerably. Gowan stood below her, surrounded by darkness.

She opened her mouth, but no words came out.

"The door is locked!" he shouted up at her. "Can you come down and let me in?"

Edie pulled herself together. She had prepared herself for this moment; she knew what to say. "I will not talk to you in the middle of the night, Gowan," she called down. "Go to bed and we can talk in the morning, before I leave."

"Edie. You cannot—You cannot mean to leave me." He didn't shout the sentence, but she heard every word clearly. So it was going to be like that. He didn't care to speak to her until he thought his possession was slipping from his grip. Bardolph's message must have convinced him to come.

"Good night, Gowan."

"You were planning to return to England without even speaking to me?" The disbelief in his voice would have made her laugh, if she didn't feel like crying.

"We could have spoken any time in the past two weeks, had you chosen to return."

"I was coming back; you knew that. I thought . . . I thought we might talk, Edie. Really talk."

"Well," Edie said, disappointment pinning her to the ground like a lead weight, "the next time you want to talk to your wife, Gowan, you'll have to give her more than an hour at dinner and a visit whenever you can spare the time from your estates. That would be your *next* wife."

"I don't want another wife!"

Of course, she couldn't flee in the morning without speaking to him. A marriage, even as brief and turbulent a marriage as theirs, had to be respected. "We will speak in the morning. I'm sure my father will agree to delay our trip back to London for another day."

"You cannot leave me!" His voice cut like a knife through the sound of the river.

Edie forced her icy, wet fingers to uncurl from the windowsill. "It's over, Gowan. I am leaving." She closed the window. And latched it.

Gowan stared up at the tower. She had refused. His whole body ached from the beating he had taken, riding for hours, being thrown off, landing in the ditch. His horse had fled, and he'd walked for an hour before reaching a village where he could get his ribs bound up and buy another mount—for approximately three times what the beast was worth. Then he'd ridden for another five hours, ribs be damned.

433

But Edie had locked the door, and then the window. A minute later he stalked back into the castle, shaking water from his cloak like a dog. He was on his way up the stairs, when he walked straight into Layla. She stopped short, her mouth falling open.

"Good evening," he said, a streak of humiliation going down his backbone. This woman knew—

The thought died at the look in her eyes. *"You!"* she said, stabbing him in the chest with her finger. "I want to talk to you."

Layla burned like a torch as she swept ahead of him into the study.

"My husband will have his own piece to say to you," she announced, pivoting to face him as he closed the door behind them.

It seemed that his inadequacies as a husband were public knowledge.

"How dare you," Layla cried, "how *dare* you act in such a despicable way to your wife!" She advanced on him like an avenging angel. "How could you say such disgraceful things to someone who is so dear, and so loving? You are a contemptible man, Kinross. Contemptible!"

It was as if one of the Greek Furies had whirled into his study: he examined her with as much bemusement as he might an ancient goddess. "Edie and I have much to discuss."

"That is an understatement."

"I want to make the point that I am not

appreciative of the role you have played in my marriage," he stated.

A flicker of guilt went through her eyes. "I should never have taught Edie as I did. I apologize."

"It was not helpful," he said, picking his words carefully. "But with time to think, I have come to realize that Edie considers you her mother. I am certain that she and I will be able to forge a new—"

"You idiot!" Layla's contemptuous voice cut his off. Whatever remorse she had felt was clearly exhausted. "You have no idea what you did to her, have you?"

"We argued," Gowan replied, anger flaring in his gut again. "That is not unheard of in marriage, Lady Gilchrist. You yourself experienced some difficulties."

"My husband and I have *never* said the things to each other that you said to Edie. Believe me, Jonas could strip me bare of every inch of self-respect, if he wished. But he would never do so, not only because he loves me, but also because he is a *decent* man."

A moment of silence elapsed before Gowan could speak. "How dare you say such a thing to me!" he shouted, every semblance of civilization leaving him.

She didn't even flinch, just crossed her arms over her chest and raked him with her scornful gaze. "Now I see the man whom Edie described. You can't frighten me with your temper. I have my faults. But I would never, not in million years, do to any human what you did to Edie. *Never.*"

What she was saying finally filtered through to Gowan past the haze of pure rage. "What in the bloody hell are you talking about? You make it sound as if I hit her. I did nothing to Edie!"

Her eyes bored into his. "Oh? You did nothing? The woman I found in your wake, stripped of all self-respect, convinced that she was a failure as a mother and a lover: that wasn't your work? Because I think it was!"

He stared at her.

"She may have pretended to have an orgasm; so what? You were so oblivious that you didn't notice. Where's the greater crime?"

She wasn't saying anything that Gowan hadn't told himself.

"You idiot," Layla said. "You sneering, despicable—"

"You're beginning to repeat yourself."

"You made her feel as if she'd done something disgusting, after the first orgasm of her life. You told her she lay like a pancake, when she had no idea what else she was supposed to be doing in bed. Now she thinks she'll never experience pleasure without drinking herself silly—because *you* told her so! Even worse, you convinced her that she had no ability to be a mother—Edie! You said that to Edie, who is one of the most loving, giving people I know."

"She had written me a letter and told me that she didn't want children." But even as he said it he remembered that wasn't quite right: she had written that she didn't want children immediately. "And when she met Susannah, it was obvious . . ."

"You *fool!*" Layla cried. "Susannah is mine; Edie didn't even have a chance. She'd never held a baby, did you know that? Her father didn't allow her to play with other children; it was too important to preserve that talent of hers. She could have won Susannah over with time, but no, you had to give the child away without even discussing it! Then you left your own wife crying on the floor, having stripped her of everything that made her a woman."

Gowan's lips had grown numb. He just stared at her, silently.

She came closer and poked her finger into his chest again. "After which, you slammed your way out of the room, upset because you had bought damaged merchandise. As if *you,* a tedious, stupid, despicable bureaucrat, were good enough to touch the hem of Edie's skirt. *You,* who didn't even know what a cello was."

Gowan couldn't speak.

"You're a philistine," Layla said, her voice dropping when he didn't fight back. "You married the most beautiful, loving woman in all

England—aye, and Scotland, too—and when you learned just how inadequate you were in bed, you blamed her. Let me tell you something, Duke." Another poke.

He felt as if he were hardly breathing, as if only scorching air was reaching his lungs.

"The only reason you haven't heard the word *inadequate* from the women who preceded Edie in your bed is your title. That's it. Don't fool yourself by thinking that *Edie* is incapable of pleasure. *You* are the problem. And those satisfied women you're comparing her to?" She actually slapped the table in her rage. "Every single one of them lied to you."

Dimly, Gowan perceived that Edie had apparently never told her stepmother of his lack of experience. Not that it mattered.

Layla's lower lip was quivering. "You smashed her as if she were a piece of china that you bought in a street market, and then you left her with a shattered heart. All she's done since you left is play her cello—because you made her believe that's all she's good for. She's lost so much weight that she looks as if she has consumption. She's convinced that she will be a terrible mother, and that no man will ever love her. She'll probably never be able to take pleasure in the bed, because you showed your disgust. You despicable—" But she was sobbing now, and the rest of her words were lost.

Gowan didn't move. Her portrait of him was so ugly that he was rooted to the spot, dimly aware that he'd gone white.

Layla had a hand braced on the table, her head hanging, weeping. The door opened. There was a second's pause, and Lord Gilchrist rushed straight past him. He gathered Layla into his arms and Gowan heard him murmur something as he pulled her head against his shoulder. It seemed the Gilchrists were together again, not that he cared.

Had he done that to Edie? What had he done? He began filtering back through his memories. Suddenly, he remembered the expression of horror in her eyes when he announced that she had no skill with children, the way she wept as she insisted that she had tried with Susannah, the mute grief in her eyes.

He remembered shouting his father's loathsome comment about pancakes, but he hadn't meant it to apply to her. She had twisted in his hands like a live flame, driving him mad with every catch in her voice, with—

He made her feel as if she had disgusted him?

Lord Gilchrist delivered his wife tenderly into a chair, turned, and slammed Gowan under the jaw with a blow so solid that he crashed to the floor like a felled tree without time to twist sideways and protect his left arm. "That's for my daughter," Gilchrist snarled, standing over him. "Don't think I can't get this annulled, because I can. I'll tell the king that a bloody Scotsman reduced my daughter to a shadow in a matter of weeks. Don't think you're keeping her dowry, either. And don't you *ever* frequent an English ballroom looking for your next wife. I'll make sure that every man in the country would rather send his daughter to the Americas than marry her to you."

Gowan's body hurt so much from slamming into yet another hard surface—though the floor was slightly better than the ditch—that he only dimly registered as Gilchrist ushered his wife from the room.

It wasn't merely the pain. It was the knowledge that he had stripped Edie of dignity, of self-respect. He'd hurt the one person he loved in the world. He'd *ruined* her. He'd taken . . .

The bleak truth of it pulsed along with the physical pain that was searing his left arm as if a hot poker stretched from his knuckles to his elbow. The binding around his ribs hadn't protected them from being jarred in such a way that he couldn't breathe.

He had just managed to get to a sitting position when Bardolph walked into the room. Gowan took a deep breath, and his cracked ribs blazed with sudden fire. "Help me up," he said, shortly.

Footsteps came toward him and he glanced up. He didn't usually think of Bardolph as being a mere decade older than he was; his customary frown made him appear thirty years older.

But now he realized that he'd never seen Bardolph when he was truly disapproving. "I'm leaving," his factor stated, staring down at Gowan without lifting a finger to help him up. "You may consider this my notice."

Gowan had braced himself on his right hand so he could get up without using his left. Bardolph stepped forward and kicked his hand out from under him. Gowan crashed down again, a stifled groan escaping from his lips.

Bardolph couldn't hate him with more virulence than he did himself.

"I didn't mean to do it," Gowan said, staring fixedly at the legs of the chair before him. "I love her."

Silence.

He wasn't even sure Bardolph was still there. Maybe he was waiting for the right moment to kick him in the kidneys.

"I love her so much." Gowan's voice broke, and for the first time since the day after Molly had disappeared beneath the floodwaters, he lost control. With the raw cry of a soul in pain, he said, "I love her more than—"

A rough hand grabbed his left arm and hauled him to his feet. The agony was so acute that he shouted involuntarily.

"Jesus, Mary, Joseph, your shoulder is dislocated!" Bardolph exclaimed.

"Ribs. I was thrown from my horse."

"That's not a good enough excuse for staying away for two weeks," his factor said, stepping back and folding his arms over his chest.

Gowan turned away. "The truth is that she's better off without me. I'm turning into my father."

"Your mother was an inebriate long before she married your father. The household knew it within a week. It's a miracle that you weren't born with your brains as addled as an egg."

Gowan absorbed that.

"You still have a chance." Bardolph's voice dropped to a growl. "She hasn't left. I did my best for you, you ignorant, ungrateful sod. I bought you time to come home by kitting out that tower. Every man in this bloody castle would have walked on their knees to Palestine for a touch of her lips, and you left her here alone, crying for you."

Why hadn't he turned around ten paces from his own front door? Why had he ever left the person he loved most in the world sobbing as he turned his back? Regret was a poker to his heart, sharper and fiercer than the pain in his arm.

Gowan went back out the front door, not even noticing the footman who pulled it open.

When he reached the tower, he leaned against it, taking refuge from the rain and trying to put it all together. He'd hurt Edie so badly that she lost confidence in her ability to love a child—a curse rose from deep in his heart—and he'd somehow convinced her that she had behaved distastefully in the grip of pleasure.

So she was leaving him. Of course she was leaving him. He straightened, but staggered as his cracked rib shrieked a warning.

Edie was the only person in the world who mattered to him. His mother and father were gone; they had been too troubled to love him, and what love he had for them had burned away. Molly was gone. His aunts were cordial, at best, and Layla had adopted Susannah.

But Edie loved him. She had said so, and he had to believe that: believe the three words that she said just before he left her. If she loved him, she might forgive him. There was a heart of darkness lurking behind his ordered life, but he was banishing it.

He had to tell her. He had to put that heart at her feet.

Intimacy was something they should have explored together, but his determination to follow a flawed plan had destroyed it. He was so desperate to please her that he ruined everything between them.

If he had just admitted his ignorance, she would have trusted him. They could have found a way together. But he had been afraid: afraid to fail, afraid that she would despise him, the way his father had. That was the truth of it.

He fell back a step and looked up at the tower. It

loomed tall and gray in the dark, its silent bulk attesting to the men who had died climbing it in a vain attempt to impress their beloveds, if the tales were true. The only one who made it past the second level was the black knight, who, according to legend, still walked the battlements.

Edie hadn't gone back to sleep. A soft glow came from her casement. She'd unlatched the window after he left, and it stood ajar.

If he called her name, she would close the window against him and keep him out.

He tilted his head back so the rain struck his face. Romeo climbed to Juliet's window, didn't he? Of course, he probably had use of both hands and intact ribs. Gowan managed to close his left hand into a fist with no more than a grunt of pain. So his wrist hurt: it still did as commanded.

He started climbing quickly, but slowed almost immediately. The stones were slick with rain, and the ascent was considerably harder than he had anticipated. Halfway up it occurred to him that he might not make it to Edie's window. But there was no way down except by falling. Whether he would survive another fall was an open question.

Even as the thought came to him, his right hand slipped and all his weight swung from his left for a moment before he caught on again. A deep grunt broke from his lips; he'd never felt pain like this before. A second later, Edie looked out the window.

Her figure was blurred by the rain on his eyelashes. But he could see her cheek, illuminated by the glow of the fire behind and to her left. She peered down and out.

Then she shrieked. "Gowan!"

He couldn't spare breath for a word, not even for her name.

"No! Go back down, Gowan. I demand that you go back down!"

He clung to the wall, cheek against the cool wet stone, and listened to his wife. When he caught his breath, he lifted his head and said, "I love you."

There was a second of silence, and then she implored, "Please, Gowan, please go back. I'll let you in. I'll do anything. Please don't keep climbing up. I'm so afraid."

"Can't do that. I love you, Edie. More than anyone. More than—more than—" He reached up with his left hand again. Cold, fierce determination filled him. *She* was there, above him. He could not allow her to leave him.

Edie leaned out the window, her face glowing against the dark stone. "You're so beautiful," he said, his breath catching between words. "The most beautiful woman I ever met. Like a fairy. Goddess."

"Drunk," she said to herself.

He was moving faster now. He didn't care about the ground, dwindling below him. His wife was leaning as far as she could out of the window, her golden hair falling forward over her shoulders and down the gray stone of the tower.

He had to rest for a moment because his wrist was on fire, and his ribs were shrieking with pain. "You cannot leave me," he said, the words coming from his mouth somewhere between a command and a prayer. He reached, and hauled himself up a little farther.

"I know I'm shite in bed," he said, not looking up because he was afraid the weight of his own tipped head would tear him from the wall. "But I can improve. We can stay in the bedroom, the two of us, for a year and a day. No footmen, Edie. I promise you that."

He reached up again with his left wrist—that was the worst and a grunt broke from his lips despite himself.

She was sobbing and the sound of it drove him higher.

"I'm your falcon." The words exploded from his heart, the way they had come to him when he'd stared into the loch and tried not to think about her . . . and had failed.

"Gowan, you're out of your mind," Edie cried, leaning out the window so far that her entire upper body was visible.

"Don't fall!" he shouted, his voice exploding into the rainy silence around them.

"I won't. Just please, please, Gowan, you're close now. Just two or three more moves."

"It's this bloody wrist," he told her. "I might have broken the damned thing."

He heard her gasp, but he was pulling himself up again. "You're not mine," he told her, just below her now, almost within reach. "I'm yours, lass. You're a net that I'm tangled in."

"No poetry," she cried, reaching down again, and then he felt her touch on his wet hair, so he pulled himself up again.

Once more.

And again.

Then over the windowsill.

The Duke of Kinross had done that thing that no man had done in six hundred years: he had conquered the unclimbable tower. In the rain. With two cracked ribs and a broken wrist. With a broken heart and a stubbornness inherited from generations of Scottish lairds.

Maybe those ancestors were at his shoulder, and pushed him up those last few feet. Or maybe it was the golden sweep of her hair, like Danaë's gold, summoning him in the rain. Or maybe it was the nightingale sound of her voice.

Or maybe it was just Edie.

The Edieness of his wife. The way he loved her, bone deep, every musical note that made up her gorgeous, stubborn, generous, joyful soul.

Forty

Gowan might have passed out, just for a moment; he came to himself to find that he was kneeling on the floor, Edie in his arms, and she was sobbing against his shoulder.

"No," he whispered. "Don't cry, *mo chrìdh*. I'm sorry," he blurted out, self-recrimination roughening his already hoarse voice. "I didn't mean to hurt you."

She raised her face, and his heart cracked open at the sight of her eyes. His body hurt too much to stand up, just yet.

"You're soaked!" She slipped away from him and came back with a towel, warm from hanging before the fire. Then she started pulling off his sopping garments until she saw the binding around his ribs and stopped in horror.

"I made close friends with a ditch," he explained, standing and stripping the rest of his wet clothing off.

"Is it painful?"

He shook his head, taking the towel from her hands. Edie watched wordlessly as he dried off his legs, then his torso and arms. Finally he lifted his arms, albeit with a wince, and gave his wet hair a rough tousle before he wound the towel around his waist. He had an erection, of course. It hardly registered anymore, not when he was around her.

But she fell back when he stepped toward her. He stopped. "I didn't mean to say that you wouldn't be a good mother, Edie. You'll be a wonderful mother. I need only think about you with our child in your arms and my heart melts." Her eyes were shuttered, and he couldn't tell what she was thinking.

"I should never have made arrangements for Susannah without asking you, but the outcome seemed inevitable. Even so, I'll never do anything like that again. I will always ask you about the smallest thing that might interest you." It was a vow.

"Susannah and Layla, and now my father, too, are happy," Edie said. The sound of her musical voice made a purr of joy ripple through him.

"Please forgive me," he said, taking another step toward her because he couldn't stop himself. "I'm a hotheaded fool, and I was in the grip of a feeling of failure. I hate myself for having been cruel."

"You said no more than you believed. Though I do think you're mistaken about my capacity for motherhood." A very small smile lit her eyes. "Susannah and I have come to appreciate each other much better in the last fortnight."

It was like a dagger to his heart. Why hadn't he been there? This was his *family*. He had been such a fool, keeping himself in the Highlands when his heart, his reason for living, was here.

He cleared his throat, finding it difficult to shape

words. "There was nothing revolting about the way you found pleasure, Edie. It was the most beautiful thing I'd ever seen. The only problem was that I knew instantly that I had failed to give you that pleasure before. I'm so *sorry* about that."

Her lashes swept down. "I don't really want to talk about it, Gowan."

"We must talk about it," he said desperately. "I can't let you go, Edie. I can't."

"I know," she said, unexpectedly.

"You do?"

She nodded. "You succeed at everything you do, Gowan. Now you have to succeed at bedding me because you cannot bear the thought of failure. Or," she added, her brow darkening, "of letting something you purchased slip away."

"I was mad to say such a thing. I should have been at your feet, thanking you for accepting my hand, and instead I was preening myself for having bought you, as if you were just another feather in my cap."

Her face didn't move, but he saw the pain in her eyes.

"I don't deserve you." The words were wrung from his heart. "I failed you in bed, and then I blamed you because I was ashamed."

Finally, finally, she stepped toward him and her hand curved around his cheek. "You didn't fail me in bed, Gowan. You mustn't think that way. We are simply not compatible."

450

"We are compatible," he said stubbornly.

"You must accept that sometimes the world doesn't go the way you wish," she said gently.

He wanted to howl at that. Go the way he wished? With his parents . . . the dog he couldn't seem to stop thinking about . . . the work that never ended. Without Edie, he faced day after day of toil. What hadn't bothered him before felt like a sentence of ten thousand years of dark loneliness. After knowing her, and loving her.

"Please," he said hoarsely. "Give us another chance, Edie. Please."

There was a long moment, and then she asked, "Why did you climb the tower?"

"You wouldn't let me in, and I had to be with you." It was that simple.

A smile wobbled on her lips. He could see that kiss tucked in the corner of her mouth, the one that she never gave away, the one that made her so kissable.

"If you leave in a carriage, I'll be in the carriage that follows," he vowed, his voice low and intent. "And when you reach home, if your father bars the door, I'll climb up to your bedchamber. It's got nothing to do with the marital bed, Edie. You are all there is for me. From the moment I entered that ballroom and saw you, I knew that."

He took her hands and turned her palms to his lips. "I can't live without you. You're my lodestone and my North Star." Very gently, he placed a kiss on first one and then the other of her palms.

Edie felt as if the tornado that was Gowan was whirling around her, imprisoning her in the still heart of his storm. What woman could resist? She fumbled for all the things he'd said that had broken her heart, and couldn't remember them . . . except for one.

Her eyes fell before his as she searched for a way to put the unsayable. "Don't," he whispered, and his hands were on her back, pulling her close. "Don't push me away."

"It must be said."

His voice was infinitely tender. "What, *mo chrìdh?*"

"I don't think I'll ever be able to be what you wish in bed," she said, telling him the truth of it. "Maybe if I'm drunk. But I really . . . I don't want to drink too much wine. I was sick after you left, and I felt dreadful the next day, and I can't play if I feel like that."

"I've come to understand that my attitude toward liquor is bollixed up," he told her, wrapping his arms around her. "When you were tipsy . . . it turned me a bit mad because of memories of my mother."

It felt so good to be in Gowan's arms. When Edie had looked down and seen him climbing the tower, her heart had stopped. The very thought made her move closer to him, her arms circling his waist, her cheek to his shoulder, nuzzling close.

With his arms around her, it felt as if the world had settled back into place. "I dislike drinking to excess, and if that's the only way I can enjoy our bed . . . I can't do it. I'm sorry."

"If you don't want to bed me ever again, I accept it," he whispered, kissing the top of her head. "It hurt, and I failed to give you pleasure. The only thing I couldn't accept is if you left me."

In this moment he probably believed what he was saying, but he was wrong. Edie knew her Scotsman. Gowan would spend the rest of his life trying to give her pleasure in bed. She thought about that, and felt her lips curve. It wasn't something many women would complain about.

And she was keenly aware that she was pressing against a sleek, strong, unclothed male body. He didn't indicate in the least that certain parts of him were rigid, but Edie could feel him through the towel.

Her hands tightened around his waist. Still, she stood frozen, afraid to make a move, to promise something that she couldn't fulfill. He would expect her to have that paroxysm of pleasure. The very idea made tension rise in her chest.

"Shhhh," he whispered, his big hand rubbing gentle circles on her back. "We don't have to do anything, Edie. We probably shouldn't. My wrist is injured."

"It's not only your wrist. You have cracked ribs, too."

"They don't hurt much. Bardolph sent word that you were leaving me. I had to come." He tipped her chin up so their eyes met. "I would climb the tower again, Edie. In a heartbeat."

A feeling of peace settled over her. Gowan was alive, not dead in a ditch or broken at the base of the tower. What would she have done if he'd fallen? The thought was so terrifying that her heart hiccupped and she turned her lips to his neck.

"Edie, sweetheart," he said, his voice a little strangled.

"Do you remember that last time we went to bed, and you said that it was about me?"

He nodded.

"And then, later, you said that I lay there like a pancake—but to be fair, Gowan, you *told* me to lie there."

His throat worked. "I should shoot myself for that comment. My father told me that about women. I was so angry that I turned into him for a moment." His eyes went pitch black with remorse.

"I don't want you to focus on me. I don't want to have to worry about whether or not I achieve a *petit mort*."

"What would you like?"

"I would like to explore you. And I don't want you to even touch me, not like that. Just for tonight?" she asked. "Please? It's so much pressure."

"I never wished you to feel anything but pleasure." Stern lines bracketed his mouth.

"So let me decide what we will do? Just so this once I needn't worry about succeeding?"

He cupped her face. "There's no success or failure between us, Edie. I would love you if we never went to bed together again."

Her smile wavered. "And if I'm never able to succeed in bed? You won't . . ."

He shook his head, his eyes never leaving hers. "It's *not* a question of success or failure. Love does not measure such things, except in kindness: and I was the failure in that respect."

"No, you weren't," she breathed. "I love you."

The joy that flared in his eyes was so sensual that she caught his head in her hands and brought his lips to hers. When they broke apart, her breathing was tremulous and she could see his chest rising and falling rapidly.

"I should bathe first," he said hoarsely. "I'll go to the castle and—"

"You smell like rain, and leather, and a bit like sweat," she stated, giving him a sultry, lazy look. "I like it. Better than I like almond soap. You smell . . . *male*. It makes me want to lick you. All over."

A curse escaped his lips but he managed to stop himself from lunging at her. Joy was like a scorching brand through him. He wanted to howl at the heavens, fall on his knees, throw himself on—

No.

"I'll do whatever you want."

"If there's any licking to be done," Edie said, "I'll do it. No touching me that way until tomorrow evening."

A look of near agony passed through Gowan's eyes. "I am not to touch you all night and day?"

"Not unless I give you leave."

He lowered those long eyelashes of his, but she thought she caught a flash of satisfaction.

"And I shall not permit it," she stated. "I promise to try again tomorrow night. I do promise, Gowan. But for the moment, I just want to put that away."

"As you wish," he said, faint reluctance underlying his words.

Still, she had no worries about whether she could trust him to keep his word. He might lose his temper again someday—and she still had to make it clear to him just how unwelcome *that* would be—but he would never be unfaithful, and he would never be untrue.

With a smile happier than she'd ever seen, he said, "Do with me what you will."

Edie felt a pulse of excitement. It was like the dreams she had, in which Gowan wasn't making love to her, but she was making love to him instead. Now he stood very still, with his hands on

456

his hips and a smile teasing the corners of his lips. Smooth shoulders, one marked by a dark blue bruise, led to a heavy plate of muscle that crossed his chest, punctuated by small, flat nipples. Just below it the white cotton bandage wrapped tightly around his ribs. Below, stomach muscles marched down in regiment. A thin line of hair ran down the center of his stomach and disappeared under the towel. And everywhere there were scratches and bruises.

Although his eyes blazed with hunger, she knew he wouldn't move until she gave her permission. And she was enjoying herself. Slowly she backed up, eyes roaming up and down the whole of him, until she reached the bed. He said nothing, just waited. It was the most erotic thing that Edie had ever experienced, knowing that this magnificent, powerful man was entirely at her service.

If she directed him to kneel, he would kneel. Not that she wanted him to kneel, but the power she held over him was dizzying. She licked her lips, and his eyes followed the motion. A blaze of fire went down her legs. She clenched her knees together, wondering what to do next.

"What would you like me to do?" His husky voice broke into her thoughts. His fingers were on his towel. "Would you like me to remove this?"

Edie took an unsteady breath, then nodded slowly.

He threw the towel off, and it was better than

she remembered. His private part was long and thick. She wanted . . .

What did she want?

"Anything you'd like me to do, my lady. Anything at all." His voice lapped at her like velvet. But at the same time, she could feel her busy mind starting to get in the way of pleasure. What should she do?

He must have seen the flicker of uncertainty in her eyes, because he sauntered around to the other side of the bed and stretched out there. "You see," he said, "I am not touching you."

She acknowledged this with a nod.

"But perhaps you'd like to remove your robe?"

She wasn't sure about that.

"I won't touch you," he said. Though he added, "Unless you ask me to, of course."

She managed to collect herself. She might as well remove her robe, because it was awkward to be clothed next to a naked man, especially a naked man to whom she happened to be married. It felt wrong, somehow. So she removed it, leaving only her nightdress. Then, before she could rethink it, she pulled off her nightgown and threw it to the side.

To her utter horror, the desire in his eyes instantly disappeared and a curse exploded from his lips.

She looked down at herself. "What's the matter?"

"I can see your ribs!" He burst from the bed, and his hands spanned her body just beneath her breasts. Then he jerked her against him and wrapped his arms around her. "I'll never leave you again." It was a vow.

"What do you mean?" Her heart was pounding, and not from pleasurable anticipation. She leaned back to see his expression.

"Layla told me you didn't eat." He had gone dead white, and his voice was hoarse.

"I—"

A look of utter panic crossed his face. "I have to feed you."

At that, Edie began to enjoy herself. She hadn't paid much attention to the fact she'd lost weight, though she had noticed that her bosom was somewhat smaller. Layla's dresses definitely wouldn't fit these days.

"Is there any food downstairs?"

She nodded. "Bardolph always leaves food, in case the river floods and the footmen can't reach me for a time."

Gowan let her go and disappeared, stark naked, down the stairs. "Good thing I don't allow footmen to stay in the tower," Edie muttered to herself. She walked over to a chair by the fire and sat down, crossing her newly slim legs, and wondering what would happen next.

She didn't wonder long, because Gowan burst back in the room, carrying a plate. He scooped

Edie up and sat down with her in his lap. She was naked, except for her bed slippers, which were remarkably elegant and decorated with narrow pink ribbons. She stretched out a leg and wiggled her toes. "What is your opinion of my new slippers, Your Grace? Layla gave them to me."

Gowan didn't even glance at the slippers. "Open your mouth," he ordered.

Against all odds, she was enjoying herself more than she had in her entire life. "What are you feeding me?"

"I don't know. I found them on the sideboard."

"Apple dumplings!" Edie exclaimed. They were shaped into a fluted flower on top. "Aren't they pretty?"

"Open," he repeated.

She obediently opened her mouth, and he popped a dumpling inside. He put the plate down, wrapped his arms around her, and pulled her tight against him. Layla was right—she had lost interest in food during the weeks Gowan had been gone, but now the dumpling's cinnamon and sugar tasted wonderful. Her appetite had returned.

"You promised not to touch me unless I asked," she observed, after she'd swallowed. "You broke your word. Is there a forfeit?"

"We are not making love at this moment," Gowan said. He reached for another dumpling, drawing in a sharp breath as he strained his ribs. "I will not have you starve yourself." His tone was fierce and he was being possessive again, but somehow it was all right this time.

But after eating three of the little pastries, she had had enough. She got up from his lap and pointed to the bed. He rose, towering over her.

Edie looked up and liked what she saw. Gowan had been alarmed by her dramatic weight loss; his face was still sharp-edged, his mouth a firm line. She'd just figured something out about the Duke of Kinross. When he was afraid, he exploded with rage.

But angry or frightened, he still loved her.

She could think about that later, though, because his eyes had now dropped below her face. His mouth tightened as he reached her ribs, but then they drifted lower, to the tuft of golden hair between her legs, her curved thighs, and, finally, her delicate slippers.

When he looked back up, his eyes had gone ravenous again. "I do like your slippers. And you have the most beautiful ankles I've ever seen." She saw his throat move as he swallowed. "May I kiss you, Edie?"

She shook her head no, quite enjoying herself.

"Your legs?" His voice sounded a little desperate.

"Absolutely not," she said.

And she pointed at the bed again. And then she did the ogling, because her heart quickened when she looked at his muscled rump. And those long legs.

Gowan lay on the bed like a man accustomed to offering himself to women. It steadied her to remember that for all he liked to claim possession, he was also hers and hers alone. He'd never touched another woman. No woman had ever touched him.

She clambered onto the bed and knelt beside him, kissing his brow, his cheeks, his nose, his lips. She investigated the prickle of his beard with the tip of her tongue, returned to his mouth, wandered to his cheekbone.

Then she pulled back and began to run her fingers over all the areas she was curious about: the strong column of his neck, his broad shoulders, his arms. She dropped kisses all over her battered, bruised warrior's chest. She ran her fingers from his wrists to his shoulders and then down to his stomach, exploring the smooth skin that sheathed rippling strength, the way he gasped, the way he started to shake.

Still, he didn't move. He let her explore him like a new instrument, caressing, inspecting, finally tasting . . .

Words broke from his throat then, unintelligible noises, finally, oaths. Edie ducked her head so that he couldn't see her grin. It was the most arousing thing she'd ever experienced to see a gorgeous, huge man panting with lust, yet never reaching for her. Not even when she ran her lips along the hair-roughed skin of his thighs.

His hands came from behind his head and dug into the sheets, but he still didn't touch her. Every groan, every oath sent a pulse through her that ended up between her legs. And every one of her touches, her kisses, and even—once she dared to be bold—her licks and nibbles sent heat through her body until her heart was beating as fast as his, and her breath was caught in her throat.

She wrapped her hand around him and experimented with that velvet hardness.

"I dreamed of this," Gowan said hoarsely.

Edie looked up. She was thinking that she could kiss him the way he kissed her. And he would like it.

"You did?"

She gripped him a bit tighter, and his hips arched into the air. "Bloody hell," he gasped. "That feels so good."

He had dreamed about her. Edie was starting to feel as if the mere sight of him was a sensual assault. She felt restless and greedy, as if her body was pulsing to a rhythm she barely understood.

"Even though I can't touch you, you can touch yourself, Edie." His voice was hypnotic.

Edie frowned at him. He was trying to turn the tables. Before he could open his mouth again, she bent her head, wrapped her lips around that part of him, and took back control.

A shout broke from his lips. She would have smiled, but she was too busy running her tongue over him. All the time her hands were moving over his legs, caressing his thighs. She discovered that she could make him roar, and his roars made her feel wet and empty and even more restless.

"You must stop," he gasped a moment later, his voice strained with need. "Edie."

She raised her head. She could feel that her lips were a little swollen so she pouted at him, watching his eyes grow even darker.

"I cannot do this anymore," he said with great difficulty. Every muscle in his arms and chest was rigid.

She smiled at how beautiful he was, and then she crawled up and said, "I love knowing that I can reduce you to begging. Are you begging?"

"Yes. I have to touch you," he said, not smiling, the words exploding from his mouth. "This is not the way it's supposed to go. Please, Edie, *please*."

She wanted his touch so much that her mind was fuzzy and she could no longer remember what she had demanded. Her hand was trailing over his stomach muscles, but maybe . . .

"Edie!"

She was starting to feel as if she'd drunk a whole bottle of champagne. She lowered her head and licked his nipple. "Mmm."

"Please, Edie." He *was* begging her, this man whom she loved more than anyone in the world.

Of course, she would always give him what he wanted. "As you wish," she said, giving his nipple a little tiny bite, just because she remembered that he—

He flipped her over so fast that her hair swirled around her shoulders and came down in a cloud. "You're so damned beautiful, Edie," he muttered. One hand ran over her breasts, over her ripe nipple, down her flat belly and then dove between her legs. Edie opened her eyes and her mouth fell open.

When he ran a finger between her legs, they both felt how drenched she was, how swollen and tight.

He groaned. She didn't say a word, because a shiver burned through her whole body at the mere touch of his fingers, rippled through her, and again. He moved his fingers and it came again, wave after wave until she was shaking all over. She cradled him with her knees and whimpered, asking without words for more, more of him, more of that.

"I meant to learn about what makes women come," he whispered against her mouth. "Up there in the Highlands."

Edie's entire self was concentrated on what he was doing with his hand. She felt as if . . . She hid her face against his shoulder. It felt out of control, as if her face might contort, or she might make some . . . some squeal or do something . . .

"Edie!" Gowan's hand stilled and after a second, she looked at him.

"Hmmm?"

"I went to a pub, the Devil's Punchbowl."

She looked at him. His face was so beautiful that she leaned up so that she could capture his mouth.

But Gowan was nothing if not stubborn. "I have to tell you this. I went to the pub to find a barmaid who could teach me about a woman's body, about what makes a woman happy in bed."

It took a moment, but that filtered in. And although Edie was not the type of person who ever shouted, she shouted now. *"What?"*

"A barmaid took me upstairs."

Edie was off the bed in one second. "You didn't!"

"I did." Gowan didn't look particularly apologetic. He rolled off the bed and stood up just in front of her. Edie was breathing fast, her fists clenched, trying to make sense of it.

"You were trying to solve the problem," she said, her chest hurting with the truth, even as she understood: Gowan was a problem solver by nature.

He nodded, and then slid his arms around her. They stood together, naked, his cheek on her hair. "I couldn't do it. I never meant to bed her, but I thought I would ask her about what she liked . . . maybe even ask her to—to demonstrate."

An involuntary shiver of disgust went up and down Edie's body, but she said nothing.

"I couldn't," he whispered, pulling her even

466

more tightly against him. "After about a moment in that room, I realized that I didn't give a damn what aroused her. I certainly didn't want her to demonstrate anything. Before I could stop her, she pulled open her bodice."

"What did you do?"

"I looked away."

Edie felt as if she'd moved into a warm room after standing in an icy rain. Heat slid over her skin. "Was the young lady was surprised?"

"She decided that I was only attracted to men," Gowan said, sounding rather pained. "She gave me a lecture about how there was nothing she could do for me. I offered her some money but she said she was too sorry for me to accept it."

Edie slid her arms around his waist, and tried for a moment to control her laughter, but to no avail.

"What I'm saying is that I'm a dunce, Edie, but I'm *your* dunce. I still don't know where I went wrong. But I'm begging you to give me another chance. You—" He stopped for a moment, and then continued. "You are the only one for me, Edie, and you always will be. I don't want to think or hear about another woman's pleasure, only yours. If you'll allow me, I will spend my whole life trying to make you happy."

It was amazing how fast tears could replace laughter. "Oh," Edie whispered. "Oh, Gowan, I love you so much."

His big hands slipped down her back. "Even though I'm an idiot?"

She pulled back just enough to look at him. "We're both idiots," she said firmly. "When you were angry—justly angry—because I deceived you, I crumpled. I need to have more backbone. I should have been honest with you from the beginning, but my impulse, my habit, is simply to smooth everything over. It was stupid."

He cupped her face in his, and gave her a sweet, sweet kiss. "I have a sense of how tempestuous your father's marriage is."

"I don't manage anger well," Edie admitted, coming up on tiptoes to kiss him back. "I don't think I ever will."

His eyes holding hers, Gowan went down on one knee, just as he had in the drawing room at Fensmore. He held her palms to his lips. "I promise never to shout at you again. I *vow* it."

The joy in Edie's body was more potent than canary wine, more heated than the sun. She sank to her knees. "I promise never to lie to you. That's my vow. And I will never love anyone the way I love you. I think we are both marked by our childhoods."

Gowan made an inarticulate sound.

Edie leaned forward. "I love you, Gowan. Just as you are: problem-solving, brilliant, domineering, beautiful, poetic. You're a poet when you're not bossing bailiffs around."

"And I love you, lass." Gowan's accent turned to a proper burr. "You're my heart, Edie. My everything."

Tears were sliding down her face, and he was kissing them away, and then somehow they were back on the bed. "I don't deserve you," he said hoarsely, "being as you love me even though I'm a proper—"

Edie stopped him with a kiss. "You survived," she told him. "I love you the way you are because you not only survived, but you triumphed. All these people depend on you, Gowan. You could have been like your father, and turned your back, but you didn't. And you never will."

Gowan wasn't listening to her, but she meant to tell him that two or three hundred times in the next fifty or sixty years, and someday he would understand.

"May I touch you, Edie?" he asked, his eyes fierce with desire.

Her heart was so open and wide that she didn't hesitate. "Both of us," she said, reaching for him.

They were kindling to a bonfire. He kissed his way down her body, put his mouth on her most delicate spots, and licked until her blood throbbed. Until she was whimpering, and crying. Until his fingers and his mouth ravished her so that she shrieked, her body arching from the bed.

Still, he didn't even stop, not until they

discovered that Edie could come again and again . . . but by then she was maddened with desire, and her begging went to Gowan's head.

"Shall we?" he asked, husky and low, when he was so overcome by a desire to be with her in the most profound way possible that he couldn't stop himself.

Edie sobbed without words, pulling at him. Gowan nudged her legs apart, braced himself, and slid in.

It didn't hurt. Not even the tiniest amount. There was just an intoxicating feeling of fullness . . . and it was *Gowan* inside her.

But he didn't move, waiting. "Is it painful?" he asked. In that moment Edie knew that if she felt the merest twinge, he would back away. The thought—his concern, his control—made flames lick at her.

She shook her head, clutched his arms, and opened her mouth, but just then he withdrew and pulsed into her again. He kissed her so hard that her scream was silenced. Then all of a sudden those feelings—that wild explosion of heat and emotion—ripped through her body again.

Gowan tore his mouth away and looked down at his wife in amazement. Edie was arched against him, her body shaking, eyes squeezed shut. Her hair was darkened with sweat, like corn silk in the rain.

He felt a joy through his body that would never

go away. So he drew back and began thrusting into her over and over and over. Her eyes flew open and she gasped, "Can you feel it if I do this?"

"Hell," he rasped, because he could feel exactly what she was doing. "If you do that, Edie—don't do that! I'm going to lose control."

She laughed and didn't obey. With every pump of his hips, she rose to meet him, her thighs clamped around his body. She was clutching him inside, over and over. He couldn't stop going harder, pounding, hurtling closer toward something that was almost frightening in its intensity.

Then Edie opened her eyes again, her lovely green eyes, and gasped, "Gowan."

Her voice was desperate, and hunger blazed down his backbone.

"Will you—"

He braced his arms, leaning down to brush a kiss on her lips. "Tell me," he managed.

Her hands slid down his back to his arse and pulled him even closer. He threw his head back. He dimly heard her gasp his name, and then she was clenching on him again, but it was tighter and sweeter than he could have imagined. Her whole body shook under him and she cried out . . .

Something in Gowan broke free. His whole body flamed up as he thrust into her.

She's all states, and all princes, I. Nothing else is.

471

Edie sobbed beneath him. Gowan threw back his head, roared, and spent himself, giving her everything he had.

She gave it back, and gave it back again.

Shine here to us, and thou art everywhere.
This bed thy center is, these walls thy
sphere.

Forty-one

Edie woke, confused, to the sound of rushing water. And then she realized that she wasn't alone. She was lying on her side, facing away from the man whose arm was curved around her waist. And she knew instinctively that if she moved, she would wake him.

"Don't even think about it," Gowan's sleepy voice growled, and sure enough his arm shifted and a hand slipped around one of her breasts. "Mmmm. I believe this is my favorite part of your body."

She laughed.

His hand slid downward. "Of course, I like this, too." He cupped her between the legs, his hand warm and affectionate. "This is my favorite way to wake up."

"Lords and ladies in polite society do not sleep together," she pointed out, a gurgle of laughter in her voice. "That is for peasants, who must keep each other warm."

His hand was back at her breast. "I love your body heat." Then, uncannily, as if he had read her thoughts, he said, "I don't think I'll ever want to sleep without you, Edie. Those endless hours when I was riding from the Highlands in the rain, when I landed in the ditch, when I found another horse—"

"When you climbed the tower in the dark and the rain!" she said, rolling over to face him. She felt a pang of fear at the memory. "I almost lost you." She dropped another kiss on his biggest bruise, the one that spread right across his shoulder.

"I thought I had lost you," he said, pulling her closer. "I was so terrified. As frightened as if the moon fell from the sky, or the sun never rose."

She slipped a leg between his, loving the way his breathing roughened at her slightest touch. "No more climbing towers."

He grinned, and her heart thrilled to the flash of wild humor in his eyes, the laughing Gowan whom almost no one glimpsed but her. "Do you know the Clan MacAulay motto? It's *dulce periculum*; danger is sweet. Go ahead and lock yourself in another tower, Edie. Danger is sweet, but you are sweeter." He leaned forward and kissed her.

She drew away sometime later, her fingers trembling. "I love you," she whispered.

He kissed her again.

"You will have to get used to sleeping alone," she said a while later, teasing him, but a little serious as well. "I can't constantly travel with you from estate to estate, Gowan."

He shrugged. "So I won't travel anymore."

"But I thought you had to move from one to the other!"

"I thought through all that while I was away. There are a few decisions that only I can make. But the world is full of intelligent men. I have Bardolph to manage them. I have you to manage me."

Edie began to smile, slowly. "Your Grace, are you, by any chance, saying that you intend to work less? That you might make a place on your schedule for a wife, aside from dinnertime?"

"I want to be with you," he said, dropping a tender kiss on the end of her nose. "I want to watch you play your cello. I want you to perform for me naked."

She laughed aloud. "I couldn't!"

He disagreed, and she ended up on her back, kissing him fiercely. After a while, Gowan rolled over, bringing her to a sitting position on top of him, because it was time to try all the things he'd dreamed of, and since he had a wife who was as confident in her sensuality as she was in her love for him . . .

Later, Edie wandered over to the window, followed by Gowan. He pushed her hair to the side and licked her neck. "Essence of Edie," he murmured. "And sweat."

She made a face at that—and then, *"Gowan!"*

"Mmmm?"

"The river," she gasped.

Overnight, the Glaschorrie had swollen to a torrent, burst its banks, and now surrounded them. The river was split in two by the tower, flowing around it and coming together on the other side, continuing its dash to the ocean.

But the rain had stopped, for the moment at least. "Imagine," Gowan said, pushing the window open wider. The sun had broken through the clouds, and the water below glinted as if thousands of gold sovereigns were hidden just below the surface. "We won't be able to leave the tower for at least a day."

Edie's eyes had grown wide. "We're trapped!"

Gowan leaned back against the sill, happier than he had ever been. "Thank goodness Bardolph left a ham and a plate of dumplings and a chicken pie."

He was more interested in the vision before him. Edie's skin was covered with a pattern of little love bites—the road map. He didn't need any maps, though he didn't bother to tell her. He was learning by sound and touch: the catch in her breath, the sob in her throat, the way her fingers tightened on his shoulders, and the way her body shook in his arms . . .

Edie leaned out the window again, transfixed by the floodwaters, which were lapping at the tower's lowest windows. "Don't," he said. "That sill is entirely too low; you might topple out."

"You're a fine one to say that," Edie retorted, laughing.

Gowan didn't argue, but wound his arms around her waist from behind, and pulled her away from the window.

"You're going to have to stop that," she said, giving him a naughty glance over her shoulder.

"What?"

"Oh, trying to get your own way."

His hands were on her breasts again. "I have an idea," he said, brushing her hair over one shoulder so he could kiss it.

"Is it about becoming a man who listens to his wife and always takes her advice and never thwarts her in any way?"

The Duke of Kinross knew better than to make promises he wouldn't keep. "A better idea," he said silkily, tucking her gorgeous bottom under the curve of his stomach.

"Gowan!"

It was amazing how a woman could sound scandalized, intrigued, aroused . . . all in the same moment.

Forty-two

Six years later
No. 37 Charles Street, London
The Duke of Kinross's town house

At eleven years old, Miss Susannah was a quite accomplished violinist. In fact, she was something of a prodigy and she knew it, even though her mama always hushed her father when he said anything about that. Her mother thought it was much more important to be a *nice* person than to be a genius.

Personally, Susannah thought you could be both. Her tutor, Monsieur Védrines, nodded at her from his seat at the piano, and she raised her bow.

She knew the piece to the middle of her bones. And she knew everyone in the room as well. There was her dear mama and papa, and Lady Arnaut, who also played the cello, although she complained that these days she couldn't play because her stomach was too great with child.

That was a paltry excuse, as Susannah could have told her, because Edie had played all the way through both of her confinements.

The first notes spilled from the piano and Susannah felt her heartbeat quicken. There was no reason that she should be so nervous, though perhaps it was because Jamie Arnaut was in the room, sitting by his father and mother. He was thirteen and seemed tremendously grown-up.

It was her turn, and her bow came down on just the right spot . . .

Afterward, she was flushed and smiling and terribly pleased. But there was still one piece left to play, a surprise for Edie. They'd all been keeping the secret for ages and ages, to the point where Susannah wondered whether Edie actually knew the truth and was merely pretending not to know. Grown-ups did that sort of thing.

Jamie came up with his father, Lord Arnaut, so she told herself not to blush, and dropped into a curtsy. And then she blushed anyway, because Jamie gave her a smile and said that he thought she was a wonderful violinist. He didn't say, *for a girl,* and he didn't even look as if he was thinking it.

Edie watched the color rise in Susannah's cheeks as she accepted young Jamie's compliments and smiled to herself. They had never been able to determine whether Gowan and Susannah's mother had remarried, so a fearful person might worry about Susannah's future acceptance in society. But it was obvious, even at eleven years old, when she was still all knees and elbows, that she would be a tremendous beauty some day. And her brother was one of the most powerful men in England *and* Scotland. Edie wasn't worried.

Layla popped up at her side and drew her to a chair in the very front row. "The recital is not over yet!" she said, giggling madly. "There's still a birthday surprise for you." There was a great deal of laughter from her assembled friends and family, though Edie had no idea why.

Monsieur Védrines sat himself back down at the piano. A footman placed a straight-backed chair next to the instrument.

"Is someone going to play a duet for my birthday?" Edie asked Layla. Layla's eyes were shining and she couldn't stop giggling, even though she was risking waking up one of her twins, draped over her shoulder fast asleep. Edie wasn't sure which one, since they were identical. All she could see was a cloud of golden hair against Layla's shoulder.

"You'll see," Layla said now.

"I can guess," Edie said, smiling. "I don't see Father. He's going to perform a new piece, isn't he?"

"Something like that," Layla replied.

Edie sighed happily. "What a lovely birthday present. Where has Gowan got to? I don't want him to miss it."

Layla looked about vaguely. "I'm sure he's here somewhere."

At that moment Edie's father strode out onto the floor, carrying his precious cello. He settled himself in the chair and nodded at Védrines. The family counted it as one of their luckiest days when the young Frenchman agreed to be their castle musician.

"We shall play Vivaldi's Concerto in D Minor, in honor of my daughter's birthday," Lord Gilchrist announced, giving Edie a smile before turning to place his music on the stand.

"He must have made a special arrangement," Edie told Layla. "That piece was written for two violins, a cello, and strings."

"I expect the piano is playing the strings," Layla said.

Before Edie could point out that, even so, two violins were still missing, Susannah had walked to the front of the room, next to the earl, and was again picking up her violin.

And then there was a murmur as the Duke of Kinross entered. Gowan had grown only more devastatingly handsome as the years passed, his sense of command polished to a fine point, but tempered by a deep love of his wife and children that made every woman sigh.

But Edie wasn't looking at his face. Rather, she was transfixed by the violin tucked casually under his left arm, as if he'd often carried an instrument that way.

He joined the ensemble, smiled at her, raised the violin, and began to play. Edie sat frozen in her chair. If the roof had flown off the town house to reveal a sky crowded with winged pigs, she would not have been as astonished as she was by the sight of her husband playing Vivaldi.

He wasn't merely following the notation, either.

Gowan played with as much reckless brilliance as he did everything else in his life. It was utterly clear that, had he cared to, he could have rivaled the world's finest players.

And she understood, in the same moment, that he did not care to.

He had learned this most difficult of arts *for her*.

"It took three years of work," Layla whispered, bending close. "Poor Védrines has been driven mad by the project."

As the last notes faded, the assembled guests burst into rapturous applause. Lord Gilchrist— father to Edie, beloved husband to Layla, papa to Susannah, and father-in-law and friend to Gowan—turned to the audience and bowed. "It is with true regret that I announce that the Duke of Kinross has played, he assures me, his first and last public recital."

More applause.

Gowan stepped forward. "The last three years have been truly happy. Learning the art of the violin from the inestimable Monsieur Védrines, with the help of my father-in-law, Lord Gilchrist, has been a pleasure."

More applause.

Gowan bowed. Being Gowan, there was no flourish of his violin or twirl of his bow.

"Will you really *never* play again?" came a voice from the back of the room.

He smiled, and his eyes returned to Edie. "Oh, I

shall play," he said. "But I shall limit myself to private duets."

The Duchess of Kinross had not stirred. Tears slipped down her cheeks. Her husband gave his violin to his little sister and picked his wife up in his arms. "Please accept our apologies," he said, inclining his head and smiling at the room. "My duchess is indisposed."

And then he strode out the door.

Susannah shrugged. Since her brother had entrusted it to her, she put her bow to his Stradivarius and played a few notes. It made a sublimely beautiful sound.

"Don't you think it was a bit odd of the duke to walk out of his own party?" Jamie asked, appearing at her elbow. A lock of hair fell over his eyes in a quite fetching way.

"My brother is like that," Susannah explained. "He's mad about my sister-in-law and he doesn't care about much else. Well, besides my niece and nephew, of course. Would you like to hear me play something?" She was longing to try out the Stradivarius.

He shoved the hair off his brow. "We could play something together if you lend me your violin. I'm not as good as you, but I'm decent. Do you know Vivaldi's *Four Seasons*? I'm learning the part of the first violin."

Susannah beamed. "That's what I've been working on! I can play first or second."

They stood facing each other, those young people, with no sense of what the future would bring. But as Susannah's melody wove under Jamie's, and then his soared above and stole back to hers, something deep inside each of them whispered the truth. Someday, a madcap girl with bright red hair would walk down an aisle toward a young man whose hair kept falling over his brow.

It was that duet, they would tell each other, years later. Even at ages eleven and thirteen, they could hear the distant echo of the music they would create in years to come.

Upstairs in the ducal bedchamber, Edie couldn't stop crying. "You make me so happy," she said finally. "You have given me everything that I ever wanted."

Gowan kissed her tears away. "You are all I've ever wanted," he whispered.

Their duet that night was a silent one . . . but thereafter, their children grew used to the sounds of a cello and violin playing together. All four of these children had perfect pitch; one of them grew to be Europe's finest violist; and only one professed that she hated music.

She was fourteen at the time, which speaks for itself.

A Note About Literature—
English, German, Persian—
and Cellos

This novel owes deep thanks to two quite different fables: that of Shakespeare's *Romeo and Juliet*, and the Brothers Grimm's "Rapunzel." Romeo's passion is echoed by Gowan; the balcony scene borrows fragments of language here and there. But Gowan also owes a debt to William Butler Yeats's early poetry: Yeats was the first to be "looped in the loops" of his beloved's hair. Toward the end of the book, more mature and hopefully wiser, Gowan learns the poetry of John Donne. I had great fun weaving bits of Romeo's language into the early scenes (the balcony and Rosaline among them), as well as into the tower-climbing scene.

If I had an obvious problem adopting the end of *Romeo and Juliet* (Edie and Gowan were young, but definitely not star-crossed nor suicidal), "Rapunzel" also offered a challenge. Her hair, for one! In a gesture toward the fable, Gowan climbs a horsehair ladder to the balcony, but in the end he ascends the tower without recourse to hair, equine or otherwise.

Yet another debt is owed to the great musician Yo-Yo Ma. I listened to his versions of Bach's cello suites and his arrangement of the traditional canon *Dona Nobis Pacem* over and over while writing *Tower*. If you'd like a playlist of all the pieces Edie mentions, just look on my website, *www.eloisajames.com*. For history buffs among you, I'll add that Vivaldi's concerti were published in 1725, and existed beyond his original handwritten manuscript. Of course, the cello is a quite new instrument at the time, so most of the pieces Edie plays (including Vivaldi's *Four Seasons*) would have been arranged for solo performance by a passionate musician such as Robert Lindley (1776–1855), who was considered one of the greatest cellists of his time.

I wanted Layla to have an exotic name for Regency England, one that connoted reckless passion, and I found just such a one in the love story *Leyli o Majnun*, written by the Persian poet, Abd-Allah Hatefi. It was published by Sir William James in 1788 and thereafter translated into English by Isaac D'Israeli, as *The Loves of Mejnoon and Leila*.

And a final literary note: Julia Quinn and I are great friends, which led to our writing, with Connie Brockway, two novels-in-three-parts, *The Lady Most Likely* and *The Lady Most Willing*. One day we were chatting on the phone and came up with the idea of embedding a couple of our characters in each other's books, purely for the delight of our shared readership. Those of you who have not had the pleasure of reading Julia's *Just Like Heaven*—and therefore have not yet met the enticing Earl of Chatteris outside the pages of this book—you have a treat in store for you!

Center Point Large Print
600 Brooks Road / PO Box 1
Thorndike ME 04986-0001 USA

(207) 568-3717

US & Canada:
1 800 929-9108
www.centerpointlargeprint.com